TO KILL THE TRUTH

SAM BOURNE

Quercus

First published in Great Britain in 2019 by

Quercus Editions Ltd
Carmelite House
50 Victoria Embankment
London EC4Y 0DZ

An Hachette UK company

A CIP catalogue record for this book is available from the British Library

HB ISBN 978 1 78747 491 8
TPB ISBN 978 1 78747 490 1
EB ISBN 978 1 78747 489 5

10 9 8 7 6 5 4 3

Typeset by Jouve (UK), Milton Keynes

Printed and bound in Great Britain by Clays Ltd, Elcograf S.p.A.

TO KILL THE TRUTH

Also by Sam Bourne

The Righteous Men
The Last Testament
The Final Reckoning
The Chosen One
Pantheon
To Kill the President

As Jonathan Freedland

Bring Home the Revolution
Jacob's Gift
The 3rd Woman

For Jonny Geller

Old friend and master agent.

This is our tenth book together, so this one's for you.

Monday

Chapter One

Charlottesville, Virginia, 2.40am

The past was present. At this late hour, he could feel it curl around him like smoke.

Normally, when he was teaching, standing before an auditorium full of students, history felt as the word sounded: distant and dusty, even to him. The same was true in the library, surrounded by people. There too the events of long ago remained beyond the horizon, out of reach.

But here, alone in this room, in the early hours, the years fell away. He had taken precautions to ensure modernity would not intrude: the phone was stilled, the computer sound asleep. It was just him and the documents, piled high on his desk. Outside, though it was too dark to see now, was the Lawn, the centrepiece of the University of Virginia's founding campus here in Charlottesville, a marvel of landscaping designed by Thomas Jefferson himself. After nearly three decades in the history department, no one begrudged Professor Russell Aikman his office with a perfect view. Even in the darkness, the mere knowledge that the Lawn was there, just on the other side of the window, narrowed the gap between him and the America of centuries earlier.

But it was the documents themselves, examined in solitude, that transported him. These were not the originals, so there was nothing sensory about this act of magic. It was not the smell or touch of these texts that sent Aikman tumbling back through time, though he knew the power of such a physical connection. He had, in the course of his career, touched the very parchment that, say, George Washington, Alexander Hamilton or, as it happens, Jefferson had scratched and etched with the hard nib of their quills. He had felt that strange kinship with ancestors that can flow through the fingertips, the sensation that both you and they had touched this same object, your skin and theirs somehow joined across the generations. But the link he felt on these late nights was not physical.

No. The grip these documents exerted on him came only from their words. For Aikman, to read a sentence set down more than two hundred years ago was to connect with the mind of a fellow human being long gone, to be allowed into their thoughts. When he contemplated the wonder of it, he pictured those images from the space age days of his youth, when an American craft would 'dock' with its Soviet counterpart. Two individuals conquering a vast distance, holding out their hands and touching.

He felt it that night, as he drilled down into the text placed at the centre of his desk. He lost himself in the words, a diver sinking deeper and deeper into dark water. Only when he heard the noise did he cannon upward, bursting through the surface and back into the present.

He bolted upright, alert as a hare, his head darting from left to right. What was that? There were occasional sounds here at night: a rumble of the heating, a shudder of the air-conditioning, depending on the season. But this was more direct. It sounded like a creak in the corridor.

'Hello?' He felt ridiculous as he called out, but he did it again. 'Hello there?'

No reply. Of course not.

He looked down and saw the array of papers on his desk as if they had been laid out by someone else. He hadn't realized how much he'd written this night, already filling three separate sheets of his yellow legal pad, along with dozens of Post-it notes. After all these years, the process still mystified him, how these scraps of scribbled half-thoughts turned steadily, over time, into something that would be called history.

He found his place once more, about two-thirds of the way through this diary of a Confederate soldier. A couple in Richmond had found it a matter of months earlier, in a stack of boxes they were about to throw out of a newly purchased nineteenth-century farmhouse. In fact, it was their daughter, fourteen years old, who had spotted it, an unbound sheaf of papers with little to announce that it was a journal. When she saw the references to battle, she thought the crumbling pages might date back to the Vietnam war. It took the family a while to understand what they had. But once they—

There it was again. Unmistakable this time. The creak of a human footstep on a floorboard, no doubt about it.

Aikman stood up, shifted around his desk and headed for the door. He felt his head grow dizzy, the colours swirling. He'd stood up too quickly.

When he opened the door, he could see nothing. The corridor was in darkness. He stepped forward, clapping his hands. He told himself his only purpose was to activate the motion-sensitive lighting. It was an unintended side effect that the noise broke the silence, providing him with the reassurance of his own presence.

'Hello?' he said again, peering into the corridor of faculty offices, adjusting his eyes to the bright light. 'Mr Warner, is that you?'

Silence.

'Is there something you need? Is there someone you need me to call?'

He scanned the doors of his colleagues, each one shut and expressionless. In the light, he noticed which doors were unmarked and which decorated, either with bumper stickers for long-forgotten, defeated liberal candidates or with a form attached to a clipboard, letting students know their office hours and when they would be available for a drop-in visit, complete with ballpoint pen dangling on a string for those keen to book an appointment. Old school, Aikman thought to himself of what had once seemed a voguish innovation: the young faculty did all that online these days. He looked at his own door, adorned only with his name.

One last try and he would go back in. Perhaps a gentler tack might coax his brilliant, but troubled, student out of the shadows. 'Adam, if you need me to take you to the hospital, I can do that. Just say the word. No need to skulk around in the middle of the—'

He was cut off mid-sentence. The lights had gone out, their automated time expired, the sudden darkness taking him by surprise. He considered requesting an extension by waving his arms around again, but thought better of it. He turned his shoulder and headed back inside towards his desk. The door behind him swung steadily back towards the latch, without ever quite meeting it.

Slower than he once was, Russell Aikman had only just reached his chair when the door opened again. When he looked up, he could barely make out the face of his visitor. The light from his desk lamp, pooled on the spread of papers, didn't reach that part of the room. He may have squinted but if he did, it was only for a split-second.

Was that time enough to see the intruder make a small movement – a small rub of the eyebrow – which seemed to act as a cue for the arm to arc upwards until it was held straight ahead, the hand unwavering, as it trained itself directly on the space just between the target's eyes? Did Russell Aikman have the time to understand what was happening to him, to comprehend that this was his very last second of life? Did he know that at that moment his present was sinking forever into the past?

Chapter Two

Washington DC, 12.05pm

Maggie Costello wriggled in her seat for the fifth time in as many minutes. She was straining to concentrate. It wasn't that the spectacle unfolding on stage before her wasn't riveting. It was. The arguments traded across the floor in this packed university lecture theatre were compelling. But still it was hard to stay focused. The noise outside was just too great.

She could hear the chants; they all could. They'd heard them as they made their way in, coming from the two armies of protesters facing off against each other, separated into two blocs on either side of the entrance path into the auditorium by a thin, struggling line of campus police reinforced by officers of the MPD, Washington's metropolitan police department.

On one side were the students, backed by allies who'd travelled in from New York, Philadelphia and beyond. They were young and unmissably diverse: Latino women, black men – one of them wearing mock-manacles around his wrists, linked by a chain to a collar around his neck – and plenty of white demonstrators draped in Pride flags, their arms tattooed and their faces multiply pierced. Their loudest, most consistent battle cry: 'No platform for racists!' and, pertinently for today, 'Slavery is real!'

Ranged against them were ranks of white men in an unofficial uniform of beige chinos and white (and occasionally black) polo shirts. Most were carrying shields, some rectangular, shaped like those wielded by riot police, some circular, like those favoured by comic book super-heroes. They were decorated with a variety of patterns that Maggie struggled to identify. Of course she recognized the Iron Cross, adopted and adapted by the Third Reich, and the Confederate flag of the old south. But the rest of the assorted triangles and crosses were new to her: they seemed to be variations on the swastika theme, hinting at some ancient Nordic pattern. Several were in a distinct white-and-red, nodding to the colours of the Crusades. At first, Maggie, watching from just a few yards away, had tried to decipher each one; a few of them she looked up on her phone. But there were so many that, after a while, they merged into a blur.

Their chants were more direct. 'Blood and Soil' was a favourite refrain, as was 'You will not replace us', often reworked as 'Jews will not replace us.' But the one that struck Maggie with greatest force, and which seemed to be tailored especially for the occasion, was, 'Don't know, don't care/Nothing happened, nothing's there.'

She could still make them out now, from her seat in the back row of the lecture theatre. They were muffled but unambiguous, even when they clashed with and overrode each other. Sometimes the words were drowned out by the percussive beat of men pounding their shields with sticks and, at intervals, the chants would merge into a single crescendo, a collective surging sound, which, Maggie guessed, meant one side had rushed against the other.

Of the three speakers on stage, improbably seated in chat-show formation around a low circular table bearing three glasses of water, only one seemed unfazed by the noise outside. His name was Rob Staat and he was the reason for the protests. He had emerged as the chief media spokesperson and defender of William Keane, the notorious self-styled historian who had become a hero to the American, and increasingly global, far right. Keane was currently at the centre of what the media had, inevitably, hailed as the 'trial of the century'.

Keane, even his enemies had to admit, was a floridly charismatic figure, in his white suits and insistence on old-world southern courtesies – all 'Yes, ma'am' and 'No, sir'ee' – and the thirty-something Staat was a pale substitute. But thanks to a constant quarter-smile that played on his lips, threatening to flourish into a full-blown smirk, he managed to arouse Maggie's loathing all the same.

Against Staat was Jonathan Baum, a scholar from Georgetown's history department. Usually a solid, methodical speaker, he was now visibly unnerved. He reached for his water glass often, the microphone on his lapel picking up the audible gulp as he drank. Perched on his lap was a large file, which he would rummage through while Staat talked, as if searching for the document that would settle the matter once and for all. Whenever the rhythmic pounding of stick against shield outside resumed, he'd look up, startled.

Seated between them was Pamela Bentham, heiress of the same Bentham family that had endowed this theatre along with the newly established Bentham Center for Free Speech to which it was attached. Besides a few opening remarks, she said almost nothing, content to let the two antagonists dominate proceedings while she maintained a studied neutrality. Maggie watched her – mid-fifties, expensively coiffed, wearing spectacles whose necessity Maggie questioned – as she swivelled to face whichever man was speaking, nodding along with each point intently. She was working hard to ignore the pandemonium outside but, Maggie noticed, one Bentham hand was gripping the other, as if to stop it from shaking.

In a way, it was impressive, Maggie concluded. Not so much the chairing, as the determination. This Bentham woman was putting her mouth where her money was, turning up in person, rather than contenting herself with a mere donation, to ensure this debate took place, despite all the pressure there had been on the university to stop it. And doing it simply to insist on the right to free speech.

Most institutions would – and indeed had – run a mile from the Keane trial. It could only bring trouble. Maggie was sure that the university grandees' collective heart had sunk when Bentham suggested airing the issues on campus. Everything about it screamed unsafe space.

And yet there was no doubting its importance. Americans had

been gripped by the trial, with plenty of the cable networks carrying long stretches of it live. That was partly thanks to Keane and his courtroom antics. But it was also because of what was at stake.

Keane had sued the African-American writer Susan Liston for libel over a paragraph in a book she'd written on the alt-right, in which she had referred to Keane as a 'slavery denier'. His case, brought before a federal court in Richmond, was simple. He could not be a slavery denier because there was nothing to deny. Black people had never been slaves in the United States.

Staat was now parroting Keane's arguments, the same ones everyone present had seen Keane make a hundred times before. Slaves' testimony was unreliable; slave owners' testimony was unreliable; the documents were unreliable. He used the word 'myth' a lot, Maggie noticed, as if it were a one-word rebuttal or perhaps an expletive. 'Myth!' he said again now, for the dozenth time.

Maggie looked around the lecture theatre. The first rows were packed with journalists, as were the seats surrounding her at the back. The entire rear of the hall was a thicket of tripods and TV cameras. As for the rest, it was a mixture of university notables, especially those associated with the Bentham Center, doubtless keen to ingratiate themselves with their patron, and handpicked graduate students. It seemed the Georgetown authorities hadn't wanted to take the risk of letting in undergrads, who were liable to whip out placards, heckle Staat or rush the stage. (Clearly, Maggie concluded, the Center for Free Speech had decided free speech had its limits.)

While Staat was off on a riff about the nature of libel, Maggie wondered about herself: was she here as a grad student or as a notable? She'd never really thought about her exact status at this institution. It was enough that she was here.

After the White House, after everything that had happened, she needed a chance to think – and that, she told herself, is what universities were for. Liz had begged Maggie to come live with her, her husband and kids in Atlanta – 'If you truly want to make a clean break, you have to leave that swamp of a city' – and Maggie had considered it, she really had. But seven days with her sister had been enough to confirm it would never work. Too much family, too much scrutiny.

She needed her own turf and, after the best part of a decade, that turf was Washington, DC. She'd never flatter it with the word 'home'. To this day, that meant Dublin. But Maggie knew her way around Washington and, for now, that was good enough.

Still, there was no denying that she needed to make a break. Writing essays and attending seminars felt like the right change. Now if she encountered a crisis, it might result in a missed lecture, rather than a nuclear conflagration and the end of the world. 'Why are academic politics so vicious?' ran the old gag. 'Because the stakes are so low.' And that suited Maggie just fine.

This lunchtime debate over the Keane trial, with the potential riot going on outside, was the closest she had got to politics since she'd left the administration. The tension in the hall, which was clearly getting to Baum and Bentham if not to Staat, who seemed to relish it, barely made a dent on Maggie's central nervous system: she had endured so much worse. But it was, at least, a reminder of the life she had left behind. She felt the first, unbidden stirrings of adrenalin.

Like a recovering alcoholic who'd risked a visit to a bar, she now cursed her own recklessness. She should never have come. She should have stayed in the library, or at home in her apartment. Studying history was meant to have been her escape from all this, a haven of calm, serene contemplation far away from political combat. This had been a mistake, a needless—

A thudding noise came from outside. Several heads turned in the hall; Baum seemed to jolt. Had there been an attempt on the door? Had one or other faction pushed forward, trying to break in? Maggie caught herself waiting. For the sound of broken glass or a scream, she wasn't sure, but something that might explain what had just happened. Instead, there was a resurgence in the chanting, louder now and angrier too. 'Don't know, don't care, nothing happened, nothing's there!'

Was this the sound of Keane's backers – the white supremacists, neo-Nazis and Klansmen – high on a frisson of triumph or, alternatively, the righteous thrill of victimhood? Were they cheering a successful charge on the building, or raging that they had been unjustly attacked by their opponents? Maggie was listening keenly, but it was hard to tell.

On the platform, Bentham was urging people to settle down. 'This, ladies and gentlemen, is exactly why this centre is so badly needed. As you can see with your own eyes, and hear with your own ears, the threat to free speech in this country is real. Yet our future depends on our being able to talk openly with each other, no matter how difficult the topic. That's why . . .'

As she spoke, Maggie noticed, the hands were trembling again. Baum was staring at the doors at the back of the hall, as if he feared a stampede at any moment. Many in the audience, perhaps following his lead, were doing the same thing. In the eye of this hurricane sat Staat, the smirk now unbound.

A sudden vibration made Maggie jump. She realized her heart was thumping as she took the phone from her pocket. A text message, from Donna Morrison, a former colleague from Maggie's first, happier stint at the White House. Morrison's response to the craziness of recent events had been to step out from the shadows, to quit the backroom, and run for office herself. She had made some history, becoming the first black woman elected as the Governor of Virginia.

The message was typical Donna: straight to the point.

I need your help.

Maggie put the phone back in her pocket. She'd not been short of job offers. There were old friends, and people she'd never met, constantly pestering her to come back to politics, to help out with this or that crisis. They always said a version of the same thing. 'You're the best troubleshooter in the business, Maggie – and I'm in trouble.'

It was flattering, but Maggie's mind was made up. She needed a break. Or, as she would tell each would-be employer: she had needed to get out, and the best way of sticking to that was not to get back in.

Her phone buzzed again.

Sighing, she pulled it out, mentally drafting her 'Thanks, but no thanks' reply.

She read the message and let out a gasp.

A man is dead, Maggie. I need you.

Chapter Three

Richmond, Virginia, 2.30pm

'How about a cookie?'

Maggie shook her head, though not because she didn't want to eat one of the chocolate chip treats, as wide as a saucer, laid out on the plate before her. Rather she had been in Washington long enough that at least some of its mores had left their mark on her. When they brought the dessert menu, you only ever ordered coffee or a mint tea. At lunch, the only drink required was a bottle of sparkling water. And in a meeting, all snacks were to be declined. Maggie struggled with the first two, but she had succumbed to the third. She now saw the little fruit platters or bowls of M&Ms left on Washington conference tables not as small gestures of courtesy but as a test, and a poorly concealed one at that.

'Baked them myself?'

'You're kidding. You're the Governor of Virginia. There's no way you've got the time to do that.'

'Oh yes, I do.' Donna Morrison looked up at the door, making sure no one was about to come in. 'I am the *menopausal* Governor of Virginia, who feels like she hasn't had a full night's sleep since the Bush administration.' Seeing Maggie's reaction, she added, 'What else am I gonna do between two and four am? There's only so much Fox a girl can watch.'

Maggie felt herself smile, wide and open. Long time since she'd smiled like that, she realized. Though, she now remembered, that was hardly uncommon in a meeting with Donna, who'd headed up the policy planning staff for the president they had both served so proudly. She was warm and welcoming, with an easy laugh. How she had come so far in Washington politics was a mystery to many in the city, including, it seemed, Donna herself. But there were lots like her in that administration, good people handpicked by a president who liked to boast he had a 'no shits' hiring policy.

'So,' the governor said, taking her place on the sofa opposite Maggie, and smoothing her skirt as she pivoted the conversation to business. 'Like I told you, a man is dead.'

'I know.'

When she'd first got Donna's text, and only for a moment, Maggie had wondered if the governor was referring to events directly outside the auditorium at Georgetown. Perhaps the commotion, that thudding noise they'd all heard, was the sound of a man crushed to death by protesters. Maybe the police had alerted the governor and she had instantly called Maggie.

But a cursory look at Twitter told her that the death her old friend had in mind was closer to home and within her state lines.

Shortly after eight o'clock this morning, a cleaner at UVA, Charlottesville, had discovered Professor Russell Aikman, long-serving member of the history faculty, dead in his office. He had been slumped over his desk, his brains sprayed over the antique maps that adorned his office walls. Which was why Maggie was now face to face with the new Governor of Virginia, fighting the urge to pick up a chocolate chip cookie.

'First question I asked, Maggie, was—'

'Is this suicide?'

'But they said no. Ruled it out within an hour. Ballistics and whatnot.'

'Which was not what you wanted to hear.'

'Damn right. I was *praying* they'd tell me he'd taken his own life. I mean, that would be horrible for his family. Just horrible. Not that this is much better. But at least, we could avoid—'

'All this.' Maggie gestured at her phone. The tweets had started straight away, as soon as word of Aikman's death had got out, which would have been shortly after the Staat vs Baum debate had begun.

One conservative talkshow host had got in early, harvesting thousands of retweets within an hour. *Tearing down statues is one thing. Taking a man's life, that's another. #RussellAikmanRIP*

But those on the other side of the argument had wasted no time either. Widely shared was a tweet by someone whose profile announced her as an activist in #pullthemdown, the campaign to remove Confederate-era statues. *Russell Aikman wrote about the history of slavery. Now he has been silenced by those who can't handle the truth. But #TheTruthLives*

'Exactly.' Donna's smile had gone. 'They're both claiming Aikman as a martyr for their cause, both blaming each other.'

'That's how things are here these days,' Maggie said. She was suddenly aware of her own voice, with its Irish accent, and worried that she sounded detached: the smug foreigner looking with pity on the basketcase nation America was becoming. Neither needed to say the name of the man they blamed.

'I know. But it's getting worse, Maggie. Let's say one or other of these groups did actually kill Aikman. Let's say that happened. That is a whole other level of serious. That's not just talking heads yammering at each other on TV or Facebook or whatever. That's . . .'

Maggie watched her run out of words. For all the folksy cookie talk, Donna Morrison looked gaunt, eaten up with anxiety.

'You think this could spread?'

'I tell you why I'm losing sleep, Maggie.' She corrected herself. 'Even more than usual. The verdict in the Keane trial is due this week. Friday, most likely.'

'The Keane trial? That guy's crazy. It's a publicity stunt. There's no way he could—'

'That's not what I'm hearing. That's not what I'm being told to prepare for.'

'You've got to be joking.'

'The defence say the signs are not good. They think there are grounds on which Keane could win.'

'That's ridiculous. He's already said—'

'Look, Maggie. You're not a lawyer and nor am I. I'm just telling you the advice they're giving me. Keane could win this thing, if only on a technicality.'

'Jesus Christ.'

'Just imagine if that happens, Maggie. A court in the southern United States declaring that slavery did not exist. You're too young to remember the Rodney King riots, but I'm not. Whole of LA blew up because white police beat a black man half to death and got away with it. This would be a thousand times worse. A thousand times. I'm telling you, Maggie, it wouldn't just start a riot. It would start a civil war.'

'Especially if the two sides are already killing each other.'

'Exactly. Think about it, Maggie. If we get into some death spiral thing here, with tit-for-tat killings, reprisals and all that – then that verdict on Friday will be like pouring a barrel of gasoline on a fire that's already raging.' She paused. 'And they're angry to start with.'

Maggie furrowed a brow.

'They've got a black woman sitting in the governor's mansion in Richmond, Virginia. The capital of the Confederacy.'

Maggie sighed. 'I hear you, Governor, I really do.'

'It's Donna to you, Maggie.'

'But I can't. I just can't. I'm out of this now. I'm—'

'Maggie. D'you know what the president – *our* president – used to call you?' She didn't wait for an answer. ' "Troubleshooter-in-chief".'

'Donna, please. Don't.'

' "You show Maggie Costello any crisis, any crisis at all . . ." ' She was impersonating his voice, and doing a half-decent job. ' "She'll get to the bottom of it. And then she'll solve it." That's what he said.'

'He was a very generous man.'

'Generous, my ass. He called it as he saw it. No bullshit praise from him.'

'I've moved on now.'

'Moved on? You're doing some hippy dropout college course!'

'I'm taking some time, to get my—'

'What? Get your head straight? Look, I get that. I *really* get that. Nothing I'd like more right now than a big long rest. Sheesh! And you went through a lot. I mean, *a lot*. We're all aware of what happened in the White House. You did something incredible. The nation owes you a great debt for that.'

'You don't need to flatter me, Donna.'

'No? Well, tell me what I do need to do, Maggie. I'm serious. Tell me what the fuck I need to do to get you to help me. To get to the bottom of this Aikman thing and shut it down, before it gets out of hand. Because I think a race war is about to erupt in my state and I am genuinely terrified that it could devour the whole country.'

Maggie stared at the floor. She didn't dare meet the governor's eye. She knew what it would do to her resolve.

'I need my life back,' Maggie said at last.

'I know you do,' Donna said quietly. 'And once this is done, you will and you must get your life back. But right now, you're the only person who can help. Please.'

There was a long silence, eventually broken by Maggie. 'I'll give you one week,' she said, rising to her feet. 'No more.'

The governor took her hand, clasping it tightly. 'We don't have a week, Maggie. We have less than five days.'

Chapter Four

Northern Virginia, 3.40pm

She was glad for the hour's drive to Charlottesville in the autumn sunshine along I-64. She would use the time to clear her head and work out something approaching a gameplan. Under blue skies, with trees rushing past in glittering shades of red, russet and gold, she would sift through what she knew as well as the larger and more important category of what she did not know.

She was drawing up a list of the known unknowns about Russell Aikman, when the supposedly alternative music station on the radio was interrupted by the sound of her phone ringing. The dashboard screen told her it was her sister Liz.

'What's wrong?'

'Well, hello to you too, Maggie. I'm grand, thank you very much for asking.'

'But it's the middle of the day. You always call in the evening.'

'For fuck's sake, Mags. I'm just calling my big sister because I feel like it. Why've you got such a big stick up your arse?'

Maggie smiled. 'So nothing wrong? You and the boys all OK?'

'All grand here in sunny Georgia. How's malarial DC?'

'Same as always.' With Liz, Maggie's instinct was always to hold back what she knew. Not out of a sense of professional confidentiality, though she was always careful about that. But because there was no point in exposing Liz to anxiety and fear her sister could do nothing about. What good would it do her?

'The same, eh? Well, I for one have just made a change in my life.'

'Oh no, don't tell me something's up with you and Paul.'

'No! Why the fuck would you think that?'

'Are you having an affair?'

'No, Margaret Costello, I am not having an affair.'

'So what is it then? What's the big "change"?'

There was a moment's silence and then: 'I don't want to tell you now.'

'Oh, come on, Liz.'

'It'll be an anticlimax.'

'Don't be like that. Tell me.'

'I don't want to.'

'Please, Liz. *Please*.'

'You're a right cow, sometimes, do you know that?'

'I do. I am a right cow. Now go on. Tell me.'

'All right. I am now seeing somebody.'

'So you *are* having an affair.'

'No. I'm *seeing* somebody. Like I told you I would. You know, a therapist.'

'Oh. You probably need to work on how you announce that.'

'Just had my third session.'

'Really? Just now?'

'Yep.'

'And how was it?'

'It was great actually. Really great. I just talked and talked.'

'Yes, somehow I can imagine that.'

'I mean, really talked. We went deep.'

'Wow. What's she like?'

'It's a he actually. Yves.'

'Yves?'

'Yves Lamarche. He's French.'

'Sounds handsome.'

'He is quite, actually. Not that that's relevant.'

'Are you sure that's a good idea?'

'Sure. Why wouldn't it be?'

'You know, all that stuff about transference. Projection.'

'Now you're just saying words. I'm ignoring you. I think it could be really good for me. Really clarifying. Yves says that—'

'What did it clarify?'

'I'm not going to get into that now. Besides, we've only just started. He says there's a lot of work to do.'

'I bet he does.'

'What's that supposed to mean?'

'Nothing. Ignore me.'

'No, what do you mean, "I bet he does"?'

'Only that he's not doing this for free, is he?'

'I'm going to ignore you and your cynical, negative energy. Because the thing is, Maggie, I bet you'd really benefit from doing it too.'

'What, seeing a therapist?'

'Don't say it like it's the weirdest thing ever.'

'And why would I do that?'

'Because it might help. Maybe you'll work out why you keep bouncing around, never really settling in one place—'

'I've lived in Washington for—'

'Never committing to one man.'

'Oh, here we go.'

'Come on, don't tell me you haven't wondered.'

'I can't bloody avoid wondering when I talk to you, can I? You talk about nothing else.'

'I mean it. Maybe it would help. Today Yves said we're going to go right back to the beginning. Talking about Quarry Street, growing up, all of it.'

'You don't even remember it, do you?'

'Some of it. But so much of it's hazy. Anyway, like you say: it's early days. But seriously, Mags. I bet you'd find it—'

'Listen, Liz, I need to go.'

'All right, be like that.'

'I'm not being like anything. I just need to go. It's the middle of the working day.' Silence at the other end. 'Talk later, yes?'

'All right. And stay safe, OK? I've only got one sister.'

It took another twenty minutes for Maggie to reach the Charlottesville Police Department, a low-rise, red-brick box next door to a multi-storey parking lot. The governor's office had called ahead, so Ed Grimes, Chief of Police, was expecting her. He ushered her into his office, where the back wall was cluttered with assorted shields, trophies and a mounted mission statement: *We aim to protect the freedom and safety of the people of Charlottesville.*

The chief was in uniform and had once been a beat cop but, had she not known that fact in advance, Maggie would never have guessed it. He had the harried face of a bureaucrat, his white skin faded under office light. He took his place behind his desk and instantly Maggie understood that he would be on the defensive, anxious that the state governor was looking over his shoulder.

'Thank you for seeing me,' Maggie began, offering her warmest smile. 'We hear great things about all you're doing here.'

'OK.'

'The governor is just very keen to be kept up to speed on the Aikman case.'

'All right.'

'What lines of inquiry you're pursuing.'

'Uh-huh.'

'What leads you have.'

The chief was looking across the table, saying nothing. If he had a deck of cards, he'd have been holding them flat against his ribcage.

Maggie tried again, more direct this time. 'So. What leads do you have?'

'Well, we're just at the start of our investigation, Miss Costello.'

Maggie repressed the urge to say 'Ms'. She nodded encouragement, before realizing the police chief was not planning on saying more.

'And which direction are you looking in, sir?'

'We're looking for whoever's guilty.'

Maggie leaned forward. 'Look, I've been doing this long enough to know that the last thing a homicide team needs is someone from up top coming down and treading all over your turf. I get that. But I promise you, it's in your interests to help me out here.'

He gave a small, tight smile that sent the blood straight into the veins of Maggie's neck. The smile of condescension. Maggie had seen it ten thousand times.

'How exactly is it in my interest, Miss Costello?'

'Because if you help me, I will report that back to the governor of this state. And if you don't, then I'll report that back too.' She smiled sweetly, allowing the unstated thought to linger in the air: big-time politicians could make the lives of small-time politicians – like the police chief of a city around the size of Charlottesville, for example – miserable if they wanted to.

Eventually, the chief reached for a pen at the top of his blotter and resettled the glasses on the bridge of his nose. He cleared his throat, as if about to deliver a formal briefing.

'As you know, Charlottesville has a recent and difficult history, especially involving activists of the so-called alt-right and their opponents on the alt-left.'

Maggie said nothing.

'This city has had a particularly active cell of the Black Lives Matter movement, centred on the university campus. We believe Prof Aikman's assailant is likely to have come from that circle.'

'And what makes you think that?'

'For one thing, students had easy access to the building in which the professor was found dead. The door to that building is opened by a keypad. Not just anybody could open that door. You had to know the code. Which dozens of students do.'

'Although there'll be others who know it too.'

'Second, Professor Aikman had clashed with the leadership of the Black Lives Matter movement. With two people in particular.'

'Clashed? How?'

Now Grimes reached under his blotter and produced a copy of a letter, handing it to Maggie.

She skimmed it, but the key lines leapt out:

As students of color, we write to express our deep concern at a pattern of grading which we believe is unjust . . . does not reflect the particularity of our experience . . . can only suggest if not bias then insensitivity . . . issues go wider than this particular case . . . lack of diversity at the highest levels of the faculty.

'You're saying that Black Lives Matter activists killed Russell Aikman because he gave them *low grades*? Besides, this is addressed to the whole history faculty, not just Aikman.'

'There's also this.' He slid another piece of paper across the desk. It was a petition, 'We the undersigned . . .' at the top and a long list of names, all of them professors of one kind or another. She scanned it, looking in vain for Aikman.

'But he didn't sign this.'

'Exactly.'

Only now did Maggie take a close look at the preamble paragraph to which 'We the undersigned' had lent their good name. It was from a year earlier, calling on the university authorities to confirm that under no circumstances would an invitation to visit the campus be extended to the President of the United States. There'd been efforts like this across the country, usually pushed by students first, with faculty trailing along behind. But clearly Aikman had refused to play his assigned role.

'Is that it?' Maggie asked, sounding unimpressed though her resolve was wavering.

'No. There's one more thing. The statue.' Grimes produced his third visual aid, a photograph of the bronze statue of Robert E. Lee, the lead general of the Confederacy, astride his horse, both man and beast now turned green with oxidization. It had always been a Charlottesville landmark, but the battle to remove it had given it a new currency. Just visible on the base of the statue, though now bleached out by frantic cleaning, were the words graffitied in spray paint: *Black Lives Matter.*

'What's this got to do with Aikman?'

'Lots of people around the university wanted that statue gone. Lots of Aikman's students.'

'And he said it should stay up.'

'Yup. Said, "You can't erase history." '

Maggie took the picture and looked at it hard. Just a man on a horse, rendered in bronze. But its presence in a city with a large black population had become a national wound. And Aikman had been on the side of the past against the future – or at least that's how the activists would have seen it.

'See it from my point of view, Miss Costello. They had the means, with access to that building. And they had the motive; several motives, in fact.' He gestured at his trifecta of paperwork. 'All we're looking for is the individual who pulled the trigger.'

Chapter Five

Court 73, Richmond, Virginia, 11.45am

'I trust your honour has Exhibit two hundred and twenty-three in front of her? I'd like the record to show that I have entered into evidence a volume entitled *Twelve Years a Slave*.'

'So ordered.'

William Keane was pacing, a panther circling the turf he had made his own: the small but crucial space between the judge, the jury and the witness box. Over the past weeks, he had grown ever more comfortable in this arena, a preacher in his pulpit, a pitcher on his mound. Here he would allow either his voice, his arms or his hands – and sometimes all three in combination – to command the court. Much ink had flowed on the question of whether his lack of legal background was an advantage – freeing him of the hidebound, stale argot that was the mother tongue of the professional attorneys he faced – or just more evidence of his phenomenal gifts. This man who had never spent a day in court until acting for himself in this trial was the star performer day after day. He was a natural.

'As the court knows, we are approaching the day of reckoning. Soon these proceedings will draw to a close. We will at last be able to leave this place, and re-enter civilization.' He turned to the jurors, with a benign, conspiratorial smile, lowering his voice: 'What a relief that will be, huh?' He returned to courtroom volume. 'At that point it will be up to this court to deliver its solemn judgement, to decide if I was libelled by the defendant when she called me a "slavery denier".'

Part of it was simply his costume. Keane understood that a courtroom was a theatre and that looking the part was an essential component of any performance. The southern gentleman in a white suit was as much of a cliche as the English gent in pinstripes, but it worked for that very reason. It tripped some deep nerve of recognition.

Besides, Keane knew not to overdo it. There was no bolo tie, no ten-gallon hat. The look he was going for was less Boss Hogg, more Atticus Finch. He wanted to convey southern decency and intellectual authority, both a match and a contrast with the po-faced, Ivy League intellectuals on the other side.

'Ladies and gentlemen of the jury, you have sat through many hours of expert, often obscure, even arcane testimony' – *testee-moan-ee* – 'but now I ask you to contemplate a text I suspect you think you know well. Why, it even became a Hollywood movie.' He gave a childish grin, as if about to offer a treat. 'We're talking about this!'

With a flourish, he produced a battered, ancient book and held it aloft. 'I suspect some of you saw that movie. I'm not going to say you *enjoyed* it. How could any decent person enjoy such a litany of horrors?' He looked at his feet and shook his head, as if lamenting the sheer awfulness of it all.

'But many of you will have an idea of the period my opponents call "the age of slavery" from that movie. It will have shaped you. It will have got into your very soul. I call as my next witness, Professor Andrea Barker.'

A marshal ushered a white woman in her mid-thirties into the box. She wore a pant suit and had long, expensively cut hair. The jurors had seen some mousy, nervous academics take the stand, but the way this woman smiled and held Keane's gaze suggested that now, at last, he had met his match.

She raised her right hand, placed it on the Bible and took the oath. She gave her name and in a strong, clear voice announced that she taught history at Wellesley College.

'And that's a women's liberal arts college in Massachusetts, am I right?' Keane was sure to enunciate and emphasize every word, so that his twelve-strong audience could not miss the signal each one carried. If he gave special weight to one in particular, it might have been 'liberal'. Or maybe 'women's' which he seemed to pronounce as 'lesbian'.

'You've written especially about this book, *Twelve Years a Slave*, yes?'

'That's right.'

'You're an expert?'

'I suppose so, yes.'

'Well, we're honoured to have you down here in Old Virginia.

Thanks for making the journey from all the way up there in Massachusetts. Hope you've been getting a fine southern welcome.'

The woman shifted in the box, unsure how she was meant to respond. Was this a barbed reference to the huge crowds penned in by police opposite the courthouse, divided into their two camps, screaming slogans at each other from morning till night? Or was it to be taken at face value?

'Thank you,' she said.

'We're obliged. Now let me begin with a simple question, Professor. Who is the author of *Twelve Years a Slave*?'

'Solomon Northup, a free man who was kidnapped and sold into slavery in Louisiana.'

'I know that's the name on the cover. But I'm asking who *wrote* the book? Who put pen to paper and wrote the sentences that appear on these pages?'

'Well, clearly a book such as—'

'Shall I refresh your memory? Your honour, here I'm quoting from Professor Barker's widely praised essay, "The Redemption of Solomon Northup". In this passage, she tells us about a famous New York politician – a liberal, so-called abolitionist – and she writes that this politician "asked a lawyer and fledgling poet, David Wilson, if he'd be willing to interview Solomon and turn his story into a book". This man Wilson – I'm still quoting Professor Barker – he "jumped at the chance". And then you go on, Professor – these are your words – "Thus, *Twelve Years a Slave* wasn't even written by Solomon Northup but by a white amanuensis." '

'What I meant there is that—'

'Oh, you'll get your turn, don't you worry. But I ain't done quoting. Your very next sentence is, "Wilson's authorship of the narrative has long cast doubt over its authenticity." My, my, Professor. What's that you say? "Doubt over its authenticity"? *Twelve Years a Slave?* Well, that's like the holy scripture of the slavery industry, isn't it? And there's you,' and at this Keane turned his back on his witness and faced the jury, 'a liberal arts professor from up there in Massachusetts,' savouring each syllable, 'admitting, *admitting*, that there are doubts over its authenticity.'

'That's not what I'm saying at all. The context is—'

'I'm a simple man, Professor. I'm just reading the words you've written. In black and white.'

'Objection. There's no point questioning a witness if the plaintiff refuses to let that witness answer.'

'Sustained.'

'Let me move on, your honour. *Uncle Tom's Cabin*. How would you describe that book, Professor Barker?'

'I don't follow.'

'What kind of book is it?'

'It's a novel.'

'A novel. Fiction. Made up. Is that right?'

'It's obviously based—'

'Is it a novel or isn't it?'

'It is.'

'And it came out one year *before Twelve Years a Slave*, is that right?'

'Yes.'

'And can you tell the court what the author of *Uncle Tom's*

Cabin said about Solomon Northup's book? What she said about *Twelve Years a Slave*?'

'Well, I don't have the exact—'

'Don't you worry, Professor. I have the words right here. The words of Harriet Beecher Stowe, the author of *Uncle Tom's Cabin*, when she read *Twelve Years a Slave* a year *after* her book came out. Here's what she said. "It is a singular coincidence that this man was carried to a plantation in the Red River country, that same region where the scene of Tom's captivity was laid; and his account of this plantation, his mode of life there, and some incidents which he describes, form a striking parallel to that history." What do you say to that, Professor?'

'Well, I would say it means that she found further vindication of her own narrative in Northup's account.'

'Or that Northup had copied a novel – *a made-up story* – to make up a story of his own.'

'No, that would be to assume—'

'But that's what you yourself said. I'm quoting your paper again. "Slave narratives were never intended to give an unbiased view . . . they contain inaccuracies, distortions and embellishments." Not my words, ladies and gentlemen, but the words of Professor Barker of Wellesley College, Massachusetts. "Inaccuracies, distortions and embellishments".'

'You're twisting my words.'

'Am I? Am I twisting them as much as Solomon Northup? Or do you not mind "inaccuracies, distortions and embellishments", so long as the cause is just?'

'Objection. He's badgering the witness.'

'Sustained. Mr Keane, I won't warn you again.'

'I'm nearly done, your honour. I have just one last passage I think merits quotation from Professor Barker's paper. It's the core of her argument. She tells her readers not to get hung up on a "false standard of authenticity". Don't let's get hung up, folks! What matters is "Northup's voice, not his facts; that voice is what makes *Twelve Years a Slave* so enduring."

'When do we say such a thing, ladies and gentlemen? When do we say, "Oh, it's not the facts that count, it's the voice, it's the *feeling*"? When do we say that? We say that when we've seen a movie or watched a TV show or read a fairy tale. We say that about *fiction*. Because that's what this is.

'*Twelve Years a Slave* won all those Oscars and was a hit movie and that's fine. You know why? Because it belongs in the movies. In the land of make-believe. Hollywood. The Dream Factory. La La Land. That's where it belongs. Because *Twelve Years a Slave* is fiction. Just like this whole slavery story is fiction, from beginning to end. Every lash of the whip, every manacle on the wrist, every chain on the ankle, it's all a fairy tale, designed to make white folks into ogres and black folks into angels. It's made up, invented out of whole cloth. And any day now, ladies and gentlemen of the jury, you'll finally have a chance to say so.

'No further questions, your honour.'

Chapter Six

Charlottesville, Virginia, 5.25pm

The light had faded to an autumn twilight by the time Maggie emerged from the Charlottesville Police Department. It was dark enough for the glow of candles on the opposite side of the street to be visible, even from here. At first, she thought it was some kind of display, designed to entice custom into the Tin Whistle pub that faced the police station. But as her eyes adjusted, she could see that the candles were, in fact, held by a small group, huddling together like carol singers on the Dublin street corners of her youth.

Except this group was not comprised of blue-rinsed Irish ladies but a combination of black and white activists, none older than thirty. They were murmuring a tune – it might have been 'Amazing Grace' – and three or four were carrying banners. *Hope Not Hate*, said one. *No to Bigotry*, declared another.

Maggie approached to get a better look. She took her place alongside two others, both with notebooks, who were scribbling down the words of the group's apparent leader: a burly, bearded African-American, he towered over them both.

'Oh, we're used to that, my friend. Anything goes down in this town, our name's in the frame. Always. But we're not going to let that happen this time. No way.'

'Police sources are telling us there was a history of antagonism between Black Lives Matter activists and Professor Aikman.' It was the female reporter, her hair so blonde and rigid that Maggie glanced around, looking for the camera.

'I know that. I know what the police are saying. They're saying it to you, they're saying it to us. To our face. All this, "Russell Aikman was your enemy." That's bullshit. You hear me?'

'Isn't it true he was on the other side of the statue debate?'

The leader smiled. 'Lot of people in this town on the other side of that debate. Lot of people in this *country*. You think we're going to start *killing* them all?'

'And the access to the building?'

'Plenty of people got access to that too. Not only black folks who got that code.' Without breaking his stride, he handed a flier to a woman who passed by, talking into her phone.

Maggie saw her moment. She held out her phone, reporter-style, as if to record his answers.

'Until yesterday, what did you know of Russell Aikman?'

'That's just it. I hardly heard of him. No disrespect to the guy, but he just wasn't one of the big players in the whole statue thing. He wasn't shooting his mouth off on CNN, you know what I'm saying?'

'Not on your enemies list?'

'We don't have an enemies list. Nothing like it.'

'But if you did?'

'He wouldn't be on it. The guy was not on our *radar*.'

In unison, the two reporters offered hurried thanks and turned around. Maggie wondered if it was something he – or perhaps she – had said. But then she spotted the Chief of Police coming out of the building opposite. They wanted to buttonhole him.

Maggie turned back to the leader and spoke more quietly now. 'Mr . . .'

'Mike Jewel. Call me Mike.'

'Mike, who do you think killed Russell Aikman?'

'I don't have a *name* for you. I ain't a detective. Mind you, they don't have a name either.' He nodded towards the police chief. 'But it's obvious. White supremacists killed that guy.'

'Why's that obvious?'

'You seen Aikman's work? You taken a look at what that guy was writing?'

Maggie shook her head.

Jewel pulled out his phone and went straight to a tab he'd kept open, apparently for this purpose. 'Look at that.'

He was holding up the screen at an angle that made it hard for Maggie to read. It appeared to be an article in an academic journal, reviewing a book by Aikman. The title of the book: *The Role of Bonded and Indentured Labor in the Virginian Economy,* 1680 *to* 1820.

'I'm not sure what I'm looking—'

Jewel withdrew the screen. 'Look, this professor went through the archives, line by line. He calculated the exact number of slaves kept at every major property and plantation in this state, including Monticello and Mount Vernon.' Still holding Maggie's gaze, he peeled off another flier and handed it to a teenage boy.

'I see.'

'He didn't just work out how many slaves Thomas Jefferson and George Washington kept. He worked out how many *died* on their watch. Aikman did the work, you know what I'm saying?'

'Right.'

'But he didn't stop with the big names. He went through the records – the wills, the auction ledgers, ships' manifests – the whole nine yards. I mean, he was relentless. He kept going till he had the exact number of slaves kept by every big family in Virginia. He had it down. Chapter and verse.'

'And those families—'

'They're *still here*. That's the whole point. They're still here. It's not that long ago, my friend. Those big plantation fortunes, those names – they never went away.'

'And you think one of them might have wanted to silence Russell Aikman.'

'Now you're putting words in my mouth. I never said that. Maybe those guys are too rich to care what some professor's saying in a book no one's gonna read. But the rest of them? The *movement*. White supremacy is real, my friend. It *lives*. And they'd have had no doubt who Russell Aikman was. *What* he was. To them, it would have been obvious. Finding out what he found out, writing what he wrote? That made him a traitor. A traitor to the white race.'

Maggie could see Jewel himself was now distracted, glancing across the street to the police department, where Ed Grimes was addressing a larger group of reporters. The key change seemed to be the arrival of not one but two cameras, their appearance acting as the cue for more journalists to gather. Maggie had seen that dynamic in action before. For all the chin-stroking essays you could read about 'the changing media landscape', it was still TV that mattered.

It was then she caught a glimpse that she processed not in her brain but in her gut. Her stomach seemed to flip while her mind struggled to keep up. She had to squint into the gloom to check what her eyes thought they'd seen.

There, by the second tripod, setting up. Could it be? She hadn't seen him in so long. His hair was a little shorter now, the loose curls tamed, but it was still thick and dark, just as she remembered it. In his boots and faded jeans, peering now into the lens, he could have passed for an American TV news cameraman, though there was that familiar reticence in his posture, a suggestion he was holding back somehow, that she recognized in an instant.

Now he looked up and met her eye. He showed no hint of surprise. On the contrary, he seemed to have been waiting for this moment, as if they'd arranged it. Without saying anything, they both moved towards each other. He broke into a small jog to cross Market Street, until their faces were just a few inches apart.

'Uri, I don't believe it.'

'Of all the race riots in all the towns in all the world, you walk into mine.'

She laughed, smiling wider than the joke merited. 'It's good to see you. You look great.'

'So do you. You always did.'

He opened his arms and Maggie stepped forward into the hug, not sure what to do with her hands, one of which was still holding her phone. She reached for his shoulder, but clashed with his arm as it attempted to make the same move. She realized that when they knew each other they never hugged this way, like two guys in a bar.

'I thought you were in London.'

'I was for a while. Then back to Israel for a bit. My mother's getting old.' He shrugged: *you know how it is*. 'And now here.'

'You live in Charlottesville?'

Now it was his turn to give a disproportionate laugh. 'New York. I've been making a film about the whole statues thing. When it kicked off, I came down.'

'That's . . . amazing. What are the chances?'

'Actually, I knew you'd be here.'

Maggie turned her eyebrows into a question mark.

'I have a friend in the governor's office.'

'Ah.'

'I guessed you'd come straight here. I wanted to see you.'

'I'm glad. It's good to see you too.' She held his gaze, looking deep into those green eyes she remembered. She felt a familiar stirring, the sensation simultaneously warm and unsettling.

'I mean, I needed to see you. About all this.' He gestured towards the police chief and the candlelit vigil for Russell Aikman. 'There's something you need to know.'

Chapter Seven

Charlottesville, Virginia, 6.40pm

They were in the lobby of his hotel in Charlottesville, a pair of townhouses in the historic district converted into a boutique 'inn'. Only now, after Uri had suggested they take the three-minute walk from the vigil outside the police department, did Maggie have a chance to take in properly the sight of this man whose bed she had shared for . . . how long had they been together? Longer than with any other man she had known, before or since.

Physically, he had barely changed, though shorter hair made him look more serious. The difference was rather in the way he carried himself and the way he looked at her. Back when they had known each other – during those first intense days in Jerusalem and then shuttling between New York and DC – there was something boyish and open about his face, a sweet eagerness that she had been unable to resist. Now he seemed warier and perhaps wiser, as if life had sat him down and instructed him in some of its harder lessons. She wondered if she looked the same way to him. Given all that had happened, she probably did.

He ordered tea for them both, then pulled out a laptop which he placed on the low table between them. He moved his chair close to hers, so that they were side by side, facing the screen. As he leaned in to the keyboard, typing in a series of passwords, she caught the scent of him – a parcel of neural information that seemed to travel straight through her skin.

'OK, so these are rushes of an interview I did about two weeks ago. Do you know this guy?' He pressed play, unspooling footage of a man she did not recognize. The man wasn't saying anything, just occasionally clearing his throat or flicking dust off his jacket. He seemed to be waiting for the interview to start, as the lighting was adjusted around him. That figured: Uri could be a pain-in-the-arse perfectionist when it came to framing and lighting a shot. But she still had no clue who this man was. He was no model or actor, even if Uri was giving him the Hollywood treatment.

'Who is it?'

Uri pulled away from the machine and sat back in his chair, prompting Maggie to shift too so that they could face each other. It seemed so strange to be in the same room again, talking together, as if the last few years of absence had just fallen away. A memory resurfaced that was once so fresh it stung.

They'd been in a bar in Washington, The Dubliner, a faux-Irish pub she couldn't stand, packed with the usual crowd of lobbyists and legislative assistants and reporters, all jostling and jockeying, forever trying to grab hold of a better place on the DC monkey bars, even if that meant edging someone else off. To her, they looked as strained and sweaty as marines on an assault course.

He kept her waiting, she remembered that. Long enough that she'd had two whiskies by the time he arrived. Maybe three.

And then he appeared, looking dark and handsome and with eyes so lost, you wanted to lose yourself in them. And he told her that he'd wanted to make it work, he really had, but he had seen what she was like, how she couldn't sit still. He reminded her how she'd been when they'd taken a holiday together – in a perfect corner of Santorini – just a few weeks earlier, how she'd been unable to lie on a beach for more than half an hour. 'I'm Irish, I burn,' she'd said. But he knew better. He saw the way she would reach for her phone, the way she needed to be where things were happening, or as he put it, 'at the dead centre of the shitstorm'. He called her 'an adrenalin junkie with a Messiah complex'. (Though on that occasion he'd been quoting Liz.)

She hadn't waited for him to say the words. She'd gathered her things, kissed him hard on the lips and said goodbye before he had the chance. She had never seen him again after that. And she never again set foot in The fucking Dubliner.

Sitting now in the lobby of this hotel, the trees flanking the entrance visible through the windows, their fairy lights twinkling, Maggie wanted to ask if he'd found with someone else what he'd been looking for with her. Did he now have a wife? Did they have children? Did he have a gorgeous little son or a beautiful baby daughter? Had he made a home?

But he did not answer any of those questions. Instead he answered the question that she had actually asked.

'His name is Mitchell Boult. He teaches history at the University of Pennsylvania.'

'OK.'

'Or rather he did.'

'What do you mean, "did"?'

'Maggie, I was following this guy for my film. About the statues campaign. He was one of the first people who got involved. He served on a state commission to advise on the future of memorials in Pennsylvania. His specialism was the civil war. He was the real deal.'

'Right.'

'Are you tired or something?'

'No, why? What do you mean?'

'It's just, it seems like you're a bit away, you know. Like maybe you weren't listening.'

'No, no, I'm listening. I mean, I suppose what I'm thinking is: it's quite a coincidence, isn't it?'

'About Boult? That's just it, he—'

'No. I mean about us.' She instantly regretted that 'us'. 'I mean, you. Being here. And me. At the same time. Guessing I would come here, and then: there I am!' In trying to sound light, she sounded heavy.

'I don't understand. You don't want me to be here?'

'No, of course not. It's great to see you, Uri. Really. It's just, you know, what a coincidence!' The voice straining for lightness again. If she could hear it in herself, so could he.

As she insisted he go on, that he tell her all about Mitchell Boult, she scolded herself – for ruining it, for being suspicious, for being paranoid, for letting her past infect her present.

'So you were saying about Boult: brilliant professor.'

'And really good guy.'

'Sure.'

'Well, last week they found him dead. They thought it was a heart attack.'

'But it wasn't?'

'I don't know, Maggie. Boult's wife was suspicious. She kept telling everyone how fit he was. He'd had a medical a couple of months ago and he was fine. All clear. Still the doctors insisted: "Look, these things can happen." '

'But?'

'But then I heard about Aikman. You know, both historians. Both experts on the same period.'

'OK. But that really might just be a coincidence.'

Maggie heard her own voice, separate from her, listening to it as it talked to Uri about these men neither of them really knew. She struggled to make sense of it. Once she and Uri had conversed in intimate whispers, their heads propped up on pillows. They had touched each other, skin on skin. And now here they were, their two voices talking in regular sentences, like strangers, in a hotel lobby in Charlottesville.

'That's what I thought too. Until I saw this.'

He angled the computer for her. It was displaying the cover page of a PDF document. *Perspectives on Public Commemoration and the Sacralization of Memory: November 21 to November 22.*

'This is what Boult was working on when he died.'

'Organizing this conference?'

'Yes. Though they called it, how do you pronounce it, a *collock-you-um*?'

Maggie nodded, remembering how she liked his rare mispronunciations, how she never wanted to correct them.

He gestured at the screen. 'Click on it.'

She opened the first page. Standard conference format, detailing registration at 09.00, introductory remarks at 09.45 to be delivered by Prof Mitchell Boult, here described as the co-convenor of the 'colloquium', then various breakout sessions, including one that caught her eye: *The William Keane trial: a roundtable.*

'Keep going.'

She scrolled through, unsure what she was looking for. Finally she reached the last page of the document, scanning it until she had reached the closing session of the final day.

Scheduled for 16.00 were concluding remarks from Prof Russell Aikman, University of Virginia. But that wasn't what had troubled Uri. That wasn't what had made him drive several hundred miles to meet Maggie again after all these years.

'See how he's described,' Uri said, touching the screen with his finger.

It was the word that appeared after Aikman's name, the same bit of academese that had described Boult. *Co-convenor.*

Maggie murmured it almost to herself. 'They organized this thing together.'

'Exactly,' said Uri, with an excitement that sounded more like relief. 'Now what are the chances that two men working on a conference both—'

'—end up dead—'

'—within a week of each other?'

She looked at him and he looked at her, their gaze unbroken. She felt that familiar longing again, a hunger that was very specific to this man. She pushed the feeling back down below the surface and listened as he spoke again.

'I know you, Maggie Costello. And I know you know that this is no coincidence.'

Chapter Eight

Court 73, Richmond, Virginia, 2.45pm

'Your honour, our next witness needs some assistance.'

Exactly as Keane had planned, everyone in court – press, public and the defence team around Susan Liston and her publishers – turned the same way at the same moment, all eyes shifting to the double-door entrance. There a tall African-American man in something akin to a nurse's uniform appeared, moving slowly. He was pushing a wheelchair, which eventually was revealed to be ferrying an ancient black woman, almost fetally curled into the seat. Both of her hands gripped the top of a cane, their fingers gnarled and claw-like. The hair on her head was flecked with silver and iron.

The judge – white, female, middle-aged and usually keen to make a great show of her impatience with verbose lawyers and long-winded experts – was now conspicuously generous, allowing both the witness and her carer to take their time.

'No hurry at all, Ms Henderson,' she soothed, as the wheelchair completed its long trek across the courtroom. Then the judge, and everyone else, watched the elaborate process required to help the witness out of the chair and onto the stand. Finally she was seated, her hands still clasping the cane, her nurse standing close by, like a bodyguard for a president.

She took the oath, identifying herself as Vivian Henderson, of Jonesboro, Arkansas. Her voice seemed to take the judge and everyone else by surprise. It was clear and unexpectedly loud.

William Keane rose to his feet. 'Miss Henderson, it's an honour to meet with you like this.'

'Not Miss. Mrs.' A high-pitched noise pierced the air. The carer stepped forward, fiddled with a device close to the woman's ear, and stepped back again.

'Oh, I beg your pardon. I was just—'

'My husband may have passed thirty-seven years ago, but that don't mean he's not my husband.'

'Quite so, Mrs Henderson. Quite so.'

Liston smiled, as did her lawyers.

'Now Mrs Henderson, my mamma always told me there are certain questions you never ask a lady, and I like to think I'm a gentleman so I hesitate to—'

'I'm ninety-nine years old.'

The whole court dissolved into laughter at that, the judge included. Liston and the rest of the defence team wore broad smiles. Over in the press seats, journalists leaned forward, wondering if Keane was, at last, about to be bettered in verbal combat.

'Oh, you are ahead of me, Miss – I beg your pardon –

Mrs Henderson. You are *way* ahead of me.' Keane theatrically turned over the first in a sheaf of papers and cleared his throat.

'Your honour, the witness has told us that she was born nearly a century ago, born – correct me if I'm wrong, Mrs Henderson – in the small town of Warren, Arkansas.'

'That's right.'

'And the reason we've called you to the court today is that you've become something of an institution in Arkansas, a state-wide *treasure*, isn't that right, Mrs Henderson?'

'I don't know about no treasure,' she said. 'I ain't seen no treasure, I tell you that.'

More laughter.

'You are modest as well as elegant, Mrs Henderson. Can you tell the court why you've become well-known in Arkansas, please?'

'Well, I suppose you're thinking about the talks I give. To the schoolchildren. About my family.'

'That's right!' Keane pivoted to face the jury and the press benches. 'That's exactly what I have in mind. Do tell us about those, please.'

'Well, I'm an old lady now. And my father was old when I was born. And his father was old when he was born. And that man, I mean my grandfather—'

'I don't want to interrupt you, Mrs Henderson, but would I be right if I simplified things by saying you are old enough to have had a grandfather who told you that he remembered slavery?'

'Didn't just *tell* me he remembered slavery. He *did* remember slavery.'

'All right. So let's start with some of what he told you.'

'Well, he told me about those long days in the fields. Starting with the sun, working till dusk. How the sweat on his back would boil, like oil on a pan.'

'What else, Mrs Henderson? Did he speak about any people in particular?'

'I remember him telling me about the master's son, John Jr. That man was so cruel, he used to set traps on his land, with alligator's teeth so sharp they'd bite through a man's ankle, clean through to the bone. Those traps. He set them in the fields—'

'He, Mrs Henderson?'

'John Jr. If any of his boys – that's what he called men like my grandfather – tried to escape or even strayed out of line, they'd get their legs caught in one of them steel traps. Like they was a fox or a hare. This John Jr, he'd leave a man in there. Wriggling and howling. Not just an hour or two, neither. But for a day and a night. Those men would be baying like wolves at the moon.' Her delivery was practised, like a tour guide in a museum. These were lines she had clearly uttered a hundred times before.

'That's what your grandfather told you?'

'Yes, sir.'

'And he named this *horrific* individual, this *monster*, as John Jr?'

'That's right.'

'Singled him out? By name?'

'He sure did.'

He nodded. 'And your grandfather, he'd seen this John Jr and his infinite cruelties, he'd seen all this with his own eyes?'

'You bet.'

'That's what he told you.'

'He told me, "A face as cruel as that, you never forget."'

'That's powerful testimony, Mrs Henderson. Powerful testimony.' Keane looked towards his feet and shook his head, as if once again moved by the agony of it all.

He lifted his eyes and quietly, sensitively, asked, 'Do you remember when he died? Your grandfather, I mean.'

'I do, sir. It was when I was ten years old.'

'And how old do you think he was then? Roughly?'

'I was always told he lived till he was ninety.'

'Thank you, Mrs Henderson. That's what I thought. That's what I've read. And using those numbers, I've done the math. I worked out all the dates. When you were born, when your daddy was born, when your grandpappy was born. And I assumed – for the sake of argument – that he was *born* right there in that plantation, back in 1840. That's the earliest he could possibly have been there. I have the records here in front of me. It's exhibit one hundred and thirty-three, your honour. Mrs Henderson, do you know what the documents say about this plantation of yours?'

'What do they say, Mr Keane?'

'Well, it's the darnedest thing.'

'What is?'

'This John Jr.'

'Yes.'

'He exists.'

'Well, I know he exists. My grandpa told me all about him.'

'But he did not exist *then*.' Keane brandished a sheet of paper, holding it high in the air, for all to see, though of course no one could read a word of it at that distance. 'There *was* a John Jr at the Stamps plantation, ladies and gentlemen of the jury. There sure was. He was the son of the first master. And he may well have been a tyrant and a bully and a wicked, wicked man. But he was dead and in his grave by the year of our Lord 1837. And that, Mrs Henderson, is fully three years before your grandpappy drew his first breath.'

'Well, all I can tell you is what he had seen with his own eyes, a man so cruel—'

'I hear you, Mrs Henderson. We all hear you. Half the schoolchildren of Arkansas have heard you tell this story. And it's a *wonderful* story. Don't get me wrong. But it can't have happened.'

'Don't you tell me it didn't happen. My grandfather, Bailey McGraw, told me what he had seen with—'

'With his own eyes, yes, yes, you said that. A man doing unspeakable things. But that man, this evil monster, was already *dead*. So I ask you, is it possible that you – or maybe your grandfather – made a *mistake*. I mean, this was a long, long time ago. You already shared with the court how old you are, Mrs Henderson. It means your grandpappy was telling you these stories – even if he told them to you on his deathbed, with his last gasp of God's sweet air – what, eighty-nine years ago? Memories fade, don't they, Mrs Henderson? I mean, I can't remember where I parked my car some mornings, and that can be a matter of eighty-nine minutes, let alone eighty-nine years!'

He laughed warmly, charitably, and much of the court laughed along with him. Susan Liston looked around the room from her table full of lawyers, with its stacks of ring binders, trying to gauge the temperature.

Now he lowered his voice. 'Mrs Henderson, is it possible that your grandfather was, in fact, telling you about John Jr's *son*?'

'What's that?'

Keane repeated his question at the same, softer volume. The old lady began fiddling with her hearing aid, sending another piercing squawk of feedback through the room.

Keane offered his question a third time, his patience now of the strained, unsmiling variety. 'Could we be talking about John Jr's son?'

'Well, maybe, I suppose,' she faltered. 'Was he called John too?'

'You know what,' Keane said encouragingly, 'maybe that's it. Maybe there were *two* John Jrs! I mean, that can happen, right? That would clear this whole thing up. Let's look right here, shall we.'

He began rummaging through his papers, as if genuinely seeking to resolve a question in his own mind. 'Here we go,' he murmured, like a librarian thumbing through a stack. 'Your honour, exhibit one hundred and twenty-nine. This records the heads of household at the Stamps plantation. There's the first John, dead in 1820. And there's the notorious John Jr, the villain of our story, dead in 1837, just like I said. And who do we have here? Yes, this is the son. And he's called . . .'

Keane let the sentence hover, incomplete, in the air for a while. A second, then another second, as he busied himself with the documents, apparently squinting and checking, when of course he knew exactly how this sentence ended. The court was hushed, waiting for the word that might answer this riddle. Finally, Keane spoke.

'George,' he said, with what sounded like heartfelt disappointment. 'The son's name was George. After that came another George – George Jr – then a Thomas. No more Johns, I'm afraid.' He looked at Vivian Henderson, saying nothing.

Then, as he knew she would, she sought to fill the void. 'I don't understand. He told me all about him, about the way the blood would splatter on his shirt during a whipping, about the metal teeth on those traps . . .' The phrases ran away from her, until she was quiet.

'Is it possible that he was talking about someone else?'

'What do you mean?'

'That maybe he got confused somewhere down the line. A different plantation maybe?'

'I don't think so. He was only ever on that one.'

'Really? I thought in one of your talks – I've seen it on YouTube – you said he was sent to Louisiana for a while. Could he have met this "John Jr" there, perhaps?'

'No, but that was later. I mean it was—'

'You mean earlier, don't you?'

'What? I don't . . . I don't . . .' The woman looked imploringly at the judge. 'Could I have a drink of water?'

The carer brought a glass of water and watched the old lady as she drank it down. He placed a hand on hers, then as he returned to his unofficial sentry post, he shot a hard stare back in Keane's direction.

'I'm sorry to labour this point, Mrs Henderson. But a moment ago you told us your grandfather was only ever on that one plantation, the Stamps plantation. But in the YouTube film of one of your talks – your honour has the reference for it in the bundle – you definitely speak about the years he spent picking cotton as a slave in Louisiana. Would your honour like me to play that extract to the court?'

'That won't be necessary, Mr Keane.'

'All right.'

'And Mr Keane?'

'Yes, your honour?'

'The witness is feeling the strain somewhat. Can we proceed to the core point, do you think?'

'I surely can, your honour, I surely can.' He smiled and dipped his head in a show of courtly manners. 'Mrs Henderson, none of us wants to keep you here too long. So if I could ask you again: was your much-loved grandfather on one plantation or two?'

In a voice quieter than the one she had used when she first took the stand, and with a slight tremble, she replied, 'He was only ever on the Stamps plantation.'

'And Louisiana?'

There was a long pause before the old lady, clutching the top of her cane and with a slight shake of her head, as if disappointed in herself, answered. 'I got confused. Maybe that was his father.'

'What's that now, Mrs Henderson?'

'I say I got confused.'

'Oh, I hear you. We *all* hear you.' He smiled kindly and then tapped his temple. 'It can get hard keeping it all straight in here, can't it? The memories get kinda jumbled and tumbled, don't they?'

Now he turned towards the jury, even as he continued to address his witness who clutched her stick and stared down to the ground.

'You see, I mean no disrespect to our elders, none at all. I only have respect in my heart for our most senior fellow citizens. But I suppose the reluctant conclusion I drew long ago, as a scholar of these events, is that we cannot always rely on personal testimony, not in matters of this import. Especially when the evidence they convey is *second-hand*. You've been relying on memories of memories, Mrs Henderson. Stories about stories that you'd picked up as a child. And as we've seen, our memories can play tricks on us.

'It's not just you, Mrs Henderson, even though you've become famous.' Here he raised his voice with a showbiz flourish: ' "The last human link with the age of slavery!" ' He shook his head with what seemed to be genuine sadness. 'We've all been relying on those same tales. And you've shown us today that we can rely on them no longer.'

He cleared his throat and said, 'Mrs Henderson, I want to thank you. I believe you've performed a valuable service for your country today and for future generations. Because if even you can't remember some of the most basic details, then what else in the conventional understanding of "slavery" ' – he put air quotes around the word – 'what else might be wrong? So I'm grateful to you, Mrs Henderson. Truly grateful. Your honour, I have nothing further.'

Chapter Nine

Charlottesville, Virginia, 9.35pm

Maggie was struggling to keep her eyes on the screen. She knew she should. She knew she could: she had removed all distractions, even putting her phone into flight mode, which these days was the equivalent of retreating to a cave and fasting for forty nights. She also knew that what she was reading was important.

The trouble was, it was also deathly dull. Page after page filled with dates, transactions and prices, with next to no narrative to connect them. After a while, she had the sensation of staring at a random collection of dots, just waiting for someone to get a pen and start joining one to another so that, at last, some kind of picture would emerge.

It reminded her why the academic life had never appealed. Her teachers – even at that bloody convent – had always said she was smart. Her problem was *application*. She lacked the patience for serious study. 'Margaret, you're the cleverest girl here, by a mile,' one of the nuns had told her, before predicting that she would amount to nothing. 'All those brain cells of yours will be as useless as a chocolate teapot if you don't learn to sit still.'

But of course that was not the only reason she was finding it so hard to concentrate. She was in a hotel room with Uri Guttman, a man she had loved so intensely he still appeared, every now and then, in her dreams. And now here he was, just a few feet away. Judging by the look of him, seated at the narrow hotel 'bureau', hunched over a laptop, he was having no such trouble: his gaze was focused intently on the words in front of him. He didn't even seem to notice when she stared at him.

She forced herself back to the screen, curled up on her knees as she sat in a rigid armchair, under a faux-retro floor lamp. (She didn't dare go anywhere near the bed.)

It had been her idea. 'This is probably a coincidence, Uri,' she had said. 'There is almost certainly nothing to it. For all we know, Mitchell Boult had an undiscovered heart condition. And it just so happened to kill him within a few days of Aikman. Just a horrible coincidence.'

'But.'

'But if there is a connection, then it will be in their work.'

He gave her that crinkled brow she hadn't seen in so long.

She went on. 'They're historians. If someone wanted them both dead, it'll be because of something they were working on. Something they wrote. Which means—'

'We get reading.'

So she had Googled a few academic papers published by Russell Aikman while Uri took on Boult. She could see, just by glancing over, that he was being methodical: he seemed to have drafted a list on a single sheet of paper, occasionally ticking off items one by one. She, meanwhile, would lose focus and click out of one scholarly article, open a new tab and find another one. Or she'd dip into a book, using that 'look inside' feature. Each time, she'd be briefly energized by the novelty, only to find her interest waning.

It was her fault, she was sure of it. She told herself her intellectual skills were eroding; she had grown so used to the near-constant adrenalin rush of recent years, her ability to do slow work had become degraded. Her faculties had deteriorated; they were desensitized. She was like those people who need to eat ever hotter, spicier food: without a shot of Tabasco they can barely taste at all.

At last, she pushed the computer to one side, with a sigh of resignation. 'I'm sorry, I can't do this.'

Uri remained fixed on his screen, pen in hand.

She sighed again, louder this time. 'I mean it.'

'Mean what?'

'This! I can't do it. Reading all this . . . stuff. It's like watching paint dry.'

He looked at her, puzzled. Was this a rare example of an English idiom that he had not yet come across?

She tried again. 'It's just too dull. OK, there's no story: I get that. No narrative, fine. Not every historian has to pretend they're on telly. But there's no *argument*. He's not actually saying anything.'

'Really?'

'Unless I'm missing it. Which is perfectly possible, given that—'

'No, no. It's the same with me.'

'Really? With Boult?'

'I keep waiting for him to argue a case. But it's just "This happened. And then this happened." Event, then a number, then a date. Then another one.'

'Fact, fact, fact, right?'

'Exactly.'

'I thought it was just me.'

'No, it's not you. It's me also.'

The sentence hung in the air, brimming with memories. Maggie smiled a cautious smile. Uri smiled back, his eyes, almost involuntarily, looking beyond her face, taking in the shape of her. Noticing that she'd noticed, he glanced back at his screen. 'Listen to this.' He began reading:

'On November twenty-third, the governor of Alabama issued an edict to the penitentiary in Birmingham, requesting the transfer of thirty-three able-bodied prisoners within the week. Six days later, the transfer was complete, so that on November twenty-ninth, thirty-two prisoners arrived. It seems the thirty-third prisoner was incapacitated by injury. That brought to one hundred and fifty-five the number of prisoners moved under compulsory requisition . . .'

Maggie was laughing now. 'That's positively dramatic compared to what I've got. Listen, listen.' She began flicking through the tabs, searching for the driest paragraph. Once she found it, she leapt to her feet, holding the computer in front of her.

'Land registry records in the Carolinas show a steady increase in transaction activity in the latter part of the decade, increasing at a rate which, when annualized, suggests a median percentage gain of between one and one point five per cent per annum . . .'

Uri raised his palms. 'I surrender! No more, please.'

They were closer now. She was standing near to his chair, separated by no more than a couple of feet. They were in a hotel bedroom. She let the laughter subside and did not fill the silence that followed. She felt the atmosphere change, grow thicker, as she knew it would. It was filled with everything they were not saying.

It was he who broke away first, showing her his back so that he could return to his screen. She felt the same sting she experienced during that dread hour in The Dubliner. Milder this time, of course. But the same message.

Not rejection, exactly. It was more pained than that; she could see it in the way he was hunching over his machine. As if this was difficult for him, as if he too were feeling what she was feeling. Though what that was, exactly, she would have struggled to articulate.

She cleared her throat, a signal to herself as much as to him. Focus.

As she spoke, she took a pace back, expanding the space between them. If there had been a barometer in the room, it would have recorded a small drop in pressure.

'This is definitely strange.'

He looked over his shoulder at her, his fingers still on the keyboard. 'What is?'

'That they're both so boring.'

He laughed.

'I mean it. You'd have assumed that a historian who gets killed would have been "controversial". You know, one of those guys who goes on TV saying "The Pope killed Kennedy" or something.'

Now Uri was standing upright. 'But they're the opposite.'

'Exactly. They're just quietly being Mr Gradgrind, compiling their little logbooks of facts.' She saw Uri's expression. 'OK, *big* logbooks of facts. But they're not letting off fireworks. They're not toppling any icons.'

'So why would anyone want them dead?'

'I don't know. But I don't think—'

There was a ping. His phone, not hers.

'What's that?'

'I set up an alert: any stories about historians or deaths.'

She stepped closer, so she could see the screen in his hand. She caught the scent of him, reviving a memory of nuzzling into his neck.

'There.' It was a story from the *Los Angeles Times*. She could make out the headline – 'Tributes paid to husband-and-wife duo, chroniclers of a century' – but had to inch nearer to read the story.

Stanford staff and students mourned the double loss of two of the faculty's leading lights Tuesday, as the deaths were announced of a couple who had helped shape the teaching of US history at the college.

Lindsey Dunn, 61, and Stuart Dunn, 64, were both tenured professors at the department, where they had taught since the mid-1980s. Known to generations of students, they were consecutive heads of the department—the husband succeeding the wife—over a period that spanned two decades. At the time of their deaths, they were still both active on campus.

The college authorities gave no indication of the cause of death, but the Stanford police department said they were not looking for anyone else in connection with the incident. Speaking on condition of anonymity, one official indicated that the couple had taken their own lives in what seemed to be a suicide pact. "We found them together," she said.

'OK,' Uri said, closing down the screen. But Maggie was already back at her laptop, Googling the names.

'There,' she said. She was pointing at the list of published articles under Stuart Dunn's name.

Patterns of slave ownership in the pre-revolutionary period
The role of the plantation in the economy of the Deep South
Agriculture and bondage: slavery and the cotton trade

Uri went back to his machine, where he now pulled up a record of Lindsey Dunn's work.

The economic impact of the civil war on the Carolinas
Mistress of the big house: new perspectives on the wives of slave owners
Race and territory: cross-currents in the antebellum south

Maggie felt herself pale. Two dead historians of slavery and the civil war might be a coincidence, but now there were four.

'Uri,' she began. 'We need to think this through. Let's see what we know—'

But Uri wasn't listening. He was still at the computer, now back at the *LA Times* story announcing the Dunns' death. He scrolled down to the bottom, reading the paragraphs they'd initially ignored.

Speculation centered on suggestions that the couple might have recently learned of a terminal medical diagnosis, though friends said they had no knowledge of any health problems. They were, however, said to be particularly subdued by the death of their colleague, former Stanford professor Jerome Payne, who was killed in a car crash on Sunday in Ithaca, New York, near Cornell University where he held his last post. The Dunns had collaborated with Prof Payne on several research projects and shared common areas of interest and expertise.

Paying tribute to the couple, a statement from the president's office praised them as, "Models of cool-eyed, methodical scholarship. In their writing and their lectures, they both preferred light to heat, led not by ideological zeal but a simple hunger for knowledge. Their only agenda was faith in the evidence and the importance of facts . . ."

'So not four,' Maggie said. 'Five. And all of them obsessed with facts, not polemic.'

Uri nodded. That look she remembered so well had returned. His eyes seemed to be imploring her for answers.

She reached into her bag and pulled out her phone. She would go back to the police department and ask—

But no sooner had she taken the device off flight mode than it vibrated with a torrent of messages. The first had been sent twenty-five minutes ago, and the rest at five-minute intervals since. They were all from Donna Morrison, Governor of Virginia, and grew increasingly desperate. The last read simply:

Maggie, please! If you're in Charlottesville, you need to get down to the UVA library right now. I mean it. NOW!

Chapter Ten

Charlottesville, Virginia, 11.53pm

Afterwards she would wonder if she had smelled it before she saw it, but the sight of it never left her. It was beautiful in its own way, a corona of orange and gold painted across the night sky.

As the car got nearer, it seemed to fill the windscreen. You couldn't look anywhere else, your eye mesmerized by those vast, round flames.

While she drove, Uri was on his phone, thumbing away at the keys. Somehow, without seeing them, she knew his fingers were trembling. Eventually, he read aloud the entry for the section of the university library the governor had told her to head for.

'"The Special Collection houses over thirteen million manuscripts, three hundred and twenty-five thousand rare books, as well as approximately five thousand maps, more than two hundred and fifty thousand photographs—"'

'What of, Uri? What of?' Maggie shouted, turning hard left on a red light.

'What?' He was staring at the orange sky ahead.

'The books, the maps – what's it a collection of?'

'Oh.' He looked back at the phone, shaking in his hands. '"American history and literature . . . with a focus on Virginia and especially African-American history." '

They were near enough to see the impromptu barricade that had sprung up, formed of ambulances and police cars, their lights flashing, and a cluster of red fire trucks. She screeched the car to a stop and they both ran out.

Only now did she take a proper look at the building rather than the sky. It was impressive, fronted by a colonnade of perhaps a dozen pillars with a tall, central arch marking the entrance. At first glance, it might have looked old, built in the colonial, Georgian style that defined so much of this university. But the brick was too clean, too new for that. Uri had mentioned that this Special Collections building was about fifteen years old and that appearances were deceptive. It was much bigger than it looked, with many of the 'stacks' of books housed underground.

And now it was in flames.

Each of the six tall windows facing out onto the quadrangle were bright with fire, two of them already engulfed in plumes of hot orange. The glass had long gone, the flames bursting outward and reaching for the sky, like curtains billowing in an unseen wind. At that very moment, a third window shattered, a ball of fire escaping from it as the glass exploded in all directions. The building seemed to be a cauldron shaken by a heat it could no longer contain. Maggie half-expected to see the roof wobbling, like a lid on a pan about to blow.

A couple of reporters were already here, gathered on the sidewalk bordering the quadrangle. They were talking to someone who seemed to be speaking on behalf of the fire department. Maggie could hear a snatch of conversation, something about the blaze spreading at a terrifying speed, much faster than most fires they'd experienced.

'We attended the scene within two minutes of the alarm being raised, but the fire was already deeply established at that time. We believe the origin may be located in that part of the facility that is below ground . . .'

At that moment, a team of four firefighters, seemingly just arrived, moved past them.

'Let's get close up,' Uri said, pulling out his phone and turning on the camera. 'As close as we can.'

'What?'

'I mean it. The only thing those guys are going to be thinking of is putting the fire out. No one else is going to be looking for who started it. You have to seize the moment, that's what you always said.'

'I know, but—'

'Come on.'

He marched off in the slipstream of the firefighters, towards the main entrance. Before the men had a chance to spot them – *Folks, I'm afraid you need to head back* – Uri took Maggie's hand and they peeled away, heading for the side of the building. Even with the adrenalin pumping through her, she felt calmed by that gesture: the two of them facing this thing, together.

The design mimicked the front, with tall sash windows on

either side of a glazed, double-height arch. Except here that arch was flanked by two external staircases leading to much more modest doorways. From what Maggie could see, the fire had not yet climbed to that upper level. All the glass was still intact.

'Now what?'

'Let's get closer, just to see.'

As they inched nearer, she could still feel the heat, the air itself cooked. As she moved onto the first step, she reached for the handrail, recoiling at the last moment: it would be scalding.

Once at the top of the stairs, she could see through the glazed part of the door and into the library. She saw a scene that was oddly calm, almost serene: the smooth, polished dark wood of a panelled corridor, lined on each side by glass cases. Inside were open rare books, antique maps and what seemed to be, though the angle was tight, a fragment of an early American flag.

She pulled down her sleeve to protect her fingers and attempted the door handle. It turned but did not open. She pressed her shoulder against the door, feeling the heat within once more. Now she pulled back and rammed her full weight into it. The door didn't open, but some part of the mechanism did seem to give, encouraging her to make another attempt.

She pushed hard, the shoulder taking the impact. Did the door buckle? It seemed to. One more go, then another and finally it was open.

The heat was instant, like stepping into an oven. It took her a few seconds to adjust. Only then did she absorb the noise, the commotion coming from below: firefighters shouting, hoses at full blast and, loudest of all, the crackle of flames.

She looked at the ground beneath her feet, checking whether she was safe to move forward. It was a floor of grey stone tiles, apparently solid. She took a step.

The heat came through her shoes, which forced her forward again, like a barefoot child skipping from one foot to another on a roasting summer beach. She was halfway down the hallway now, able to read the place names on the eighteenth-century map behind glass: *Charles City County*, *Warwick County* . . .

She looked over her shoulder, checking for Uri. Was he still at the door? Had it slammed shut after she forced it open?

With a glance upward, she clocked the series of sprinklers studding the ceiling, each of them dry and inactive. In the corner was a CCTV camera, which she looked at for a half second longer than it demanded. Something about it was not quite right.

The rational voice within her was becoming more insistent: time to go. Uri had suggested they take a look and she had taken a look. Maggie had just made the executive decision to side with reason over intuition and leave when, in an instant, the entire space filled with thick black smoke.

It was coming from the open stairwell, with its wide, curving staircase, at the end of the hallway. She'd glimpsed the staircase when she first broke in. It was clearly the architectural centre-piece; all corridors and hallways led to it. But it meant this upper level was vulnerable to what was happening below.

Some door must have yielded downstairs. She pictured it, the billowing cloud a living thing, hammering against the door down below, pressing against it, until the door could take it no longer and finally gave way. And then the smoke, free to roam, rushing for the stairs and filling every corner it could find.

Now it was here and Maggie was choking. A moment later she was down on the ground, whether because she had been knocked to her feet by the force of the cloud or because she had once read that firefighters drop to their hands and knees to stay below the smoke, she wasn't sure.

The task was to get back to that door, and to Uri who was surely on the other side of it, hammering to get in. The door was there, she knew that, not ten yards away. She just had to get there.

She began to inch along the floor, holding her breath to avoid taking in the acrid fumes that now enveloped the hallway like the thickest fog. She was moving forward when, sooner than expected, she hit something solid.

Surely she couldn't be by the door already. She extended her fingertips. Solid wall, hot to the touch. She moved her hands left and right to where the door should be. But just wall.

She reached upwards. Ah, glass. But it was a large expanse of glass and it was thinner than the panel of the door she had rammed open just a few minutes ago. She let her hands pad either side, expecting to sense either timber frame or more solid wall or even, please God, the cool of outside air. But it was all glass, now too hot to touch.

Of course. She was not by the door at all. She had merely crossed to one side of the hallway. These were the display cases she was touching.

But which side was she on? There were glass cases on both. She looked in the direction she felt sure must be the doorway out, but all she could see was black smoke. She squinted the other way: more smoke. She was in the centre of a dark cloud. Perhaps it was the fumes, or the heat or the panic, but she had no idea which way was out. She needed to breathe, though she didn't dare.

Finally, there was a light. To her right, she saw it and for a precious, deluded split-second she thought it must be the world outside – perhaps the flashing lights of the emergency crews coming through that door she'd forced open. But as the light got stronger she understood. This was a fireball, perhaps fifteen foot across, and it was coming towards her.

The next three or four seconds passed like long minutes. First, she calculated that, given that the ball was coming from inside, the exit could only be the other way. Lying flat on the roasting ground, she hauled herself forward, like a commando in the mud of an assault course. The movement made her choke and, in a reflex action, she took a breath.

Its impact was instant, as if she'd been punched hard in the head. She was dizzy and sick. Everything in her body cried out for rest. She wanted desperately to surrender, to succumb to the sleep that seemed to be enveloping her just as surely as the smoke. She felt her head dip onto her hands. The temperature, already scalding, rose. The ball of fire was getting closer.

Chapter Eleven

Northern Virginia, three months earlier

Some people would hate to think of themselves as a cog in a machine, a link in a chain. But Ben Hudson found it reassuring. There was a system and so long as he did his bit, nothing could go wrong. He could begin his shift at seven am, clock off at four and know that he would be paid for that day and, if he did the same for four more days that week, he would be paid for the week.

Better still, there was no grey area about whether he was doing his bit right. He'd once worked in a flower shop, during that first summer after he'd left school, and he'd regularly be pulled aside by the manager, to be told how he'd looked at the customer wrong – *You need to look them in the eye, Ben* – or been too friendly or not friendly enough.

There was none of that in this job. If you got it right, the bar scanner made a single beep and displayed a green tick. Get it wrong, and you'd see a red cross and hear a different noise. Green or red; no greys.

So as he drove the armoured van away from the centre of the city, following the instructions on the company-mandated GPS system, he knew he was doing his bit right. He could hum along to the music on the radio knowing that he had completed the first stage of the 'work order' on his handheld device and that he was on his way to completing the second.

That first task had been to drive to the library, park in the designated area, then present himself at the front desk where he'd been met by a woman from the library's IT department. She had handed him a sealed blue box, the size of a small briefcase, which he had duly scanned – beep, green tick – and taken from her. He had then followed procedure by turning the two separate locks on the van and placing it in the secured storage area. And now he was returning to head office.

He didn't have to think about anything else. If the traffic light showed red, he would stop. If there was a detour, he would follow the yellow signs. But as to the blue box in the hold, he didn't need to think about that at all.

So it did not cross his mind for a moment even to consider the larger process he was involved in. If someone had asked him, Ben Hudson would have struggled to explain that he was helping store a back-up, digital copy of all the information contained inside one of the most important libraries in America.

All the hard copies – the books and papers themselves – were kept in the building in Charlottesville. But these days the library did not put all its faith in the physical realm. It needed to guard against fire or flood, and so it had made, over a period of several years, high-quality digital scans of those texts and documents that were unique to its own collection.

Those were stored and backed up on computer drives inside the library. They were safe – just so long as there were not, say, a computer worm or virus, despatched from afar and tunnelling its way into those disks, moving from machine to machine, steadily erasing data.

Still, even if that happened, all would not be lost. The data was also stored on back-up tapes, physical objects that could be kept far away in an offsite tape vault, a well-defended warehouse, maintained by a professional data storage company. If catastrophe struck and a library burned down and its computers were wiped, there would be one last line of defence: those back-up tapes, filed and guarded around the clock many miles away.

That's where Ben Hudson was driving now, back to base with that blue box of magnetic tapes in the back, into which was etched the back-up copies of the data held by the library.

Once he'd arrived at HQ and parked up, there was more scanning – of the pass that was attached to his belt, of the blue box and then of the individual tapes inside the box, as each one was taken off to be stacked in racks in protected vaults. Happily, that was someone else's job. Ben didn't even have to think about it.

Which meant that, even if someone faraway had interfered with the 'work orders' that were sent as automatic instructions to those handheld devices that he and everyone else used, he wouldn't know about it. Nor, more importantly, would he be especially bothered. All that mattered was that Ben Hudson had done his bit as ordered, handing the tapes to someone else. That person was now the next link in what the company called its 'chain of custody'.

So Ben had no interest in where his co-worker actually took the tapes that he'd ferried from the library. His colleague would surely just follow whatever instruction was displayed on their scanner. And if that meant the tapes were now labelled as 'expired' – even though the librarians back in Charlottesville had never classified them that way – then they would be taken to the secure shredding area, where machines specially engineered to dispose of electronic material, including magnetic tape, disks and drives, would get to work.

If the work order was in the system, no matter that it was only there thanks to skilled, long-distance hacking, then it would be obeyed – if not by Ben, then by one of his like-minded fellow employees. They would keep doing it too, quietly destroying back-up tapes month after month.

Meanwhile, the curators and librarians back in Charlottesville would assure themselves that they were doing the right thing, cheerily unaware that when they sent those tapes off for supposedly iron-clad safekeeping, they were in fact sending them to oblivion.

They would be similarly unaware of the slow, almost imperceptible corrosion that was underway inside the library's electronic index system: steadily gnawing away at the database which acted as the indispensable guide to those countless back-up files, explaining what was held where. Should calamity strike, and the collection have to be reassembled from digital copies, the index would be the indispensable starting point. Without an index, such a vast store of knowledge was all but useless. As librarians knew better than anyone.

As it was, no one – not at the library and not at the offsite tape vault – knew that any of this was happening. It was slow and stealthy, a steady drip-drip-drip of damage. And if similar efforts were underway elsewhere, who would notice? Certainly not the loyal, obedient army of Ben Hudsons. They saw nothing.

Beep, green tick.

Tuesday

Chapter Twelve

Charlottesville, Virginia, 12.11am

It felt like the faintest breath on her face, that hint of cooler air. Not the air itself, but the promise of it. Maggie Costello was near that door she'd opened, she was sure of it. She heaved herself forward and upward, certain that, after this, she'd have no energy left.

Her head met the door: it was jammed shut. She lacked the strength to reach upward for the handle; the heat had surely sealed the door closed anyway. Feeling the glass panel that stood between her and the outside, she realized there was only one option left. With her right elbow as her weapon, she focused all her remaining strength on that point – and charged it as hard as she could into the barrier before her. She felt the glass give and, on a second attempt, shatter. Uncertain what shards still remained, jagged and lethal, she threw herself forward all the same, onto the external stairs, tumbling down them in a single move. The momentum carried her a yard or two away from the building, but she was still close enough to feel the glass descend on her like snowfall when, a second later, the fireball crashed through that double-storey window with an almighty roar.

How long did she pass out? For a few seconds? For half an hour? She had no idea. But she remembered a team in uniform – paramedics or firefighters, she wasn't sure – surrounding her, the texture of their uniforms thick and comforting. She remembered the clamour, the dangle of tubes, the vivid yellow of oxygen tanks and the heat of her skin. She remembered the change in the air as she got further away. She seemed to be floating, certainly not walking or running. It took her a while to understand she was on a stretcher.

And suddenly she was sitting on the kerb, wrapped in a foil blanket like a woman in a front-page photograph. Hesitantly, she looked down at her hands. Scratched and bloody but, to her surprise, they still looked like hands. She touched her cheeks, she checked her hair and then her arms and legs. Her mind was working. She made a sound, to establish beyond doubt that she was alive and not in the hell the nuns had promised her. The sound that came out of her mouth was 'Liz'.

She looked up to see Uri, walking around as if in a daze, his face drawn, his eyes desperate.

'Uri,' she called, surprised by the thinness of her own voice. 'Uri. Here.'

He turned, saw her and instantly rushed towards her. She tried to get up, but she couldn't do it. He crouched down and put his arms around her shoulders. 'Thank God,' he said. 'Thank God. I thought you were—'

'I'm OK,' she said. As he hugged her, she said, 'Where were you? What happened?'

'I don't know. I was filming from outside the building and I looked around and you'd gone. It was like you'd vanished. I tried all the doors, but they were jammed. I went around the back, but I couldn't get in.'

'I couldn't find you.'

He was holding her tight. Wasn't that what she had wanted, even yearned for just an hour or so ago, when they had stood a few inches apart in his hotel room? It was. And yet, here – now – she found herself fighting the urge to remove his arms from her, to disentangle herself.

She looked upward. There were lots of people now. TV crews – was that the rigid blonde from yesterday? – spokespeople for the fire and police departments and plenty of officials looking busy, doubtless from the university and City Hall.

But there were also clusters of people just looking stunned. None of them was in a silver blanket like hers, but they seemed equally dazed. They stood in groups of three and four, and most kept their gaze fixed on the building, which was still burning. She could see the flames reflected in their eyes.

Some of the faces were white, but most were African-American. Maggie recognized several of them from yesterday's demo outside the police station, but this time there was no anger or defiance, just shell-shocked grief. One man in his late forties, who she identified without evidence as a pastor, was talking into a news camera. The TV shot would have shown the blaze just behind him.

'Right now, while we speak, books are burning,' he said,

gesturing over his shoulder. 'Old books, rare books, books on parchment and books on goat skin. Books as old as this country. Books *older* than this country. Books of science, books of geography, books of poetry and books of history. Books full of maps and drawings and songs and scripture. And they're all burning, stack after stack of them. By morning they'll be gone.'

Even in her state, Maggie couldn't stop looking at him. His eyes seemed to be brimming with tears.

'Inside that building are the documents which record what happened to our people. The plantation ledgers, the ships' manifests, the diaries, the testimonies, the records that show that our ancestors – my ancestors – were held in the Commonwealth of Virginia and in these United States as chattel and property. As slaves. And now—'

But then the TV light that had been trained on him went dark, leaving him lit only by the raging orange of the fire behind him. His interviewer and the rest of the press had rushed over to the fire chief, who was apparently about to give a formal statement.

'Uri, look. He's saying something.'

Uri straightened himself up and helped Maggie to her feet. They got closer to the cluster of reporters and to the chief, an African-American man around the same age as the pastor, now himself illuminated by the klieg lights of television.

'. . . operation is still ongoing. But what is already clear is that the men and women of the Fire Department of Charlottesville have devoted themselves to this mission with their customary dedication and professionalism.'

'Sir, have there been any casualties?'

'So far, we don't believe there have been any fatalities from this incident. But as you can see, this incident is still active.'

'Any ideas how the fire started, sir?'

'There will be ample time for investigations in due course, starting at first light.'

'But initial indications?'

'This facility is a state-of-the-art building, highly protected against any catastrophic incident. We believe it was well-guarded against any accident or accident scenario.'

'You mean, a fire couldn't have started by accident? It was deliberate?'

'I'm going to let my words speak for themselves. Now, if you'll excuse me.'

Maggie turned to Uri. His look confirmed they were thinking the same thing.

They moved silently for a while, among the vigil clusters of black activists who were standing, dumbfounded, as close to the library as they could get. Eventually, there was another rustle of movement among the press pack as a two-vehicle convoy of black SUVs pulled up.

Donna Morrison got out of the second car, striding purposefully towards the fire chief whose hand she shook. Soon the mayor joined them, as well as the police chief. There was much pointing at the blaze, some sombre nodding and finally a few words from the governor for the cameras. Boilerplate about 'every effort', 'first responders' and 'a dark day for Virginia'.

Eventually, as she was heading back to her car, Donna caught

Maggie's eye and, with the slightest tilt of the head, she motioned for her to follow. Only once the door was closed, the two of them sitting in the deep leather back seats, did the governor speak.

'What the hell happened to you?'

'I went in.'

'You what? What the hell were you thinking? You're no use to me burnt to a crisp, Maggie. You're no use to me dead.'

'I thought I might . . . see something.'

'And did you?'

'Maybe.'

'Jesus Christ, Maggie. Don't go getting yourself killed on me.'

'I'm sorry.'

'I mean it. This is happening, Maggie. It's real. Forget that bullshit about investigations "starting at first light".'

'You know already?'

'Of course. It's arson. No doubt about it.'

'Right.'

'It's exactly what I feared.' Donna paused to look out of the window, contemplating the raging fire that was devouring her state's history with each passing minute. Then she turned back, her expression as grave as Maggie had ever seen it.

'I'm begging you, Maggie. Make this stop.'

Maggie did not need persuading. She shared the governor's fury and her fear. For she had known within seconds of entering that building that this was no accident. And that this was no ordinary arsonist.

Chapter Thirteen

Swiss Cottage, London, 12.10pm

Judith Beaton took one last look in the mirror in the hallway. She dabbed at her cheek, to ensure the colour was spread evenly. A memory pricked at her, as it always did. She tucked away a stray hair. A word popped into her head from her childhood, a word of her mother's: *fligel*. Her mother would say it when brushing her daughter's hair in the morning, applying it to any stubborn curl that refused to lie flat. Only later did Judith discover its literal meaning. It was the Yiddish word for 'wing'. But her mother was gone by then.

She was still looking. She straightened the line of her sweater, checked her earrings, touched her brooch. The lines on her face: well, there was nothing she could do about those. You get to her age, you're going to be wrinkled. But everything else? There's no excuse.

One last check of the kitchen. The stove off, the lights off. She opened the fridge again and then the cupboard under the sink, noting the dozen cartons of orange juice and equal number of tins of tomato soup. She looked at her watch, then again at the phone her grandson had given her, with its uncanny ability to tell her when the bus was coming. She had to press that button, then that one, then that one . . . Ah, there we are. Eleven minutes.

She would leave now. One more peek at the stove, then out.

As always, she bypassed the lift and took the stairs. Three flights, it wouldn't kill her.

She took her place at the bus stop, checking her watch and taking a third look inside her handbag. Purse, phone, bread roll wrapped in foil: all present and correct.

When the bus came, she had no struggle to find a seat, though these days people usually gave up theirs if they saw her standing. 'These days', who was she kidding? She was eighty-seven years old: people had been standing for her for decades.

Still, she preferred these afternoon visits. True, the children were often restless after lunch, or sleepy. When you got them at nine o'clock in the morning, it was easier. But the rush hour was not for her. She liked to have the morning to prepare, to have a bath, to take her time getting dressed.

But not to think about what she was going to say. She had no need to give that a moment's thought. She did not have some set spiel that she had learned off by heart, though she knew plenty of the others who did exactly that. She had never even written it out as a text. She simply described what happened, starting at the beginning and getting to the end. As for the questions, she just had to answer whatever they asked. She didn't need notes for that either. Why would she? She remembered every detail. It was her life, after all.

She took another look in her bag. The bread roll was still there, freshly wrapped this morning. Only rarely did a question faze her. It had happened a few months ago, when a child – maybe sixteen years old – asked whether there was anything that had happened in those years that she could *not* remember.

She had paused, trying to think. She had scanned her memory, looking for gaps. And then, for the first time – after giving, what, more than nine hundred of these talks? – she found tears coming. She thought about ducking the question. *No, my darling, I can recall those events as if they happened yesterday, every detail.* She could dab her eye with a tissue and move on to the next question. No one need notice. But the obligation to be honest – otherwise, what was the point? – had overruled her.

'Sometimes I cannot remember my brother's face,' she had said. 'He was younger than me, just eight years old, and they took him away as soon as we got to Auschwitz. I never saw him again. And sometimes I cannot see his face. I try and I try, but I cannot picture it.'

She had already told the children, arranged in row after row in front of her, how she had worked as a slave labourer for eighteen months in Auschwitz, and how she had then been despatched to another camp at Nordhausen. 'There was a group of us and we went by train, travelling for six or seven days without food.'

They survived, she explained, by constructing a box, attaching it to their belts and lowering it outside to scoop up the snow below. Sometimes it would be covered with oil from the train, but if it came up clean they would push the snow into their mouths, sucking out its moisture.

She had told the children, their eyes locked onto hers, about the work they had to do on that journey. 'We'd have to take off the dead people,' she'd said. 'You'd have to pick up the dead people and lay them like you lay herrings, one this way, one that way. I was carrying them. They weighed nothing, they were like skeletons. I carried them under my arm.'

Judith Beaton, once Yehudit Botsky, had explained all this, just as she'd told the children how she had lied about her age to survive, how she'd pretended to look fitter and stronger than she was to survive, how she would sometimes prick her finger, rubbing the blood onto her cheeks to survive, because if you looked too pale, you didn't work, and if you didn't work, you didn't live. On that day a few months earlier she had explained all this with perfect self-control, her voice never wavering. But when she admitted that she could not remember her brother's face, she could not hold back the tears.

The memory of it had troubled her, nagging at her for weeks afterwards. But on this afternoon visit to a comprehensive school in Brent, nothing like that happened. The teachers were polite, the children were overflowing with questions. Children whose parents were from Nigeria, Somalia or heaven knows where else; along with children whose parents were from Poland or Lithuania or Latvia, whose grandparents had done heaven knows what. Judith preferred not to think about it. But if she did think about it, she liked to see her survival, and the chance to teach this next generation, as a little victory over the murderers.

She was back on the bus, her eyes closed. She was exhausted, though she would find the strength to do it all over again if she had to. She had been giving at least one of these talks every week for nearly twenty years, sometimes two or three. She had to. They all felt the obligation, the survivors, or at least the ones she knew. They were all so old. In a decade, give or take, they'd all be gone. What if the memory of the Holocaust were to die with them? Who would be left to tell the truth?

If she hadn't dozed off, would she have noticed the woman on the bus who had been watching her since she had waved goodbye to the headteacher at the school? Would she have even given her a second glance? Judith Beaton had experienced much in her eighty-seven years, but she was no spy and no soldier. She had no idea what to look for.

So she had not seen that this woman had followed her into the underground station, onto the platform and onto the train, keeping just far enough away to remain out of view. She had not seen her get off the train a couple of seconds after Judith. She had not seen her hang back at the bus stop, taking care to board last. She did not see her now, watching and waiting.

Judith woke up just in time for her stop, gathering her bag and stepping through the buggies and mothers glued to their phones to climb off. It was nearly dark; she had to watch her step. But she made it. Habit made her check her bag, to see that the bread roll was still there. She was not four minutes from her front door and, behind it, her kitchen and fridge, both fully stocked. But the habit had never left her. As she would have told the children if they had asked: once you've known real hunger, you will never risk knowing it again.

She took the stairs upward, another habit that had refused to loosen its grip all these years later. The lift might be quicker and easier, but it was a confined space and those were to be avoided.

Besides, there was no hurry. There was ample time to stop on each landing, to pause and catch her breath. By the time she had got to the third floor, it would have been an effort to say hello to the woman who had appeared just behind her or, given that she did not recognize her, to ask her if she was lost and did she need any help, dear?

But, as it happened, there was no opportunity for such pleasantries, nor even to notice the woman make a small, fleeting movement – more a nervous tic than a gesture – as she briefly reached for and rubbed her left eyebrow. For the woman came up from behind and, in a swift, practised movement, placed a handkerchief over Judith's mouth, so that she could make no sound. Then, in an equally efficient move, she pulled her backward so that the old woman's back was against the bannister. After that, it was a simple pivot, requiring next to no force. Gravity took care of the rest, sending Judith Beaton to the bottom of the stairwell.

For Judith, the shock and the terror lasted only two seconds, three at most. Even then, as she plunged through the air, the fear was not pure. After what she had seen nearly three-quarters of a century ago, nothing could ever be as frightening. Not even this. A threat, even a mortal threat, induced in her only a kind of resignation. Ah, here comes death. Again.

But there was room for one more thought as she felt herself heading for the ground. Yehudit Botsky wondered if she might, if only for a split-second, glimpse her brother's face at last.

Chapter Fourteen

Charlottesville, Virginia, 7.53am

Breaking news on the Charlottesville fire that has stunned the nation. Reporting live for us this morning, correspondent Laurel Berry. What do you have for us, Laurel?

Chuck, this tragedy just got more tragic. As we've been reporting since late last night, the fire at the University of Virginia destroyed millions of precious documents as well as priceless rare books from the civil war era and earlier, ripping the heart out of this key archive. But now there's more. Anthony Gowdridge, the man in charge, has just told a news conference here in Charlottesville that not only were the hard, physical copies of those books and documents destroyed in last night's blaze – but the digital back-ups have also vanished. Let's roll that tape.

'Meticulously and over the last two decades, we have been digitizing our collection here at UVA, in part guarding against a catastrophe like this one. Today it is my grave duty to tell you that that digital archive has, it seems, also been taken from us. Our technicians are

investigating the situation, but their preliminary conclusion is that the UVA archive has been the target of a sabotage operation that did not begin last night but has been underway for several months. It was subtle and my deep regret is that it was not noticed until now. For that failure, I bear ultimate responsibility. Which is why I have submitted my resignation as University Librarian and Dean of Libraries, effective immediately.'

Chuck, that resignation is a big blow to Virginia officials as they deal with this crisis, but historians are saying this loss represents a devastating blow for the nation itself – the destruction of millions of key texts depriving America of some of its most cherished documents. One historian telling CNN this morning: 'We are a tree that has been severed from its roots.' Chuck?

Maggie clicked the remote, muting the TV. Jesus Christ, what the hell was happening here? She resettled herself, returning the pillow to her side, letting out an involuntary yelp of pain.

That prompted Uri to leap out of his seat at the desk, readying himself for emergency action. He was placated by a smile from her, an act of reassurance she had made a thousand times, even if she had not needed to deploy it with Uri for several years. She waited for him to return to his machine and then let out what she hoped was a silent sigh.

She had been re-examined by paramedics at the library building, at the insistence of the governor. Shaking her head, and with an expression of exasperated admiration that Maggie had grown used to in those she worked for, Donna Morrison had had her driver escort Maggie over to one of the dozen ambulance teams on the scene, most of them idling since, it appeared, the library had been unoccupied when the fire struck. 'Do not come back here until you've seen her get serious medical help!' the governor had called out. 'I know her tricks.'

Two nurses had examined her and their advice was clear, repeating the verdict of the paramedics who'd first seen her but which she'd been too dazed to absorb: she needed to get to a hospital.

'Am I burned?'

'Exposure to such intense heat can lead to—'

'Is that a no?'

'Well, you've got severe cuts and bruises here, here and—'

'But no burns?'

'Skin damage does not always appear straight away, there can be blistering—'

But Maggie was already on her feet, clambering out of the vehicle and joining Uri. She promised the nurses she would rest up. He had driven her back to his hotel, where she had had an ice-cold shower – any hotter and the water seemed to scald her. She felt as if she'd been out in the sun for twelve hours without suncream or a hat – and just as stupid.

'You know, if you'd have told me I would find myself in Uri Guttman's bed, this is not exactly what I'd have pictured,' she said now.

Uri turned away from his screen. 'Me neither.' His smile suggested he was relieved that at least one of them had had the courage to nod towards the elephant in the room.

He turned his chair so that he was facing her. 'You've had a busy few years, Maggie Costello.'

She shrugged a modest shrug.

'I read what you did: you know, the whole president thing. Everyone did.'

'It wasn't just me.'

'I cheered for you, Maggie. Like millions of others.'

She adjusted her position in the bed. 'And what about you, Mr Guttman? What have you been up to?'

He talked about a couple of the films he'd made, a prize he'd won at a festival in Europe. But they both knew that wasn't what she meant.

'I got married, Maggie.'

She smiled widely, the same smile she'd seen on the faces of runners-up at the Oscars. 'Who's the lucky woman?'

'Who *was* the lucky woman, you mean.'

'Oh my God, Uri, what happened?'

'No, no. Nothing like that. It just . . . didn't work out. She was lovely. *Is* lovely. A doctor. From Boston. And we tried really hard. But somehow . . .'

Maggie nodded. 'I'd say I know what you mean, but actually . . . I've never been married so I don't—'

'Yet.'

'What?'

'You've never been married *yet*.'

At that, Maggie contrived to resettle herself once more in the bed, even though she didn't need to. She made a small whelp, more by way of diversion than pain. 'So, fucking hell. They destroyed the entire library. Hard copies and back-ups. They know what they're doing. I could see that when I was in there.'

The memory of being there alone, of looking for Uri and not finding him, returned and, with it, her puzzlement at the extraordinary synchronicity that had led them both to be in the same southern town at the same time.

'How do you mean? What did you see?'

'The CCTV cameras in the library. They'd all been turned off.'

'How the hell could you tell that?'

'No little red light. They'd been disabled. Remotely, I reckon.'

'Jesus, I can't believe—'

'That, and taking out all the key experts. They're serious, these people. They're skilled. And they've been planning this a long time.'

' "They"? You think it's the same people doing this?'

'Bit of a coincidence if not. Five historians of the slavery period, all found dead in a matter of days, at least one of them very obviously murdered. And now the key records of the same period wiped out completely, print and digital.'

'You're certain this is all one operation?'

'I'm not certain. But there's one person I'd very much like to ask.'

Chapter Fifteen

Richmond, Virginia, 11.27am

One of Maggie's regular complaints about America, one she shared frequently with her sister, was that the place was so new, it was hard to take seriously. She remembered telling Liz about a trip she'd taken in Houston, Texas.

'So they do a "Historic Houston" bus tour, you know, open-top, tour guide, the whole thing.'

'Right.' Liz knew where this was going.

'And the guide goes,' and here Maggie attempted a Texan accent, ' "So welcome, ladies and gentlemen—" '

'So the guide was from Cork? Why didn't you say?'

'Fuck off. He goes, "Welcome, ladies and gentlemen, to this tour of Historic Houston. We'll be looking at homes and sites that date as far back as 1912." '

'He never said that.'

'He did!'

'Nineteen twelve?'

'Nineteen fucking twelve!'

'Wasn't Nan alive in 1912?'

'"Historic". Can you believe that?'

For two girls from Ireland, where you could walk past a thousand-year-old church and barely notice it, the United States seemed positively infant. On some days, Maggie liked that about it: to be in a land unladen with centuries of baggage, a land so unlike her own. It held out promise, the chance to start over and not be judged for it. The country had invented itself anew, so why couldn't you? In other words, the opposite of Ireland.

But there were also days when it was unsettling to be in a place whose roots felt so shallow. You could feel unsteady.

And then there was a third sensation, and she felt it now as she pulled into Richmond. Here, in the one-time capital of the Confederate south, there was plenty of history. You couldn't move for statues and memorials. But that history was dark and troubled and, crucially, insufficiently distant. Race was still dividing America, not yesterday but today. This wasn't like visiting old churches or ruined monasteries back home. Here the past refused to be past.

Still, that was only one source of her disquiet. Mainly, she was worried by the prospect of her next meeting. Oh, she had faced – and faced down – powerful men before, men much more powerful than this one. She had worked in the White House, at the side of more than one American president, for God's sake. But, still, she could not deny the feeling. She feared the man she was about to meet.

Her phone told her she had reached her destination. If only. She found a spot and parked the car.

William Keane had made great play of the fact that he was acting as his own attorney in his libel action against Susan Liston and her publishers: it nicely reinforced his casting of himself as the plucky little guy, daring to challenge the establishment. But his choice of venue for this meeting with Maggie suggested there was some spin at work in that narrative. He'd asked to meet at the downtown offices of Harper Montaigne Brice, a Richmond law firm. Outside was a small knot of Keane supporters, holding out buckets for cash donations. They wore T-shirts bearing the slogan Maggie had heard at Georgetown. On the front: *Don't know, don't care*. On the back: *Nothing happened, nothing's there*.

Getting a meeting had been easier than she'd expected. She'd played the 'Governor Morrison's office' card early and it had worked. But that only made her warier. She'd been in Washington long enough to know that people did not agree to meet out of politeness. They met only if they saw some advantage for themselves. The last thing she wanted was to get played.

She was ushered into a boardroom and asked to wait. She refused the offer of a seat. An instinct told her that you wanted to be at full height when meeting a man like this for the first time.

And then, after three or four minutes – just long enough to make her feel like a supplicant, but short enough not to be rude – he strode in, as if he'd rushed in from another appointment and would be off again shortly: a man in a hurry and in demand.

'Miss Costello, the pleasure is mine,' he said, extending a hand. The white suit, the baritone voice, the confidence of a tall, broad man used to commanding space. 'I can barely abide unpunctuality in others, so I apologize for committing that sin myself. As perhaps you can imagine, we are in the very final stages of this case and time is just not my own. Interviews, TV appearances – I have even, and this surprises no one more than me, just fended off a request to do what I believe they call a "photoshoot". Absurdity in this country reaches new heights – or should that be depths? – every day. Why the readers of *Vanity Fair* would want to have their dreams darkened by the image of a pot-bellied bookworm from James City County, Virginia, the Lord alone knows. The sooner I can return to my study and my work, the better. One thing I have learned about myself through this process, Miss Costello: the spotlight is not for me.'

Maggie's face had adopted the rictus grin that came to her whenever she was in the company of the American far right – and she'd had no shortage of practice. In those few months when she served in the administration of the current president, as a holdover from the previous one, she had been surrounded by men just like Keane, most of them supported and enabled by a phalanx of ultra-conservative women whose look was as uniform as their politics, all of them equipped with long, straight hair in a shade she called Fox News blonde. (Working in that White House, even Maggie's hair colour – Irish red – had seemed like an act of rebellion.)

'Well, I appreciate you seeing me, Mr Keane.'

'I'm a loyal citizen of this fine commonwealth, Miss Costello: I'd always bow to a request issued by the governor.' He dipped his head in a courtly little bow.

'This is a sensitive matter and I want you to be assured that we're speaking in confidence.'

'Consider me assured.'

'It's about the fire last night, at the library in Charlottesville.'

He suddenly looked aghast. 'Forgive me, Miss Costello. Where are my manners? Put it down to the stress of this case. Please. I should have asked you the moment I walked in this room. Of course, I heard you were caught up in that horrific disaster. How are you managing?' He cocked his head to one side, in a show of sympathy.

'I'm sore, but I'm fine. Now about that fire—'

He held up a finger, as if correcting her. 'That *tragic* fire.'

'Yes. About that tragic fire. As you know, there are dozens of libraries in Virginia, thousands in the United States. There are even several collections held by the University of Virginia at Charlottesville.'

'Yes, indeed.'

'And yet the one that was hit, the one that was targeted—'

'Forgive me interrupting you, but you say "hit"—'

'Yes.'

'And "targeted".'

'Yes.'

'Well, do we *know* that?'

'The working assumption of the fire and police departments, shared with the governor, is that this was arson, yes.'

'Assumption. That's their working *assumption*.'

'Based on their preliminary investigation, yes.'

'So they don't know for certain. Not yet. They can't know for certain.'

'With respect, Mr Keane. We're not in your courtroom now. I

don't want to play your little games about what can't be known and what can't be proved, and how every document is a forgery and every witness is a liar. I'm not playing that game, do you understand me?'

She was surprised at her own anger. She could hear the quality of rage in her voice, and judging by his face, so could William Keane. He retracted his neck, like a jungle animal that has just glimpsed a fellow predator. She continued.

'Here's my question. Of all the libraries that could have burned down last night, the one that did was the country's – and perhaps the world's – pre-eminent archive of the era of American slavery. I know you're going to tell me that there was no such thing, but here's what I can't help thinking: that case is a whole lot easier for you to make now that those documents have gone, isn't it? I mean, all that proof, all that evidence – it's gone up in smoke.'

Keane smiled at her and then, making a little explosion mime with his hands, he made the sound: 'Pufff.'

'Should I take that as a yes?'

He smiled, waited a beat and then changed his expression. Once again, he was a professional, abiding by the accepted norms. But this readoption of the mask only confirmed the sense that she had briefly glimpsed the face behind it. For that second or two, she had seen a playfulness that knew, and took delight in, its own cruelty.

'If I may, there is a small lacuna in your argument, Miss Costello.'

'A lacuna.'

'Yes, a small gap in your—'

'I know what the word means.'

'Forgive me. Occasionally, I forget the education system of almost every other English-speaking nation is superior to our own.' He cleared his throat. 'The lacuna is, in a word, timing.'

Maggie said nothing.

'Let's say, purely for the sake of your argument, that the disappearance of these records somehow aids my case.'

'It obviously does!'

He held up his palm in a plea for patience. 'As I said, let us follow your logic. Let us suppose this helps me. The question you would have to answer is: why would I do this *now*? As we've already discussed, this trial is in its very closing stages. If I were going to take such drastic – nay, barbaric, action – I should have done it months ago, when it might conceivably have helped me. Now it's too late to make any difference.'

Of course, Maggie had considered this. She had turned it over in her own mind during the hour's drive from Charlottesville. He was right. It made no sense. Why would he destroy the documents in the UVA library, but not touch the ones with which he'd been confronted during the course of this trial? Why would he kill the likes of Aikman and Boult, but leave alive the historians who had taken the witness stand? Why on earth would he embark on this rampage of death and destruction after the trial and not before it?

She had wrestled with it and come up with only one answer.

'Because this is much bigger for you than winning a court case. You want to expunge slavery from the record. You want to rip out that page of history altogether. You thought the trial might do it, and – who knows – you might just win it. But that would be on a technicality. You'd persuade the jury that this or that document is a forgery, but what about all the others? What about the millions and millions of pages kept in archives like the one in Charlottesville? You can't explain all of them away. How much better for you if they were all gone.' And here she mimicked his little mime of an explosion, complete with sound effects.

He smiled. 'I like you, Miss Costello. You've got spunk.' He paused, as if he was considering telling her something and then thought better of it. 'But you're wrong.'

He began to pace, looking not at her but at the leather-bound volumes that lined the shelves of this boardroom. 'You know, I've learned a thing or two about the law doing this case.' He spun round and with a genial twinkle added, 'I've had to! An amateur like me up against all those fast-talking city slickers from New York. Imagine that: a southern boy taking on the Aronsons and Goldsteins, with all their friends in the media.'

Maggie felt her hackles rise. She resorted to a technique she had relied on when surrounded by all those bigots during her final few months in the White House. She gripped the table. If she channelled the rage through her hands, then it might not come out of her mouth.

'So I've learned a lot of law. And now I know what all these law books' – he stopped to gesture at the shelves – 'come down to, when you boil it all away. Means and motive. Means and motive.' He carried on pacing.

'I certainly don't have the means.' He indicated his suit which, now that she looked at it, Maggie could see was fraying at the lapels and sleeves. He nodded towards a stack of Office Depot cardboard boxes, each one labelled in a simple marker pen. She could make out one from here: 'Northup'.

'You see, it's just little ol' me and a few ten-buck donations from the odd generous old lady.' He gave her a butter-wouldn't-melt grin. 'And when I say odd, I mean odd!

'So how on earth would I have the resources to stage what happened last night? A big fire an hour away, while I was here, watched and observed by the national media around the clock. You think I have the wherewithal to organize such a thing? To hire the people, to lay the fuses or what-have-you? Besides, didn't you see the news? They've said the digital archive has gone too, methodically hacked and destroyed over a period of months. Now, how much of an evil genius do you think I am?' He laughed warmly, pleasured by his own joke.

'Which brings us to motive. Your theory sounds all well and good. But here's the thing. I don't need to *destroy* anything.' He returned once again to the table, sitting closer to Maggie this time.

'You been in court, Miss Costello? You seen the way this jury are reacting to the evidence they're hearing? To the arguments I'm making? I'm *winning*, Miss Costello. I'm winning.' He sat back, and dusted some unseen fluff from his knee.

'I'm winning this case. Not only do I not need to start burning historical documents, especially when this trial is nearly over, but it could only do me harm. Why would I take that risk? Here I am, on the brink of vindication. Why would I risk being brought down as nothing more than an arsonist and online saboteur? Can you imagine what the *New York Times* would do with that?' He adopted an East Coast accent to declaim the imagined headline: '"The Cracker Hacker!" It doesn't stack up.

'Moreover, it does not fit my argument. What is the case I am making here, Miss Costello? I am not arguing that the key records of that period don't *exist*. I am not pretending that these stacks of paper aren't *there*. I readily concede that they *are* there. It's just that we've misunderstood them all these years. We've *misread* them. We've read novels as if they were history books, we've—'

'What about the Constitution?' Maggie couldn't help herself. It blurted out.

'Excuse me?'

'The Constitution. Of the United States. It refers to slavery. It *abolishes* slavery. How can it have abolished something that didn't exist?' This was exactly what she had vowed not to do. She had promised she would not play William Keane's parlour game with him. He had been doing this for years; he was in finely tuned form, having played the game at the highest level in that courtroom for weeks on end. He would wipe the floor with her. But now it was too late.

'Do you want to know something odd about me, Miss Costello? Something *strange*.'

'What's that?'

'I know the entire text of the US Constitution by heart. And I have done so since I was nine years old. Go on.' He paused, waiting for her. 'Go on. Test me.'

'No, Mr Keane. I will not test you.'

'What was the passage you referred to just now?'

'I was thinking of the Thirteenth Amendment.'

'The one that abolishes "slavery", you mean?' The quotation marks were audible.

'Yes.'

' "Neither slavery nor involuntary servitude, except as a punishment for crime whereof the party shall have been duly convicted, shall exist within the United States, or any place subject to their jurisdiction." The Thirteenth Amendment, ratified on the sixth day of December, 1865.'

'Very impressive. And it makes my point.'

'But what exactly were they abolishing, Miss Costello? The legal effect of that amendment was to nullify Article Four, Section Two, Clause Three. And do you know what that says?'

'No. But I have a feeling you're about to tell me.'

He looked upward, addressing the ceiling as he began to recite. ' "No Person held to Service or Labor in one State, under the Laws thereof, escaping into another, shall, in Consequence of any Law or Regulation therein, be discharged from such Service or Labor, but shall be delivered up on Claim of the Party to whom such Service or Labor may be due." '

Maggie knew what was coming.

'Did you hear what word was missing, Miss Costello? "No person held to Service or Labor in one—" '

'Slavery. It doesn't mention slavery.'

'That's right! All it speaks of is persons *held to Service or Labor*. Why, it's speaking of workers bound by contract.'

'So you think that America fought the civil war over a dispute about *employment law*?'

'Oh, I do like you, Miss Costello. I *like* you. You remind me of one of my most interesting students. Though she wasn't quite as bright as you. But the *passion*. It's most charming, I confess.'

Maggie could feel herself shudder. 'None of this explains why you had no motive to burn down the UVA library.'

'Oh, but it does. I don't need to *destroy* inconvenient documents or texts or books or novels or any of it. That's far too crude. I just need to *explain* them. And, as I think I have just demonstrated, I can explain them all.'

He rested his hands on his lap and dipped his head, like a concert pianist who's completed a recital and who now waits, exhausted yet moved by the immensity of his own talent, for the applause.

Maggie rose to her feet. 'I think I've heard enough, Mr Keane. You've been generous with your time.' She was about to mention the evidence she had held back – the deaths of Aikman, Boult and the others – when there was a light knock on the door. Without waiting for an answer, a young woman, also helmeted in blonde, poked her head around. She looked nervous.

'Mr Keane?'

He broke from his reverie to swivel around.

'I'm sorry to disturb you, sir. Mr Brice asked me to come here with a message.'

'Yes?'

'He says you need to put on the TV. Right away.'

Keane got up, and began searching for the remote. Eventually, he found it on top of one pile of cardboard boxes and aimed it at the opposite wall.

Fox News burst into life, with a 'breaking news' chyron across the bottom of the screen. The voice was urgent.

. . . live pictures coming to us from Israel's Channel Ten this hour. This is the scene in Jerusalem, which seems to confirm initial reports we brought to you just a moment or so ago. And, Katya, the building we can see in the middle of our screens there, that is Yad Vashem?

That's right, Bill. The world's most famous Holocaust museum, a landmark in this country, a must-see destination for visiting dignitaries and world leaders, is in flames. The fire is far advanced and, according to Israeli government sources, it has already caused devastation. One minister saying, 'We are watching the memory of the Holocaust turn to ash.'

Chapter Sixteen

Melita Island, Montana, 8.31 am

Until now, if you'd have asked him, he'd have always said he grew up in the middle of nowhere. But that was before he moved to this place, which made his home town – just outside Cedar Rapids, Iowa – look like a throbbing metropolis. Occasionally, he would go online, drop a pin to show his current location then zoom out. It would confirm that he was a pinprick on a tiny island, alone inside a wide, endless lake, inside a vast national park, inside the state of Montana, itself one of the least populous states in the union.

His home these last six weeks was Melita Island, its sixty-four wooded acres inhabited for most of the year by mule deer, osprey, woodpeckers and a nesting pair of eagles. 'Most of the year' because, for two summer months, hordes of Boy Scouts would row across the lake to this deserted spot to learn how to build a raft or forage for food among the cottonwoods and firs for their annual summer camp. But that was some way off. For now, the

Scouts' empty log cabins, still carrying a scent of summer that instantly took him back to his own boyhood, had become home to a camp of a different kind.

Some still had their bunks, but the rest had been replaced with banks of computers resting on simple trestle tables, the floor covered with thick coils of exposed cabling. The connection was faster and steadier than any Jason Ramey had ever known – 'We're plugged into the spinal column of the internet,' Jim, the 'project co-ordinator', had announced when showing them around – and, crucially, secure. Every search, every electronic communication that went in or out of Melita Island was, they were assured, triple-encrypted and impregnable.

Jason had been struck by the degree of secrecy that cloaked everything they did here. Of course, he'd mixed in these circles long enough to know that no one would take any chances. Everyone always took it as read that, as Jim put it, 'They're listening.' (He went on to say: 'They're *always* listening. The trick is to make sure we give them nothing to *hear*.' No one had asked Jim to identify 'they'.)

Still, the precautions here were more extreme than anything Jason had encountered before, and he considered himself a seasoned traveller in this world. The day each one of them had arrived, they'd been handed a non-disclosure agreement which contractually bound them to total and blanket silence about everything they saw, heard or did on this project. Jim literally did not speak until Jason had signed the piece of paper, agreeing to be gagged on pain of a penalty 'of no less than ten million dollars'. In return they would receive 'the greatest possible reward' for their efforts.

Only then did he meet the other recruits. Most were just like him: men in their twenties or early thirties. The instant he saw them all, two dozen of them gathered together in the largest cabin on that first morning for an hour's 'orientation', he could guess who was who and, it turned out, he was mostly right. The largest group were the basement dwellers, introverted men who had been raised like indoor plants in the artificial light of a computer screen. They, in turn, divided into two sub-groups: some were professional geeks, paid in adulthood to maintain their adolescent vocation in programming or coding, while others were activist types, equally skilled in tech but who, so far as Jason could tell, spent their lives online reading, posting, agitating for the cause. The final group, and there was some overlap of course, were ex-military or law enforcement.

Jason counted a total of four women, two of them tattooed, one of them conspicuously attractive. He allowed himself to wonder what the early autumn on this unspoiled island might have in store for him, conscious that the same thought was surely passing through the head of every single man in the room. Well, maybe not every man: he suspected the incel community had a couple of representatives here.

They were set to work on that very first day and that ethos held thereafter. The work was constant and pursued with total discipline. They worked in shifts, around the clock, their focus moving around the globe with the sun. Early evenings, you worked on

Asia; small hours of the night, Europe; mornings, the US East Coast; afternoons, California and the west. Eight hours at a stretch, meal breaks taken like Boy Scouts: food served in the dining hall, canteen-style.

As for the work itself, it began with an order sheet from Jim. He would present the target list for that shift: sometimes a place or an object, usually a person. Then the researchers – that was the term Jim used – would be tasked with finding out all they could. Precise location, usual daily movements, domestic arrangements, access points to place of work or home. They would then devise what Jim called a 'work plan' so that that person or object could be 'filed'. That was the preferred term and they all now used it.

Jason was on the day shift, which meant his focus was on the continental United States. He looked hard at the screen, staring at the face that was staring back at him. He was looking at a digitized version of an old newspaper cutting, taken from the *Detroit Free Press*. This was the first item he had found, before he had checked – hacked might be another word – local hospital records, along with the databases of the social security system, Medicare and the Department of Motor Vehicles. He now had the basic details: exact address, contact telephone number and so on. This one had been especially easy. The target was on Facebook: she might as well have left her front door unlocked.

Officially, then, there was no problem. He had the basic information that was requested of him. Drawing up a work plan would be simple, not least because their human resources were, if not quite unlimited, then plentiful. Jim had made clear that, just as their online connectivity was state-of-the-art, so they had abundant 'assets' IRL – in real life. If they did not have someone on the ground or nearby already, an asset could be brought on board quickly, reliably and discreetly.

In this case, as with several others, the target was in an assisted living facility which posed some superficial difficulties – closed circuit TV cameras, witnesses and so on – but also had significant advantages: people were in and out of those places all the time. Whichever on-the-ground asset was deployed, Jason was confident that they could get to the target without any need for forced entry, without arousing suspicion at all. They could pose as the great-nephews from Oak Park that, thanks to Facebook, Jason had identified and located within minutes.

No, the problem was not at the operational level. Rather it was with the necessity of this particular task. Their instructions were clear: they were to do as they were told, simply implementing that day's order sheet. Decisions about priorities were the preserve of Jim or, he implied, those above him – those who the researchers had never met, heard from or seen.

And yet, every now and again, Jim had hinted at a degree of discretion in their work. Or at least in Jason's work. Sometimes, as he hunched over his machine, staring at his triple-screen display, Jim would lean over Jason's shoulder, watch the profile he was constructing take shape and say, 'What do you think? Based on what you've got, would you say this one needs to be actioned right away? Or could it wait?'

He never spelled out the criteria by which Jason was meant to make such a judgement. But recently, especially after their work together on that London operation – involving that woman in the stairwell – he had formed a sense of it. And now, given what he'd learned, he wondered if this latest target failed to meet the unspoken standard.

Her face was still looking back at him. He skimmed the details of the newspaper once more. Esther Gratzky of the Detroit suburb of Sherwood Forest, who had introduced a local screening of *Schindler's List* in 1993. Then aged sixty-four, she had taken questions after the film as she recounted her own experience of life in a Polish ghetto. The newspaper reported that most of the audience had been moved to tears, while Gratzky herself remained dry-eyed throughout.

There had been more such talks, noted on Facebook. But her activities had dropped off. The health records suggested no dramatic developments, but she was very old now.

All of which lent force to the question now nagging at Jason, as his finger hovered over the button that would action this work plan. Esther Gratzky, Holocaust survivor, now living in Detroit, Michigan: did she deserve to be 'filed' or not?

Chapter Seventeen

Washington DC, 6.55pm

Maggie had been staring at Uri for the best part of two minutes before she realized what she was doing. Watching him working intently at his laptop at her kitchen table, she was daydreaming, drifting somewhere between memory and fantasy, as she pictured – recalled, really – the two of them in bed together, in this very apartment. Their lovemaking had been intense, and somehow *serious.* As if they were engaged in an ongoing conversation of great import, the two of them unpeeling more and more of themselves each time their bodies met. The sex with Richard, her last boyfriend, just a few months ago, had been compulsive, even addictive. But it lacked whatever it was she had had with Uri. Looking back now, she supposed that difference was love.

'What?' Uri's eyes hinted at a smile.

'What do you mean, "What"?'

'What are you looking at?'

Maggie wanted to answer truthfully. She wanted to say, 'You.' But she worried that would load more weight onto the moment than it could bear. Or more than she could bear, anyway.

So instead she said, 'Nothing.' And then, after a pause that lasted a half second too long, she said: 'What have you got?'

'I don't know. It might be nothing. I mean, there might be an explanation.'

'For what?' She moved from her chair too fast, so that her scalded skin seemed to pull tight. She grimaced as she said, 'An explanation for what?'

'We know the UVA library lost its digital archive, right? So I was checking at Yad Vashem.'

'To see if the same thing happened to them?'

'Right.'

'And?'

'Look.'

The screen displayed an error message: *This site can't be reached*.

Maggie took it in and said: 'So what's the other explanation?'

Uri flicked to another tab on the screen, opened to Twitter. It showed the list of trending topics, with Yad Vashem at the top. He pointed at it. 'It's the big story, people are curious, they google Yad Vashem, system gets overloaded, system goes down.'

'OK. Well, that makes sense.'

'Maybe. We'll see if it comes back up. What about you? Found anything?'

Maggie looked down at the pad on which she'd scribbled a few disparate items that she'd spotted after a wide, but shallow, Google trawl. First on the list was a story she'd picked up already.

It had led the local news on the radio as she'd made the two-hour drive back to DC from Richmond. Several guides at the National Museum of African American History and Culture in Washington said they had been assaulted on their way to and from work in the preceding twenty-four hours, in what appeared to be an organized, even systemic attack. The home of the museum's director had been daubed with graffiti, including the slogans *Fake news* and *Stop the lies*. At the museum itself, a crowd had surrounded one official guide, badgering him to tell the truth, jabbing him on the chest and calling him a liar.

Maggie also noted an outbreak of E. coli at an academic conference – on reparations – in Oklahoma and a remarkably similar outbreak at the history faculty in Maine. An eminent historian of the nineteenth-century United States – specializing in slavery and the American civil war – had been found dead in Amsterdam, where he had been on a one-year sabbatical. Police said that he appeared to have been caught up in an armed robbery.

There was one more story that didn't quite fit the pattern, but which she noted nonetheless. In London, the family of Holocaust survivor Judith Beaton rejected a provisional police finding of suicide after the woman was found dead at the bottom of a stairwell in her apartment building. The daughter's words, quoted in the news report, had leapt out at Maggie. 'My mother lived to tell the world of her experience in Auschwitz and on the death march in 1945. She regarded every day she had been granted as precious – as a gift – and was determined not to squander even a moment of it. The idea that she would have taken her own life is absurd and an insult to her memory.' The Beaton family said they were sure that once the coroner had assessed the evidence, they too would 'throw out' any talk of suicide.

Maggie mentioned all of this to Uri who, on hearing the Beaton story, suddenly sat upright, as if he'd heard an alarm bell ring. He opened up a new tab on the computer and Maggie watched over his shoulder as he typed the words 'Shoah testimony project' into the search bar. The first answer came up announcing something called the Shoah Foundation. Uri clicked.

To Maggie's relief, there was no error message like the one at Yad Vashem. This page did load, bringing up the About Us page, which confirmed that this was the archive founded by one of Hollywood's biggest directors in the early 1990s, an attempt to record on camera the testimony of every last living witness and survivor of the Holocaust. It announced that it had so far collected fifty-five thousand interviews in forty-two languages, a monumental effort to ensure the horror was fully documented while it still remained in living memory, to record it before it was too late.

'Thank God for that,' Maggie said, watching as Uri clicked his way towards the search option and then typed in the name 'Judith Beaton'.

The machine recognized it and rapidly generated a page with a paragraph or two of information below a small video player screen. It showed a still image of an elegant woman, her chin raised. Uri clicked the play button but nothing happened. He clicked it again. Still nothing. And then, as he tried a third time, the machine did something strange.

The page appeared to melt before their eyes. The words, the graphics, the small, unresponsive screen within the screen – they all began to lose shape and drip, like candlewax. The molten letters tumbled to the bottom of the page, where they gathered in a pool, useless and illegible.

'Try another one,' Maggie said.

Uri backed out of that page and found the search bar again. His fingers hesitated. Maggie couldn't keep the urgency out of her voice: 'Anyone, Uri. Anyone.'

Uri muttered something about an old friend of his father's, a fellow archaeologist who had been in the ghetto in Kaunas, Lithuania. He typed the name, and the page appeared. A man, then in his seventies, wearing what appeared to be a safari suit. Once again, the play button on the video player was useless. And a second later, the page began to melt.

'What the hell is this?' Maggie said.

Uri was frantically jabbing at the keys. 'It's some kind of hack.'

'I can see that! But what the fuck is going on?'

'It depends if the people behind this are—'

'I'll tell you what's going on, Uri. This isn't just about slavery. Someone is trying to destroy the evidence of the greatest crimes in human history. And as of this moment, they're succeeding.'

Chapter Eighteen

Washington DC, 8.55pm

Maggie needed water. She felt her temperature rising, though whether that was the result of the burns on her blistered skin or the realization now coursing through her, she could not tell. She went into the kitchen, filled a glass and drained it before she could even set it down on the counter. She filled it again, then left the tap running so she could splash a few drops on her face.

Her phone buzzed. A one-word text, from Governor Morrison. *Anything?*

She thumbed out a two-word reply – *Not yet* – and filled another glass for Uri, then headed back out into the living area. It was now converted into an impromptu research centre, with piles of papers, take-out cartons and notepads arranged around the two computers and the tangle of cables and phone chargers that lay between them.

'I mean,' she said, continuing out loud the train of thought that had been running through her mind and which she assumed

Uri would automatically follow, the kind of assumption that she had made only with him. 'I've dealt with some shitty people in my time. Doing really shitty things. Driving a good president from office. Keeping a bad president *in* office. Sabotaging a Middle East peace deal.' For that last one, she gestured in Uri's direction, as if to say: *You don't need me to tell you about that, you were there*. Which indeed he was.

'I've seen plenty of bad stuff, I really have.' She took a swig of water, which did nothing to reduce the heat on her face. 'But this? This is something else completely.'

Uri looked at her and listened, as he had done a thousand times before.

'It's killing those people all over again. It's enslaving them all over again. You put a person in chains, you're saying: you're an animal. Your life is worth nothing. Your life *means* nothing. And then, years later, you say it didn't happen? You pretend it didn't happen? You're saying the same thing to them all over again: your life has so little value, we'll destroy all the proof you ever existed. We'll *forget* you were ever here.'

'Maggie—'

'And the Holocaust, Uri? Can you believe that? The world did nothing for those people. They stood by and let it happen. Six million people. Why am I telling you? You don't need me—'

'Maggie, please.'

'It's OK. I'm OK.' She took another chug of water, wishing the burning would stop. 'I'm all right. I'll be all right. I was just going to say: remembering is all we can do for those people. It's the *least* we can do. Literally, the very fucking least. Otherwise, we're just the same as the people who stood and watched and maybe tutted and said, "That's a shame, dear", and just let it happen. And I don't want to be one of those people, Uri. I don't want to live in that world.'

She let herself fall into a chair. The stinging sensation made her eyes smart even more, but somehow she welcomed the physical pain: it would provide a cover for the tears' true source.

Uri passed her a tissue. He took her hand and said, 'You know, maybe this can be healing.'

At first, she thought he was talking about them. That sharing this moment, enduring this horror together, might bind them together. But his eyes said otherwise.

'What could be "healing"?'

'All this. What's happening.' He pulled his hand from hers, confirming her hunch. 'Wiping the slate clean.'

'Are you serious? Tell me, for fuck's sake, you're not serious.'

'Well, if you think—'

'These people are torching *libraries*, Uri. They're burning *books*. I mean, that surely rings a few bells.'

'Obviously I hate the way they're doing it, Maggie. Obviously. No one in their right minds could support that. But if this is about there being too much history, then . . . then, I understand where they're coming from.'

'I don't believe this.'

'It's possible to have too much history, that's all I'm saying, Maggie. I come from a country buried up to its neck in the past. Not up to its neck; up to its eyes! I grew up in Jerusalem. You know what that place is like. All around, every little side turning or alleyway, it's a stone from the time of Abraham or it's the tomb of Rachel or the cave of Jesus or the rock of Mohammed – people who may, or may not, have lived thousands of years ago – and people fight and kill each other now, *today*, over the "memory" of these people. People that of course they don't remember. Not actually remember. But they *tell* themselves they do, with all that bullshit about "collective memory". Worshipping every stone they pull out of the ground, every grain of dust, saying, "This proves it! This proves we belong here." Or more often, "This proves that here belongs to us."'

'It was your father's work, Uri. His life's work.'

'Oh, don't worry, I know that. Like it wasn't enough that I got all this history in school, and on the radio, I had it every day in my home, thanks to my father, the great Shimon Guttman, archaeologist and excavator of the heroic Jewish past! The past filled my home, Maggie. Every inch, every shelf. The air in that house was filled with dust, no matter how hard my mother worked with her cloths and her polish and her broom. The dust of thousands of years of history. History so thick you could choke on it.'

Maggie was shaking her head. 'But without history, Uri, why on earth . . . I mean, it would make no sense. None of it would make any sense. Why would you be in Israel? Why would any of us be anywhere? We'd just be like . . . animals. Dumb, pointless animals.'

'We'd be people, Maggie. Not "A People". But real people, individuals, not little bit players in some bullshit epic story. And the story is almost always bullshit, isn't it? Some murderous butcher whipping his people up, saying, "We must rise up and kill those people, over there, to avenge what they did to our ancestors. They humiliated us a thousand years ago. They killed your grandparents. They did a massacre here in the year eleven hundred and bullshit. Now it's time to settle the score." It's the same story wherever you go. It can be Israel, it can be Rwanda, it can be Bosnia. I go with my camera, and I hear it again and again. "We owe it to the dead. We must honour the past." '

Now he smiled. 'Shit, Maggie, listen to me. I'm lecturing Maggie Costello on *this*? Maggie Costello from *Ireland*. Our countries are the joint champions, yours and mine, Ireland and Israel, top of the leaderboard in history mania. You're as bad as we are. All those flags and slogans demanding revenge for deaths that happened four hundred years ago, as if they were just yesterday. You were brought up to be as crazy as us!'

Maggie tried to be calm, to adopt her quieter, steady voice. Even though Uri would know the instant he heard it that Maggie was, in fact, more livid than if she were screaming.

'I understand that it's possible to be stuck in the past, Uri. But the solution to that is not to destroy the past. It's not a solution to wipe out the historical record. We need that record. It's such a cliche, it's embarrassing to even say it, but it's true. "Those who cannot remember the past—" '

'Are condemned to repeat it. Sure. But we can't keep saying that any more, Maggie. We just can't. Because we *do* remember the past and we still repeat it.'

'I don't—'

'Like "Never Again". I mean, that's the fucking national

anthem in my country. "Never Again shall a people commit genocide against another people." But it *did* happen again. It happened in Cambodia. It happened in Rwanda. It happened in Srebrenica. We had all the museums, Maggie. We had all the libraries. And all the movies. And all the great novels that I had to read in school. And all those historians. We had it all. Everyone knew what happened in the 1940s. But did it stop anything? I don't have your accent, Maggie, but like you would say, "Did it fuck?" '

There was silence now, while Maggie stared at her fingers. She'd forgotten this side of Uri, the passion that he forced down below the surface, as if keeping the lid on a cauldron filled with spitting, boiling oil. She once thought she liked it, but now he just felt far away. Unbidden, she remembered being in that burning library and looking over her shoulder to see that Uri had . . . gone.

'The funny thing is, Maggie, I learned this from you. When we met, you were a peace negotiator. Sent into the Jerusalem madhouse to deal with all those crazy Israelis and Palestinians. And what you always said was – and it stayed with me – you said, if you want to end a war, you have to choose. Sometimes you get peace, sometimes you get justice, but you don't get both. It was a choice. "Either you get a reckoning for the past, or you can have hope for the future." That's not me saying that. It's what you said. I remember it, because it made so much sense. And it was so wise. And so few people in my country ever, ever talked like that.'

'But not like this, Uri. It can't be like this.'

'I agree. Not like this. It's horrible and it has to stop. But maybe something good can come from it, all the same. I just know that the one thing my country needs most is a chance to forget.'

'"We should raise a monument to Amnesia and then forget where we put it."'

'Exactly.'

'Just because I know the quote, Uri, doesn't mean I agree with it.' She sighed. 'If we don't know about the past, I don't know who we'd be. We'd be like goldfish, living in this moment, then this one, then the next, then the next. Living for two seconds, forgetting it all and then starting all over again. We'd never get anywhere. We'd be trapped in this permanent present. I'm only me because I remember my past, where I've been, what I've done. Who I've loved and who's loved me. Otherwise, I'm just a bunch of . . . I don't know, neural fucking inputs. And that's not just true of individual human beings, that's true of the human race.'

They were silent for a while before she spoke again. Again, her voice was soft.

'I can't believe I'm on my own.'

'You're not on your own, Maggie.'

She looked up, fixing him in a cold stare. 'I am alone if I'm up against a gang of book-burners and murderers and you're on their bloody side!'

She stood up and moved towards the front door of the apartment. 'I know it sounds hysterical, that you probably think I just need to calm down. But if we're not on the same side, then I need to do this alone.' She opened the door and held it open, watching in silence as he packed up his things and left.

*

At moments like this, Maggie tended to have two forms of pain relief. Either whisky or a phone call with her sister. This time she opted for both.

'Maggie?'

'Hi Liz.'

'You sound weird. Is something going on?'

'Thanks a lot, Liz.'

'I just mean, usually, I call you. Unless, you know, something's up.'

'Did I tell you I ran into Uri?'

'No, Maggie, you did not tell me that *major* piece of information.' The excitement in her voice was audible, even from six hundred and fifty miles away. 'Don't tell me, he's married. I don't want to say, "I told you so." '

'Well, then don't.'

'So he's married?'

'Was.'

'Divorced? Or—'

'Divorced.'

'It's just I was hearing about Dolores. Do you remember her? Year above me? Had plaits till she was, like, twelve? Apparently her boyfriend left her when she got the diagnosis. I mean, we knew he was a prize wanker, but I didn't think even he was capable . . .'

As Liz spoke, Maggie was thinking about Uri. What the fuck was he talking about? *Maybe this can be healing.* How could he of all people even think like that about the torching of archives and libraries, including a Holocaust museum? And if he did think like that, why the hell was he helping her?

'. . . he doing now?'

Half an antenna picked up that her sister had asked a question. It demanded a response.

'What's he doing now?' she said, stalling. Of course. Uri. 'He's still making documentaries. We were in the same place.'

'Yeah, that's kind of essential if you're going to run into each other. Jesus, Mags, can you cut to the chase? Did you, you know?'

'No, I don't know.'

'You bloody do know, you stupid cow. Did you shag?'

'Elizabeth Costello, can I remind you that you are now a married woman and a mother of two and you're not meant to talk like you're still bunking off Sister Agnes' scripture class to have a quick fag.'

'Did you or didn't you?'

'All right, I'll tell you. We did not.'

'How come?'

'To tell you the truth, I think maybe he's changed.'

'Why, has he gone fat? It can happen. I mean, Paul gets a bit lardy if he misses his bike ride, though I always—'

'No. He looks good actually. It's just I'm not sure we see eye to eye any more. We had a bit of a row, actually. Just now.'

'What about?'

'I threw him out.'

'You threw him out? You're kidding! You'd only just seen him.'

'I know.'

'You don't mess about, do you?'

'It's a long story. Tell me, how are the boys?'

The long answer that inquiry always yielded gave Maggie

time to think. A feeling that she had pushed down below the surface now rose to the top. Last night, at the library, it was Uri who had suggested they get a closer look, he who had suggested they go in, even though that had meant exposing themselves to grave danger. She had done as he had suggested but when she looked round, he was . . . gone.

'And how's work?' Maggie offered, as if poking at a logfire that might otherwise flicker out.

As her sister spoke about the new academic year and a change in the testing system that was making her timetable a nightmare, Maggie went back to the way she and Uri had bumped into each other in Charlottesville. *Of all the race riots in all the towns in all the world, you walk into mine*. It was smooth, no doubt about it. But was it a bit too smooth?

'Sure. So what did you say?' she asked, tuning into Liz's monologue just in time to maintain the illusion of dialogue. As her sister replied, Maggie reminded herself that she had been played by men before, that she should have learned her lesson by now.

Liz was running through the pros and cons of her applying for the Head of Computer Studies job at the school rather than waiting to be offered it, especially since Ryan seemed to be needier now that he was in elementary school. Meanwhile, another voice in Maggie's head was telling herself that this was now, not then. Uri was Uri, he wasn't the same as those others. Letting the past strangle the chance of something good: that too was a habit from her past.

'So you know this new therapist I've been seeing?'

'The handsome French bloke?'

'He says I need to be very careful to avoid repeating childhood behaviours.'

Maggie sat up. 'What kind of childhood behaviours?'

'He says I avoid confrontations, that I put my head in the sand.'

'Like what?'

'That I go into denial rather than deal with things.'

'And what's he basing that on?'

'I don't know, just what we've talked about, I suppose.'

'And how often are you seeing him?'

'Twice a week. Three this week, because of all the stuff we're working through.'

'Jesus.'

'That's his method. He does an extra session if you have the time.'

'And the money.'

'Thing is, Mags. We got deep into the childhood stuff this morning. It was strange. A whole lot of things I remembered, which I didn't know I remembered, do you know what I mean?'

'I've heard about this. False memory syndrome.'

'No, I can tell they're real. It's just I'd forgotten, if that makes any sense.'

'That's because you've actually got a life. Which means living in the present, not obsessing over the past. If therapists had their way, we'd spend every single fucking day going over how we felt taking a shit when we were three. But some of us actually—'

'All right, don't bite my head off.'

'I'm sorry, Liz. But these people, really. How much are you paying him?'

'I told you, it's nothing to do with money. I'm finding it useful. There's a lot that happened that I feel confused by.'

'Well, I think people like this – like this "Yves" – they thrive on that. On making their customers feel confused. So they get hooked and have to keep coming back.'

'I don't believe this. Why are you trying to sabotage this, Maggie?'

'I'm not sabotaging anything.'

'Yes you are. You're trying to undermine this process. Now why do you think you'd be doing that? What's that about?'

'Now you're even talking like a fucking therapist!'

'Oh, fuck off, Maggie.'

Neither of them hung up. They held the silence together for about twenty seconds until Maggie let out a long sigh. 'I'm sorry, Liz. I don't know what's got into me.' It was true; she didn't. 'It's probably this thing with Uri. Blame that.'

'All right.' Liz's voice was tight, several stages away from forgiving.

They said goodbye. Maggie drained the whisky glass, wondering as she returned it to the kitchen how many more relationships she could ruin before the day was out. And as she washed her face in the bathroom, she wondered if her sister had a point. Had she been trying to sabotage this therapy thing? And if she had, what would be the reason?

Gingerly she removed her clothes, inhaling sharply at the sting the burned skin still sent to her nervous system when touched, and slipped under the covers, trying not to think of Uri and therefore thinking only of Uri. Sleep came eventually, bringing dreams of talking statues and falling gravestones, so that Maggie Costello was wholly unaware of the burning havoc being unleashed thousands of miles away, as she lay unconscious and in the dark.

Wednesday

Chapter Nineteen

Bodleian Library, Oxford, 2.05am

The stillness was complete at this hour, the air silent but for the low hum of the electrics which kept this place safe and dry. The books remained where they had always been, lined up on shelves, stiff and straight-backed, standing to attention, like soldiers waiting for their orders.

Waiting was their vocation. Some of them had done it for hundreds of years, right in this very place. Waiting day after day, night after night, for weeks which turned into months, months which turned into years, years which turned into decades and decades which turned into centuries. They were patience itself, ripe with the knowledge that they would disgorge just the moment it was required. They would not force their knowledge on anyone. They would hold it within their pages, yielding it only when required. But there it sat, ready, waiting for the moment.

Line after line, row after row, of books, packed together in the dark of night. Added together, they would stretch for hundreds of miles, girdling the nation if not the globe with their facts, their memories, their observations, their quotations, their dates, their disagreements, their discoveries, their ideas and their proof of all that had gone before.

And not just books. Crammed together in this warren of rooms, this catacomb of pages, were maps and stamps and drawings and sheet music, as well as poems, speeches, novels and reports. There were computations from the dawn of science, as well as sermons from the Middle Ages and ruminations on the birth of modern philosophy – all, in their own way, attempts to touch the face of God.

If any of those long-dead authors had stalked the empty corridors of the Bodleian Library that night, what might they have heard? Not a sound as the fire alarm system was hacked and disabled, for that was a noiseless process easily done from many miles away. Nor would they have had any clue as a distant hand took similar charge of the climate control system, preparing it for use as a crucial tool. Or, more accurately, weapon.

Next came command of the power-assisted doors and the system of fire curtains, the blinds woven from fibre-glass material that were coiled up in boxes ready to roll down like shutters when needed. No less important: cutting off selected cameras from the closed circuit TV system. This was the beauty of the fully connected, fire-conscious building: everything was computerized through a single, state-of-the-art system.

And surely any spectral presence walking through the ancient rooms of the Bodleian would have paid no attention to those objects which were to be found on every floor, stashed away in the ceiling ducts: the heating and ventilation units, glorified metal boxes inside which would be stored a heating element, capable of warming the box up the way an element heats up a kettle, and a refrigeration unit ready for when cooling air was required.

Almost as invisible, out of sight and out of mind, would be the 'riser'. To the untutored, walking past them each day, they would look like nothing more than a big store cupboard, centrally placed, one on each floor, their doors almost always closed.

But inside were the electrics, a series of panels fixed to the walls for each of the fire and burglar alarms, as well as lighting, heating and ventilation. Along with the main power supply, it was all here, the wiring spidering out to reach all points on that floor. If you could speak of a building having a central nervous system, this was it.

The first move came invisibly, with the remote despatch shortly after two am of an instruction to the heating units on each floor, dialling them up to their maximum setting. Soon the metal became red-hot. The wiring inside began to smoulder.

But of course, no alarm sounded. How could it? That was the job of a fire warning system that had been silently disabled by remote signal.

The ducts in an old building like this were rarely cleaned. Inside was the accumulated dust – the hair, the human skin – of years, if not decades. It would take just a single spark from those wires melting in the heat to light that kindling. But the distant hand was not relying on that. Instead, at a moment calculated with precision, it turned on the fans that were essential to any ventilation system, so that they now breathed all that super-heated air over the dry dust, igniting it as surely as a Boy Scout blowing on a pile of tinder.

The flames would come quickly. The silent witnesses on the shelves, bound in aged leather, would see them – but the CCTV system would not. Carefully selected, the camera with a view of this particular corner had been quietly taken out.

The night security guards, facing their bank of monitors, would see nothing out of the ordinary. And why would they get up out of their chairs to go and look? Foot patrols had been replaced long ago, deemed redundant thanks to the network of motion-sensitive infra-red sensors. If anyone were moving around, they'd know about it.

The air around the vents was dry. Of course it was. Expensive climate control technology always ensured the environment inside this centuries-old building was just so, guarding against the humidity and dampness that might spoil all those precious volumes. There were no sprinklers overhead for a similar reason: water damage was deemed an even greater menace to all those old, dusty pages than fire.

Indeed, the precautions against fire had created the perfect conditions for it. For what lay inside each fire control panel, also now in the grip of remote instruction, but a contingency put in place precisely for an emergency like this one? A set of lithium ion batteries that might fuel the panel in case of a power cut. The trouble was, those batteries were highly flammable. Thanks to the heat and the flames, they would eventually catch fire too.

And of course the smoke did not remain contained. It leaked into those spaces no one ever thought about, but which fire craved: the voids between the ceiling of one room and the floor of the room above. Contained in that space, the smoke swiftly got hotter and hotter. The void was full of cables of all kinds – telephone, electricity, internet – each of them sheathed in a rubber that began to melt. The raw wire was now exposed, so that one cable could touch the naked current of another. The result was another spark. And then another. Those sparks touched the smoke – so hot it was capable of reaching temperatures of six hundred degrees – which promptly burst into more flames.

How long did it take for those flames to spread through the ceiling void of this entire floor? Seconds. And from there into the wall voids, until the fire had the building in its grip from all sides. A library like this one could barely resist the licking tongues of those flames. It offered itself up to them eagerly. It made such perfect tinder: all those dustbins, all those ancient wooden desks and shelves, all those books, all that *paper* and all of it so fastidiously dry. It was ideal kindling, ready to burst at the first caress of fire.

And from afar, the blaze could now be directed and choreographed. Had the system been working as it was meant to, the air-conditioning system would have shut down at the first breath of fire. But it was an accomplice to this crime: it had helped start the fire in the first place. Turned on at full strength, it continued to send gusts of oxygen to feed the flames. It was nature's accelerant.

Like a conductor using every instrument to shape the swell and sound of the orchestra, the distant controller was also using the fire curtains to direct the blaze. The conductor might drop down a curtain in one area, allowing the fire to build up and intensify in that confined space, then raise it, encouraging the fire, now grown more fierce, to spread into the next room. The electronically operated doors could serve a similar purpose.

And through it all, those delicate texts, those old scrolls and battered parchments, those documents that recorded civil war, reformation and counter-reformation, empire and revolution, remained silent, save for the crackle and whisper they uttered as they turned into cinders and ash.

Chapter Twenty

Washington DC, 7.38am

The moment she saw the news about the Bodleian, and about the fires on a similar scale at national libraries in Paris and Beijing, Maggie wanted to send a message to Donna Morrison, Governor of Virginia: *This is much bigger than we thought.*

But as she typed in the letters – D, then O, then N – the phone, which usually completed the rest, did nothing to bring up Donna's name or her number. Impatient, Maggie went into the 'contacts', but the device told her starkly, *You have no contacts.*

She went to her archive of text messages. She would find the governor's last one and simply reply to that. Except that too was empty.

Maggie looked at her phone and then, in a gesture that made no sense, shook it, as if she might stir it from its slumber, or as if it were an old transistor radio with sand in the works.

Second best, but she would email the governor instead. But

when she went to the Mail app, her inbox was also empty. Everything had been deleted, her entire phone wiped.

She went to her laptop and went to the section marked *Photos*. As the machine processed her request, she felt the anxiety rising like bile. She heard herself muttering: *'Please no, please no.'* But it was no good. Blankly, the computer let her know that that part of its memory – and hers – had been obliterated. The photos – of Liz, of her nephews, of Uri, of Stuart, of her life – had gone. If they had once sat in the cloud, they were now no more than vapour.

It was clear. Someone was destroying her personal history. They could erase her past by a simple hack, doubtless the work of a few keystrokes from anywhere in the world. They had the ability to do it and, they wanted her to know, they had the will.

She went back to the keyboard. She had her contacts backed up there, also stored, along with her email in the cloud. Unless . . .

Yep, those too had been erased. Jesus Christ, if you wanted to drive somebody mad in the twenty-first century, this was how to do it.

She would have to call Liz. She would remind her that, ages ago, Liz had done some kind of back-up of Maggie's data on an external hard drive. She would ask her where that was and what she needed to do.

But of course she could do none of that, because she didn't have any numbers in her phone – which was now a husk, dumb and empty – and, this was the insanity of it, she didn't know Liz's number. Her own sister.

Maggie fell into a chair and murmured out loud the landline

number of the Dublin house they had grown up in. Nine five three, seven five nine nine. And then the number for Kathleen McEntee, her best friend in primary school. Four five eight, two one six one. And then the number for their Auntie Deirdre, who she was always to call if their ma . . . was having one of her bad days.

She was finding it hard to see. The tears were obstructing her vision. She hardly ever thought about her childhood, about the tiny house on Quarry Street, but suddenly she missed it. The simplicity of it, of life before inboxes and hard drives and 'contacts', when clouds were in the sky and friends were people you knew. She missed the days when you knew where your sister was and how to reach her and, if you wanted her to give you a hug, you didn't have to get on a fucking plane.

Maggie went to the bathroom to clean herself up, catching sight of her face, still a throbbing pink on one side from the fire: she looked sunburned. And also, she reflected, as she saw the auburn hair that framed her pale skin, so stubbornly Irish.

It was then she caught just the faintest hint of the dream she'd been having seconds before she woke. She and Liz were swimming with their mother, in a pool on a summer's day. Liz was a toddler, so their ma was keeping her afloat, with her palm under her tummy. Maggie was paddling around them, but then she suddenly realized that Liz was sinking, that Ma was failing to keep her head above water. Maggie had started to scream and then to flounder, splashing wildly as she tried to reach her sister. Some water got in her mouth, but it didn't taste like water. It tasted strong and sharp . . .

The phone was ringing in the kitchen. She dashed back in and looked at the screen: a string of digits that her phone no longer recognized and to which, therefore, it could not attach a name.

Which meant all Maggie could manage was, 'Hello?'

'I'm in DC.'

It was Donna Morrison.

'I've been trying to reach you. Donna, this is way bigger than—'

'I know. Maggie—'

'I mean, it's not just buildings. They're killing historians too. And survivors and eyewitnesses. The point is—'

'You can fill me in on your way over here. Maggie, you need to get in a car.'

'Where to?'

'I'm in with the Director of the FBI. Come here right away. There's something you need to see.'

Chapter Twenty-One

Melita Island, Montana, 8am

'OK, listen up, gentlemen. And, of course, ladies.' The latter added as if it were somehow charming. 'Things are proceeding as we thought they would, and as we planned. I want to congratulate you on your work so far. We're making steady progress. And so far we've managed to do that without drawing attention to ourselves. Let me reiterate, however, that this is no time for complacency. None whatsoever. We are where we are – we've achieved what we've achieved – by adhering scrupulously to our practice of total confidentiality. That's why we've come all the way here and why we've taken such steps to maintain one hundred per cent secrecy. Is anything I've said so far unclear?'

They were in the dining hall, the same room where they had gathered on day one for orientation. Jason watched from the back row, assessing his colleagues as much as he was listening to Jim, their team leader or boss or commanding officer: he used none of those titles, though his role had elements of all three. He would have been ready to bet that Jim was ex-military, though personal disclosure was very much frowned upon, especially by him.

Jason was curious to see how they would react to what was about to unfold. Jim had not told him much, just enough to know that it would require a shift on the part of his fellow workers.

Until now they had simply had to draw up work plans for the targets they were given: starting with location, movements, weak points and then, from those, devising a suitable method of 'filing'. But in the last few days, as the implementation phase had gathered pace, there were other decisions to take.

Jim had given Jason an early sense of that shift. Perhaps Jason was flattering himself, but he liked to think Jim had singled him out for a greater degree of respect than the others by hinting that there were some judgements that had not already been made by the unseen high-ups, but for which his input might be of value.

These were judgements that had arisen only now, questions that had not been foreseen in the planning stage. Jim had made the point twice, first by saying that, 'In the wise words of Field Marshal Helmuth Karl Bernhard Graf von Moltke, Chief of Staff of the Prussian General Staff, "No battle plan ever survives contact with the enemy",' before adding, 'Or, as I like to put it, quoting Field Marshal Mike von Tyson, "Everybody has a plan until they get punched in the mouth."' How exactly they had been punched in the mouth, he didn't say.

If all this was a tactic on Jim's part, designed to strengthen Jason's commitment to the project, to the cause, by appearing to include him in the circle of trust, then it had worked. Jason was devoted to what they were doing.

But he worried about his colleagues. Not that they lacked application to the task. Far from it. But he suspected that most of them – even the ones with the tattoos and the 'Live Free or Die' belt buckles – were ultimately worker bees. They were built to work on tasks they were given, their little bit of the assembly line, rather than looking at the bigger picture. Jim had been right to include him, Jason, in the decision-making circle – even the outer rim of it – but these others? Not so sure.

'What I'm going to ask of you is mainly operational, where I know you all have proven expertise. But there is also a strategic element. A values dimension, if you will. In some ways, I'll be asking you to make a *value judgement*.' His voice italicized the last two words, as if they were in a foreign language and needed to be spoken slowly to be understood.

'So here's the deal. The focus of the question I need to raise with you, the targets if you will, are inanimate rather than animate. High-value items, all of them. I want you to prioritize, based on a combination of both operational factors and relative worth. How easy are these targets to achieve and how much are they worth it.

'What I want you to do is to rank the three items that I'm going to give you in order of priority. Which ones should we move on first, bearing in mind those two different sets of criteria: both how possible is it that we can get to them, and how important is it that we do. Blending those two factors, rank these three items in order. All right, are we all clear? Good.'

Jim now clicked on a device in his right hand which Jason hadn't noticed until now. Instantly, the wall behind him lit up, illuminated by the beam of a projector. It had become an impromptu screen. Jim clicked the device again, which appeared to divide the screen into three parts. The first two showed images of scrolls or parchment; only the third was a bound, if ancient, book.

'These are the three items. On the left, gentlemen, is the original, signed text of the United States Constitution, preserved under permanent, climate-controlled surveillance in Washington, DC. In the middle are the Dead Sea Scrolls, similarly protected in Jerusalem's Israel Museum, documents dating back two millennia, some of them three centuries older than Jesus, including manuscripts of texts later included in what we think of as the Holy Bible. And finally, fragments of the first known edition of the Koran, the sacred text of the world's nearly two billion Muslims, a manuscript which scholars believe was hand-written by someone who had themselves heard the Prophet Muhammad preach – a document kept under lock and key at the University of Birmingham, England.

'So that's the choice we need to make. I know, given the nature of this project, we'd like to target all three. The world would be a better place if we could. But we have to prioritize. So what's it to be, gentlemen? Which of these is our target?'

Chapter Twenty-Two

FBI headquarters, Washington DC, 8.30am

Rule one for Washington meetings: never be late. It wasn't a courtesy thing. It was a power thing. Walk in late, and your first words were an apology, even if you tried to mouth it silently to minimize disruption. That put you on the defensive from the very start. In the Washington shark tank, you'd left blood in the water.

Yet here was Maggie, having dashed out of the cab on 9th Street, introduced herself at the lobby – thereby marking herself out as that inferior creature in any landmark Washington building: one without a pass – and then waited for the elevator to take her up. From there, more introductions at the desk of the FBI Director's administrative assistant, who guided her through a vast conference room until they finally reached the inner office of the Director, before uttering the dread words, 'They're waiting for you.'

It didn't matter that none of this was Maggie's fault, that she had come as quickly as she'd been summoned. Nor that, unlike the Director and the Governor of Virginia and the rest of the half dozen people who now rose to their feet, she was no longer a public official, but someone who'd been drafted back in less than forty-eight hours ago. The instant she'd walked into this room, she was back in the Washington ecosystem, judged once more by their standards and set to be placed somewhere in the all-important DC hierarchy.

That process was underway right now, Maggie could feel it. Of course, Donna and the Director would not be involved. They were 'principals' and therefore above such things; they would only care about their status relative to other principals. But everyone else in the room would be working out where exactly to slot in Maggie Costello.

On the one hand, she was a 'former', a lower form of Washington life, no matter how elevated the post one formerly held. On the other hand, that could give her a stature the others lacked. She was no one's employee. She was no mere worker bee, invited here because of the job she happened to fill. She was here on her own merits, requested by the governor herself because she had some expertise that could not be supplied by any other part of the federal bureaucracy. In other words, she had been deemed indispensable by a principal. Which in turn made her – and this, Maggie understood instinctively – a threat. She was here as an individual, untethered to any bureaucracy. It was as if, in a room full of suits, she had walked in wearing ripped jeans. She hadn't done that, but she *could have*. And in Washington terms, that amounted to the same thing.

All of this went through Maggie's mind in the seconds it took for her to move from the door to her place in the circle of stiff-backed, though cushioned, chairs loosely arranged in front of the Director's desk, in a kind of homage to the choreography and upholstery of the Oval Office.

'I think you know everyone here,' he said, though that was not true, before giving half-line summaries of each person present. What followed was a jumble of Deputy Directors, Associate Deputy Directors, Executive Assistant Directors and Assistant Directors. But she got the idea.

The Director himself, Craig Lofgren, was someone Maggie had come across a few times, usually in meetings like this, back when he'd been shuttling between senior jobs at Justice and Homeland Security and she'd been serving the previous president from her perch in the White House. Crucially, he was not an appointee of the current incumbent, a fact which, in Maggie's eyes at least, vouched for his good character. Like Donna, he did not carry that taint.

White, early fifties, with hair still brown and cut so short and neatly it begged not to be noticed. For a certain kind of Washington man, and plenty of women, when it came to matters of personal style, 'efficient' and 'functional' were compliments, with 'practical' the highest form of praise. Maggie's loose, flame-red hair, still long enough to reach her shoulders, marked her out as positively maverick.

'OK, just to bring everyone up to speed, let me loop you all in real quick. As you know, Governor Morrison brought in Maggie Costello to assist with what she believed was a potentially explosive situation in her state, following a series of racially charged incidents.'

Racially charged. Another one of those Washington-isms designed to swerve around words that would sound too intense for meetings like this one.

'Overnight,' Lofgren continued, 'it's become clear that the threat goes beyond racial tensions in Virginia and perhaps beyond race as the central aggravating factor. It seems we're dealing with a wider threat penumbra.'

Wider threat penumbra. It had only been a few months, but Maggie had almost forgotten that Washington had its own language.

'The attacks on libraries and archives in Oxford, Beijing and Paris suggest an organized and international effort to destroy key repositories of documents, many of them precious. Our colleagues in Langley, in discussion with their counterparts around the world, suspect this might be a concerted attack on the so-called Alexandria Group, a network of a dozen of the world's leading libraries. And, in case any of you were thinking it, that name predates these fires.'

'Kind of tempting fate though, don't you think?'

It was Andrea Ellis, Lofgren's deputy, a woman Maggie knew of only by reputation. Word was, Lofgren outsourced his emotional intelligence to her: she was there to 'complete his skill set', which translated as 'deal with other human beings'. That remark of hers just now prompted Maggie to smile in her direction.

'We're already liaising with Langley and of course with colleagues around the world,' the Director continued, his software only briefly jarred by the intrusion of an unscripted joke. 'A working group has been established linking MI5 and SIS in London, MSS in Beijing and DGSI and DGSE in Paris. We will obviously prioritize the immediate threat inside the United States, with a focus on the sole American member of the Alexandria Group, namely the Library of Congress. But we will also play our part in the international effort. With that in mind, I wanted our own dedicated leadership team on this matter until it's resolved. That is the group in this room. Codenamed, Florian.

'OK, two developments you need to be aware of, both of them strongly indicating a single perpetrator or group of perpetrators behind this threat. First, on the screen behind me is the image that now displays when you go to the website of the Bodleian Library in Oxford, the Bibliothèque National in Paris or the National Library of China in Beijing. The website for each of those institutions appears to have been destroyed. This is all you see now.'

Like everyone else in the room, Maggie was transfixed by what she was looking at. It was a short animation, a luridly bright child's cartoon, showing a line of green bottles wobbling on a brick wall. She quickly added them up: nine. There were twelve Alexandria libraries and now three were down. So whoever was behind this was offering a little riff on the old children's song, with an extra two bottles added for good measure.

'Apparently these images changed during the night. The Beijing site went down first, replaced by a GIF showing eleven green bottles. Then Oxford, showing ten. After Paris, they all went down to nine. That's where we are now.'

'Jesus Christ,' Maggie murmured, bringing a nod from Donna and a sharp look from one of the others.

'Second,' and now Lofgren pointedly checked his watch, 'fifty-three minutes ago, a package was opened in the mail room of this building, addressed to me. It is a treatise some thirty-five thousand words in length, entitled "Remembering to Forget, Forgetting to Remember". Needless to say it's anonymous. Equally needless to say, it has been scrubbed of all identifying marks. Obviously, we have agents at work right now, both reading it for content and examining the envelope, print quality and ink to see if there are any clues as to origination. It appears to have been hand-delivered, so we'll be examining CCTV footage too. But at this very early stage it seems that what we have here is a manifesto.'

'Seems our Bookburner has written a book,' Donna said, signalling that none of this was news to her. 'And they say irony is dead.'

'And what does it say, this manifesto?' Maggie asked noticing the man next to her slowly writing out the word 'Bookburner' on his yellow legal pad.

The Director replied, even though Maggie had been looking at the governor. 'Early days, but the first pass suggests that it consists largely of the intellectual case for destroying all evidence of the past. The introduction speaks of "a return to an Edenic state". As I say, we're getting it read and analyzed now. We'll have executive summaries for you soon.'

Maggie frowned. 'Edenic?'

One of the Assistants, or maybe it was a Deputy Assistant – it was hard to tell since all the men, bar one who was African-American, looked and dressed alike – leaned forward. He seemed, whether consciously or not, to be aping the body language and speech patterns of the Director. She'd seen that in Washington before too: the underling who aspires to be a miniature version of the boss.

'As in the Garden of Eden.'

'I know what the word means! I went to convent school, for Christ's sake. I'm just thinking—'

'Well, religious language may indeed be a significant factor,' Lofgren said, keen to retake control. 'If this is an initiative of global jihadism, then it would not be surprising if this document were to be full of such references.'

'Is that the working theory for this, that it's jihadist terrorism?'

The Director looked over to his deputy. 'Andrea?'

She cleared her throat. 'That's always going to be our starting assumption in a case like this. Multiple, iconic targets; simultaneous attacks; destruction of historic sites; violating western norms. Does kind of check all the boxes.'

'But China,' Maggie said. 'That would be a departure, wouldn't it?'

'It would,' Ellis replied. 'But if we're right that they have the Alexandria Group in their sights, then it won't just be western locations. Western sensibilities might well be the ultimate target. If you think back to Palmyra: trashing it was partly about erasing Syria's pre-Islamic past, and partly about outraging western opinion. Same with the Taliban blowing up the Bamiyan Buddhas.'

'But we shouldn't forget the killings. That's not their usual MO, is it?'

'Excuse me?' It was Lofgren's mini-me. 'What killings?'

Governor Morrison looked over at the Director. *This is what I was telling you about.* Now she gestured for Maggie to explain.

'OK. Even before the destruction of the library at Charlottesville, there was a murder. Of a historian at that university. That's what the governor first asked me to look at. A Professor Russell Aikman. But it turns out he was not the only one. We found several historians killed—'

'Who's we?' Mini-Lofgren again.

'Er, sorry. Me. Just me. Force of habit.' Maggie smiled broadly, as Uri walked into her head and then out again. 'In the past few days, several historians were killed in very rapid succession and in very suspicious circumstances. I can give you the details. And not only in this country. And not only historians. We've also seen the murder of crucial eyewitnesses to historic events. Holocaust survivors initially, but there are also now reports of the killings of survivors of the massacres in Rwanda and in the Balkans.' She thought of Uri and his ingenious system of Google alerts; a string of text messages had arrived from him as she rode in the cab. A peace offering perhaps.

'To say nothing of the destruction of Yad Vashem, and denial of service attacks on a range of websites whose sole purpose is documenting these events. This looked like a wide-ranging, international effort aimed at destroying the record of history's greatest crimes. And now, after what happened last night, the target seems to be even bigger. History itself.'

She took a breath. She suddenly felt self-conscious. This, she realized, looked like grandstanding: a Washington offence, even if everybody did it all the time.

'All I'm saying is that this might be jihadism or it might not. We don't know.' Maggie looked around the circle. 'We need to keep an open mind.' She saw two of the Deputy Assistants, or Assistant Deputies, look at each other. She was being difficult.

As she spoke, the secretary who'd brought Maggie to this room came in noiselessly, approached the Director and handed him a small square of paper. He took it and carried on nodding, allowing Maggie to finish her point. Then he cleared his throat.

'It's from the analytics team. Confirmation that our work here is now much more urgent. First, this document fits our initial assumption: it makes clear that the Alexandria Group of libraries and archives is indeed the central target of a worldwide operation, apparently aimed at destroying the historical record.

'Second and more alarming, the manifesto includes a deadline.'

'A deadline?' said the governor, now looking petrified. 'What kind of deadline?'

'Whoever is behind this effort wants it completed by Friday of this week.'

'Friday? Why Friday?' It was Lofgren's echo.

Andrea Ellis was checking the calendar on her phone. 'Does that date have any particular significance?'

Donna Morrison sighed. 'I can think of one. That's the day we're expecting a verdict in the Keane case. You know, "history on trial".'

There was a silence as each person in the room tried to process the implications and to calculate the relative probabilities of coincidence or intent.

'Either way,' said Lofgren, 'we have only two days.'

Chapter Twenty-Three

Mountain View, California, one month earlier

Jen Goodwin checked her watch. Her contact here, Katy, would be down in a minute or so. Jen would have to pretend not to recognize her immediately – even though she had spent a good part of the last week scouring her every social media post, learning so much about her, she'd almost become a friend. Almost.

She felt that familiar frisson – part guilt, part thrill, each related to the other – that this job still supplied, even after several years. If asked at dinner parties, she would usually say she was in 'IT', a response which elicited either a turned back, a look of strained pity or undisguised panic: *Oh my God, how dull, what on earth are we going to talk about?*

Occasionally, she would say infosec or information security or, if speaking to someone over forty, cybersecurity, which might trigger a raised eyebrow or, more often, an inquiry about passwords. What Jen Goodwin never said was that she was a pentester: a penetration tester, hired either alone or as part of a 'red team' to test the defences of companies' computer systems against intrusion.

Her task was to break through by whatever means necessary. That might mean sitting at the keyboard of a machine hundreds, if not thousands, of miles away, prodding and poking at a company's digital plumbing until she found a weak join. Or it might mean deploying what she and her colleagues called 'social engineering': exploiting the single weakest part of any company's digital infrastructure, namely the human beings who supported it.

When Jen Goodwin had received this commission four days ago, she'd known instantly it would be the hardest of her career to date. The target company was just too important, too central to the internet, to take chances with its security. And, of course, it was stupendously, unimaginably rich, with a bottomless well of resources. To attempt a virtual break-in would be ridiculous. Whatever trick of hackery might work with a regular company was doomed to fail against this one. Which left only one option: physical penetration.

But a quick look at the available OSINT – open-source intelligence, your regular publicly available information – was, if anything, even more discouraging. It took Jen barely a glance at Google Maps – and yes, she was aware of the irony – along with various satellite images, to see that the Network Operations Center, or NOC, which was her target, was all but impregnable. It was built like a maximum-security prison: no windows, heavy iron gates, electronic card scanners, biometric security controls – doubtless including iris-recognition – as well as swipecard-controlled turnstiles at every entrance. Sometimes, you'd be surprised; Jen could waltz into company offices by simply tailgating, attaching herself to a group of visitors and slipping in without anyone noticing. That was not going to be an option with this one.

But, and this was one of the things Jen loved about her job, that very fact prompted a thought. What must it be like to work inside such a place? All that security: pretty soon, you'd feel like a prisoner yourself. Maybe she could use that to her advantage . . .

Her next move was her LinkedIn account. Or rather one of her half dozen fake LinkedIn accounts. It took a while, but before long Jen's screen displayed several profiles of people who worked both in the NOC and in the 'data integrity' centre nearby. She then simply cross-checked those with accounts held by those same people on social media: Facebook, as always, was the most generous source of personal information. Which was what had led her to Katy.

Katy was just darling, you could see that. Such a sweet person. Newly hired at the data centre, fairly low level and so eager to share the details of her life. Scrolling through her (public) Facebook page, Jen learned it all: mother's maiden name, high school, childhood pets. That stuff they ask in those 'security questions' when you need to change your password? It was all there. Oh, and so was the location of her children's school. Just in case that became relevant.

Anyway, that wasn't what leapt out. No, the detail which jumped off Katy's Facebook page was her involvement with, and commitment to, a local maternity support centre. She was a volunteer there, and a passionate one. Once Jen saw how much Katy cared for new or expectant mothers, she knew what she had to do.

The first move, as always, was a phone call. Not from her phone, but from her laptop, via spoofcard.com. The webpage greeted her with its familiar message: *Easily disguise your Caller ID. Display a different number to protect yourself or pull a prank.*

What she was doing was somewhere between the two, she decided. She selected the 'free demo' option and then followed the steps: entering the number she wanted to call, then the number she wanted to display and finally, as she put her earphones in, clicking 'Place Call'. It really was that simple.

Now, as she called the data centre's switchboard, the incoming call would appear to be from the target company's headquarters. She asked to be put through to Katy. She cleared her throat and got into character, the first of three roles she would be playing for this job.

'Hi Katy, my name is Helen. I'm a project co-ordinator with facilities management? We're upgrading a few of our facilities. The good news is, we're sending out an interior designer to you tomorrow so she can take a look around, then put together a scheme for renovating your workspace?'

'That's great,' Katy said, just as sweetly as Jen had hoped. 'We really could use the help!' A little laugh and then, 'But isn't this a little short notice?'

Jen had assumed Katy, no matter how good a person she was, would be suspicious. And she had prepared for it.

She sighed and said, 'You're right. You should have heard from me sooner. I have just been completely buried in work. And I know I'm falling behind, but with the baby due in five weeks—' She let her voice quaver. 'If my boss finds out I screwed this up, he's going to freak out.'

'Oh, sweetheart, don't worry. We'll figure this out. Forget I even mentioned it. Tell me about the baby! Is it your first? Do you know if it's a boy or girl?'

Jen dived in, talking about names and birth plans, the fact that she'd had to switch her ob-gyn a month ago – all of it coming easily, since she had, in fact, been pregnant with her first child two years earlier. All she had to do was maintain the slightly higher-pitched voice she had allocated to 'Helen'.

'Anyway,' Jen said, as if reluctantly getting back to business. She gave Katy the name of 'Greta', the interior designer who'd be coming to the data centre at eleven am the next day.

Which was who Jen was to play right now. She looked up and there was Katy, her face a picture of warm welcome. Instantly Jen knew that the fake business cards and website she'd cooked up for Greta would scarcely be necessary. She was in.

Seconds later, now issued with an all-important pass, she was with Katy and her colleagues in the data integrity department, chatting away helpfully about what they wanted from their office environment, what was working well and what would be 'even better if'.

'I like to call those EBIs,' Greta said enthusiastically, as she scribbled down each of their suggestions. Before long, they were all thumbing through swatches and talking ergonomic keyboards.

There was a long discussion about the optimal location for the water cooler.

After an hour or so, Jen took a bathroom break, which gave her a chance to walk around the office and be seen. She didn't rush, smiling instead as she brushed by Katy's co-workers, so that as the morning passed and as lunchtime neared, she had all but become a familiar face around the office. The company's official policy may have demanded that all visitors be escorted but that was for *visitors*. By now Jen had been seen walking around with, even getting coffee for and laughing alongside, trusted insiders. She no longer looked like a visitor, so no one questioned her. (Mega tech giant this might be, Jen thought: but human nature is human nature.)

Eventually, 'Greta' put away her tape measure and said, 'Thanks so much, guys. I think I have all I need here. You've all been so great.' She checked her watch. 'Eek. I need to be over at the NOC for my next appointment. Can any of you wonderful people point me in that direction?'

Katy's face became a picture of concern. 'When do you need to get there? It's quite a ways.'

'Really? I'm meant to be there in, like, ten minutes.'

Instantly, Katy scooped up her bag and her keys and said, 'You know what, I'll give you a ride.'

'No, that is completely un—'

'I insist. It'll take you far too long to walk over there from here. Come on. I might even get coffee for all these losers.' A round of warm laughter and rushed goodbyes from Katy's co-workers, as they thanked Greta once again for all she was about to do for them.

In the car, Katy chatted away about the long hours in this job and how she was adamant that that would not affect her volunteering. Greta nodded and murmured her agreement, careful to leave no doubt that she was hearing about it all for the first time.

As they spoke, Katy's car twice pulled up at gates where a camera scanned her auto-pass and the boom lifted automatically – barriers that, had Jen attempted them alone, would have kept her out. The closer they got to the NOC, the more intense the security became.

'All right, here we are,' Katy said as she pulled into the parking lot directly in front of the building, which looked every bit as forbidding as it had online. 'Do you want me to take you in?'

'No, you've done more than enough. I'll take it from here.'

Katy said her last goodbyes to Greta and, as it happens, Jen did the same. As she strode through the NOC entrance, careful to walk with the confident stride of an employee rather than a guest, she left 'Greta' behind.

Attached to her waistband was the pass which she had lifted from Katy's desk nearly an hour ago. Except now it was modified, the face of Katy replaced with the face of Jen. It had been easy enough to do: some basic recon the day before yesterday to discover what the passes looked like, then some fiddling around on Photoshop before printing onto a vinyl sticker a partial mock-up of a pass, using a picture of her own face. The finishing touch had come when she'd taken that bathroom break: in the stall, she'd pulled the sticker out of the zipped compartment of her purse and slowly pasted it onto Katy's pass. Now, with any luck, the pass would ID her as herself, but scan as Katy.

It worked. She was in.

Now for the part most fraught with risk. She went to reception and asked them to call up to Greg Turner.

Her searches through LinkedIn had proceeded along two tracks. First, the hunt for Katy, but second had been her quest to find a SysOp, a man – it was bound to be a man – in system operations, established in the NOC, inside the belly of the beast.

Thanks to LinkedIn, in combination with Tinder and two other dating sites, she had found Greg. Early thirties, uber-geek and, crucially, if predictably, single. Which hardly narrowed things down in this place. But the point about Greg was that he was looking. Seriously looking. What's more, and admittedly Jen had much less to go on than she did with Katy and the maternity centre, Greg came across as a guy who still had a touching faith in romance. Perhaps even in fate.

'Greg?' she said into the phone handed to her by the guard at reception when the message she had asked him to convey became too complicated. Jen asked the question in a voice that was shyer, more tentative than either Greta, Helen or, in truth, Jen. The profile she'd constructed of Greg in her mind told her he was after a woman who didn't scare him. Actually, 'woman' was probably not the right word. 'Girl' was closer to the mark.

'Oh hi there, I'm Katy from over at data integrity? Apparently you're the designated fire marshal guy in your area, so I'm really sorry but that's how I got your name. So, here's the thing. Facilities management just had an interior designer with us, looking to improve our workspace – you know, maybe get us new chairs and all that – and she wanted to be shown around the NOC. So obviously we said no, we couldn't let an external contractor in. So instead, she's given me some questions to ask you all, which I can then feed back to her. It will take, like, five minutes?'

There was a pause, a moment of silence into which Jen read any one of a hundred possibilities. He was suspicious. Or he was busy and didn't need the hassle. Or, despite her best efforts, her voice didn't appeal to him and he had decided she wasn't his type. (Maybe she sounded too much like a mom. Was that it? The thought had crossed her mind before and, given her line of work, it was troubling.)

But then he said, 'OK. Sure. I'll be right down.'

He emerged from the elevators about two minutes later, in a pair of chinos and polo shirt in a shade that would be identified as Nerd Blue on a colour chart. Exactly as Jen had hoped.

Shyly, she offered her hand. He took it just as shyly. 'Katy,' she said. 'Greg,' he said.

Rein it in, she told herself. Don't give him the full eyes or the wide smile. It'll scare him off. Sidelights, not full beam.

In the elevator, she pulled out her notebook and began running through the kind of questions she'd been asked to ask. 'And she gave me these books with, like, fabrics in them.'

'OK,' he said, before looking up at the display which showed which floor they were on.

Soon, though, they were at his desk and she was asking him to sit in his chair and lean back and lean forward. Slowly a couple of other guys drifted over, and she felt like the girl allowed into the boys' school on the last day of term.

To her surprise, they had lots of questions of their own about the angle of incline on the lumbar bar and the adjustability of the tension in the mesh. But still she managed to get them interested enough in carpet colours that the swatches soon came out. And of course there were long discussions about keyboards, as she asked Greg to log in and show her how he typed. Only fleetingly did she touch his head and neck to demonstrate what the interior designer had showed them all that morning – but just long enough for her to see that the touch had registered.

She waited for the group to disperse and only after Greg had hesitantly asked if he could get her a coffee, did she wonder out loud whether she could perhaps sit for a few minutes at that empty desk just over there and email over to the designer the details she had asked for.

'She said it's much better to get it all down when you can actually see the space in front of you.'

Greg said that was no problem and offered to log her into the system as a guest. 'Your usual login won't work here,' he explained. 'Tighter security,' he added, with a flicker of macho pride. As he helped settle her in, promising that no one would disturb her here, she gave him her widest smile so far. It's possible that her fingers brushed his for a second. Accidentally of course.

What he didn't know, and what she didn't tell him, was that all that fussing over the keyboards earlier had allowed her to place a tiny device at the end of the cable that connected his keyboard to his machine. This little wonder was one of Jen's trustiest allies: the keylogger, which had faithfully recorded Greg's keystrokes, including at the moment when 'Katy' had asked him to demonstrate how he typically used his machine. She had made a point of looking away as he obediently typed in his username and password, concentrating instead on his posture – safe in the knowledge that, quietly, the keylogger was storing all the details.

Of course, Jen knew that wouldn't be enough. A company like this one would rely on two-factor authentication. First, the password you remember. And then a second password, a one-off code, either sent by text to your phone or generated by a YubiKey, a small dongle allocated to each employee and usually found on their keyring. That's what Greg and his fellow system administrators used.

Grabbing that had been simple enough. Once 'Katy' had covered his desk with the fabric swatches she said 'the designer' had given her, and as they were being passed around, it had been easy to nudge Greg's keyring into her bag.

Now, armed with both the keylogger and the YubiKey, she logged out and then logged in again, not as a guest this time but as Greg. With a system administrator's level of access, it wasn't hard to get first to the monitoring system, and disable that, then move to the system whereby the company backed up all its data. She set to work, issuing the electronic instructions that would steadily overwrite those back-ups, eventually moving to the live system itself.

She did it as swiftly as she could, always keeping one eye on the shifting dynamics of the office, ready to clear her screen if anyone came too near.

At last she was done. She logged out of and powered down the desktop machine, then returned to Greg's desk to thank him and his co-workers for helping her out.

He was awkward, unsure how to say goodbye, so 'Katy' decided to make it easy for him, giving him a hug – which he maintained – noiselessly using the opportunity to place his keys back on his desk, just behind the coffee cup where they might plausibly have been obscured. She said her goodbyes to the rest of the SysOps team, making a little fingers-crossed gesture as she left, to signal their shared hope that their workspace might soon be getting more comfortable.

The walk back to her car was long, but she wouldn't rush. No need to look guilty. As she adjusted the mirrors and pulled out of the space, and as she put away Greta, Helen and Katy, at least until the next time, she pictured the electronic ones and zeroes she had sent into battle, steadily advancing like digital infantry, overwriting the drives on which was stored the indexing system that had become indispensable to the population of the entire world – a tool so essential that not only had the company's name entered the language but their core product had become humanity's electronic memory bank. People no longer bothered remembering facts, because they knew they could just look them up. This company's product had become nothing less than an outsourced part of the human brain.

That the test had been so easy to run was almost chilling. Thank God, she thought, she was working for the good guys, a firm that specialized in exposing the gaps in tech companies' defences so that they could plug them before any real damage was done. Within the next few minutes, she comforted herself, the people who had commissioned her for this project would tip off the target company and alert them to the threat. She had injected a lethal bacillus into the bloodstream; very soon they would stop it in its tracks.

She reached for her phone, to send the message that said, 'Task complete.' Only as she typed it did it strike her that this particular project had been arranged entirely over encrypted text. She had never even spoken to her clients, let alone met them.

Still, she did not dwell on that. Instead, she took in the gorgeous blue sky on this warm autumn day and felt the satisfaction of a job well done, watching as the world headquarters of Google receded in her rear-view mirror.

Chapter Twenty-Four

FBI headquarters, Washington DC, 8.51am

'All right,' Lofgren said, his voice signalling a new urgency to their deliberations. 'We clearly need to see the full report of this preliminary read of the manifesto. Once we have that, I shall be working with the White House, notifying Homeland Security, the CIA and other key agencies, as well as allies around the world and specifically those nations with institutions in the Alexandria Group. I will also be proposing enhanced security arrangements at the named libraries.'

Now his deputy, Andrea Ellis, chipped in. 'Can I suggest that immediately after this meeting, Maggie has a quiet word with the leadership of the Library of Congress? Less . . . formal than if we do it. Our embassies can talk to the international institutions.'

The Director nodded towards Ellis and then to Maggie, indicating that it was agreed. Addressing the group, he said, 'The approach has to be one of increased vigilance, without causing undue alarm. We know that terror threats of this kind are—'

'Shouldn't we talk about *why* we have this document?' Interrupting a principal, the host of the meeting, in his own office. At a moment of great gravity. Quadruply bad form, but Maggie ploughed on. 'I mean, why would they do that?'

'Because these groups are proud of what they do?' It was Lofgren's mini-me again, with a smirk of condescension.

'They *are* proud of what they do, that's true,' said Maggie. 'Which is why they put statements – including *really* long ones – online all the time. But they didn't do that. They handed it straight to you.' She was alternating her gaze between Donna and the Director. 'Which suggests this was something else. A leak.' She left a beat and, surprised that no one jumped in, she carried on. 'Let's say this is a group. What if there's someone inside that group who thinks it's gone too far? Who's now getting worried.'

'OK,' said Mini-Me. 'But then you'd leak information that might actually thwart their operations. Dates, times, co-ordinates.'

'Unless you were terrified. Unless you'd concluded that the only information you could get out without exposing yourself – to punishment and even fatal risk – was this document. And you did it because you knew that, read the right way, this document would indeed blow the whistle.'

The Director was nodding. 'All right. And given the urgency, what's your advice, Maggie?'

'Well, obviously, you do what you're already doing. You put the manifesto through intense linguistic analysis, see what else it matches. Books, essays, speeches. See who else writes like this.'

'Obviously. What else?'

'You publish it.'

'What?'

'It's the Unabomber move. When the *Times* and the *Post* got his manifesto, the FBI recommended they printed it. Which they did. In full.'

'Director, if I may.' It was the sidekick. 'This is a very different situation. The Unabomber was threatening to send another bomb, "with intent to kill", if his manifesto wasn't published. We've received no such demand in this case. To run it now would be to give the terrorists the oxygen of publicity and to do so voluntarily. I'm afraid you yourself, Director Lofgren, would face accusations of doing the terrorists' work for them. Given the questions that were raised during the confirmation hearing, and the assurances you gave, I would strongly recommend—'

'I don't care about "facing accusations". We get accused of things all the time. *I* get accused all the time. The point is, would those accusations be right? Maggie, why should I even consider publishing this thing?'

'The small reason is that, if we are right about it being a hostile leak, it will wrongfoot the Bookburner. You'd be pre-empting their big moment. They wanted to launch this at a time of their choosing, and now you're doing it at a time that suits you. That'll throw them off balance.'

'Unless this is *exactly* what they want us to do.' Mini-Me again. 'And we're walking right into their trap.'

'That's possible,' Maggie said, breaking another Washington rule by conceding ground to an opponent. 'It's definitely a risk. If they are nodding to the Unabomber thing, which they might be, then publication is what they'll be expecting. But none of that outweighs the big reason to do it.'

'Which is?'

'The wisdom of crowds.'

'What?'

'Look, you'll have the best computer analysts in the world here, no doubt about it. They'll spot all the idiosyncratic punctuation and all that. But out there,' Maggie pointed at the picture window with its view of the US Capitol, 'there'll be someone who knows more about this than all of your computers. Whoever they are, they just need to read it. It might not work. But it might.'

Andrea was shaking her head. 'I worry we'll just be acting as their recruiting sergeant. I've seen that happen too. This world is so messed up, ISIS only had to put out a video of a beheading or of burning that guy in a cage, and people *flocked* to join them. And that can happen very quickly. There might be all kinds of crackpot arsonists who will see the Friday deadline as a challenge. You know, let's give it a helping hand. As Governor Morrison knows, Friday is already incendiary as it is.'

Mini-Lofgren saw an opening. 'Where would you suggest we publish this, Maggie? On FBI.gov?' He looked around the circle, hoping for supportive laughter. Maggie replied that, if it were up to her, she'd give it to everyone: *New York Times*, *Washington Post*, BuzzFeed, all of them. But, sure, why not, FBI.gov too. The more the merrier.

The secretary was back, her head around the door with another bulletin. The Director stood up to meet her, took the piece of paper from her hand, skim-read it and then, still standing, made his announcement.

'I have to tell you that, as we've been speaking, the National Library of India, held at Kolkata, has been burned to the ground.'

There was a silence of a moment or two. Lofgren bowed his head. Maggie half wondered if he was about to lead a moment of prayer. In this town, you wouldn't rule it out.

Instead, the Director shook his head quietly, as if in despair of what man was capable of, and then returned not to the circle but to his desk, signalling that the meeting was over. As he moved, he promised to circulate the preliminary analysis of the manifesto to the group as soon as he had it: until then, sight of the text itself would be limited to the analytics team. 'I don't want this going any wider until we know exactly what's in it,' he said. Once that exercise was complete, and barring any surprises, he would organize online publication across multiple outlets, 'probably as soon as tonight.'

As they filed out of the room, one of the colleagues who'd been silent finally spoke. 'Oh, one last thing. Why Florian?'

The Director, already at his keyboard, didn't shift his gaze from the computer screen. 'Saint Florian. Patron saint of firefighters.'

Maggie left with Donna, who briefly fussed over her bag, picking up Maggie's, which was similar, by mistake, then swapping them back. As they walked out, the governor confessed that, though she rated Lofgren himself, she had much less confidence in the federal bureaucracy. 'We worked inside it, Maggie. We know better than anyone its strange gift for turning things to shit.'

The governor broke away as they reached the elevator, apparently to have a further chat with Andrea, the Deputy Director. It meant Maggie had to get into the lift with three of the others, one of them being Lofgren's little helper.

Pointedly, she thought, they conducted a conversation without her. Suddenly she was back at school, frozen out by Bernadette Clark and her sidekicks for the crime of having said something intelligent in class.

But now she noticed something different. As they reached the ground floor, all three of them fell into a stunned silence as they checked their phones, looking back at her, then looking down to their phones again.

She assumed they'd seen some breaking news – perhaps yet another library was ablaze or a celebrity historian had been found dead – but she was damned if she was going to ask them. She would check her own phone once they were gone.

But as they left the lift, there was that look again – away from their screens and directed squarely at her. It was a look that combined both pity and contempt.

There was no doubt about it: these three senior FBI officials had just seen something on their phones that was directly related to her. But what was it?

Chapter Twenty-Five

Capitol Hill, Washington DC, 9.41am

It had not taken her long to see what the men in the elevator had seen. Once she was in a cab and holding her phone, heading towards Capitol Hill, it took Maggie only the slightest amount of clicking and swiping to find it.

Her first port of call was Twitter. Her account had disappeared along with everything else, so she had to poke around as a mere onlooker. But once she had typed her own name into the search window, there it was.

The initial item had been posted by a journalist in the Washington bureau of one of the cable TV networks, a twenty-something who specialized in dredging up embarrassing items from the archive. His usual prey were politicians caught in contradiction. They'd failed to turn up to vote on, say, an abortion rights bill and, hey presto, there was a tweet from two years earlier:

Simply no excuse for elected representatives who don't do their job. If there's an important vote on an important matter – like the lives of our unborn children – then the least you can do is vote. #Youhadonejob

But now he'd posted this:

Remember White House operative and former peace negotiator Maggie Costello? Turns out she wasn't always such a, er, diplomat #emaildump

There then appeared screenshots of internal White House memos, sent by email, with dates going back several years, back to when she served under the president who'd first appointed her. If she squinted, she could make out the words.

Vietnam vets won't like it. They never do. But you know what, a few shots of cripples waving their sticks – who's going to care?

Then there was one, apparently from Maggie to Donna:

In light of recent events, it's clear that the usual approach can no longer be relied upon to work. Much more drastic action required. I have good connections with the groups involved. Why don't I meet their representatives and suggest financial benefits – personal, not institutional – will be available to them, should they agree to roll over on the bill? Happy to discuss further. M x

And another, from Maggie to her mentor, the late Stuart Goldstein:

Can I just say, if anyone needs to get fucked in the ass, it's our friends on the Hill. They've had this coming for such a long time. Especially Hansen and Schilling. Trouble is, they both look like they'd enjoy it. M.

She read each one again, in turn. That was her old White House email address and the dates tallied with when she was in the White House and, in the case of the third one – sent from the personal email address she still used – when Stuart was still alive.

But those words were not hers. They couldn't be. Mocking veterans as 'cripples'? Blatantly discussing a bribe? Referring to two respected female members of the United States senate as needing to get 'fucked in the ass'? It just wasn't how she talked or wrote. Was it?

Maggie clicked out of that to check the other results of her Twitter search. Someone she'd never heard of had posted a link to a story that had gone up within the last hour on that new political website, DC Wire.

Former White House official engaged in misogyny, bigotry and possible corruption, leaked emails reveal.

Washington, DC—A top former White House operative described Vietnam veterans as "cripples", floated possible bribes to lobbyists and fantasized about the anal rape of leading female senators in internal correspondence which has just emerged.

Maggie Costello, widely admired for her role in exposing the . . .

She scanned the rest, stopping at this sentence.

No word yet from Costello, whose Twitter account appeared to have been deleted soon after publication of these emails.

She felt her stomach heaving as she handed a ten-dollar bill to the cab driver and faced the vast complex that was the Library of Congress. What she wanted to do was get straight back into the cab, head home and either deal with this madness or, ideally, hide under the duvet. Instead, she girded herself for what she knew would be a mammoth exercise in compartmentalization. She would have to keep this lunacy out of her mind – and keep this meeting short.

The library consisted of three buildings: the Librarian's working office was in the tallest and most modern, the Madison, a six-storey structure that boasted it was the biggest building in DC after the Pentagon and FBI headquarters. Andrea Ellis's office had called ahead, so that when Maggie told reception she had a meeting with the Librarian – an unusually archaic title in this city of Directors and Administrators – an assistant was already hovering to play usher.

As they took the elevator, Maggie realized that the insanity she'd seen pouring out of her phone had caused her to break her usual practice. She'd been scrolling through Twitter instead of checking out the person she was about to meet. Now, with just seconds to go, she typed in the name Denise Wherry, and saw a picture of yet another identikit Washington conservative woman, whose blonde hair was so straight it could have been ironed. Needless to say, she had only recently been named to the job – and by this president. Maggie remembered the appointment: there had been a ruckus because Wherry had no experience in the field whatsoever. She had never worked as a librarian or archivist, but was instead a TV producer. No prizes for guessing for which network.

Wherry was waiting for her, standing in front of her desk with her hand outstretched. Maggie took it and then turned to shake the hand of the two other people in the room. There was an aide in his late twenties who was introduced as 'chief of staff' and a man who might have been the chemical opposite of Wherry. Tall, middle-aged, bearded and unkempt, he was what you'd have expected in a library: eyes twinkling with intelligence, he looked part scatty professor, part Old Testament prophet.

'I'm the Principal Deputy Librarian,' he said, a small smile playing on the edge of his lips, apparently at the absurdity of the title. 'Irving Herman.'

Soon they were in the small seating area, as Maggie explained the threat as the authorities now saw it. Wherry nodded at all the right moments, and then said, 'We'll work with all the relevant authorities, metropolitan and federal, to ensure that our security arrangements are at the right level.' She ended the sentence looking at her chief of staff, who picked up.

'If that means lockdown, we'll lock down.'

Maggie was about to say that she was glad they were all on the same page and that there was therefore little more to add, when Herman spoke up.

'What my colleagues say is reassuring, but only up to a point, Lord Copper, only up to a point.'

Herman continued, oblivious to the look of bafflement on Wherry's face. 'Perhaps I'm too close to this institution to see it the way others would. Thirty-three years does tend to warp one's perspective! But this is the foremost and most precious collection of books in the United States, and perhaps the world. It stands to reason that this institution will be a prime target.'

'Right, and we just agreed to take immediate action to be guarded against that threat, Irving.' It was the chief of staff.

'No, we agreed to take immediate action to be guarded against all *known* threats, using known and established methods. But the point is, unless Miss Costello corrects me, the method here is *unknown*.'

Maggie nodded. 'That is true. As things stand, we don't know how the perpetrators are burning down these buildings. The investigations are necessarily at a very early stage.'

'Exactly. So until we do, I think we have to take extraordinary measures to protect these extraordinary books.'

The chief of staff rolled his eyes, a gesture rapidly explained by Wherry. 'Irving thinks we should close the library completely. Right away.'

'Just until we—'

'We cannot wave the white flag, we cannot let them change our way of life. Ring of steel, fine. Airport-style security at every entrance, fine. Limited public access, fine. But we can't close the library down. We can't let the terrorists win.'

'That sounds very good as a soundbite on television,' Herman said, 'but does nothing to protect this precious, irreplaceable collection.' He was addressing Maggie, as if she were the chair in a debate at the Oxford Union. 'Anyway, I've had a better idea since then.'

'What's that?' Maggie deliberately kept her gaze on Herman, ignoring the sighs of exasperation coming from Wherry and her helper.

'I suggest we call for volunteers to come to the library, to occupy every room, to stand by every doorway. Around the clock.'

'Irving wants a permanent sleepover in the Library of Congress.'

'It's happened before.'

'With kids, Irving! It was ridiculous then too. Hundreds of children and teenagers in a building of this status, lying around in sleeping bags.' Turning to Maggie, she went on, 'My predecessor said it "forged a connection with the next generation" but it was not practical. I eradicated that programme very early on in my tenure, and now Irving wants to revive it – for adults!'

The chief of staff joined in. 'Our view is that that could be an additional security hazard, admitting uncredentialled adults into the estate. It raises the risk threshold, given that they would be unsupervised.'

'We could limit it to Friends of the Library,' Herman said, but his heart was not in it. He took off his glasses and rubbed his eyes. 'I just fear for these books. For their pages. For the wisdom they contain. For our ancestors who wrote them. For all the people who have read them and will read them in the future. For the proof that we are not just random atoms of flotsam and jetsam, but links in the great chain of human civilization.'

Wherry and her lieutenant were shifting in their seats, staring either at their feet or each other. But Maggie was ignoring them and so was Herman.

'I'd do anything to protect these books. I'd stand over them myself if I could,' he said and then, as if to break the tension, he raised his chin and the register of his voice. 'I'd stand at the entrance to this great library with my rod and stave, warding off all intruders and men who threaten harm!' He smiled at Maggie, but she could see his eyes were moist. In a quieter voice, he said: 'We saw what happened to those other libraries. We watched them burn. I could not bear to witness such a sight here, Miss Costello. I know I could not bear it.'

Maggie brought the meeting to a close by giving out her cellphone number – though only Herman took it – and urging them to stay in touch. She was keen to wind things up, partly because she was not sure what more she could say and partly, perhaps mostly, because she was itching to get back online and deal with the other fire that was blazing in a separate, if poorly sealed, area of her mind.

'Mr Herman might be right,' she said finally. 'Guarding against past threats, using old methods, may not be enough. You need to think differently. We all do.'

For perhaps the thousandth time in the last decade, Maggie

left a Washington meeting uncertain what good she'd done or whether she'd done any good at all. But as she hailed a cab and headed to her apartment she put that out of her mind. As one compartment was closing, another, more painful, was opening once more.

Less than twenty minutes later, her hand was trembling as she tried to put the key in the lock and open her front door.

Once inside, she flipped open her laptop and looked again at the tweets and DC Wire story, as if somehow they might have disappeared in the twenty seconds that had elapsed since she had read them all over again on her phone, sitting in the back of that taxi.

She paced the kitchen, then went into the bathroom, then back out again.

Think, she told herself. She tried, but those words kept returning. *Misogyny, bigotry and possible corruption . . . fantasized about the anal rape of . . .*

Never had she missed Stuart more than she did now. In moments like this, she needed to hear his voice. She fell into a chair and, with eyes closed, tried to summon it. What would he say, right now?

First things first. Did you write those emails?

She went back to her laptop and found the DC Wire story, into which was embedded a PDF file, so that you could click to see the original emails.

She looked hard at them, examining the headers and timestamps. They'd redacted the address details for the recipients, but her own email details were as they were, back when she worked in the West Wing. They looked accurate.

But are those your words? Did you say those things, Maggie? Did you write them? Did you think *them?*

Suddenly, Maggie felt not quite relief, but the intimation of it, like seeing the first swell of a distant wave on the horizon. No, she thought. No, I did not write those things. Of course I didn't.

So they're fakes. We don't know how they were done or who did it, but they were fakes. Yes?

Yes.

So now you need to say so. Publicly. And quickly. Remember, a rebuttal loses its force by a factor of ten every minute it's delayed. That's a law of physics.

Right.

So get out there. Now.

Maggie went to the laptop and called up her email. Normally, the inbox appeared instantly but now there was a delay and a request that she log in. She tried, using the same password she'd always used. But the computer looked at her blankly.

She wondered about contacting the TV reporter or the woman who'd written the story for DC Wire. But how? She couldn't tweet at them: her own account had disappeared. Deleted by her own hand, in an act of mortified shame, according to the tacit implication of that story.

She could set up a new account, unverified and with zero followers that would immediately look bogus and would surely be ignored. If anything, it might only add to the sense that Maggie Costello had gone way off the reservation.

This time she didn't wait for Stuart. She reached for her

phone, dialled the number for information and asked for DC Wire. With a pen in her hand, she wrote down the number they gave her. It rang perhaps two dozen times before someone picked up. She pictured a big Bakelite phone, coated in dust, like the one that used to sit on her nan's hall table in Delvin Road: the last landline phone in the office.

Maggie could hear the confusion at the other end as she explained that she wished to speak to a person whose cellphone number she didn't have. She felt as if she were a hundred years old, calling Uber and asking when the horse and carriage might arrive.

Eventually, they gave her a number and she was on the phone with Gaby Hutton, who'd written the story.

'Hi Gaby. This is Maggie Costello. So I just wanted to clarify something about those emails? They weren't "leaked", Gaby. They were totally fabricated. Literally made up. I never wrote a word of any one of them. In fact, this "leak" happened hours after my email archive was wiped, phone contacts were destroyed and my Twitter account zapped.'

'Why would anyone do that?'

'I don't know, but you may have noticed that libraries and archives are being destroyed all around the world—'

'And you're working on that?'

Maggie had to think quickly. She never operated in public. And now she didn't even have an official title to hide behind. She would have to resort to the non-denial denial.

'I can't talk about that, Gaby. All I'm saying is that records of the past keep getting destroyed. Important archives – like the National Library of India today – and totally trivial ones, like mine. So given that people are destroying evidence of the past—'

'We shouldn't be surprised if they start inventing evidence of the past?'

'What?'

'Is that what you're saying?'

'I don't know. Maybe. Anyway, I'd like it if you could tell your readers—'

'Total denial?'

'Exactly. Every word of those emails is bogus.'

'They've been well done though.'

'That's true. Anyway, if you can correct your story. And tweet it, that would—'

'Already done.'

'What, the story?'

'The tweet.'

Cradling the phone in her neck, Maggie reached for the laptop and refreshed the 'Maggie Costello' search. Sure enough, there it was. A new tweet.

Latest: Costello denies emails were hers. "Totally fabricated," she tells me.

'Wow. That's great. Thank you so much.'

'No problem.'

'So when will the story come down?'

'Excuse me?'

'The story. You know: me talking about "cripples" and all that. When will you remove it?'

'I don't understand. I'll update it with your denial. "Totally fabricated" and all that. I'll get that included right away.'

'But the story itself will stay there? So everyone can read these wholly bogus things that I've just told you I never said or wrote?'

'Yeah, and then they can read your denial that you said them.'

'But . . . this is crazy. Somebody just sat at a desk and made up fake emails, pretending I'd sent them. And then you publish them, so that millions of people read them. Even when you know they're fake.'

'All I know is that you *say* they're fake. Which is fine. I'm not doubting that. But I can't say I *know* they're fake.'

'But you don't know they're real either.'

'No. Which is why we include both. The emails and your denial. Both sides. And then the reader can decide.'

'So, so . . . what you're saying . . .' Maggie could hear herself spluttering. 'You're saying that someone could just sit down and with a bit of natty software they could produce a whole lot of, I don't know, text messages that suggest you're a paedophile and a raging racist and all they have to do is press send and then the right thing to do is, is, is publish them everywhere so that everyone then thinks that's what you are – and that's right, is it? That's journalism?'

'Well, obviously we have to make sure something is credible—'

'Credible?'

'Yes. We check to make sure a claim is credible before we—'

'And how exactly are these totally fucking fake emails "credible"?'

'Well, we checked them against White House emails we've seen before and they have the same characteristics.'

'You mean the forger got the email addresses right?'

'More than that. You know, the timestamps, the fonts.'

'So fake documents are fine, just so long as the faker is good at it. Is that it? And let's say they were real – which they're not – didn't we go through all this? Forces hostile to the United States dumping emails to mess with us and mess with our politics? I mean, seriously, did we not learn our fucking lesson?'

'Look, I can see why you're upset. But right now the only thing preventing me getting your denial into the story is the fact that we're still talking on the phone.'

'This is so . . . fucked up.' Maggie had a strong urge to scream which she only just managed to repress. 'All right. Run the denial.' And then, remembering Stuart, she added, 'And put it high up. First paragraph.'

'I'll see what I can do.'

'All right.'

'Before you go—'

'Yes?'

'What's the deal with all these libraries?'

Maggie sighed. 'I don't . . .' She remembered Stuart again. 'I'll talk to you on background if you promise to get my denial into that first paragraph.'

'OK.'

'Deal?'

'Deal.'

'The truth is, we don't know. But it's serious. The attacks seem co-ordinated.'

'Terrorism?'

'It's definitely that. And now all the agencies are on it. FBI, CIA, Homeland Security. International co-operation.'

'Anything else?'

'It's not just libraries. They're killing historians too.'

'And is there any—'

'I've got to go, Gaby.' One thing Maggie had learned watching Stuart: no journalist ever ends any conversation voluntarily – they'll always have one more question.

'OK. And this cell is good for you? If I need to know—'

'Sure.'

Maggie exhaled deeply. She resolved not to look online and not to check Twitter, to try to put this whole business out of her mind. Yes, the messages from friends – and, oh God, from Liz – as they saw the story, would start piling up. But she had to ignore them. She needed to focus. They had just two days, before everything was lost.

After all, wasn't it obvious that this was what they wanted? Whoever had ginned up those emails had certainly wanted to destroy Maggie's credibility, but a parallel motive might have been even more basic. Aware that she was in pursuit, they wanted to divert her attention, to tie her up with hassles that had no connection with the operation they were conducting. If she was on the phone to DC Wire, if she was having to look up old, deleted phone numbers, if she was embarrassed about emails she hadn't even sent, then she was distracted from the fight against them. She was taken out of the game. It was what they wanted and she was damned if she was going to give it to them.

So now she would concentrate. She put the phone over on the other side of the room. She would have cable news on, but muted: that way she could know what was happening in the world, while avoiding any tweets or messages about herself.

She opened her bag to pull out her notebook, but there seemed to be two in there. Side by side, two full-size, spiral-bound pads. She took them out and realized what must have happened. In that confusion over the bags, Governor Morrison had accidentally put her notebook in Maggie's—

Hold on. This was no accident. Tucked inside the second pad was a document that Donna had obviously sought to conceal, a document that the FBI Director had explicitly said was not to be shared or circulated. Clearly the governor wanted to give Maggie a head start on the manifesto, rather than making her wait till Lofgren released it into the public domain. She had smuggled her copy to Maggie, who now held it in her hands.

Maggie took in the title page, felt a chill shudder through her and prepared to read.

Chapter Twenty-Six

'Remembering to Forget, Forgetting to Remember' by Lethe

1. *Memory and its consequences have been a disaster for the human race. Every war has been the result of one side seeking to avenge the remembered calamity inflicted upon it by another. The calamity may have been real or exaggerated or no calamity at all, but no matter: it is the "memory" of it that drives men on to take up arms and kill their fellow man. They hate a stranger from a distant land because they "remember" what that faraway stranger did to them, and so they must act in the name of that memory.*
2. *This destructive habit has been the curse of mankind from the very start, a terrible cast of mind imposed on humans by God or the Bible (depending on your religious or philosophical opinions). This need to avenge spilled blood, to honor the memory of the dead by acts of vengeance, starts with God. After Cain killed Abel, what does God say? "What hast thou done?" he asks. "The voice of thy brother's blood crieth unto Me from the ground." We have lived with that curse – that delusion that blood cries out from the ground – ever since.*

3. *But blood does not cry out. As has been noted, when Charles de Gaulle wanted to withdraw from Algeria and concede independence to that land, one of his advisers protested: "But so much blood has been shed." De Gaulle replied: "Nothing dries quicker than blood." We do not have to be slaves to the past. The dead do not hold us to any pact or obligation. The dead forget.*

Maggie skipped ahead.

16. *Others have understood this truth before us.*
17. *In 1598, Henri IV issued the Edict of Nantes, as he sought finally to end the wars of religion that had brought such pain to France. He understood the scale of the task: wars are easy to start but hard to stop. For sometimes events have a momentum of their own. So his edict sought to do something wonderful. It sought to make memory illegal. Henri forbade all his subjects, whether Catholic or Protestant, from remembering. "The memory of all things that took place on one side or the other from March 1585 [onward] . . ." the edict decreed, "and in all of the preceding troubles, will remain extinguished, and treated as something that did not take place." Henri was eventually murdered, but he stands as proof that this urge to erase history itself has a history.*
18. *A more recent example can also be provided. Spain recovered from the civil war that divided that country by means of the* pacto del olvido, *the "pact of forgetting." Both sides, right and left, fascist and republican, initially agreed to bury the past along with their dead. They would dig up no bodies, they would bring no charges, they would hold no trials. That, they agreed, was the only way to guarantee the transition to a democratic system following the death of General Francisco*

Franco. Those who seek justice insist we must remember. But those who seek peace insist we forget.

Maggie's gaze drifted away from the pages in front of her and to the window, where evening was coming. Not twenty-four hours ago, she had heard this same argument made, in this very room, by the man she once loved. Uri had not used identical language. He hadn't burned down any libraries. But these were his views. That peace mattered more than justice and that sometimes you just had to let go of the past.

An unwanted thought returned to shiver through her. Why exactly had Uri turned up like that, after all those years? No matter how good his contacts in the governor's office, which – now that she thought about it – was also a stretch, was it really plausible that he just happened to be in the same part of Charlottesville at exactly the moment she was? And then sending her into that burning building? She remembered again the quality of his fury at his archaeologist father. How had he put it? *History so thick you could choke on it.*

Was it possible that Uri's rage against the past had led him into some dark place, ready to join those who would literally burn it all down? Was he part of this group, sent to lead Maggie astray, to divert her, to weaken her resolve? He would not have been the first man deployed against Maggie that way. It had happened before. And it had worked.

But surely not Uri. He had helped her, hadn't he? Even sending her those texts when they were officially not speaking. He had to be on her side, surely.

She went back to the text, skipping ahead a few more paragraphs. One section jumped out at her.

128. *We teach children the story of Adam and Eve and the Garden of Eden and, depending on our views or education, we blame Eve or the Serpent. But we do not pay sufficient attention to the true source of the couple's downfall. What is the tree from which the first man and first woman ate? What is the tree whose fruit was forbidden? It is the tree of knowledge. It is the acquisition of knowledge that sees Adam and Eve expelled from the Garden and humankind deprived of its Edenic gifts forever after.*

Maggie took out a pencil and circled that word. *Edenic*. She read on.

129. *Every child knows this and yet we continue to seek new knowledge and preserve at all costs the knowledge we have acquired. We guard it in libraries, which are as tightly protected as bank vaults, controlling the climate and the light, as if these shreds of paper are holy. But the truth is the opposite. It is knowledge that has kept us from our Edenic state. This is not a question of wrong and right, but of simple happiness. We were happiest and even holiest when we were innocent, literally lacking in knowledge.*

She moved to the concluding sections.

229. *Revolutionary movements have failed and failed again throughout history by making the same error. They stare with shining faces towards the future, promising to build the world anew and that*

another world is possible. "We have the power in our hands to remake the world," they tell themselves. But they fail to see the obvious gap in their reasoning. They fail to follow their own logic through to its unavoidable conclusion. If you are to make a new world, you first must destroy the old one.

230. *In truth, some revolutionaries have understood this, but they have lacked the full courage of their convictions. In Cambodia, the Khmer Rouge saw the necessity of Year Zero and they removed some of those "intellectuals" whose historical knowledge threatened to be an obstacle. But they did not complete the task. In the Soviet Union, the Bolsheviks shot the Tsar and his family, but they did not destroy their memory: the paintings, the palaces and, above all, the documents remained. They were not strong enough to go further.*
231. *The next revolution will not suffer from that timidity. It understands that partial success is no success at all. To be free of the past, one has to be free of all of it. No trace can remain. If it does, all the old habits will persist: they will simply attach to whatever scrap or shard of memory survives. There needs to be nothing.*
232. *We need to renew ourselves by starting afresh. The slate must be wiped clean. Even machines understand this about themselves: sometimes the drive must be erased of all data. So it is with humankind. We have to cut down the Tree of Knowledge which brought about our fall. Only then can we return to the Garden.*

Maggie sat back and briefly closed her eyes. Jesus Christ, what were they up against? The terrifying certainty, the absolute conviction – the declaration that the only vice of Stalin and Pol Pot was that they were too moderate.

Was this the work of an individual or a committee? A man or a woman? Was it an American or perhaps someone from somewhere else entirely, their work rendered in translation? And who was Lethe?

She googled and was not wholly surprised by the answer. *Lethe: one of the five rivers of the underworld: those who drank from it experienced complete forgetfulness. Lethe: the name for the Greek spirit of oblivion.*

So whoever wrote this manifesto had attributed it to the goddess of amnesia.

Maggie was about to reread those last few paragraphs, to catch something that had jogged a thought, when an image on the TV caught her eye. Was it fate or a premonition, but there, holding forth on the screen, his face bright with glee and the Richmond courthouse as a backdrop, was William Keane.

Chapter Twenty-Seven

Washington DC, 1.22pm

Maggie reached for the clicker and jacked up the volume. While his mouth moved silently, all William Keane was conveying was smugness. But now she began to hear his voice.

'. . . in the final stages of this remarkable case. But I am here to tell you, ladies and gentlemen of the press, that as soon as I am done here, I will be going into that building to deliver this letter to the presiding judge, urging her to see what is surely now obvious, not only to the twelve good men and true who are sitting as jurors – and yes,' he was rolling his eyes and sighing simultaneously, 'before the snowflakes start writing to their congressmen, I know there are women on that jury too – obvious not only to them, obvious not only to the citizens of the Commonwealth of Virginia and these United States of America, but to the entire watching world. Namely that her solemn duty under the law of the Commonwealth and, indeed, under the basic principles of natural justice, is to direct the jury to rule in my favour!'

Maggie watched Keane work himself up, his face getting more flushed, the blood vessels under his skin almost visibly cracking under the strain, and found she could not tear herself away. What they said about William Keane was true. His charisma, especially on television, was powerful. You could not stop looking.

'What possible evidence of so-called "slavery" can my opponents point to now? All their supposed evidence is disappearing by the hour! It's on the ash-heap of history. In fact, history is an ash-heap! That's all that's left!'

His glee was disgusting. But the sheer, shocking nerve of it, the sight of a man welcoming a series of events everyone else had lamented, refusing to mouth the politician's pieties about 'loss' or 'tragedy', but instead standing there and *celebrating* a fire which had destroyed the archive in Charlottesville, and all those other blazes around the world, it was . . . mesmerizing.

'The records of so many so-called events are up in smoke now. I mean, that centre in Jerusalem' – *Jerr-oooz-ah-lem* – 'that's gone now. So we won't be hearing too much more about the "Holocaust".' His fingers made air quotes around the word. 'I mean, these are revolutionary occurrences, ladies and gentlemen.'

There was a muffled question, off camera.

'What's that?' Keane cupped his ear, prompting the unseen reporter to speak up. Now Maggie could hear the question.

'Are you saying those documents that were destroyed in Charlottesville *would* have proved the existence of slavery, but now they're gone we can't be sure? Because in that case—'

'No, no, Matthew. You know that's not right. You've been following this trial. I could have proved that any one of those documents in that library was either a forgery or exaggerated under duress or for profit or otherwise unreliable. Don't you worry about that, I'd have proved that. My point is, now I don't have to! They don't have any fake documents to wave at me any more.

'I mean, this is a game-changer, folks. All these "crimes" they keep saying we've done? Well, how they gonna prove any of them now? Let me give you just one example. I mean, how sick and tired are you of hearing that our great founding father, Thomas Jefferson, was a "slave" owner?' More air quotes. 'About his supposed siring of children with a Miss Sally Hemings? Well, I have to tell you, all the documents that were relied on to make that spurious case are now gone. They were there in that institution in Charlottesville. And now they are but dust in the air. So we'll hear no more of that.'

He was still talking as the screen split and a 'breaking news' alert flashed along the bottom. The other half of the picture showed a night sky, filled with patches of raging orange. Now the words appeared. *Massive blaze at National Diet Library buildings in Tokyo and Kyoto.*

Good God, thought Maggie. A masochistic urge propelled her to the website of the Japanese library. Sure enough, it displayed an image of seven green bottles.

They were moving so fast. She pictured the volumes housed in the building she could now barely make out in the TV footage: the texts and treasures of an entire civilization, some of them no doubt dating back to the very birth of Japan. And she, like millions of others, was just sitting there, watching them turn to smoke.

A new sentence appeared on the TV screen, crawling along the bottom: *Curator feared dead, killed in bid to save collection, Tokyo officials say.*

She could bear to look at Keane's gloating face no longer. She went back to the document whose pages were spread out on the kitchen table: the manifesto. Again it came to her, that thought she had had so fleetingly before Keane's face had appeared on the television. But it broke the surface only briefly and then was gone, like the shimmer of a fish in a river. She was trying to grab at it, like snatching a fragment of a dream in the seconds after waking. *Come on*, she thought. *What was it?*

At that moment, there was a chime from her phone and then, a moment later, another one. As she fumbled it, there was a third. No names, only numbers: because all her contacts had been deleted, the phone didn't recognize them.

The first read simply: *Am looking for a reaction quote to the latest drop. Gaby.*

Fuck. More bloody emails.

The next one was obviously from Liz. *Mags, call as soon as you get this. L xx.*

The third struck hardest. *I'm getting calls about this. Pressure on me to ask you to step down. Donna*

Maggie shook her head and prepared to call the governor. Even if there were new emails, she'd have hoped her blanket denial to DC Wire would have covered it. Surely people would have understood that if the first lot of ridiculous emails were fake, this next batch were too? Why didn't Donna see that?

Now the phone was ringing. From the number, there was no

sure way of telling if it was Liz or that reporter, Gaby. She thought of screening it and then, after four rings, pressed the green button.

'Jesus, Maggie, what the fuck?'

'Liz. I promise you, whatever you think I said, I didn't say it. Those emails are fake. Someone's forged—'

'What are you talking about?'

'Whatever it looks like I said, I didn't. This whole thing—'

'It's not something you *said*, Maggie.'

'What? What do you mean?'

'You know damn well what I mean.'

'I seriously don't know what the fuck you're talking about, Liz. What?'

'You haven't seen it?'

'Haven't seen what?'

'There's a video of you, Maggie. On the internet.'

'What kind of video?'

'Maggie, please. Don't make me say it.'

Chapter Twenty-Eight

Washington DC, 1.40pm

Instantly Maggie pictured herself caught on camera during some unguarded moment, probably slagging off the president or some of the wankers in his party. She could imagine it: herself slouched on some bar in Washington, dodgy sound picked up by a hidden camera. Nightmare. She braced herself, glad that she was going to hear it from her sister rather than Gaby bloody DC bloody Wire. She closed her eyes. 'Go on. What is it? What am I saying in it?'

Liz replied quietly. 'Like I said, Maggie. You don't *say* anything in it. Words are not exactly the issue here.'

'So what is it then? Come on, Liz, for fuck's sake. Spit it out.'

'It's, you know, a tape.'

'What kind of tape?'

'A *tape*. You know, a tape tape.' Hearing the silence at the other end of the line, Liz said a babble of words that came out as, 'I can't believe you're making me say this fuck fuck fuck it's a sex tape. That's what it is. A sex tape.'

'Of me?'

'Yes. Yes, yes, yes. Oh God.' Liz sounded as if she was curled into a ball.

'Are you joking?'

'I wish I were.'

'And you've seen it?'

'Yes. It's on the internet. Don't look! I mean, you can look. But maybe don't. Oh, Christ.'

'But I've never . . . I don't understand. Is it . . . is it a hidden camera or something?'

'No. In the tape, you're totally, you know, looking at the camera.'

'Looking at it?'

'Yes. Sort of . . . performing for it.'

'Oh my God.'

'I know.'

'But I never did that.' Maggie was remembering the sex with Richard. It did get intense, compulsive even. But he'd never produced a camera. He'd wanted to, but she'd refused. Point blank. Unless. Had he filmed her anyway? Had he hidden a camera behind a mirror?

'Is it Richard in the tape? Is that who I'm having sex with?'

'No. I don't think so. It doesn't – listen, I think you'd better look at it yourself.'

'How do I find it?'

'Oh, I don't think you'll have any trouble finding it.'

'Liz.'

'If you go on Twitter and search "former White House official sex tape", it comes up pretty fast. Call me back.'

Maggie's hands were trembling as she typed in the words. It came out as *former whote hoiuse official seex tape* and therefore brought the response: *No results for former whote hoiuse official seex tape. The term you entered did not bring up any results.*

She did it again, one button at a time. She felt herself paling.

Now the screen filled with tweets. The top one was from Drudge:

Breaking: Sex tape featuring former White House official.

It linked to a celebrity gossip site, which had a few words of text – including Maggie Costello's name and the name of the president who first hired her and whose campaign she served on – above a video player. There was a warning. *This video features explicit language, nudity and explicit content of a sexual nature.*

She pressed the play button.

It began with a glimpse of a naked torso, male and taut, and the waistband of a pair of boxers. The image was shaking as a pair of hands, the man's hands, fidgeted with the camera, settling it into position. Then he withdrew, turning his back to the viewer.

Now you could see the room. Or rather the bed, wide and stacked with cushions, all in various shades of brown. Above it, a bland, abstract canvas. At a guess, she'd have said it was an expensive hotel room, lit for the late evening.

And now, at the left of the screen, there appeared the figure of a woman, standing side-on, in profile. You couldn't see her face, because she was looking down, her long red hair a curtain. She was wearing only underwear, black and lacy.

She mounted the bed and crawled across it, on all fours, slow and panther-like, until she was at the centre of the frame. The head was bowed, still looking downward, the hair still a curtain. The image suggested submission, surrender. She stayed like that for a half second, offering her body to the gaze of the camera.

A moment later the man was in shot, standing over the woman. He put his hands on her hips and began to peel off her underwear. Only then did the woman turn towards the camera, so that at last her face could be seen.

Maggie was looking at herself.

She gasped, putting her hand over her mouth. There was no mistaking her own face, staring back at her from the screen.

She looked at her on-screen self, with her mouth open and eyes eager. She watched as this woman, herself, brushed her hair away, and as the man's hands – you could only see the back of his head – removed her bra and began cupping her breasts.

Maggie hit the pause button. It was both unbearable to look and impossible not to. It was herself she was looking at, and yet she had no recollection of that room, this moment or that man. She clicked ahead on the video, only to see herself performing oral sex. She clicked ahead again, and there she was underneath the man, as he pushed himself inside her.

She got up and went to the kitchen. She reached for a bottle of Ardbeg whisky, grabbed a tumbler and poured out what may well have been a quadruple measure. She drank half of it and welcomed the sharp sting at the back of her throat and the warmth that followed it.

She tried to process what she had seen. Who was that man? It didn't look like Richard. The build was roughly the same, so was the height. But the hair colour wasn't right, and nor were the glimpses she had caught of his face.

Maggie could hardly bear to go back into the room and touch that computer, let alone look at more of that video. But she had to know: who had she had sex with on camera like that, and how on earth had she no memory of it?

With a finger on the controls, she clicked in and out, watching a few seconds each time. She listened closely, but could hear only fairly muffled grunting and moaning. (For whoever had filmed this, sound was clearly not the top priority.)

It was then that, for the first time, she allowed in the thought that she had kept out. Other people would be watching that tape. They would include people she knew – friends and former colleagues – and people she didn't know. Some would be looking out of curiosity. Some would be journalists at work, in offices, looking because it had suddenly become a 'story'. Others would be acquaintances, long-forgotten contacts or rivals, looking to enjoy the brief delight of schadenfreude at the trials of another.

But that's not who she was thinking of at this moment. Instead, her head filled with images of men on their own. Men in mothers' basements or in potting sheds, in single bedrooms or in locked bathrooms, on phones or at their keyboards, men looking at her, naked and apparently flushed with sex – men who, right now, would be touching themselves.

As that thought dug its fingernails in, refusing to let go, she glanced again at the screen, and watched as this man plunged into her from another angle. She looked away, a reflex response to what felt like a physical strike. Actually, strike was the wrong word. To see yourself penetrated that way was itself a kind of penetration. Violation. That was the word.

Unable to bear any more, she pressed pause again. The image froze at a point at which she was once again on all fours, this time in apparent raptures as this man remained lodged deep inside her. Maggie's eye, though, was not on him but on her. There was one part of her body in profile in particular that she stared at, her focus unwavering.

Hold on.

She grabbed the phone, hit the 'recents' button and dialled the last number that had dialled her.

'Liz, that's not me.'

'What?'

'On the video. It's not me.'

'Maggie, please. Anyone can see it's you. I'm sorry, but I recognize my own sister's face when I see it. That's—'

'It's not my body. Have you seen the thighs on that girl? Last time I had thighs that thin I was twelve years old.'

'The camera's weird like that, it can—'

'And those tits are not mine either.'

'What, too big?'

'Actually, it's more the shape. Anyway, the point is, it's not me.'

'But the face—'

'The face is me, that's true. But it's not me.'

There was some rustling at the other end, as Liz explained she was 'relocating', doubtless to be a safe distance away from her children before she watched explicit sex on a computer.

'OK. I'm looking at it now.'

'Oh, please Liz, don't. Not with me listening.'

'I just want to check something. Wait.'

Maggie could hear some clicking and then grunting sounds emanating from the machine. 'Liz!'

'Wow, that is incredible. I did wonder, but I thought it was too good for—'

'What's incredible?'

'The pace of progress with this stuff is just unbelievable.'

'Liz?'

'OK. Click about two minutes in. Two minutes sixteen seconds, just watch that bit.'

Maggie did as she was told and contemplated her on-screen self adjusting her position, readying to receive her lover's tongue between her legs. She was looking directly at the camera.

'See?' said Liz.

'Yes, I can see, thank you very much. What am I meant to be looking at?'

'Look at your face.'

'Hold on, I'm rewinding. OK . . . Oh, that bit? When it sort of moves but doesn't move?'

'Yes. It's not tracking properly.'

'Like the face is slightly slower than the head or something?'

'Exactly. The processing can't make a perfect match. I'll find another one.'

Liz began firing out timings – four minutes twenty-three, seven minutes forty-one – when she had spotted similar moments. 'See?' she said. 'That's a total uncanny valley right there.'

'Is that some porn term?'

'Oh, Maggie, come on. Do you not read *any* of those articles I send you? "Uncanny valley": like when a robot looks so close to a human being that there's only a tiny gap between the fake and the real thing. And that gap freaks us out much more than if it wasn't even close.'

'And in this video—'

'It makes me throw up mainly because it's my own sister but also because my brain can tell it's nearly there but not quite. In those bits especially. It's jarring.'

'Jarring. That's how you'd describe this video? Jarring?'

'It's a thing now. Deepfakes, they're called. When you use AI to face-swap someone for porn. They do it with celebrities usually. No offence.'

'So someone has put my face on a real woman in a real sex tape?'

'It's not even that difficult. You just use a machine learning tool, which are open-source these days. I bet they used something like TensorFlow, which is actually available to anyone who's into deep learning algorithms. I have this student, Cameron, who—'

'Liz.'

'I think there's even an app. And they used to be so obvious. You could spot them instantly. But the processing is getting better and better—'

'Liz!'

'Sorry, what?'

'I need to know what I can do about this. But before that, I need to know you're a hundred per cent sure. About it being a, what did you call it?'

'A deepfake. I'm sure. And you know what? Somewhere out there will be the original sex tape.'

'The one they put my face on?'

'Exactly. That'll prove it.'

'Liz?'

'Yes?'

'Thank you. And sorry that you had to, you know.'

'Too late. I can't unsee it. Listen, Maggie. Before you go.'

'Yes?'

'Weird time to bring this up, but I saw Yves again today. You know, my therapist.'

'Sure.'

'We were talking more about my childhood. Quarry Street, Ma, you. Everything.'

'Right.'

'Yves feels we're on the verge of some kind of breakthrough, that my memories are piecing things back together.'

'OK.'

'Anyway, I have another session on Friday.' There was a pause. 'I just wanted you to know.'

As Maggie pressed the red button to end the call, she wondered why she felt the way she did – as if she had been given yet another deadline.

Almost physically filing that thought away, she began texting the governor, offering as concise an explanation of what she'd just heard as she could manage. Then she called Gaby, the reporter, and did the same, urging her to get a corrected story up as fast as she could. As it happened, the reporter knew all about deepfakes, checking off the names of the famous singers and actresses who'd become inadvertent and unwilling porn stars.

'Are there lots of regular pictures of you around?' she asked. 'You know, on the internet?'

Maggie thought of those campaign events she'd attended with the former president, the footage of her at negotiations, the news coverage of the craziness that unfolded with his successor. 'A few. Enough.'

'Well, they only need a few hundred apparently.'

Maggie told the reporter that she planned to write to the major tech companies, formally requesting the video be removed from their platforms, and that she'd be starting with Google.

'Good luck with that,' Gaby said. 'Reckon they might have a *few* other things on their minds right now.'

Maggie ignored that and thanked the reporter – again – clocking that same tone of scepticism which had greeted her earlier denials of the bogus emails, a tone she could have frankly done without. She wished she was dealing with one of the journalists she knew well from her White House and State Department days. She thought of Jake Haynes, still working the intelligence beat at the *New York Times*. They'd done some big stories together; there was a solid basis of trust. Besides, he owed her. It was obvious: she should call him.

Except his number was wiped, along with the rest of her contacts. And even if she did get hold of him, how mortifying would that call be? She imagined herself talking to this man she actually knew and saying, *No, fast forward to when I'm sucking the guy's dick: can't you tell, that's definitely not me.*

Maggie went to Twitter, avoiding her own 'mentions' and heading straight to the account of Gaby Hutton. Her latest tweet was posted four minutes ago:

> *Maggie Costello tells DC Wire #DCsextape is "100% fake, 100% bogus." Describes it as a "deepfake", a face-swap porn video like those that've targeted Hollywood stars, models. Demands Google, Facebook remove it*

Gaby had threaded it to her previous tweets about the fake emails. The casual reader, Maggie knew with a sinking sense of dread, would be thinking: 'This Washington woman is waving her arms about to clear a *lot* of smoke. No way you get all that smoke unless there's a little bit of fire. So we're meant to believe those emails were fake *and* this porno is fake: come on, who's she kidding?' Or, in what would doubtless be the arsehole formulation of choice: the lady doth protest too much.

She drained the rest of her whisky and went back to the kitchen for more. All she could think of was that video. The horror of it. But also the way it seemed to mix in her head with actual, genuine memories – of nights she'd spent with Richard, of nights she'd spent with Uri. She tried to remember sex with Uri especially, the last man she had loved. But the only images that would come were those she had seen on that screen a few minutes ago. Her, but not her. The uncanny valley.

This was what filled the mind of Maggie Costello, even as

CNN flashed the news that the National Archives and Library of Ethiopia in Addis Ababa was burning to the ground.

She barely considered the text that had consumed her attention earlier, where buried in those thousands of words was the prompt for the thought she had had, but let slip away. The key words were there still, waiting for her to look at them, waiting to offer up their secrets.

Chapter Twenty-Nine

Washington DC, 2.14pm

Another call on her phone, another string of indecipherable numbers. It could be anyone. A friend, another reporter or, she hoped, someone from the Florian unit at FBI headquarters. Maybe there was news of the analysis of the manifesto. They must have something by now . . .

'Hello there. Is that Maggie Costello?'

'Yes.'

'Hi there, Maggie. Hope you're having a great day. This is Justin, from TMZ. We wanted to reach out to you, to see if you might want to share with us the story of the tape? You know, from your perspective?'

'Is this a joke?'

'Ha, no, Maggie,' he said warmly, his voice offering a nice, illustrative chortle. 'Not at all. There's just great interest in your tape right now and so—'

'*My* tape?'

'That's right. You know, people are kind of *intrigued* by politics and Washington right now, and it's so rare for them to have this kind of insight into life in the nation's capital and so we'd love for you to do one of our "TMZ on TV" spots—'

'It's not my tape.'

'No. I understand. Your boyfriend seems to have released the—'

'He's not my boyfriend!'

'I'm sorry. Your *former* boyfriend. And that's part of the story? Do you feel betrayed maybe by what he did? Is this a revenge porn kind of a deal?'

'What I mean is, that's not *me* in the tape. It's some kind of face-swap, digital, algorithm thing.'

'Right,' Justin said in a tone that translated as, *Whatever, honey, if that's what you need to tell yourself.*

'I mean it. Haven't you seen the DC Wire story?'

'I haven't looked at that yet, no.'

'OK. So why don't you "look" at that and then you can—'

'One thing, Maggie, real quick? Can you tell us who the man in the tape is?'

'I've no idea. I've never met him!'

'You'd never met him before. OK, I've got that.'

'No, no. Not "I'd never met him before", I have never met . . . Oh, you know what? Just fuck off.' She hung up, savouring the thrill of telling that dickhead where to get off. It lasted all of two and a half seconds before she accepted that she had just made the hole she was in deeper still.

The phone rang again. Another fucking set of mystery digits.

She willed herself to keep calm as she took the phone into the kitchen and eyed up the bottle of Ardbeg.

'Hi Maggie?'

'Yes?'

'This is Dan, in Governor Morrison's office.'

Strange, Maggie thought. Normally Donna always called directly.

'Yes?'

'So I just came off the phone with the governor and I'm afraid it's not good news. We're going to need to release you from your work on the current situation.'

'Release me?'

'She's spoken with Director Lofgren and he's reached the same view. About your involvement with Florian. It means we're going to be revoking security access for you on this and all related matters.'

'But she wanted me to . . . What about the Keane trial? The verdict's on Friday, she was worried it could turn into—'

'Hey, I'm just the messenger here.'

'But I'm making progress. I'm finding—'

'As I say. My role is limited to conveying the decision which the governor feels it is necessary to take at this time.'

'Necessary? Why's it necessary?'

'Well, that's clearly something you'd need to put to her. But in light of the current controversy, both she and Director Lofgren have come to the view—'

'You mean this tape business? It's fake! I've told her. It's bogus. It's a total invention.'

'Well, it's now a story and, given the gravity of the situation nationally and internationally, their shared view is that there can be no further distractions from this work. It's too important. She said that you'd understand.'

Maggie stopped herself. 'She said that?'

'Her exact words were, "Maggie Costello of all people will understand." '

Half of her wanted to say fuck off to this jerk as well. But she could hear Donna saying those words and could imagine her meaning them too. Because of course she understood.

We're stage hands, you and me, Stuart had said. *Our job is to make the people out front look good. We're the ones in the black pants and black T-shirts, maybe even black gloves, so that no one even knows we're there. The second the audience notices you schlepping the scenery, the spell is broken – and it's time you got out the way.*

She had become the story. And right now the Governor of Virginia and the Director of the Federal Bureau of Investigation had more important things to do than field questions about whose face belonged to whom in a porn video. Donna had made the right call. If Maggie had still been on the team, and thinking straight, she'd have advised her to do it.

What's more, this was surely a chance to get back on track. Hadn't she wanted to take a break, to study and use the time to collect herself after everything that had happened at the White House? She had resisted Donna's efforts to pull her back in. Well, now she was free again. She could get back to her life. (Even her 'so-called life', to use a phrase Liz had hurled in her direction more than once.)

Maggie didn't allow herself to dwell on that thought. There was no way she was going to retreat into playing at being a semi-academic now. There was too much at stake. Underway was a global plot to erase history, to destroy what human beings knew about their own past – and so far, it was enjoying great success. On the TV at that very moment were mute images of the blaze in Ethiopia, turning one of the great archives of Africa into clouds of grey smoke. There were pictures of a crowd watching, looking upward at the sky. As the camera lingered on an old man, Maggie saw that his face was slowly becoming coated in ash.

The twelve great libraries of the world were vanishing in a matter of days. And once they were gone, the original texts they once held would be lost forever. They had housed records and documents that were stored nowhere else, proof of the events and deeds that comprised the story of humanity's life on this planet. Just as bones and fossils were our only record of the age of the dinosaurs, so these were our only clues to the infancy of human culture. And within forty-eight hours, they would almost all be gone.

True, there were plenty of books that had been printed by the million and that would surely never disappear completely: there would always be Dickens or Shakespeare. But if the first editions were gone, as that first folio of Shakespeare had been burned in Oxford, then what was to stop the likes of William Keane casting doubt over the authenticity of any text he singled out for questioning? With no original to go back to, what was to stop him and his ilk from playing the same games he had played in that Richmond courtroom? Anyone could get up at any point and say, *You claim this is the opening line of the Magna Carta, but how can you know? How can you know for sure?*

There'd been people willing to say it for years about the Holocaust. Keane had made it acceptable to say it about slavery. But with all the libraries gone, anybody could say it about anything. Did the Catholic church in Spain burn heretics at the stake? Who knows? Did Henry VIII have six wives? Search me. Given there are no documents left to prove it, it might just be a fairy story. This town you're from: sure, the street signs say Dublin, but how do you know it's not all a big, elaborate trick?

Maggie didn't want to live in a world like that, where anyone could lie about anything. Because if no one could be certain about history, with all its mistakes and its warnings, then they could do whatever they liked right now. Agreed facts were the boundaries that marked out the public square, where people could meet and discuss and debate how to proceed. Beyond those lines lay the jungle, where the law was dictated by the mightiest beast and history was whatever the powerful said it was. You needed the past. Without it there was no future.

A picture floated before Maggie's eyes of her grandmother back in Ireland, and her gradual slide into dementia. The less Nan had remembered, the less she was herself. Eventually she couldn't place her granddaughters' faces, she couldn't remember her own children or her late husband or, by the end, even her own name. She stopped being Nan Costello, she became . . . empty.

The day she died, somebody – was it a counsellor from the hospice? – had tried to comfort Maggie and Liz by saying, 'Your grandmother left us long ago.' And in a way, she was right. If you can't remember what you did or said yesterday or last month or last year or even fifty years ago, then who are you today? And if that was true of people, surely it was true of societies too. Without memories we were nothing. Just packs of animals, scrapping for survival.

So Maggie might have had her access withdrawn and her privileges revoked. She might be off the team and on the outside. She might not have access to a single email or text message that was more than an hour old, – though Liz was working on that – an empty contacts book that was worse than useless and no photographs save for those in the biscuit tin she kept at the top of her closet and which she had not taken down in years. And she might, even now, be the subject of global ridicule and shame, either laughed at or wanked over thanks to that video. But she couldn't give up. She would do whatever she could to find these people who were burning the past – to find them and stop them. What else was she going to do, submerge herself in a post-grad reading list and a bottle of Ardbeg?

Hang on. She very nearly said it out loud. She had given herself an idea.

She rushed to the kitchen, poured herself a large glass of water, downed it in one, and then poured another, in an attempt to dilute the forty-six-per-cent-proof whisky in her bloodstream. She all but sprinted back to her desk and the manifesto and, with a pen in her hand, got to work.

Reading list. She went through each page, picking out the references the author or authors made to other works. Not simply quotations, like those from the Bible, but citations, aspects of the argument that leaned on the writings of others. Soon enough she had jotted down the names of E.H. Carr and C. Vann Woodward and then Herodotus, Tacitus, Gibbon, Carlyle and Macaulay as well as Ibn Ishaq, Michelet and Taine. She looked for some more current names, but besides Rieff and the Spanish writer, Javier Cercas, there weren't many.

She went to her laptop and typed the words 'reading list' into the search bar followed by the full list of names. It was slow, the page seeming to take an age to load, but eventually hundreds of results appeared. The links were to history faculties at universities everywhere from Northwestern in Illinois to Nuremberg in Germany, from Miami to Manukau. She clicked on one at random and saw that it was indeed the undergraduate reading list for a course on 'historiography: the study of historical method and the emergence of history as an academic discipline'. The next entry she opened at random also spoke of historiography, which it preferred to describe as 'the history of "history"'.

She needed to narrow it down. She went back through the text, looking for anything she'd missed. Only then did it strike her that she needed to break her old student habit of skipping all the footnotes. Her attitude to reading academic books of any kind was consistent: if it was important, they wouldn't shove it in a bloody footnote, would they? So she'd had an iron rule of ignoring anything in a smaller font, endnotes and footnotes alike, especially if they appeared in a report back in her State Department or White House days: height of pretentiousness. But now she went through each one that appeared in the manifesto, as if scavenging for gold.

That yielded a whole new crop of names: Burckhardt, Bloom, Hughes, Reiter, Toynbee, Eisenstadt and Spengler. Excitedly now, she typed in that list, again with the words 'reading list'. Once more, the search engine seemed to be coughing along at quarter speed.

Eventually, though, she was looking at a page showing perhaps fifteen substantive entries, most of them relating to history courses in the US, Canada, the UK, Germany, Australia and Holland. Maggie scrolled down the page of results where, lurking at the bottom, was one that looked less official than the rest. While the others linked to official university websites, this one directed to a personal blog. What's more, for this result Google had bashfully crossed out two of the names on her list – Hughes and Spengler – as if it had drawn a blank on those. The article it was offering would include references to only five of the historians she had typed in.

She clicked and in an instant could see that the blog was both old and defunct. Its design was from the web's infancy. Sure enough, the article had been posted in 2004. She didn't recognize the author's name, but she skimmed the text.

To her surprise, the article was not a dense academic treatise but far more personal. It was a reminiscence of college days written by a graduate of Stanford University.

. . . eccentric, to say the least. The ethos that semester was something like "know thine enemy," as we were guided to master existing approaches to history in order to expose their flaws. "You will be a feeble opponent unless you know the devil's battalions as well or better than he does," that kind of thing, always delivered in that same

trademark, melodic voice with its rising and falling, almost musical, cadences. The room was packed, as always. There'd be people there who weren't even history majors, all squished up sitting on the stairs, some of them sitting cross-legged right in front of the podium, lining up outside the lecture theater. I can't tell you how much history we learned that semester, though I can probably still recite that monster reading list in my sleep – Bloom, Eisenstadt, Reiter, Toynbee, Burckhardt – as well as all the old favorites, from Herodotus to Gibbon, Tacitus to Macaulay . . .

Maggie scrolled up and down, searching for the name she was looking for. Maddeningly, there seemed to be no reference to it, the blogger working on the assumption that his readers would know it already. Finally, at the very end there were two initials. The ones she was expecting. The ones she was hoping for.

She would cross-check it first, just to be sure. It took a while – interestingly, that particular academic posting was missing from his résumé – but on Stanford's own website, she found confirmation.

It couldn't be a coincidence. She reached for her phone, the urge strong to text Donna and tell her what she'd found. But then she imagined how such a message would look, as if Maggie was too thick-skinned to have got the message, as if she was desperate to be allowed back into the circle, like a spurned lover calling up to the bedroom from the street below.

No, she would have to call a virtual stranger, one who instinct nevertheless told her she could trust. As it happened, she had the phone number because Donna had written it down in her notebook, the one she had accidentally on purpose slipped into Maggie's bag.

Slowly, checking each digit, she dialled the number of Andrea Ellis, Deputy Director of the FBI.

'Ellis.'

'This is Maggie Costello. I think I have a suspect for you.'

Chapter Thirty

The Vietnam Veterans Memorial, Washington DC, 7.07pm

The official version, the story she would tell friends in Dublin when they gathered in the pub on Christmas Eve, was that Maggie hated Washington. The stuff-shirted, buttoned-down men; the po-faced women all badly in need of an irony infusion; the obsessive power games; the preening of the media bigwigs; the smallness of a place that somehow made Dublin seem like a metropolis – she could rail against them all. (Though she had stopped doing that with Liz, lest it bring another wave of 'So leave! Move back to Dublin. Or come live here in Atlanta, so you can be near your sole surviving family, you daft cow.')

But the truth was, there were parts of this town that she had grown to love. There were still few better places to see a band than the 9.30 Club. She loved to walk through Rock Creek Park. And, though she'd pretend to find it a chore taking visitors around and playing the tour guide, she had become a sucker for the memorials.

Climbing the steps to see the seated Lincoln still had the power to awe her. She found the circular colonnade on the Tidal Basin which housed Jefferson a place of rare tranquillity. And flying over the city, seeing the simple needle for Washington, was a sign that she was back, even if not quite home.

So she was glad when Andrea Ellis had suggested this place to meet. A phone call was too risky and so was any electronic communication, even, apparently, the messaging apps which boasted of their end-to-end encryption. (Maggie noted that reluctance and filed it away: if it wasn't good enough for the top brass at the FBI, it probably wasn't good enough.)

Maggie was there first, taking in the long wall of black marble as she approached it. Instantly she greeted it the same way she always did, the same way most visitors did: with her hands.

The Vietnam Veterans Memorial all but cried out to be touched. Partly it was the cool dark stone, stretching so high and long, metre after metre of it, as if it might go on forever. But mainly, Maggie thought, it was the names, etched in gold. Touching them seemed obvious, a gesture of tribute, but also the only way to make them real, to make the one name your eyes and your fingers had picked at random become a person.

At night, it was especially beautiful, at least to Maggie. The wall was picked out by a series of lights studded into the ground, forming an avenue pointing towards the Washington Monument. There was bound to be some elaborate essay written somewhere about the symbolic meaning of that proximity – something, no doubt, about patriotism and military sacrifice – but for Maggie it was simpler than that. It was a reminder that noble ideals so often ended in blood and grime and wasted lives.

But on this evening, she was nagged by another thought. How long till they came after this place? After all, the wall was a kind of document too. Its list of names was a record. Surely it too would have to be destroyed eventually. Whoever was doing this would want it vanished. Or perhaps they'd be content to say that 'nobody really knows' how many died in that war or what the war was about or whether it even happened.

'Hi there.'

Maggie turned to see that Andrea Ellis had appeared at her shoulder. She had materialized out of nowhere, making barely a sound. A former field agent.

'Andrea. Hi.'

Ellis was looking at the wall, her eye running over the names. They were at the point where the Bs turned to Cs. 'Should I be looking for a Costello?'

'As it happens,' Maggie said, also staring ahead, 'there are five. I always say hello when I'm here. Look, there's Lawrence R Costello.'

'Family?'

'Not that I know of. But lots of Costellos got on the boat, back in the day.' Involuntarily, Maggie touched the name, letting her finger trace the C and the O. Mutely, she sent something like condolences or commiserations across the decades to the young Lawrence, whose face she had never seen.

'So, Maggie,' Andrea said, shuffling slowly along the wall, her eyes now on the block of Ds. 'You haven't dropped this.'

'I haven't. I never do.'

'That's what I hear.' Ellis said it with a smile which, even glimpsed side-on, confirmed that Maggie had not called the wrong person.

'I've checked the document, the manifesto. I've read it closely.'

'We have computers doing that right now. Pattern recognition analysis.'

'And I'm sure that's going to yield great results.'

'But?'

'But,' Maggie began, 'I've seen something else.' She explained about the citations and how she'd cross-checked them with university reading lists, and how that had led her to a blog post apparently aimed at alumni of a course taught at Stanford in the 1980s. Now she prepared for her big reveal. 'The man who taught that course was—'

'William Keane.'

Maggie turned away from the wall to look at Ellis directly. The FBI official did not react, keeping her gaze trained on the wall. She was looking towards the Es.

'Yes, William Keane,' Maggie said. 'So you knew.'

'Actually, I didn't know. Not about that specific course, I mean. But I guessed that's what you were going to say.'

'Because of the trial?'

'Because he brags that he's in the history-busting business; because he's high profile; and because he's one of the few people out there cheering the destruction of all these libraries. Which makes him an obvious target.'

'And now there's a link between him and the manifesto. That document cites the very books he recommended when he taught that course at Stanford.'

'Which would be important—'

'The very same ones. Even quite obscure books. I can show you.' Maggie reached into her bag, ready to produce the reading list. Andrea put her hand on Maggie's wrist.

'It's not him, Maggie.' She was still scanning the names.

'What?'

'Keane. It's not him.'

'How can you be so sure? He's very manipulative and very—'

'I know. But it's not him.' Now she turned to look at Maggie, which stilled her. For a few seconds, the silence lingered between them like vapour: two pros who knew that the best way to get the other person to talk was to say nothing.

It was Ellis who spoke first, continuing her slow march along the wall.

'He's been under tight surveillance for months. We've been all over his calls, his meetings – including with your good self shortly before twelve hundred hours on Tuesday – his emails, his social media. If he changes the channel, we know about it. If he has fries with that, we know about it.'

Maggie waited for more.

'There's no way he could have pulled off anything like this without us knowing about it. Directing an international operation on this scale – targeted assassinations, arson attacks timed and co-ordinated in multiple cities – that's a major enterprise. Would have left a huge footprint.'

'And there's nothing?'

'Not quite nothing. A few meetings with supporters. Some events for his legal defence fund. All exactly what you'd expect him to be doing given that he's fighting a court case that has got every wingnut in this country dusting off his Klan costume.'

'Right. OK.'

'You're disappointed.'

Maggie exhaled. 'It's been a tough day.'

'So I hear.'

'Those emails, that tape. They're fake, you know.'

'I thought so.'

'But Donna – the governor's fired me anyway.'

'You don't need me to tell you how politics works.'

There was silence for a moment or two. They both took in the names.

'I wouldn't be too down on yourself, Maggie. The reading list thing, that's good.' Suddenly her tone changed. 'Obviously, I cannot disclose any information derived from or related to an active investigation by the Bureau,' she said, the words delivered with a hint of ironic detachment so slight it was barely audible. 'Given that legal restriction, I am unable to confirm or deny that your conclusions mesh with the Bureau's initial findings of linguistic analysis. For the same reason, I cannot confirm if they mesh very precisely with what the pattern recognition software is indicating.'

'You mean, the analysis points at Keane too?'

'That is obviously not something I could officially confirm at this time.'

Maggie turned to look at the Deputy Director, but Andrea Ellis was still examining the wall. There was no smile, no wink. Just a woman looking at a memorial.

'And yet you know it was not Keane? That it can't be Keane?'

'It's been good to talk, Maggie,' Andrea replied. 'But I'm going to have to say goodnight now. I need to have a word with my dad.'

Maggie followed the woman's gaze as it came to rest on the name of Henry R Ellis. She watched his daughter trace the letters with her fingers, one by one.

Maggie said nothing, turning away quietly, with one last glance at the Washington Monument, which seemed to shine on this early autumn night. Was it that sight which made her see it? Or perhaps that hint of encouragement from the Deputy Director? Whatever it was that had done it, Maggie Costello flagged down a cab suddenly knowing exactly where she had to look next.

Chapter Thirty-One

Melita Island, Montana, 8.55pm

The characters on the screen were beginning to swim. And dive, turning triple somersaults as they plunged from the top board down to the bottom of the page where they made no splash. Jason Ramey closed his eyes and when he opened them again the words were straight enough, but the lines seemed to be wobbling, curving and dipping at the ends like the bending spoons of a trickster illusionist. He reached for the can of Diet Coke, which was very possibly his seventh of the day.

Though 'day' was too quaint a term for a unit of time as he now experienced it. His life was divided into shifts, but those were barely divided from each other. One shift merged into another, broken only by stretches of intermittent unconsciousness that barely deserved to be called sleep. There were no meal breaks now; he hadn't sat in the communal dining hall for days. Instead, he ate here at his desk, staring at his three screens which now seemed to represent the frontiers of the known world.

Only when he walked the few yards from this cabin to the dorm did he remember that he was, in fact, living in a beautiful spot, an island surrounded by smooth, untroubled lake water. For a precious few seconds he might hear the song of a chickadee. One morning, after working through the night, he caught a glimpse of a loon. Maya, she of the tattoos, saw it too: they'd smiled about it.

But that was a blink of an eye next to the endless hours he spent in that chair, staring at the pixels and ones and zeroes that now comprised his waking life. The exhaustion had spread far beyond his brain or his muscle or his joints. It seemed to have seeped into his marrow.

Jim appeared next to him, pulling up a chair. Jim too looked like shit. The lids of his eyes were thin and raw, the stubble on his cheeks resembled a crust. He looked like he needed to sleep for forty-eight hours straight. They all did.

'Jason, listen.'

That was the new greeting. The 'Hey there' or 'How you doing?' of the early days had gone. There was no time for such pleasantries and certainly none for an inquiry that risked an answer. ('I'm fine thanks, Jim.') That was nearly a full second gone. And they needed every minute they had. They all knew how long they had to get this done.

These chats with Jim were getting more frequent. Jason did his work well and on time and so, he guessed, Jim had come to trust him. But he also suspected that his boss – commanding officer? – needed to share the load with someone. It was clear Jim was getting his orders from somewhere, but here on Melita Island he was in sole charge. Jason's experience of leadership was zero, so what did he know, but he suspected it was tough running an operation like this alone.

'Given the time constraints, like I said the other day, we have to prioritize. The instructions are to zero in on this list of targets.'

Jim stretched across the desk to start typing on Jason's keyboard, giving the latter a brief blast of his odour. Maybe they all smelled like that these days; showering had become a luxury.

Jim was unlocking a password-protected file which now revealed itself to be titled: *Right here, right mow.*

He leaned back and let Jason read what was on the screen. Reflexively, Jason moved to correct the spelling of the last word.

'That's not a typo,' Jim said.

Jason crinkled his forehead into a question mark.

'It's an acronym. M-O-W. Stands for Memory of the World.'

Jason scrolled further down the document, learning that the Memory of the World project was a UNESCO initiative whose website proclaimed it to be engaged in the fight against 'collective amnesia', protecting everything from ancient manuscripts to cave paintings from the ravages of time, neglect and a changing climate as well as wilful and deliberate destruction. Jason gave a sideways glance at Jim at that last one.

'The important thing is this,' Jim said, scrolling down. 'The Memory of the World Register.' He clicked a couple of times and there it was, a list of more than three hundred and fifty documents deemed by the UN to be worthy of international protection. He started at the top.

The 1703 Census of Iceland

The Abolition of the Army in Costa Rica

The Abolition of Slavery in Tunisia

Jason skimmed ahead, noting the predictable independence declarations, constitutions and decrees and stopping at the unexpected. From Uzbekistan: the archives of the chancellery of Khiva Khans, including papers dating back five hundred years. From Holland: the archive of the Amsterdam Notaries 1578–1915. From Japan: the archives of the Tōji temple. From England: the Mappa Mundi of Hereford. From Barbados: sheet music of a song chanted by African slaves in the sugar fields for two hundred years, starting in the mid-seventeenth century.

'Wow,' Jason said. 'That's quite a list.'

'Rich pickings, huh?' Jim smiled. 'And all neatly listed and tabulated for our convenience.'

'It's like they knew we were coming,' Jason said.

'Yep. So let's not disappoint them. Can you assemble a team? Maybe Dan? And Maya? Make this a priority. Work your way through that list. I know we're all slammed right now, but this is what you might call a target-rich environment. So let's get targeting. OK?'

Jason nodded.

'Good. Because with every one of those you get, we're making the world a better place. Am I right?'

And at that, through their exhaustion, both men smiled.

Chapter Thirty-Two

Washington DC, 7.54pm

More mystery numbers on her phone. *Who could this be?* For a second, Maggie was returned to her Dublin adolescence, when the phone would ring at home and it was anybody's guess who was calling. You might screen it, letting the answering machine take it, but that was fraught with risk. What if it was a boy and he began broadcasting his private message to you all over the house? Avoiding that catastrophe was incentive enough to trigger a sprint to the phone, to ensure you got there before Ma and, more importantly, Liz. Sometimes the two sisters would be in a duel that was part running race, part wrestling bout, each one grabbing or tugging at, or tripping over, the other so they could get to the phone first. If Liz won, and it was indeed a boy at the other end, Liz would insist on engaging the poor, ambushed creature in tortured conversation, usually ending in: 'And may I ask what your intentions are with my sister?'

This time there was no race with Liz, but the same sense of the unknown as the phone rang in her hand. And as it happened, it was a boy who was calling.

'Hello?'

'Maggie, it's me.' A pause. 'Uri.'

'Hi.'

Another pause, as if he were waiting for her to say more. But she wanted him to move first.

'Listen, Maggie. I want to say I'm sorry. But I don't want to do it like this, on the phone. I'm downstairs, outside.' She looked out the window, and she could see him, standing under the tree on the other side of Corcoran Street. He didn't look up. 'Can I come in?'

'Sure,' she said, in a voice that stressed that entry was not to be read as a concession.

Minutes later he was at her kitchen table. He didn't do what he could have done – putting himself near her, allowing the chemistry between them to overcome her resistance. He was going to let the words do the work. It told her he was serious.

'I'm sorry,' he began.

'Sorry? For what?' Most men would have taken that as absolution. *Sorry? What do you have to be sorry for?* But Uri knew her better than that. He knew she needed to hear him say it.

'I'm not sorry for the opinions I hold. It's not a crime for me to have a different view from you. I grew up . . . my bringing-up was different from yours.'

Bringing-up. Uri's English was so good that the rare lapse was always unfailingly charming. She wondered if he had done it deliberately.

'OK.'

'But that was not the time to get into it. You didn't need a philosophy seminar. Not then.'

'No, I bloody well didn't.'

'You needed an ally.'

'Exactly.'

More silence. Was she waiting for more? Would he give it?

'You always said that that's what you need in life. A comrade.'

'Was that the word I used?'

'Sometimes you'd say "friend". But then you said Facebook ruined that word, so you went back to comrade.'

Maggie laughed at that, the first crack in the ice. There was a time when he'd have seized on that opening, made another joke and the shared laughter would have rapidly turned into an embrace which would, inevitably, have turned into something more. But he didn't take that route.

'The thing is, I know the past is everything with you. You're wary of me now because of what happened with us before.'

'Yeah, that and also the weirdness of what happened at the library. You're there and all of a sudden you're not there. And I'm on my own in the middle of a fucking fire.'

'I cannot tell you how sorry I am about that, Maggie. I was taking pictures and I turn around and you're gone, and I was just so desperate to find you. I was terrified that maybe something had happened to you. And I thought: *Please, don't let me lose her again.*'

Maggie let that last sentence sink in. Then, quietly, she said, 'I didn't like that feeling, Uri. And I wondered why you'd turned up here out of the blue, as if maybe it was . . .' She was embarrassed to say it. 'You know, a trap.'

'Me, a trap?'

'Because it's happened before, Uri. With other people, I mean.'

'There we go again, with the past. That's the point, Maggie. We're not teenagers any more. There's always going to be a past, more and more of it. The question is, which past matters more?'

'What do you mean?'

'The past you've had with other men – all the bad experiences – or the past you had with me. The past we had together.'

She didn't reply. Instead she sat opposite him at the kitchen table and tried to absorb what he had said. The silence hung between them for a good while, neither awkward nor tense. It was like a blanket that covered them both.

Under it, she was thinking about what he had said – and she was also remembering. She was remembering Richard, the nights she had spent with him in this same place, and the way it had ended. And she was remembering Uri too, the days and nights they had shared together in this room, in the bedroom, in every corner of this apartment; the closed, private world they had built together – their faces inches apart under the covers, their skin touching, hiding nothing.

Had she got that wrong? It never felt wrong. Not once. Mind you, it hadn't felt wrong with Richard either – not until it was too late. But Uri had never betrayed her. She might have feared it, after what happened in Charlottesville, but what were those fears really? They were scars left by Richard, not Uri. Was she really going to carry them around with her forever?

She got to her feet and walked the tiny – and enormous – distance over to him, placing her hand on his shoulder. Gently, he covered her hand with his own, looking up at her, directly into her eyes. Without planning to, she bent down until her mouth was close to his, her hair falling like a curtain to cover them. They didn't kiss straight away, but rather reverted to what had always been their habit, letting their lips linger close to each other for a second, then another second, allowing them to feel the proximity of each other's breath, letting the desire build. And then, with no decision she could remember, their lips were touching, the kiss instantly becoming urgent in its intensity. The taste of him was such a relief after so long.

The desire that followed almost shocked her. It moved so fast and so completely, seeming to reach every part of her, as if it were carried through her bloodstream. When his hand cradled her neck, just the touch of him on her skin made her moan.

From then on, their movements required no direction or conscious thought. Their fingers, their tongues, knew exactly what to do. Only later, once they were lying together in her bed, naked and spent, did the thought strike her: that whatever goes on in the heart or the head, the body too has a memory.

She was coming back from the bathroom, marvelling at how good he looked, propped upright on several pillows, when Uri smiled and said, 'Since I'm here, why don't you tell me what's happening?' They grinned at each other, aware that, for both of them, work, even when it looked like a war zone, was also a comfort zone.

Within minutes Maggie had told him about the manifesto, the reading list and her visit to the Vietnam Memorial.

For now, she had said, let's assume Andrea Ellis is telling the truth. In which case, she explained, Keane is not the man behind these arson attacks and killings. And yet we know that the manifesto has got Keane's fingerprints all over it, drawing directly from the course he taught at Stanford in the mid-1980s. Logically that left only one possibility. The author of that document – the arsonist, the murderer – was not the professor who had set that reading list, but one of the students who had followed it.

Uri understood immediately and was just as swift to realize why Maggie was telling him. 'You want me to come up with a list of everyone who took that course in that period?'

'How did you guess?' Maggie smiled, leaning in for another kiss. She had missed the sex, no doubt about it, but this – the easy familiarity – she had longed for almost as much. 'There's no one better at that stuff and you know it.'

They got dressed and she saw Uri to the door. Within an hour, helped in part by the alumni blog that had first led Maggie to connect Keane with the manifesto, he had sent over a list of names. One by one, she looked them up online. The responses were painfully slow.

Thanks to Liz, her email was working again, but was something up with Google? She was tempted to Google it, but instead went over to Twitter and typed in 'Google'.

The tweets from a few hours ago were variations on a theme.

*Is it just me or is Google like *crawling* today?*

Am Googling the words 'glacial pace'. Still no results . . .

*Just Googled 'slowest search engine in world history'. Google response: *About four results (0.43 weeks)**

Before long, the meme artists had got busy, several of them riffing on an image of Albert Einstein scratching his head.

Grandpa, was this what life was like before Google?
Hey, remember when we actually remembered stuff?

A more po-faced version came from the blue-ticked author of a global bestseller on human evolution:

A reminder that we were once a species that relied on its own collective memory rather than on a single algorithm

Finally, Maggie followed a link to a story from the *Washington Post.*

PALO ALTO—Internet users the world over suffered an unprecedented loss of service late Wednesday as Google, the world's biggest search engine, reported what it described as "an exceptional drop in performance."

The tech giant refused to confirm that it had come under cyberattack, but senior figures in the company's Mountain View headquarters speaking on condition of anonymity told the Post they believed they had indeed been the victim of a "serious, sustained assault aimed at Google's central nervous system."

Users in the Middle East and Europe were the first to report a problem early Wednesday evening, as the search engine's usually lightning-fast search function began to slow. The trouble spread westward, affecting service in the US by 1pm EDT. As the malaise widened, it also deepened, with initially sluggish response times grinding to a virtual halt.

Google sources said this was not a conventional "denial of service" attack, but one they deemed more sophisticated. One executive hinted that the source of the virus may well have been internal. "The call is coming from inside the house," he said.

Others suggested that "thinking in terms of a virus may be the wrong template" and this might have been a deliberate act of sabotage embedded deep inside Google's own coding several days or weeks ago.

Internal investigations are already underway, with the company's senior management team—including the founding duo—said to be in permanent session. "We are working around the clock to restore Google to the consistently excellent level of service our users have grown used to," a spokesperson said.

Maggie sat back in her chair and bit hard on the pen top she had been chewing. She had seen a tweet which distilled the conclusion she had already reached.

Google down? Don't worry. We can look up whatever we need at the library. Oh wait . . .

So Operation Florian would have to widen its scope. Not content with destroying the world's libraries, whoever was doing this was obviously determined to go much further: to destroy not only the physical foundations of the world's knowledge, but also the electronic means by which human beings had come to access it. The author of that manifesto was not exaggerating the seriousness of their intent. They were out to rob the human race of all it knew.

There were other search engines and she would have to use them. They too were slow – perhaps they'd come under similar attack – but name by name, she began to work through Uri's list.

Keane had taught for three years. His had been a fairly niche course – *New perspectives in historiography and the case for radical scepticism* – with perhaps no more than forty students a year. The eventual total should be around one hundred and twenty names. So far Uri had sent over about fifty.

She scanned the one-line summaries of the former students. Uri had eliminated six names from the start: they were dead. But it was hard to make even a crude cull of the rest. She saw at least four graduates who were now involved in banking or high finance. Not her area, but if one of these four (three men and a woman) had made serious money, they might have the resources to mount an operation like this. She would come back to them.

Two worked for NGOs, one fairly high up in an international medical charity, the other as head of an LGBTQ organization in Canada. Ordinarily, if Maggie were drawing up any kind of list of suspects, she'd eliminate such palpable, neon-lit do-gooders first. But something stopped her this time. She thought back to that argument she'd had with Uri, the philosophy seminar, where he had expressed sympathy with the notion of shaking off the burden of history, of having a fresh start. Even him.

She thought of the manifesto, with its tone of moral purpose.

Those who seek justice insist we must remember. But those who seek peace insist we forget. The author believed he was on the side of peace and a better world.

She kept the two NGO names on the list.

There were a couple of journalists and an academic historian: surely destroying knowledge was anathema to them? The Director of Strategy to the Mayor of Omaha was a former student of William Keane's. What possible motive could he have for torching libraries the world over?

On the other hand, she had seen the crowds cheering for Keane. She knew his appeal stretched far and deep. What was to say it did not extend to a local government official in Nebraska? As for the academic, well, wasn't Keane himself a historian?

She got back up and went to the kitchen, where she poured herself a small – or small-ish – glass of whisky. Her skin still tingled from its encounter with Uri: the body with its own memory again.

This was more difficult than she had anticipated. If she was looking for someone involved in, say, a corruption scam or a political manoeuvre, a process of elimination would always work quite swiftly. But this was different. From what she could tell, this threat did not arise from personal greed or ambition, venality or lust – her usual stocks-in-trade – but from something more nebulous. It seemed to be driven by principle. Fanatical, extreme, unhinged principle, but principle all the same. She would have to approach it differently.

She was exhausted, but there was something keeping her awake. It was a nagging thought, like a dream that slips through your fingers the moment you try to grasp hold of it. Now, she recalled, that sensation had first surfaced when she had sat in this room, reading the manifesto.

She reached for the hard copy that the governor had smuggled to her, sat up on the bed and started reading it again, from the start. She couldn't have said what exactly she was looking for, though she told herself she would know it when she saw it. It wasn't a thought or idea so much as a sensation: she was waiting to feel as if something had snagged, like the thread of a sweater caught on a barbed wire fence.

More than once she dozed off. The author of this manifesto was a fluent writer, but also an obsessive one. Packed with academic references and, unexpectedly in a call for the eradication of history, replete with allusions to relatively obscure historical events, the manifesto was not an easy read.

178. *A phrase worth examining is "war memorial". It is embedded deep in our language and rightly so. Most people think it refers to those monuments that exist in almost every place in America and elsewhere to "honor" those who died in wars. But the reason it resonates is that we understand that wars are themselves acts of memorial. They are almost always fought to avenge, honor or reverse some prior loss. And yet, we should know from even a basic reading of Sun Tzu or Clausewitz, that wars are seldom truly fought for those purposes. They are fought over resources and wealth, whether that be spices in the sixteenth century or oil in the twenty-first. Avenging the past might be the rallying cry, used to stir the masses, but it is rarely the genuine cause. Still, it works because of a weakness in men's minds: a weakness for our own past.*

Her eyelids were heavy, but she forced herself to read on.

179. *Very few people are honest enough to admit this, which itself is revealing. It shows that we understand that this obsession with history is a weakness. Consider the phrase "ancestor worship". It denotes primitive thinking. Yet when Slobodan Milošević suggested that a battle that had been fought in* 1389 *needed to be avenged in* 1989, *what was he doing but engaging in the worship of ancestors that had lived six centuries earlier? He presented this as a matter of death and life, but really it had no bearing on the actual existence of the people of Serbia in the last years of the twentieth century. Such is the . . .*

There it was, that snagging sensation. It was familiar, not just from when she'd first read this document, but from much longer ago. She and Liz had been out in the park, and Liz had lost a ring. A silly bit of plastic costume jewellery, but she had liked it and the pair of them had marched the length of the park together, up and down, eyes fixed on the ground, like detectives in a missing persons inquiry, searching for that stupid ring. Eventually, Maggie had found it. But first came the sensation she had now, the *feeling* that she had glimpsed it somewhere in her peripheral vision. Twenty-five years ago, it had been a tiny shard of colour that had made Maggie turn around, retrace her steps and stare even harder at the ground.

She had that feeling again now. As she read that last paragraph, word by word, clause by clause. What was it? Not 'history is a weakness'. Not 'ancestor worship' either. Was it the reference to Milosevic? She tested each phrase on herself, to see if it triggered that response from her unconscious. She was waiting for the snag on the wire.

He presented this as a matter of death and life . . .

There it was. *A matter of death and life.* At first she was disappointed, for this was no great discovery: it was a formulation that would trip up any reader. The usual order – 'a matter of life and death' – had been reversed. It might have been no more than a mistake when typing, or a curious idiosyncrasy of the author's.

Her phone buzzed. The screen lit up with a news alert: *FBI release 'Bookburner's manifesto', document said to be penned by arsonist behind terror attacks on world libraries.*

So it was out there now. Whatever else the linguistic analysis had yielded, it clearly hadn't produced anything to alter the conclusion the FBI Director had drawn, at Maggie's prompting, that morning: that their best hope was to publish the text and wait for someone, somewhere, to read it and spot the word or phrase that identified the author.

The nagging itch in Maggie's brain had not gone away. She went to the *New York Times* website where the lead item was a news story about the release, including a few details on the FBI mission a source had revealed was codenamed Operation Florian. Embedded in the first sentence was a link to the text in full. Once there, Maggie ran a word search for 'A matter of . . .' It brought up no instances except the one she'd already found. She closed her eyes, her body desperate to surrender to sleep but her brain adamant that it settle this question once and for all.

Question.

Now she tried that, searching for: 'A question of . . .'

There were three results. The first offered a sentence that included the words 'a question of historicity'. The next came up with 'a question of jurisdiction'. Finally the third read: 'This is not a simple question of wrong and right . . .'

Wrong and right.

The same reversal of the usual order. So perhaps this was a habit. She typed in 'black and white'. Nothing. She typed in 'white and black'. Still nothing. She tried a few more stock phrases, looking for that curious reverse. No luck. She had just two instances to go on.

That's when it came to her. There was only one person she'd ever known who shared that same verbal tic. What was strange was that she had only ever half-noticed it. She had never articulated it to another person or even to herself. But it had registered just enough to have snagged her both times she had read the document.

If she was right, it meant the author of the Bookburner's manifesto was no mystery. She knew who it was.

Chapter Thirty-Three

Capitol Hill, Washington DC, 11.05pm

She'd had to go via several circuitous routes to get his home address, pulling in multiple favours with old Washington contacts. That was harder than usual, and not only because of the hack into her phone book. Several texts went unanswered, several more calls went straight to voicemail. Thanks to that video, Maggie Costello carried a taint. For now, the DC calculus held that the safest bet was to steer well clear.

She could have done it officially, through the Bureau. But that risked an advance tip-off: there would be a faction in the FBI loyal to this man, she had learned that much a while ago. The element of surprise was one of her few advantages and she was not about to squander it.

And now here she was, parking up around the corner from the Capitol Hill townhouse that was, despite everything, still his. He was living proof that, in politics, most people, most of the time, got away with it.

She climbed the three steps and knocked on the door which revealed itself on impact to be unlocked. She pushed it to find another, inner door that was secured. Next to it was a buzzer that appeared to include a video camera. She pressed the button and a hand instinctively went to her hair.

A voice came through the speaker. 'No, don't change a thing! You look great just like that.'

Just hearing him again made her shudder. She considered turning on her heel and heading back to her car. There had to be another way of doing this. But it was too late. He had already flung the door wide open and was standing there with his arms outstretched, as if expecting a hug.

'If it isn't Maggie Costello, as I live and breathe! Star of the hottest sex tape of the *year*, ladies and gentlemen.'

His eyes were redder than when she'd last seen him, the paunch larger, but otherwise Crawford 'Mac' McNamara was so unchanged, he made it look like an act of defiance. The former chief strategist to the President of the United States was unshaven, barefoot and still in his trademark cargo-style shorts and rock-themed T-shirt. Today, and perhaps yesterday judging by the stains around the armpits, it was Metallica. The look said: *unrepentant*.

'Maggie, come in. Please. We can't have you on the streets. I don't care what you did in that video, it hasn't come to that!'

She stepped inside, reminding herself of the resolve she maintained for most of the five months they worked in the same White House: do not take the bait.

He gestured towards a living room, though it more closely resembled a cross between a bookshop and a campaign office. On the floor, apparently awaiting hanging, were framed newspaper front pages and the odd poster. On the tables, on the floor, even on the improbably chintzy chairs, were piles of books. Maggie noticed a cardboard box, from which were spilling copies of a single volume whose cover was filled with an up-close portrait of Mac's face, so intimate you could see individual pores. The title was *Burning Down the House*.

'Go on,' McNamara said. 'Take a copy. You know you want to. Everybody in America wants to read that book.'

'So this is the period of "penance and quiet reflection" you talked about? You've been writing your memoirs.'

He smiled. 'I know you didn't fall for that bullshit, Maggie. Everyone else in this town, yes. But not you.' He affected the English accent of a Hollywood villain and dipped his head in a bow: 'You were a worthy adversary, Miss Costello.' And then, in his own voice: 'It is still "Miss", right? It's not "Mrs"? I don't want to offend anyone.'

Do not take the bait. Do not take it.

'Look at me, standing here. Where are my manners? Sit down, sit down. Please. What can I get you? Coffee? Scotch? Crack?'

'Nothing, thank you, Mac.' She crossed to the seat carrying fewest books, removed them and sat down.

'You do look gorgeous, I gotta say,' Mac said, still standing. 'Life outside the White House suits you. OK, maybe I'm swayed a *bit* by that tape. Once that's in your head, it's hard to shake, you know what I mean?' He suddenly stood taller, closed his eyes and with his curled right hand mimed the few jerking strokes of a man masturbating himself to a climax.

'You are a truly disgusting man.'

'Ya think? But guess what's great. I am now free to be a truly disgusting man and no longer give a flying fuck what all the headshakers and teethsuckers of the liberal elite – your crowd – think about me.' With his arms wide, he simulated a child pretending to be an aeroplane as he spun around singing tunelessly: 'I'm freeeeee as a bird!'

'Mac, I need to tell you why I'm here.'

'I did wonder,' he said, slumping into a chair, apparently exhausted by his brief pirouette, and putting his bare feet up on a coffee table, resting them on a particularly fat biography of Benito Mussolini. Maggie was close enough to see the dead skin and broken toenails.

'It's about the so-called Bookburner's manifesto.'

'My God, what kind of asshole am I?' He was out of the chair and off to another room, calling out from over his shoulder, 'Publishing that thing was your idea, right? I should have congratulated you the second you walked in here: Maggie Costello back at the heart of government!' So her instinct had been right: Mac did have a mole inside the FBI.

He was back clutching two empty flutes and a bottle of Krug, which he held close to his groin, uncorking it inches from Maggie's face. She saw the foam explode. 'Now what does that image remind me of?'

'For fuck's sake, Mac, that video wasn't me. As you well know.'

Now the voice of a small-time New York gangster from a Jimmy Cagney movie: 'A fella's gotta right to dream, ain't he?'

Maggie put the glass down on the table, next to the Mussolini book, without taking a sip. 'Now, listen.' She was back in the West Wing, feeling the way McNamara always made her feel when she had the misfortune of working for him: like a 1950s schoolmarm, prim and uptight. This was what he wanted, what he always wanted: to unsettle, to wrongfoot, whoever he was talking to. 'I've read that document and it bears the specific linguistic imprint of one person.'

'Old news, Maggie. William Keane. The FBI got their computer geeks on it. Pattern recognition, language analysis, the whole nine yards of horseshit and it's him.' His inside sources again, this time getting it only half-right.

'Not Keane, Mac. I'm not talking about him. I'm talking about you.'

McNamara made a show of spluttering on his champagne. 'Me? Are you kidding?'

' "A matter of death and life." "A question of wrong and right." You're the only person I've ever met who does that. You and the author of the Bookburner's manifesto.'

'You're sounding like a crazy woman again, Mags.'

'Don't call me Mags. If the language analysts haven't picked it up yet, it's because it's a thing you do when you *speak*, and so far they've only been looking at published writing. Look, I can see that, on its own, that might seem like insufficient evidence. But then I took a little look at your résumé, Mac.'

He emptied his champagne glass and poured himself some more.

'And what I saw is that not only did you, the great scourge of the Ivy League, study at both Harvard and Yale, but you also did a semester at Stanford.'

'Architecture.'

'That's right. But it just so happens that the one semester you were there coincided with the period when Professor William Keane was teaching a blockbuster course that, I'm told, absolutely *everyone* went to.'

As she spoke, she recalled the lines in that alumni blog. *There'd be people there who weren't even history majors, all squished up sitting on the stairs, some of them sitting cross-legged right in front of the podium, lining up outside the lecture theater . . .*

Mac put down his glass and allowed a sly smile to pass his lips. 'You know, given what happened the last time you and I had a chat, and how that worked out, I need to ask you something, Maggie.'

'What is it?'

'Are you carrying a cellphone?'

'Yes.'

'OK. So I need you to put that on the table.'

'I'm not recording this conversation.'

'All right, I believe you. But as St Ronald of the Shining City on the Hill taught us—'

' "Trust, but verify." '

'Precisely.'

Maggie did as she was told. McNamara picked up the phone and turned the power off. 'Any other recording devices, Maggie?'

'No.'

'Don't make me frisk you. I'll enjoy it, but you won't. So. Is there a wire under that underwire bra? Tell you what, why don't you put that bag of yours in the next room. Just in case.'

Maggie did that too. A price worth paying to get this over with.

Once she was back and facing him, Mac cleared his throat. 'Maggie, I think you're very smart, you know that. One of the few over there I had to think about. The rest I could deal with in my sleep. But you were a cut above. And yet do you know where you let yourself down?'

'I have a feeling you're about to tell me.'

'You get too hung up on the "who". Who did this, who did that. Whodunnit. When the real question, the only question, is always *why*.'

'Why.'

'Yes. *Why* would anyone want to start burning books or killing historians or wrecking libraries and databases? Why would anyone want to do such a thing?'

Maggie waited, allowing McNamara his little performance.

'It's not a rhetorical question, Maggie! Tell me: why?'

'Because they want to destroy the past.'

He got to his feet and started pacing. His legs were pale and unexpectedly thin. 'Because facts are elitist and we are all about taking down the liberal elite.'

'You're joking, right?'

'I am definitely not joking. Facts are elitist. So's science. All knowledge, in fact. Elitist, to its core.

'Just think about it. I'm a guy in, I don't know, Wisconsin. I lost my job two years ago when they closed the steelworks down. And I see some Chinaman or Mexican working in a steel plant owned by the same company that shut my factory down. Now that guy *feels* in his water that that Chinaman and that Mexican took his job. That's what he feels.

'And then along comes some wonk from MIT or the *Wall Street Journal* or the *Economist* who tells the guy in Wisconsin that he's wrong. That, actually, the *facts* say globalization is good for the economy, because it's making everybody richer. Or that, actually, GDP has increased by 2.2 per cent in the last fiscal year. That's what the facts say. "I'm merely citing the evidence",' McNamara added in his best hoity-toity accent, as he walked around on tiptoes, like a prissy ballerina. ' "I'm merely following the data." '

'Or immigration. I lose my job to some spic who's happy to work for half what I used to get, and then you tell me that immigration is a net boost to the economy. That overall we gain more than we lose. So I should be happy. Because "those are the facts". And you know what I say, if I'm that guy in Wisconsin? I say, fuck that. FUCK THAT, Maggie.'

She hoped he hadn't seen her jump when he shouted.

'You see, what if I don't like those facts? Huh? What if I think those facts have nothing to do with me or how I feel? What if I want some "alternative facts" that say something about my life? What, Maggie, if I'm sick of your crowd ending every argument by pulling out your killer so-called facts? Don't you think it would feel real good to stop you doing that, once and for all? And do you know how I stop you? Because there's only one way. I need to *destroy* all your facts.'

'They're not *my* facts, Mac. They're *the* facts. They're not on anyone's side.'

'Really? Because it sure don't feel that way to our folks. If what you just said was right then sometimes the facts would break their way, sometimes they'd break for the other side. Like a ref in a ball-game. But it's not like that, is it? The facts *always* break your way. My guy in Wisconsin sees a murderer, he wants to fry him in the electric chair. "That'll teach those motherfuckers once and for all," he says. And then some professor gets on her hind legs and says, "Actually, all *the evidence* suggests that countries with the death penalty have higher murder rates than countries that don't." Ah, come on. Don't give me that.

'You got bad guys shooting people. Give me a gun, then I can protect my family. That'll make us safer. And then, here we go, the pointy-heads and the know-it-alls at the *New York Times* or NPR pipe up, "Actually,"' – he was on tiptoes again – '"there are more gun deaths in America than in all these one hundred and sixty-four countries that ban guns put together." No way, that can't be. Don't tell me that.

'D'you see what I'm saying to you, Maggie? It's *tiring* when the elite keep saying you're wrong every hour of every day. Two men fucking each other in the ass, that's just unnatural. "Actually, there are same-sex relationships in the animal kingdom." Actually, actually, always fucking "actually".

'But what if we just stopped you from doing that? What if we took "actually" right off the table? Let me put it in terms your crowd might understand. Scrabble. I bet you love Scrabble. Am I right?'

As it happened, Maggie had never had the patience for it. Liz was the master, her brain computing all the possibilities in seconds. Maggie never quite saw the point. But she nodded, knowing there was no stopping Mac now.

'So imagine you're playing Scrabble against this guy who keeps dipping his hand in that bag of letters, keeps on pulling out an X or a Q or a Z. Pretty soon, you get sick of it. You get tired. So you take the goddamn bag and chuck it right out of the window. See how he likes that. See how well he plays now. That's tempting, right?

'You take away all the knowledge and history and facts and science that the elite love using to keep the little guy down. You just take it away. Level the playing field.'

He sat down and drained his glass. His face was becoming flushed.

'So that's what this is about?' Maggie said in the pause. 'Torch the libraries, then when everyone knows nothing, we'll all be equal.'

'I didn't say that. Don't try pretending I'm some kind of communist or something.'

'All right: everyone will be equally ignorant.'

'I'm talking about robbing the elite of their weapons, the ones they use to keep the rest of us down. But no. That's not what this is all about.'

'You mean there's more?'

'People want a story, Maggie. They want to be told a *story*. "America was in the toilet, now we're making America great again." That's a terrific story. And he tells it so well.' He didn't need to spell out who 'he' was. They both knew.

' "We've created more jobs than ever before." That sounds good. "Wages have never gone up so fast. Before I came in, they were falling. Now they're going up." That's another great story. It's hopeful, it's encouraging.'

'And it's totally false. Jobs and wages were already going up.'

Mac put the index finger of one hand on his nose, and pointed directly at Maggie with the other. 'That's it! You see, you did it right there. Exactly that. *Ruining* the story with some pesky, annoying, pedantic "fact".' He made air quotes with his fingers.

'He wants people to feel good, Maggie. To let them think that, now that he's there, sitting behind that big desk, they can sleep easy at night. Daddy will look after them. That things were shit before, but they're getting better now. That the country was overrun with rapists and murderers and criminals before, but now it's getting safer. And the world respects America now. Like never before.

'Now isn't that nice? Isn't that a happy story? But then you and your crowd have to ruin it, with your "reality checks" and "truth squads" and your itemized lists of "demonstrable falsehoods" and "misleading statements". I mean, what a downer. Such kill-joys, every one of you.

'Because "the truth" is a serious party-pooper, Maggie. We're about to break out the champagne, and then you put your hand in the air and you're all, "Miss, miss! Miss, I don't think that's quite right", and you've ruined everything. And then you get smug and say your job is to point out "inconvenient truths", like we're meant to be grateful. I mean, this is what I don't get about liberals. You think "inconvenient" is something to brag about! Like it's a selling point. Well, I've got news for you: inconvenience is not a good thing. No one wants your inconvenient truths. We'd rather enjoy the bedtime story he was telling us, all tucked up in bed with our warm milk and cookies, before you spoiled it, thank you very much.

'And you know what's so great? And for this, by the way, I give him one hundred per cent of the credit. I don't know whether I'd have ever even *seen* it, if it hadn't been for him. He understood that the truth is *weak*.

'That's right, Maggie: weak. All this stuff – the historical record, the facts, the truth – you guys always big it up like it's some terrifying adversary. But now, thanks to him, I know that the opposite is true. It's *fragile*.'

He was out of his chair again, pacing, apparently revived by the point he was about to make. 'Oh, for years, we all acted like the truth was the mightiest force in the known universe. The second someone dared stray from the facts, the media jumped all over them. The *Times* would have an orgasm because it found the documents that showed that Governor This or Mayor That had "uttered a falsehood" and there'd be calls for their resignation and then the politician would shuffle up to the podium, head down, tail between his legs' – Mac had moulded his body into the sullen shape of a guilty schoolboy – 'and they'd say, "I must apologize. I misspoke." Misspoke! Whatever the fuck that is. And usually they'd have to quit. Because everyone accepted that they'd done the worst thing anyone could ever imagine: they'd *lied*.' Mac put his hands over his mouth, and collapsed back into his chair like a Victorian lady on her fainting couch, shocked at a glimpse of ankle.

'Not to play the boring old guy, but I came up after Watergate. Do you know what single question gripped – I mean, *obsessed* – this country for two years? One question: did Nixon lie? That was it! As if that was the ultimate crime.

'And Nixon – so innocent, so naïve – went along with it! He didn't see that through all those denials, all that "I am not a crook" bullshit, he was *accepting* – tacitly, of course, implicitly – that lying was the greatest crime known to man. Tying himself up in knots, torturing the English language, just so he wouldn't be caught in a lie.

'It was the same with you-know-who getting his dick sucked in the Oval Office. "I did not have sexual relations" and "It depends what the meaning of 'is' is." All these pathetic politicians doing backflips, just to stay on the right side of "the truth".

'And then along comes the man who is now our president – and guess what? He refuses to play the game. He doesn't tangle himself up this way and that to stay on the right side of the line marked "truth", because he doesn't give a fuck. He just says what he wants. He tells people he was against that shit-useless war, and then they find a tape of him supporting the war, but he doesn't care and here's the thing: no one else cares either.

'There's some policy of his everyone hates? "That wasn't me," he says. "That was my opponent." No, all the media bigwigs say. That was you. Here's the order you signed, just a few weeks ago. "No," he says. "It's their policy and I'm trying to fix it. If only they would help me."

'I mean, you gotta hand it to him, Maggie. Even though he's wrong, and there's hard, written, documented proof that he's wrong – that he's *lying* – his followers all believe him. Forty per cent of the country say he's telling the truth. And a whole lot more don't know who to believe.'

McNamara started clapping. 'I mean, give that man a round of applause. What fools he's made of the rest of us who grew up terrified, trembling in the face of "The Truth".' McNamara intoned those last two words in a deep, Hollywood voice-over baritone.

'I mean it, Maggie. I was petrified. As a kid, I pictured it – the truth – like it was this real thing, two giant tablets of stone in a Cecil B. DeMille movie, looming over me. All that stuff – "The truth will out", "The truth will set you free" – that could make a kid shit himself. We were all like that, trying to stay on the right side of the truth, until this great, extraordinary man comes along and says, "Fuck that." *Fuck* that. He just lies and gets away with it. Because no one cares. They move on to the next thing. That was his great insight. *No one cares.*

'That's what I mean when I say the truth is weak, Maggie. It is weak and feeble. We thought it was so strong, but it relied on everyone bowing down to it. The minute someone had the balls to say, "Fuck that", it just crumbled. It just took one little boy with the courage to point at the naked emperor and say, "That man is fully clothed", and the truth collapsed into a heap. It didn't even have the stomach for a fight.

'Its fatal flaw, you see, Maggie, was that it relied on *shame.* Truth relied on shame. People were embarrassed to be caught in a lie. They were ashamed of it. Before him, no one wanted to do it. But then this once-in-a-generation, hell, once-in-a-millennium man comes along and he couldn't give a rat's asshole. He doesn't even blush. He feels no shame. He doesn't care. And because he doesn't care, you don't need to care either. And, just like that, it's over. Truth is dead.

'It's funny, don't you think? All these great thinkers and philosophers, and it takes this man who they all think is a moron and a fraud to point out something they never saw. To teach them this huge lesson. That the truth is powerless against a man who does not mind lying and lying brazenly. It is powerless against a man with no shame.'

Mac drained the last of the champagne, then leaned down to pull a bottle of water from a pack of twelve below his desk and chugged most of that back. He looked as if he'd just run a ten-K. Crawford McNamara was an aerobic talker, the only person Maggie knew capable of working himself into a sweat just through conversation or, more accurately, monologue.

'I don't blame you for not getting this, Maggie. I really don't. Because you're not American. So you're off the hook. But the others? Don't they realize, this is what America is *about*? It's what America is *for.* America is the land where you write your own script, tell your own story – whatever you want it to be. Don't let a few tedious, Ivy League, dry as a nun's snatch, UN-backed, peer-reviewed, limp-wristed, European "facts" get in your way. Leave that to the bores in the reality-based community. Write your own story. That's what America's about. And that's what he's doing. And that's why he's still there, behind the big desk in the Oval, despite your best efforts.'

As he took in some air, Maggie jumped in. 'Which means you – he – could just keep lying. Who cares if "my crowd" hit back? None of what we say matters anyway, not with the true believers. His base. They accept everything he says. So just keep saying it. Why bother destroying all the facts that could prove you wrong?'

'Besides the sheer pleasure in seeing you all go out of your minds, you mean? Which, don't knock it, by the way. I mean, that's a thrill. Next time he says, "No president has ever achieved so much in such a short space of time" and you all run back to the record books to prove him wrong and you start looking for all the great things FDR did or Lincoln and – guess what – *there's nothing there*. All the records and books have burned to a crisp! I mean, man, that is just gonna be a priceless moment. And it's already happening, by the way. After that big library went up in Oxford, how can you *prove* there ever was a Queen Elizabeth the First? I mean, really prove it. Maybe it's just a fairy story. Virgin queen, virgin birth: maybe it's all bullshit. Who can tell?

'But while I truly believe that the tears of liberals are the elixir of life – you can take your whisky and champagne, give me a keg of liberal tears, neat, every day of the week – that's not the main reason. More a happy byproduct, if you know what I mean. As always, and add this to the ever-expanding list of things liberals don't know shit about, the real deal is – drumroll, please, maestro,' and here Mac mimed a furious pounding of a snare, 'power. *Power*.

'You know all that horseshit about a "well-informed citizenry"? How it's necessary for a healthy democracy and that's why we need a free press and all that crap? Well, maybe I believed that before I worked in the White House – *maybe* – but I can tell you, now that I've been there, if you're the people running the show, that is the very *last* thing you want.

'Confusion. That's what you want. Confusion is your best friend. The ideal people to rule over are either people who love you or, if you can't have that, people who are *confused*. The more confused, the better. When the folks don't know what's true and what's false, and they don't know who to believe, well, then you can do what the fuck you like.

'Like, and I love this one because we did this and it actually worked, let's say you want to give your pals a big, fat, juicy, T-bone tax cut. You can say: "We're passing this new tax bill, it's going to make you all ten per cent richer." And then all the liberals will say, "No, it won't! There's independent economic modelling which shows that scheduled over six fiscal years, while there might be some benefit for the bottom two income deciles, that will be more like four point three per cent, tapering to three point two per cent" and on and on, and we just go, "Ten per cent richer!" And we keep saying it. And then they realize that their fancy study was too complicated and no one understood it, so they try to make it simple and say: "It won't make you ten per cent richer. That's a terrible lie!" And they produce another "independent, academic" report *proving* your ten per cent figure is wrong. And they're completely right, by the way. The ten per cent thing is pure bullshit. But guess what's happened? Two things, both of them good for us and terrible for you and your crowd.

'First, there's now only one figure that everyone remembers. *Ten per cent*. All the four point threes and three point whatevers, no one can remember any of that. The only thing normal people remember is ten per cent. "Hey, wasn't there that ten per cent tax cut?" Nice round number, easy. And you know why they remember it? Because *you folks* kept saying it. Even when you were denying it, you were saying it over and over again – ten per cent, ten per cent, ten per cent. All you've done is reinforce it! Which is so beautiful.

'But let's say some people kinda half listened to all your belly-aching. If you ask them, "Will this tax bill make you richer or poorer?" they either say, "Ten per cent richer!" or they shrug. Because they're confused. Which is just great. I love those people who shrug.' He sang to the ceiling, ' "Give me your shrugging masses, yearning to breathe free!" Seriously. I love them. Almost as much as the poorly educated, although there's an overlap obviously. But the confused, they're just the best. Because no one goes out onto the streets when they're confused. They stay home or watch the ballgame or mow the lawn or jerk off into their wife's underwear drawer or whatever, but they don't protest.

'Incidentally, you ever notice what the president's favourite phrase is? Uses it all the time? Don't worry, I won't make you guess. "Nobody really knows." He loves that one. "Nobody really knows who shot down that plane, nobody really knows." "Nobody really knows what's going on with the climate, nobody knows for sure." He doesn't care if you don't agree with him that climate change is a hoax. That's OK. Main thing he wants is that you *don't know*. That's good enough for him. If you agree with the statement, "Nobody really knows . . ." then God love you. If you shrug your shoulders – not one of those neurotic Jew shrugs, but a genuinely dumb shrug, like you're indifferent to the truth – that's the best. That's what he wants. It's like the title of that book: *Nothing Is True and Everything Is Possible*. I love that title. Love it. Because when nothing is true, everything *is* possible. Did we just blow all that money on some failed policy? Did we just do a deal with a hostile foreign power to funnel some cash to the president's kids? Did we just drop a bomb in the wrong place and kill a whole bunch of civilians?' He shrugged. ' "Nobody really knows." You see, when nobody knows anything, you can *do* anything.'

Not for the first time, Maggie marvelled at McNamara's candour. It made him compelling in a way few backroom operatives ever were. It was why he'd been so powerful in politics once and doubtless would be again, just as soon as his spell of enforced purdah had passed. (There was a time when such a period would be measured in years if not decades. Judging by those copies of his newly minted memoir, what counted as a 'decent interval' was now measured in months.) It was risky for him to talk this way – a recording of this conversation would be terminal for him. Or at least it would have been once: these days you could never be sure. But it was the only way he knew.

'So you're telling me all this – the destruction of the human memory bank – is just another power grab?'

'Just? *Just?* You are hilarious, Costello. "Just another power grab." Like it's a small thing! Like having that kind of power is not *everything*. No wonder your crowd are always losing. You don't want it enough. My side *craves* power. We know it's the whole ballgame. Everything else is just chin-stroking and dick-tugging. Fun, but useless.'

He moved as if to make the masturbation gesture again, but was deterred by Maggie raising the palm of her hand.

'All right. Since you ask, it's not the whole story. I'll save you the Googling: I sent a cheque to Keane's legal defence fund. You want to know why?'

'It's not a *defence* fund. He brought the case. He's suing *them*.'

'Whatever. The reason why I wrote a big cheque for Professor Keane is—'

'—because you liked him at Stanford.'

'Just *listen*, would you? The reason I back what he's doing down there in Richmond is that our side, we are *hobbled* by all that history. I mean, we have been dragging this ball and chain around for decades. In Europe no one wants to be called "extreme right" or "far right". Why? Because those words mean "Nazis" and that word means "Holocaust". I mean, that is quite some baggage to carry. And here, it's not much better. You say you're on the right here, before you know it the media'll have you in a white sheet burning a cross. If you say you're on the far right, then brace yourself, my friend: you're the Imperial Wizard.

'You gotta shake off that legacy. Why do you think we invented "alt-right"? Alt to what? It was a way of saying, we're not the scary KKK crowd. We're *alternative*. But that was never going to work, not really. Too defensive. The wise Professor Keane understood that. Bowing your head and apologizing? Doomed. You say sorry, they'll tell you you didn't say sorry loud enough. You bow your head, they'll ask why you didn't get on your knees. And if you get on your knees, then why didn't you lie flat on the floor, prostrate before me? Same with reparations. Bad idea. However much you give, it will never, ever be enough. So don't give a cent!

'Keane understood you had to attack the problem at its root. If people think you're guilty of a crime, your only way out is to get them to believe *there was no crime*.

'I mean, it was ambitious. More radical than any idea on the right for decades, maybe a century. I wasn't sure he could pull it off down there in Richmond, but by God, he just might. We've been limping around with that ball and chain on our ankles all these years and along comes Keane with his giant pair of bolt-cutters to break it off. Like he's saying, "Don't associate me with the evils of Holocaust and slavery. You know why: because there was no Holocaust and there was no slavery!" It's genius, if you think about it. Thanks to William Keane, we white conservatives can sing it loud and sing it proud: "Free at last, free at last, thank God Almighty we are free at last!" '

Maggie assessed the moment as an opportunity to come in with a question of her own. At the very least, Mac looked like he needed to take a breath. But clocking that she was about to speak, he pre-empted it, raising a palm and picking up where he left off.

'Oh, and don't go thinking this is anything but the American way. I know that'd be tempting. But, come on. What do you think this country was all about if not *starting over*? A fresh start. They even called it the "New World". That was the whole, beautiful idea, Maggie. In Europe they were buried under all those layers of dust and shit and *past*. They could hardly breathe, for all that history.

'And then Christopher Columbus sails the ocean blue, the founders land on Plymouth Rock, they feel the virgin sand under their feet and they think, "We can start anew. *Tabula rasa*. We can be born again."

'That's the promise of America. We're the blank slate nation. Amnesia is right there in our genome. You know the story,

Maggie. We came to this land, killed almost everyone who already lived here' – he raised his hand in the shape of a gun and, like a boy playing cowboys and Indians, made a *piow, piow* sound – 'and then we promptly forgot all about them. Forgot we'd even done it. Like we'd just taken out the trash or something. I mean, that is a mighty, mighty thing, the power to forget like that. It's what makes us great.'

Maggie could feel her revulsion rising, which was not good. She knew it could cloud her judgement. She needed to conclude this conversation soon, which meant steering McNamara towards the information she needed. But asking a direct question was doomed: he would clam up.

Finally she said, in a voice that was calm and casual, modulated by a detached intellectual curiosity, 'But Keane's approach was all about the law. Fight it in the courts. He never preached this doctrine of destroying the evidence, did he? That was new.'

McNamara broke out of his reverie and suddenly looked at her. She'd blundered, she could feel it. Now he was staring at her; whatever effect the booze had had on him seemed to have faded.

'And here I am, chatting away as if you might be genuinely interested in the issues at hand. Treating you like an intellectual peer. Have I made a mistake here, Maggie?

'The funny thing is, what irritates me is not the crude effort to get me to speculate about the identity of the so-called "Bookburner" that all the hot chicks on MSNBC are soiling their panties about. Though that is irritating. No. What's disappointing is the narrowness of the liberal mind.

'Because you're still looking for the mastermind, aren't you? The evil genius pulling the strings. I mean, that is the liberal failure in a nutshell, isn't it? That's what you thought when the big guy won too. "It must all be an evil plot. Someone was pulling the strings, but who?" Maybe it was Moscow! Maybe that batshit data company and their secret, scary algorithms! Maybe it was both of them! Same with the Brits and that Europe thing. You and the rest of the cool kids keep looking for the Wizard of Oz, the master villain who's cunningly making it all happen.

'Which is funny, because it makes you as dumb and as naïve as those saps in their mothers' basements, the losers who lapped up all that shit I served them and made me a millionaire. You're as bad as they are, with their wingnut conspiracy theories. OK, you guys point the finger in a different direction – though, it's gotta be said, you often end up in the exact same place – but the one thing that never crosses your minds, any of you, is that maybe this is not about a single super-bad guy that you and the rest of the vegans can hate. Maybe this is something much scarier.'

'Scarier?'

'Yes, Maggie. Way scarier. Because what if the truth is that what got the president elected, or that referendum won, wasn't some monster like me, with a cat on his lap and a big scar down his face, but a *movement*? What if it's *lots* of people who feel this way, millions of them? I mean, how much worse is that?

'And guess what, Mags: that's the truth. You seen the crowds outside that courthouse in Richmond? He's got a following, Professor Keane. Always did have. Could have run for office himself, back in his prime. Became a bit, you know, eccentric.

But still. One of those guys you can't take your eyes off. Like you-know-who.

'But fuck the messenger. It's the *message*. There's a real big market for Keane's message, believe me. Get all this history off your back? All this guilt? Oh yes, there's plenty of people ready to buy that. In this country, for sure. You tell some white guy in Alabama that, hey, how'd you like a world where slavery never happened and all those moaning, whining liberals can do shit about it, and all you gotta do to make it happen is light a match here and there. You'd have some takers for that, no doubt about it. Where do I sign! And in Europe? Get that Nazi monkey off your back? No more apologizing for all the "sins of empire" and all that crap? They'd form a nice, orderly "queue"' – the English accent again – 'for that.

'And that's just the ones giving you active help. You also need the others who stand by and let it happen. They're crucial, those folks. I love those people too, I gotta tell ya. "All it takes for evil to prosper is that good men do nothing." I agree! We'd be nothing without the people who do nothing. The bystanders. And we have *millions* of those. I mean, have you seen the poll numbers on the Keane trial? No wonder that friend of yours, the governor, the African Queen, no wonder she was reaching for the panic button and calling for Maggie Costello. She saw the way things were going.

'Even now, all these buildings on fire, these historians waking up dead. Oh, sure the PBS *NewsHour* is having a stroke and the *New Yorker* is weeping buckets, but out there? You think they care about a few old books that no one ever read? Even if you call them "documents", you think they could give a flying fuck? Give them a job, keep the price of gas and beer down and they couldn't give two shits whether some old scrolls are on fire in Ethiopia.

'So call off the search, Maggie. You're not looking for Mr Big. It's the *people*, that's your enemy. The people, who keep voting the wrong damn way in all these elections, stupid little fuckers. They're the villain you're after. But what're you gonna do? You can't put *all* of them in jail, can you?'

He sat back in his chair, tilting it onto its hind legs so that he could return his feet to the little coffee table, where they invaded Maggie's space. He was pleased with himself, she could see that. Maybe these days he didn't get the chance to sound off like this that often.

Maggie cleared her throat. 'It's very impressive, Mac, it really is. The way you tell it, everything's always so clear. Unambiguous. None of those infuriating shades of grey.'

'Well, sometimes that's how life is. Sometimes things really are white and black. I know you liberals love to overcomplicate things—'

'See. You did it again.'

'Did what again?'

' "White and black". Most people say "black and white". Or "life and death". Or "right and wrong". But you have this strange tic. You always do it the other way around. You and the author of the manifesto. Funny that, don't you think?'

McNamara looked at his fingernails, picking at the cuticles. He glanced up at Maggie and then back to his nails. It was the first time she'd got here that the great torrent of words had stilled, even for a few seconds.

The words were forming in her mouth: *It's you, isn't it?* But she held her tongue, and kept her eyes on him. Eventually he spoke.

'Look, there were a few of us. On one of those private forums. Password-protected, two-step verification, the whole thing. If you were a European faggot, you'd call it a *salon*.' He put the emphasis on the last syllable. 'We were trading ideas, working on language, honing arguments.'

'Who's we?'

He sighed, an errant child reluctantly confessing to his mother. 'Keane's boys. His favourites.' There was something else in that sigh, Maggie understood: wistfulness, nostalgia for an earlier, golden era when Mac was young and singled out by his charismatic teacher.

'And you're saying these writings formed the manifesto?'

'Seems that way. When I read it, I recognized chunks of it as sounding like me. Some of it sounds like Keane. Hard to tell. Maybe we all just sound like each other.' That wistfulness again. 'Maybe we all just sound like him.'

'Like Keane, you mean? Does he do that "white and black" thing too? Is that where you got it?'

Mac shrugged. *Maybe*.

'So who were the others?'

He looked up. 'I told you. Private forum. That means confidential.'

'Oh, for Christ's sake, Mac. You don't think the FBI are not going to work this out sooner or later? They'll crack open your "private forum" soon enough. And then you'll be looking at charges of conspiracy. Several people are dead, here and abroad. That's jail time.'

'I've got good lawyers, Maggie. You know that.'

She did know that. She'd had him on the hook months earlier. And yet here he was.

'So you knew that what you were writing was a manifesto for what is basically a global terrorist operation, perhaps the biggest in history?'

He looked at her with an expression she had not seen before, at least not on the face of Crawford McNamara. She guessed it was sincerity.

'I absolutely knew no such thing. None of us did. Including Keane. We were debating, we were arguing. We were perfecting the intellectual case against memory, against history. Jesus, none of us realized some looney tune was going to take the idea and *implement* it.'

'So who did, if it wasn't you?' Maggie felt a wave of frustration so strong, it was physical, a surge of bile that seemed to push through her gut and into her throat. 'Who was it?'

'I don't know.'

'Come on, Mac. It's me or Lofgren's agents. If they talk to you, they'll want a conviction. All I want is to know what the hell's going on.'

'So you can stop it?'

'Exactly.'

There was a silence between them. Oddly, it was the closest they'd come to dialogue since she'd got here.

'The truth is, I don't know who's doing it. No one in the group knows either. No one knows how they got access to the writings.'

'You're sure about that?'

'I'm sure. It's our words, I grant you. But it's not us who are . . .' The words trailed off.

'So who the fuck is it, Mac? Who?'

'I truly don't know. I can only give you one piece of advice.'

'I don't need *advice*, Mac. There are only six Alexandria libraries left in the world. Six. When they're gone, it's over. This is not some college prank any more. This is not some intellectual thought experiment, taking an idea to its logical conclusion. This is the real world. And whatever you know, you need to tell me. Otherwise, the next knock on that door is going to be Director Lofgren with a warrant for your arrest.'

'My advice to you, Maggie, is: follow the money.'

'Don't give me the Deep Throat shtick, Mac. Please.'

'I mean it. This operation is sophisticated. It will have cost big money. The technology to pull all this stuff off, hiring contract killers, if that's what they've done, none of this comes cheap. I've told you as much as I know. But if I were in your shoes, that's what I'd do. Follow the money.'

Maggie collected her things and said goodbye, carefully avoiding so much as a handshake, let alone an attempted kiss on the cheek. As she returned to her car, she reflected that Mac had ended their conversation in typical fashion: with a knowing nod to Washington folklore and nothing concrete enough to use.

And she was left with a question that, even just formulated in her head, sounded absurd: could she trust a word he had said? If he was involved, if that manifesto was his, would he admit it? His ego was enormous, but he was not stupid. Even his parting observation – that the Alexandria operation would be costing big money – was as incriminating as it was exonerating. McNamara used to be a senior figure in the administration, the former lead strategist and continuing close counsel to a president who, by his own admission, was the chief warrior against the truth. If it came to it, who had deeper pockets and bigger reach than the US government itself? Once she'd have dismissed that thought as deranged paranoia. Now she ruled nothing out.

She checked her phone. There was a breaking news alert: *Reports of serious fire at National Library of Mexico in Mexico City.* She went to the library's website and, sure enough, there they were, five green bottles, hanging on the wall.

A few routine emails and then one from a woman whose name she didn't recognize. The subject line was *Operation Florian.*

Maggie clicked it open and read it twice before she had absorbed its meaning.

I know who wrote the manifesto that's on the internet. I know because he's my son.

Thursday

Chapter Thirty-Four

The following podcast contains explicit language.

Welcome to the gabfest, where we are talking about a development that has only now come to light – a lethal fire at an Amazon warehouse, or 'fulfilment centre', in Kenosha, Wisconsin. The company waited several hours before revealing information about the fire, which at first was said to be an accident but which is now known to have been an act of arson by an employee or an 'associate', to use Amazon's preferred term, who lost his own life as a result. Emily, what's this all about?

You know what, David, I admit I'm confused by this story. At first, I was, like, 'OK, it's a fire at a warehouse. That happens.' But the fact that the company seems to have changed their story—

A complete one-eighty—

Right. So that's kind of fishy. But just given everything else that's going on, it does make you wonder if perhaps—

Perhaps, what?

Well, if perhaps it's related to the Operation Florian story.

You know, I can see why people might think that. Sorry, I interrupted you, Emily.

John, you go ahead and then back to Emily.

Well, I get why people might see a connection. Like, here are all these fires in libraries all over the world and suddenly there's a serious fire at Amazon—

In the books *area of the warehouse. The books!*

I know, and I get that. But the logic doesn't quite work here. You see, what we know – just from the targets so far – is that whoever is behind this has a very clear objective. It's indefensible, but it is clear. They want to take out the twelve core libraries of the world. And, this is a slight tangent, but let me just say, that's a smart choice: because the Alexandria Group really does cover the core documents of human history. You take them out, you deal a fatal blow to the global historical record.

Remember, John, we don't do endorsements on this podcast.

That's a low blow, David.

We're strictly non-partisan! We're always aware you have a choice of homicidal arsonist murderers!

Guys, come on.

OK, all right. Finish your point, John.

I'm just saying, on the Bookburner's own logic, targeting these major deposit libraries makes sense. But on that same logic, hitting Amazon – even the books section of the warehouse – does not fit at all. Because there were no canonical documents stored in Kenosha, Wisconsin! There were no original, precious texts. There were, like, stacks of recipe books and Martha Stewart and self-help and vegan diets and Harry Potter which – no disrespect, I love all those books—

Especially the vegan diet—

Love them all. But the point is, it's kind of whack-a-mole. You burn one crate of Trusting Your Inner You *and there's, like, another gazillion copies in a warehouse somewhere else. So it doesn't achieve anything. It doesn't deplete the sum total of human knowledge by even a single microgram.*

Unless—

All right, Emily, you come in here.

I was just going to say, John's right. It does seem pointless to burn a bunch of books in an Amazon warehouse—

Fulfilment centre.

At an Amazon fulfilment centre *unless, that is, your aim is to . . . Well, let me back up here. There's two ways this might be connected to the Florian stuff. First, it could just be a copycat thing. So there's a bunch of libraries on fire, everyone's seen the pictures on TV, and some guy working the night shift in Kenosha thinks—*

'That looks fucking cool.'

Right. So kind of on a whim, he just sets fire to a stack of books. And kills himself in the process. So that's one way it could be connected.

Like school shootings.

Exactly. The copycat effect. We know that exists. And that could be a danger going forward. So it's not nothing.

All right. And what's the other way this could be connected, Emily?

Well, this may seem a stretch, but hear me out. Let's say you really were determined to wipe out human knowledge, like the manifesto says. It wouldn't be enough just to wipe out a few big libraries.

And their digital databases. Don't forget those.

Sure. But even that wouldn't be enough. You'd basically want to stop people reading books. And so let's say this incident in Kenosha is not the only one. You saw that report out of Staffordshire, England? Another fire in the 'fulfilment centre' there too. Also in the books department, as it happens. So what if this is a concerted effort? What if this keeps happening? My guess is that, at some point, somebody at Amazon corporate headquarters says, 'Guys, I've run the numbers. I've done the math, and it's just not worth it. The money we make from books is just not worth the risk.'

So you're talking about a deterrent effect?

Or a chilling effect. But yes, basically. Do you remember with Salman Rushdie and the fatwa and all that? There were attacks on publishing offices and, like, a translator got killed?

The Japanese translator.

Yep. And for a while there, people were thinking maybe this isn't worth it. The price is too high. And that was about publishing one book. So what if whoever is doing this wants the entire book industry to come to the same conclusion? You know, this is too risky.

You're getting all that from one fire?

Well, there's now been two at Amazon. And there have been petrol bombs thrown at bookshops in Utah and in Chicago yesterday. And in Turin. And two in France.

So you're saying this is a plot to eliminate all books?

I don't know. We don't know yet, do we? But we didn't know about Florian at all until a few hours ago. None of us had heard of the Bookburner and his manifesto either. So I think this might be part of it.

David, can I ask a question?

Go ahead, John.

Wouldn't this make sense only if the Bookburner planned to get every last bookshop? Like, if a copy of, I don't know, Great Expectations *still exists somewhere, then that book still exists. So I suppose I come back to my question. What would be the point?*

I think, John, you might be being too literal.

That is a very frequent criticism levelled in my direction, I grant you.

No, no, you're brilliant in every way. What I mean is, you really don't have to destroy every single copy. If there are fewer books around, if it becomes really hard to get hold of Great Expectations, *if only one copy exists behind a glass case in a museum somewhere, you know, under armed guard and you can't even get it online because the digital back-up has been destroyed and Google is so wrecked you couldn't even find it anyway, well, in that sense the book does gradually cease to exist. It begins to fall out of our collective memory.*

Look, I hate to be the voice of doom on this podcast – again! – but if this steps up, if there are more arson attacks on bookshops and libraries, if not just Amazon but everyone gets out of the book business, well, pretty soon, the Bookburner will have got his way. It may not happen overnight, it may take some time. But bit by bit we'll be chipping away at the sum of human knowledge, in the sense of what human beings actually know. And I got to tell you, that scares the living shit out of me.

Chapter Thirty-Five

Cleveland, Ohio, 8.57am

There was a line of bottles on a wall. None of them was green. Instead they were clear and empty.

Maggie could see that something or someone was just behind them, but through the glass it was impossible to make out more than a vague shape. She got closer but the image was still hazy, distorted by the glass. And the closer she got, the more the bottles began to wobble, trembling, the way they would if they were being held in an unsteady hand. She got nearer, readying herself to catch the first one that fell.

A bottle did fall, but it was not the one she expected. She tried to reach it, but was too late. Then another one went, and she missed that one too. And then another. And another. Until, eventually, all but one of the bottles were gone.

Now she could see who was behind the wall. It was her mother, her mouth stretched in a wide, wild smile and her eyes crazed. Maggie looked down and she saw her baby sister, crawling on the floor, splinters of glass piercing her skin . . .

Maggie jerked awake, her chest thudding into the steering wheel. She opened her eyes wide in panic, bracing for the sight of oncoming traffic, and heard her heart thump for two beats, then three, before understanding that the car was still. That it remained where she had parked it last night, on a quiet residential street in the Garfield Heights neighbourhood of Cleveland. Outside the local branch of the Cuyahoga County Public Library, in fact. (She figured that a woman sleeping in her car would arouse less interest outside a public building than in front of someone's house.)

'Last night' was not quite accurate. She had pulled in at around six o'clock this morning, having driven solidly through the small hours, save for a ten-minute nap at a rest stop, interrupted by instinct as a couple of truckers approached, exhibiting a bit too much interest in the redheaded woman curled up alone in the driver's seat of a stationary car.

She was still in the grip of that dream. It had come from somewhere deep in her subconscious, dragging with it memories and pain she had buried so long ago she had almost forgotten them. Almost. She remembered the Friday deadline hanging over her: Liz's next session with her therapist.

She pulled out her phone and looked again at the email that had arrived last night.

I know who wrote the manifesto that's on the internet. I know because he's my son.

It had come from a woman named Edith Kelly. At the bottom of the email she had put an address: Shady Lanes Retirement Home, Cleveland, Ohio. That would fit: anyone old enough to be a parent of one of Keane's former students at Stanford would be in their seventies or eighties by now.

What gave Maggie pause as she sat in the driver's seat was a more basic question, one she had chewed over through the long night's drive. Why would this woman have contacted Maggie? The *Times* and *Post* had both given the number of an FBI hotline for people to call with information. Why hadn't she called that?

How she'd got Maggie's email address was, unfortunately, no mystery. The big news websites that had run the fake emails purportedly from Maggie had been careful to redact her email address from the screenshots they'd run. But others had not been so diligent. Her contact details were out there now, a fact confirmed by the barrage of garbage, abuse and pornographic fantasy that had been filling her inbox over the last twenty-four hours.

Still, if this were genuine, why would an elderly lady sitting in an old people's home get in touch with Maggie when she could contact the FBI itself? A couple of stories had linked Maggie's name to Florian, but why would she—

Of course. *Kelly*.

She could hear her nan's voice. *Call me all the names you like, Margaret, but sometimes it's nice to talk to one of your own.*

It was that thought that took root once Maggie had followed her gut and decided not to wait for a dawn flight, but to get in her car and make the six-hour drive from Washington to the heart of the American Midwest.

Maggie opened the car door and got out, stretching wide. The details of her dream were already slipping from her grasp, but the sensation of it lingered. The powerlessness, the inability to do anything about . . .

It was just after nine am. Maggie could see that the library was opening. Through the tall glass of the entrance she glimpsed a woman unbolting the door, then poking her head out and looking left and right. *Even here*, Maggie thought. Even here, at a suburban Midwestern library – where kids would come for reading class and retirees might come to flick through a magazine or borrow a detective story or romance – even here they were frightened. Books had become dangerous. Merely to be in possession of the printed word now posed a mortal threat.

Maggie attempted to straighten herself out, tugging at her top in a feeble effort at removing the creases. Posture, she decided, would have to do the rest. If she walked in confidently – head up, shoulders back – she might just succeed in looking like a woman who had not slept in her clothes. In her car.

She did just that, eyeing the sign for the bathroom as soon as she was inside. There she splashed water on her face and did her best to freshen up. She found some rudimentary make-up in her bag and applied it. Never had concealer been more aptly named.

When she emerged she caught the eye of the librarian one more time, who was standing as stiff as a sentry at the 'returns' desk. The poor woman looked terrified.

Maggie got back in the car and prepared to make the five-minute drive to Shady Lanes.

The local NPR station was broadcasting the news from the BBC.

. . . the grief here is palpable, with many Egyptians weeping openly on the streets. This man tells me Cairo is the birthplace of civilization. To lose the Dar al-Kotob, the National Library and Archives, he says, is like 'ripping the heart out of the Arab world'.

So now, thought Maggie, it was four green bottles, hanging on the wall.

There's disbelief here that this could happen, not least because the library was under twenty-four-hour armed guard by the Egyptian military. Among the treasures believed to have been lost in the fire are an estimated fifty-seven thousand of the oldest, most valuable manuscripts in the world, including several parchment texts of the Koran, some of them inscribed by renowned practitioners of the art of Islamic calligraphy. The library held illuminated manuscripts, Arabic papyri that were nearly fifteen hundred years old, Arabic coins from the same period, as well as ancient marriage certificates, tax records and land contracts. It was, says the library's director, the 'record of an entire world'. And now it is gone.

How on earth were they getting past armed guards to burn these libraries? What kind of sorcery was this Bookburner capable of?

There followed an interview with an Oxford professor of medieval Islamic history, who described himself as heartbroken.

He talked about the specific loss of Cairo, and the significance of an attack on the Alexandria Group member closest to the ancient city that gave those dozen libraries their name. 'It's fair to say that Egypt never really did recover from the fire that destroyed the library of Alexandria nearly two thousand years ago. There are some cultural losses that can never be made good again.'

Then he broadened out, his sorrow turning to anger. 'When you look at what's happened around the world, and when you consider what's been lost – the human race has destroyed in a matter of days what took our ancestors many centuries, millennia really, to build up. I know this is not a war or a genocide, where millions of people are killed. But this is one of the greatest tragedies in human history. They are destroying unique documents that have no copy. They are destroying the digital back-ups. It seems that whoever is doing this is determined that there will be nothing left. We won't remember our past at all.'

Maggie pulled out her phone to check the address for the retirement home. Twitter was abuzz with the publication of the Bookburner's manifesto, with everyone suddenly an expert on counter-terrorism. She saw that Mac had weighed in, condemning the *Times* and the *Post* for the ethics of their decision. *Americans of all generations, old and young, will be appalled by this move – the liberal media insist on acting as enablers to those who wish us harm.* Those in favour of publication commanded much less firepower. Typical was the tweet that came from the woman Maggie had seen vainly try to hold the middle ground during that debate at Georgetown. According to Pamela Bentham of the Bentham Center for Free Speech: *In moments of crisis, free expression makes us safer. Airing this "manifesto" should enable both citizens and leaders to make better informed decisions.*

Maggie paid more attention to a report from the *Post*'s London correspondent, saying that the Alexandria project was now the focus of unprecedented global co-operation among intelligence agencies. *In Downing Street, the "Cobra" group of ministers and officials is meeting twice daily, hoping to protect Britain's libraries after the loss of the Bodleian and lending what support they can to counterparts overseas. As to identifying a perpetrator, the authorities admit privately that they have made little concrete progress.*

Maggie set off, arriving just as soon as the app on her phone said she would. As she parked up, she wondered whether Edith Kelly would prove to be a delusional fantasist or the woman who might just stop the world being robbed of its past.

If ever there were a slamdunk candidate for prosecution under truth in advertising laws, 'retirement homes' were surely it. The names alone were almost always a lie. 'Sunny Side' would turn out to be a battery cage for the elderly, permanently shrouded in cloud. 'Sea View' would be a barracks, housing the aged in a penitentiary whose only glimpse of the ocean would come from the twenty-four/seven TV sets permanently tuned to the Weather Channel. And though they would always claim to be a 'community', too often they consisted of individuals seeing out their last days in atomized solitude.

In other words, Maggie Costello had low expectations of Shady Lanes. Expectations which turned out to be wrong.

This was a cluster of low-rise, one- or two-person units set in landscaped gardens surrounding a reservoir. There were signs here and there, pointing out the birdlife that had been lured back to the area by means of reedbeds and marshes. The reservoir was circled, and the buildings linked, by narrow pathways, just wide enough for a couple to walk two abreast or for a mobility scooter. Maggie thought of her own mother and how she might have liked it here. Maybe.

Edith Kelly also confounded expectations. Sitting on a lawn chair in front of her ground-floor apartment, its compact verandah behind her, she was not the wizened old Irish lady Maggie had decided upon en route here. Instead, she was tall and agile, leaping to her feet when Maggie arrived, shaking her hand firmly. Her hair was white, but her first words on seeing Maggie were, 'A redhead, just like me. Back in the day.'

She explained that she was an avid consumer of news, had been even when her husband, Terence, God rest his soul, was alive, but especially these days: 'You have to be, don't you, love?' Her accent was New York via County Cork. Maggie felt like she was visiting an aunt.

She had seen the stories about Maggie, both the emails and that awful business with the pornography. 'I tell you, I wouldn't be young now for all the tea in China. Much harder for all of you than it was for us, love.'

And then she had read the manifesto. 'I'm not saying I understand every word in it, because I don't. But I read enough to hear his voice. Not how he spoke when he grew up and lived under our roof, mind, but how he talked after he'd been off to college. How he spoke, how he wrote. How he *thought*.'

'You're talking about your son.'

'That's right. Martin.'

Maggie decided to say as little as she could. She would sit and listen and assess. She reminded herself that the right starting point for such a conversation was, to quote William Keane, radical scepticism. For one thing, as soon as the scale of this threat had become clear to her, Maggie had assumed that this was not the work of a lone individual – how could it be? – but that of an organized, collective operation. For another, it would have required enormous resources: men capable of burning landmark buildings to the ground without detection did not come cheap, and nor did the contract killers who had doubtless been hired to murder the likes of Russell Aikman in Charlottesville or Judith Beaton in London.

So for all those reasons, Maggie's working presumption was that Edith Kelly was a liar or seriously disturbed – and she would wait to be proved wrong.

'Going on about the Garden of Eden, and talking about God as if he doesn't exist one minute, as if he does the next, and you're never quite sure, and all those fancy names, the experts and the writers, quoting this one and that one. When I read that on my iPad here,' she gestured towards it, 'it sounded like Martin was at the dinner table all over again. It was like he was right here talking to me.'

'And have you told him this?'

'What, *Martin*? I have not.'

'Because you're frightened of how he might react?'

'Because I haven't spoken to him in eleven years.'

'Oh. I see.'

'No. No, you really don't.'

In the silence that followed, Maggie sat back and signalled that she was ready to listen, without interruption.

'Martin was our only child. Imagine that, a Catholic family with just one. But that's what the Good Lord intended and so that's how it was. But my word, what a clever child he was. The cleverest boy in his class. I know every mother says that, but it happens to be true. This is when we lived in the city and there was no shortage of clever boys there. But Martin, we wondered if he was, you know, some kind of genius. Terry, my husband Terence, was convinced Martin would be president one day. I never thought that for one single moment. Never. He was far too shy. And he was a thin-skinned child. Hated being teased. He went on Scout camp in the summer, but I'm not sure he ever fitted in.

'But Stanford! Well, that seemed to be the making of him. He was captivated by it. Especially by this man, Keane. It was "Professor Keane says this" and "Professor Keane says that". Terry didn't like it. I think he was jealous. But I was pleased. To see Martin grow like that, to see him spread his wings and soar. I thought it was wonderful, to be quite honest with you.'

Maggie nodded and smiled, topping up Edith's glass with some water from the jug. Solicitous, interested, kind: Maggie was playing the Irish daughter-in-law-to-be.

'Well, we all took it for granted that after Stanford – graduating summa cum laude, if you don't mind – Martin would write his own ticket. He could do whatever he liked. But for some reason, things didn't quite gel, if you know what I mean. He'd apply for jobs and he'd get them, but then he'd walk out in a huff. Or he'd have a fight with the boss.'

'An argument, you mean?'

'No, I mean a fight. With his fists.' She held up her clenched hands, to demonstrate. 'I think he had what these days they'd call "anger management issues".'

'And this was in California?'

'Yes. At first. He said he wanted to be near Professor Keane, so he hung around Stanford a year or two. While Keane was still there. I didn't think that was healthy.'

'The attachment to Keane?'

'Sticking around his old college. Like he was Peter Pan. Eternal student. "Time to move on, Martin," I'd say. His father too. "Come on, Martin, time to grow up." But he didn't want to leave. I wouldn't care, but it's not like he had so many friends there.'

'At Stanford?'

'Yes. I mean, don't get me wrong, there was a tight group. That history class. Keane's class. Martin would mention all the names, this one and that one. But I was never convinced that the feeling was mutual, if you get my meaning.'

'You weren't sure that—'

'I suppose I began to worry that Martin was a bit of a loner. Like he was on the outside looking in or something.' She was gazing into the middle distance now, watching a swan at the water's edge. 'Anyway, he was drifting. He would pick up something, then drop it. He would learn everything there was to learn about computers and Terence and I would get our hopes up – "Pet, maybe this will be his calling, you know?" – but then he'd be disappointed or get bored, I don't know what. Such a bright boy.'

'And was he in touch with Professor Keane in this period?'

'I don't know. But he still talked about him plenty. The few times he came home. Though he came less and less often. And when he was here he started saying some strange stuff, winding up his father something rotten.'

'Like what?'

'He got into these conspiracy theories. "Everyone's lying. What you think is true, Mom, is almost never true." '

'What kind of things? JFK? The moon landings? That sort of thing?'

'9/11: that was the main one. Hours he would spend on his computer, examining pictures of this side of the building, or that joist. Terry was in construction, you know. A foreman. He told Martin he was talking nonsense, but Martin wouldn't listen. He knew best.

'That was the last straw, for Terry. You see, Terry's brother . . . he lost his brother in the towers. Michael, his name was. Terry's brother. He was a fireman. Firefighter, you're meant to say now, aren't you? Well, that's what he did. And of course he rushed down there like the rest of them. Only, he was one of those who went back in.' The old lady's eyes were starting to glitter.

'Well, one day, Martin went too far, talking about the second tower and the "explosions" and that. "It's all a lie," he was saying. "The government staged a great big hoax and you all fell for it." '

'Well, you can imagine. Terence had the rage of Samson himself boiling up in him. "How dare you say that," he said. "You take that back, for the sake of your Uncle Michael, may God rest his soul." And then Martin looks at him, his own father, and says, "Uncle Michael wasn't a hero. He was an extra in a fucking movie." Pardon my language, Maggie. But that's what Martin says, to his father's face. Well, Terry slaps him hard and Martin punches him straight back. Just like that. Knocks him out cold. And then he walks out and I've not seen him from that day to this.'

Maggie sipped her own glass of water and let Edith Kelly collect herself. She knew more was coming.

'After that, I picked up the odd fag-end here and there. That's all. No more letters, no phone calls. Even after Terry died. But reading that manifesto last night, I tell you: it was like I had a long letter from him. Like I was holding it in my hands.'

'The way it was written?'

'It *sounded* like him. Do you know what I mean? Just the way he talked. Crazy and so sure of himself, and so convinced that heaven was around the corner. That line about returning to the Garden of Eden? I can hear him saying it. And numbering every point? "Eleven . . . Thirty-four . . . One hundred and thirty-one." Martin did that. In his letters, and he used to send me *long* letters. But he even did it when he was talking.'

'So you're sure?'

'I wish I wasn't. It's a terrible thing to believe your own flesh and blood, the child you fed from your own breast, is capable of such wickedness. But I know it, Maggie. I know it.'

'How do you know?'

'Because everything in that document is what Martin wanted most. A fresh start. A chance to start over. I know he's talking in that manifesto about society and the human race and all that. But I think that's what Martin wanted for himself. Every time he started a new job, he'd say it: "A clean slate. I want to wipe the slate clean." It's insane and it's evil, but I think that's what my son thinks he's giving the world.'

Maggie nodded quietly and then, in a gesture that surprised herself, she reached out and placed a hand on the older woman's hand. As if Edith Kelly were a Dublin aunt, grieving at a wake.

The next few minutes were taken up with practical questions. Did she know where Martin lived now? His last known address? His email or cellphone?

Finally: would Edith allow Maggie to share this information with the federal authorities, even if that meant Martin would be arrested and perhaps, eventually, charged with these crimes?

'I've been thinking of nothing else since six o'clock this morning. I've been asking myself, what would Terry say.'

'And what would he say?'

'He'd say, "What do *you* think, love?"' She smiled. 'And maybe he'd say we should ask the priest.'

'And have you done that?'

She made a face. 'What, ask advice from that slip of a lad who calls himself the chaplain here? You must be joking. He's younger than you are, no disrespect, and the only thing he knows how to do is the last rites. Mind you, in this place he gets plenty of practice.' A mischievous smile.

'So what did you decide?'

'I decided that I'm a mother and the last thing a mother should ever do is betray her own child. Her only child.'

Maggie could feel her shoulders slump.

'But,' Edith continued, 'this can't only be about my feelings. There are other mothers involved here too. The mothers of those historians killed in cold blood, those librarians, who died trying to save their collections. Those survivors of all those terrible wars, the Holocaust and what have you. And they're just the ones who've been killed already. What about the others who are going to get killed today or next week? Those mothers' feelings matter too. In what way, exactly, would I be doing my duty as a mother if I shield Martin, and that means all those other mothers' children die? You don't need to be a priest to see that that's not right. So, yes. You tell the FBI what I know.'

Maggie nodded.

'But will you do me one small favour, Maggie?'

'Of course.'

'Will you ask them not to be too rough with him? I don't know exactly what he's done, but he's not as tough as he seems, whatever he likes to say. The truth is, he's a gentle boy.'

As Maggie said goodbye, she was filled with the urge to praise Edith Kelly for her wisdom, for her act of human generosity, for her selflessness. She also wanted to give her a hug, as she guessed what pain she was about to endure. But instead she asked one last question.

'Edith, you never told me. Before you retired, did you work?' The woman nodded. 'Can I ask what you did?'

'Oh, I thought you might have guessed that one. Most people do, from the way I go on. But maybe it's not as obvious now as it once was. I was a teacher, Maggie. I taught history.'

Chapter Thirty-Six

FBI headquarters, Washington DC, 6.35pm

There was the real one and there was a fake one. This was the real one. The giveaway was the absence of cameras.

Over at 1600 Pennsylvania Avenue, the president and a few handpicked senior White House aides, all but one of them men, along with a couple of generals in uniform, were gathered in the Situation Room. The president was at the head of the cramped conference table, naturally, and his gaze, like that of the other dozen or so crammed around him, fixed straight ahead. They all appeared to be staring at a TV screen.

Maggie knew all this because she could see it. It was being televised and live-streamed online, by direct order of the president. 'It'll make great TV,' he had said. 'The ratings will be sky high.'

Which explained the presence of the uniforms. Of course the operation now unfolding in Montana, which they were watching so avidly on the Situation Room screens, had nothing to do with the army or any other branch of the military. But the president wanted them there anyway. For the pictures.

'They look the part,' he had explained.

The military were not involved, because this was an FBI show, directed and run from FBI headquarters. Which was why the real event was here, in the Director's office. As it happened, here too they were gathered around a conference table, though it was slightly larger than the one in the Situation Room where, Maggie remembered well, your knees would touch those of the person opposite and you really hoped everyone had brought a supply of breath mints. Here too the tableau may have borne an uncanny resemblance to *that* image of an anxious president and his team watching a faraway raid by an elite unit, but in this case that similarity was entirely coincidental. Craig Lofgren was not staging this session for the cameras. This was for real.

'Can you get closer on the aerial image, or improve the resolution maybe?' the Director was asking. Instantly the central image on the video wall opposite began to change. Still bordered by a set of white lines and numbers – time of day, precise GPS co-ordinates – it now zoomed closer, so that Lofgren, Maggie and the rest of the command team of Operation Florian could see in precise detail what was on the roof of the isolated Montana cabin – hidden deep in the Coeur d'Alene National Forest, far off Route 200 – which Martin Kelly had called home for the last nine years. Unmistakable was the sight of an oversized satellite dish, perhaps the only means by which someone in that part of the rural, remote northwest could have high-grade access to the internet.

Andrea Ellis gave Maggie a glance which, despite its brevity, signalled affirmation. *See the size of that thing? You weren't wrong, Maggie.*

That Maggie was here at all was proof that Andrea's view was now the official one. Once Maggie had called the Deputy Director with what she had – the testimony of Kelly's mother, validated by his presence on the Stanford alumni list – her transition from outcast to trusted member of the team was swift. She was put on the first flight out of Cleveland and told not to worry about her car.

It turned out that the tech team had been running the manifesto through the linguistic pattern recognition software, comparing the text with everything ever published online, and had narrowed the search down to a few hundred possibilities, but they had not yet lighted upon Martin Kelly. The trouble was, he had written so little that was available on the internet – a mere fraction of the number of words he had used in the hundreds of letters he had sent his mother, at least until they had broken off all contact. The computer barely had enough to go on. Once the machines had his name, of course they could see the match straight away. It was unmistakable. Once they'd found their needle, they knew it was theirs. But knowing where in the haystack, where in the millions of haystacks, to look, that had been Maggie's achievement.

Maggie was happy to take the credit, if that meant rejoining the hunt for the Bookburner. But in truth, she knew that the person they – America and the world – needed to thank was Edith Kelly. It somehow warmed Maggie to think that, in this world of algorithms and artificial intelligence, it was a mother's love, with its unique intensity, that had seen what the machines could not.

What about the money? That had been Maggie's first question. But the Bureau team had an answer to that too. Preliminary analysis of online activity traced to Kelly's cabin suggested manipulation of the crypto-currency market. 'Enough to amass some serious cash,' as Ellis put it.

There was a crackle on the speaker placed in the centre of the table. 'This is gold command. Awaiting your order, sir.' One of the nine screens on the video wall indicated that the gold team was in the woods east of Kelly's cabin. 'This is red command. Awaiting your order, sir.' They were behind the cabin, close to a stream. And finally: 'This is black command. Awaiting your order, sir.' Those were the agents directly in front, the ones who would charge through Kelly's front door.

Maggie saw Lofgren swallow, a motion visible chiefly because of his effort to hide it. 'This is Director Lofgren,' he said. 'Do it.'

There was then a cacophony of voices, several of them saying, 'We are a go, we are a go.'

Maggie watched the raid unfold from multiple angles, her gaze mostly focused on the images provided by black command, doubtless from cameras attached to their helmets, as they rammed the door. A second later the screen showed Kelly, in boxer shorts and a T-shirt, instantly fling his arms up in the air in a gesture of abject surrender. (That, Maggie thought, will be the image that goes around the world.) He had been at a desk, on a computer: online and yet utterly unaware of the fate that was about to befall him.

Now Maggie saw the federal agents, helmeted, encased in bulletproof vests and armed with semi-automatic weapons as they moved to surround Kelly. At a guess, there seemed to be at least twenty of them jammed into the tiny space of this one-room cabin, with perhaps eight guns pointed directly at the man in his boxer shorts.

But then Kelly made a sudden movement, reaching with his right arm back to the desk. In almost that same instant, he fell forward – a move that happened so fast it took Maggie, and apparently everyone else in this room, a second or two to realize what had happened. Confirmation came from the voice on the radio.

'This is black command. The suspect is down, repeat the suspect is down.'

The room around her seemed stunned into silence. Lofgren took off his glasses, closed his eyes and rubbed the bridge of his nose. Maggie's gaze remained fixed on the screen, where the cabin seemed to have erupted into controlled pandemonium. Paramedics were now jammed into the small room, so that it was thoroughly congested, as packed as a subway train filled with bulked-up soldier-agents, the letters 'FBI' huge on their backs. The medics were trying to clear a space, but even from this distance, even from three thousand miles away, it was obvious: Martin Kelly was dead.

Maggie looked over to Andrea Ellis. She mouthed a suggestion. 'Get them to find what he was looking for.'

Ellis mouthed back. 'What?'

Maggie leaned in, so that she was whispering distance from the Deputy Director. 'He was reaching for something. They thought it was a gun. But it was something else. See if they can find it.' Ellis nodded and turned to Lofgren.

Maggie's eyes returned to the monitor. It was hard to see through and beyond that thicket of people, forming a perverse guard of honour for Kelly's stretchered body, but what Maggie could make out struck her.

The room was simple, monastic even. A metal-framed single bed; a table which seemed to serve a double function as a desk; a stiff, wooden chair. There was no bathroom she could see; perhaps Kelly used the stream out back. There were no pictures on the walls, and yet they were covered in colour.

It took her a while to work out what she was looking at, but when a couple of the agents filed out, she got a clearer view. Almost every inch of available floor space was filled with tottering piles, wobbling columns, of books. Apparently Martin Kelly, the Bookburner, had decided he could live without running water, without human company, without a cupboard for his clothes – but that he could not live without books.

Chapter Thirty-Seven

FBI headquarters, Washington DC, 7.08pm

Maggie stood towards the back as she listened to Craig Lofgren praise the 'team effort and professionalism that made today possible'. The Director did not hint at his disappointment, but everyone present knew this was not the outcome he had wanted. Much better to apprehend a prime suspect alive rather than dead. But still, he wanted to acknowledge those who had 'removed the threat which the FBI concluded Martin Kelly posed to the nation and the world'.

There was a smattering of applause in Maggie's direction when the Director said, 'We would not be here were it not for the tenacity and ingenuity of one individual who is not even a member of the Bureau: Maggie Costello.' She tried to feign a smile, even though all she could see was the face of Edith Kelly and all she could hear were the words the old lady had left her with: *Will you ask them not to be too rough with him? The truth is, he's a gentle boy.*

Maggie dipped her head to recognize those who applauded

her, even though she knew those same people would have crossed the street to avoid her twenty-four hours earlier. Those same people who had sniggered, or worse, when they thought they had seen her naked and on her back in a #sextape.

She had also listened politely as a huddle had watched the president address the nation on television, his live statement intercut with still photographs of himself in the Situation Room, apparently commanding the operation to 'bring Kelly to justice', as the White House statement euphemistically referred to his death. She had clocked the fleeting side-eye she received from Andrea Ellis when the president said, 'People said we wouldn't find the guy behind these terrible crimes. Horrible crimes. But I found him and I took him out.' The team around her were too self-disciplined to groan audibly at that.

Her phone buzzed with the arrival of a text, associated with a list of numbers she once again could only guess at. She clicked on it.

M, I know you understand why we had to do what we did. But I couldn't be more grateful. I owe you a great debt of gratitude. D.

Maggie registered the 'we' for the bitter pill and the 'I' for the sugar coating. Politicians, even ones who used to be your friends: they couldn't help themselves.

It was during all this, not twenty minutes after the fatal raid in Montana, that word came through of the fire at the National Library of Iran, the largest library campus in the Middle East. As Maggie headed back to her apartment, she listened to the talking heads – the audio of cable TV, carried on the radio – as they reassured their audiences that this latest development did not undermine in any way the significance of Kelly's 'elimination'.

There's a delay, a time lag, if you will, in these things. Clearly, this was a huge undertaking masterminded by Kelly and he'd have set some of these wheels in motion days, weeks or even months ago. Of course, those wheels will still be turning for a day or two longer. That's perfectly natural.

I think that's right, Kirsten. It's not like, say, a serial killer where, once you get the guy, the murders stop. This was clearly a vast operation and law enforcement sources are certainly clear in telling this network that they would always expect some 'momentum' in a situation like this. This is not denting their confidence in any way. Besides, and this is new reporting this hour, they are already looking closely at financial transactions involving Kelly, bank transfers and the like which put the Montana recluse at the centre of a global network of—

Because of course the question of financial resources has been a big one here, right? However Kelly organized this thing, it would have cost a lot of money.

That's right. So this new information could supply that missing piece of the puzzle . . .

Maggie went back to her phone, scrolling through the texts. *I bet you had something to do with this*, from Liz. *I knew you'd do it*, from Uri.

She looked at Twitter. The Iran news – complete with graphic now showing just three green bottles – had set off yet another argument about jihadist violence. One camp said the destruction of a library in Tehran, a world capital of Islamism, was further proof that 'radical Islamist terror' had not played any role in this wave of terror. Others denounced such thinking as moronic: surely it was obvious that this was a Sunni attack on Shia Islam, whose global centre was Tehran. That latter group further subdivided into two camps, one that believed that evidence would soon emerge showing that Kelly had recently converted to Sunni Islam and had been radicalized online, and another that insisted the hermit in the Montana cabin was clearly a fall guy for a larger, more shadowy conspiracy.

None of it persuaded Maggie and yet something didn't feel right. Part of it was the notion of a lone wolf, an oddball, like Kelly, at the centre of such an accomplished and advanced global enterprise. The picture Edith Kelly had sketched of her son made clear that he was smart, dogmatic and, potentially, violent. But did that make him plausible as a criminal mastermind, funnelling cash and instructions around the globe? She wasn't sure.

And part of it was the whispered exchange she'd had with Andrea Ellis as she'd left. Ellis had explained that she was not getting 'full co-operation' from the agents involved in the raid on Kelly's cabin. She suspected they were covering their traces in the matter of his shooting. She had, however, received a tip, as yet unconfirmed, that in his final seconds Kelly had not been reaching for a weapon at all, but for a black notebook held in his desk drawer. Before Maggie had a chance to speak, Andrea told her that of course she was getting the notebook fully analyzed, but so far the handwriting it contained was 'barely legible'.

Maggie pushed her apartment door open and felt her foot catch on something as she walked in. She looked down and saw a large envelope, unaddressed and unstamped. She picked it up, shook it and, unaccountably, held it to her ear. It did not rattle.

She didn't dare risk falling onto the sofa: once down, she'd never get up. So she headed to the kitchen, poured herself a shot of Ardbeg and, still standing, though with her bottom resting on the kitchen counter, she opened the envelope.

Inside was a photograph. It was a group portrait, in landscape format, like a team photo. It was black and white, the resolution furry. Maggie wondered if it was a reproduction: a photo of a photo.

Judging from the hairstyles, this was from the mid-eighties. At the centre was a face she recognized.

She looked back in the envelope and was relieved to see another sheet, more relieved still when she saw that it was a handwritten note from Uri.

Took a while, but here it is. Keane's class, plus a few others, Stanford 1986. Not nailed everyone yet, but I'm getting there.

She turned the sheet over to see that Uri had provided an extended caption, identifying those in the picture: *back row, left to right . . .*

Maggie scanned the names, confirming that the familiar face dead centre was, indeed, a young or younger William Keane. In the bottom corner, three from the right, and staring straight ahead, was Martin Kelly.

She thought of his mother, sitting alone in that room in the

Shady Lanes retirement home. What torture was she putting herself through now? If she had not emailed Maggie, her son would be alive now. If Maggie had not made that call to Andrea Ellis . . .

His face stared out. While the others were smiling and basking in what looked like summer sunshine, Kelly seemed detached from the others. Had he set himself apart? Or had they rejected him, the son of a New York construction worker disdained by all these Ivy League prodigies?

As she pictured Stanford in the eighties, Maggie's eye was caught by another familiar face. Jesus, he'd changed. There he was, with a full head of hair. He looked cynical even then, his smile knowing. He was standing just a couple of places away from Keane. A young, lean Crawford McNamara.

Hardly any women, Maggie noticed. A couple of gorgeous young things, a cool customer in shades, a bluestocking in Coke-bottle glasses. She consulted the caption. Uri had found names for two of them, but nothing that Maggie recognized. They'd be middle-aged women now, Maggie reflected. And they clearly hadn't been at the centre of the action then.

It was brilliant work by Uri, and utterly typical of him. His documentaries always won praise for their archive footage; somehow he was able to find pictures that eluded everyone else. He'd done it again.

More than that, though, he was signalling that she was not alone, that she had an ally. Forget roses or chocolates or candlelit dinners. To her, exhausted to the point of hallucination, the hand-delivery of this photograph, and the work that would have unearthed it, seemed the most romantic gesture she could imagine.

Her plan was to look closely at the picture in the morning, guided by Mac's advice to follow the money. But the thought of Mac brought back something else he had said, albeit with less of a flourish.

He had been talking about his fellow students of William Keane, how they had stayed in touch. *On one of those private forums. Password-protected, two-step verification, the whole thing. If you were a European faggot, you'd call it a salon. We were trading ideas, working on language, honing arguments.*

She reached for her phone, found the text from Liz and used it to dial her number.

'Can I ask your help with something techie?'

'Have you tried turning it off and turning it on again?'

'Ha ha. Listen, I'll spare you the details. Someone's told me about a website – I mean, it's more a closed chatroom kind of a thing. I'm not asking you to hack into it or anything – I know your rules – but I basically want them to know that I went there, tried to look around. Like, when the post leave you that note: "We tried to deliver your parcel but you weren't in", that kind of thing. Is there a way for me to do that?'

'Why would you want to do that?'

Maggie felt the pitch of her voice rise. The strain of keeping it light. 'You know, like giving a dog a gentle poke. I want them to know that I know they exist.'

'So that they know you're on to them?'

'I wouldn't put it exactly like that. But yes, sort of. And I don't want it to look deliberate. I want them to think I've left my fingerprints by accident, if you know what I mean.'

'What the fuck are you up to now, Margaret?'

'You don't want to know. Just my usual stuff and nonsense.' A phrase their mother had used. 'So. What do you say? Can it be done?'

'It *could*. What you'd need to do is get control of the DNS entry for your IP address, which is normally governed by your ISP. But if you *did* control it, you could create a reverse DNS which would point back to a domain name, which could identify you. So yes.'

'And now in English?'

'Your internet service provider – you know, whoever you pay for your broadband – issue you with a unique number—'

'You know what: when I said, "Can it be done?" what I really meant was, "Can you do it for me?" Please.'

There was a silence at the end of the phone. Maggie had another go. 'Like that time you took over my machine and you had the cursor whizzing around by magic—'

'It's not cute, you know, Maggie, your ignorance in this area. Not cute at all. It's completely irresponsible in this day and age. What about that coding course I found? I sent you a link.'

'Yeah, that did look really good. But I think the dates clashed—'

'Christ, Maggie! You have to learn this stuff. Promise me.'

'So you'll do it?'

'Only if you promise.'

'I promise.'

'Swear.'

'I swear.'

'On our ma's life?'

'Ma's dead, Liz.'

'All right. But you know what I mean.'

'OK. I swear on Ma's life.'

'Good. I'll do it. But this is the last fucking time, I mean it.'

'And you'll make it look like it's me? It won't show up as you?'

'No. I'll rent a virtual machine and set up the reverse DNS on that.'

'I don't know what that means but it sounds great.'

'You are so doing that course.'

'And they'll notice you? Being me, I mean.'

'That's a point actually.' Maggie could hear her sister thinking. 'Depends on the nature of the host site. I'll just search for pages that don't exist, or have them running around searching for things, using up capacity. Basic denial of service stuff. That'll get their attention.'

'But not too much, right? It's got to look like it's just me, rooting around.'

'Don't worry. I'll do just enough to get them looking at their logs. It'll be fine. The kids are asleep: I'll do it right away.'

Maggie gave her sister as much information as she had – Keane, Stanford, McNamara, the dates – and thanked her again. They promised to talk soon.

A last check of Twitter before she staggered into bed brought the news that, by now, had become numbingly familiar.

Breaking: Russian State Library ablaze, says TASS

There were photos, like those she had now seen a dozen times, of a night sky filled with plumes of orange. The grand, classical porticoed entrance of the Moscow building was already obscured behind clouds of that same black smoke, generated by the burning of wood and paper. Maybe it was her near-delirious state of sleeplessness, but as she watched twenty seconds of video footage, she was sure that, if only for a moment, she could see a trail of Cyrillic characters rising into the air like vapour, the letters scorched off the page and soaring into the sky, where they – and the poems, novels and scholarly histories they once formed – would be lost forever.

The instant commentary had begun, of course.

The "It must be Moscow" crowd have gone very quiet, haven't they? All those who accused Russia of these library burnings should hang their heads in shame.

Another had the words *Waiting for an apology from the Russiaphobes like . . .* attached to a GIF of a child drumming his fingers on a table.

I hope those who've been blaming Russia for the #BookBurnings will publicly recant.

And no less swift were the replies.

*If you were in the Kremlin, widely blamed for #BookBurnings, wouldn't staging a fire in the Russian State Library be *exactly* what you'd do? #bitconvenient #falseflag*

Someone else had posted a screengrab of the Moscow library website. Only two green bottles, wobbling more precariously than ever.

At last she was in bed. Maggie turned off the phone and felt herself descend into sleep even before her eyes were fully closed. In her dreams, the flames were sending not just letters, but whole words, along with punctuation marks and page numbers, high up into the clouds, higher and higher until they were gone.

Friday

Chapter Thirty-Eight

Washington DC, 3.40am

The noise sounded primal, like a throbbing from deep in the bowels of the earth. It broke into her dreams, where it seemed to emerge from a dark, narrow pit, perhaps a dry, long-abandoned well. The sound got louder, as if it was rising higher from the well and was about to reach the surface.

Maggie opened her eyes to hear her heart thumping. It took her a full second to understand that the sound was continuing, that she had not left it behind in her sleep. It was here, right now. A loud, thick pounding: wood against wood. And it was very near.

She got out of bed, glimpsing the clock on the nightstand: 3.40am. Wearing only shorts and a vest, she opened her bedroom door.

What did she see first? When she tried to recollect the moment later, it would prove hard to disentangle the multiple shocks she sustained in the space of a single second, to separate one from another. But, oddly, the first image to surface in her memory was the cluster of red dots that suddenly appeared, hovering like fireflies on her white vest.

She saw the front door of her apartment, flattened and off its hinges. Framed in the open doorway were two men, gripping a thick wooden battering ram, one handle each. It had the same dimensions, the same unarguable solidity, as the central roof beam you might find in an old Irish farmhouse. It made no sense, but somehow the beam itself looked guilty, sheepish even: for it had just knocked down her front door.

Only then, last, did her mind take in the dozen or more armed men whose machine guns were trained on her. Clad in black, their giant, hulking bodies bulked up with protective armour, equipment and squawking radios, they filled every corner of her field of vision: four inside the apartment, two on each side of the narrow hallway, two more on the other side of the front door, two more lying commando-style on the communal staircase, one on the landing above, the other spreadeagled on the steps below. Every barrel of every gun was aimed at her and now, though only slowly, she understood the red dots. Instinct told her there were more red dots, more fireflies, that she could not see: concentrated, no doubt, on her forehead.

And then, as if she had been underwater, holding her breath, and only now burst up through the water's surface, there was a sudden rush of noise in her ears.

'Put your hands in the air!'

'Right now! In the fucking air!'

'Freeze! Do not fucking move!'

It sounded like every one of these men was shouting at her, deploying the full force of their lungs. The saliva of the one – what was he? A soldier? A police officer? – closest to her landed on her left cheek as he bellowed his command: 'Don't move, bitch!'

Now she let out a scream as someone, or something, gripped her arms, joined the wrists and pulled them back down behind her back, a manoeuvre whose speed seemed to rip her shoulder muscles.

The fog of semi-consciousness, which had persisted for the ten or fifteen seconds since she had woken up, now lifted.

'What the *fuck* do you think you're doing? Who the hell are you?' she shouted.

Their answer was a question: 'Is there anybody else in the apartment with you?'

'First tell me who the fuck you are.'

'I repeat, is there anyone else in this location?'

They pushed her towards her bedroom, her walk a stagger with her arms cuffed behind her back. They went in ahead of her, their weapons aimed at every possible angle to cover against an ambush.

'Do you have a firearm in this location?' Before she had a chance to process the question, it was repeated at full volume and with great urgency. 'DO YOU HAVE A FIREARM, YES OR NO?'

'No.'

They proceeded to search the room anyway. Maggie heard the other men do the same in the rest of the apartment. They checked the bed first, ripping off the covers and then the mattress, to allow a look through the wooden slats to see if anyone was cowering underneath. Next it was the bathroom and then the closets. They observed a routine. One would open the door, another would cover him by aiming his automatic weapon at anyone who might be hiding within. The commotion as they flung open doors or overturned chairs was ferocious. Maggie stood in the centre of it, two guns still trained on her despite the handcuffs, suddenly conscious how little she was wearing.

Now there was a shove in the middle of her back, pushing her forward, out of her bedroom and towards what used to be the front door. Behind, she could hear the clang of crockery and cutlery, as they pulled out every door and cupboard in the small kitchen.

They led her downstairs, still at gunpoint. Maggie thought she spotted the door of one of her neighbours' apartments ajar just wide enough for a pair of eyes to follow her.

Now she was outside on the stoop, the stone cold under her bare feet. They pushed her further forward, down the two stairs and onto the sidewalk, where she felt a nick as her right sole was cut by a sliver of broken glass. The passenger door opened on a large SUV, parked right outside her building, its windows tinted. A hand placed itself on her head, pressing her to duck as someone pushed her into the car.

Now she was seated, wedged between two uniformed men, their bulk pressed against her. She was acutely conscious of the bareness of her legs, the thinness of her sleepwear, as they sandwiched her between them, her hands still manacled.

She resolved somehow to get a grip on this situation. In a voice that was calm and quiet, she said, 'You need to get me some clothes right away. And then you need to explain why you have just broken into my home and searched it without a warrant, which is so blatant a violation of the Fourth Amendment of the Constitution of the United States that I could sue every single one of you.'

'I need you to confirm your identity for me.' The voice came from the passenger seat at the front of the car, where another uniformed man was sitting, his head fixed on the laptop in front of him. Maggie could not make out his face. She guessed he had been inside the car throughout.

'I'm not going to confirm anything until you give me some answers.'

The man in front gave a glance to the man on Maggie's left. He repeated, 'Can you confirm your name is Margaret Costello?'

'Tell me who you are and then I'll think about telling you who I am. Because if you don't already know my name, that suggests you're handcuffing random strangers. Which is not good for you at all.'

The man sighed and half turned towards her. Now she had a glimpse of his profile. 'We are a Special Weapons and Tactics team deployed at the instruction of the United States Secret Service.'

'A SWAT team?'

'Now, can you confirm you are Margaret Costello?'

'Yes. But why on earth would—'

'Margaret Costello, I am arresting you under United States Code, Title Eighteen, Section Eight Seven One, for the felony of threatening—'

'What?'

'—and the issuing of violent threats directed at—'

'What the fuck are you talking about? This is completely crazy. Who am I meant to have threatened?'

'You need to listen, Ms Costello. Do not interrupt me again. I am arresting you for the crime of threatening the President of the United States.'

Chapter Thirty-Nine

It's six o'clock and this is Today. *Good morning and these are the headlines.*

A devastating fire has ripped through the British Library in London, destroying the country's biggest collection of historical documents and rare works. The prime minister has called it 'an attack on our nation's memory and our very soul', but the government has been criticized by those who say the intelligence services and even the armed forces – who were guarding the library – clearly did not do enough to protect it.

We'll have coverage throughout the programme with leading historians on what this loss represents, as well as with security analysts and counter-terrorism experts. But first, our home affairs editor filed this report from the scene in central London a few moments ago:

The blaze is said to have begun in the early hours and to have accelerated at what a spokesman for the London Fire Brigade called 'lightning speed', reaching temperatures of more than six hundred degrees centigrade. It burnt through the Rare Books collection first, then spread through the Humanities and then into rooms holding priceless works relating to music, including the original score of Handel's Messiah. *Among the most cherished treasures reported destroyed is the* Diamond Sutra, *thought to be the world's earliest dated printed book, traced to the year* 868.

Also lost: multiple Bibles including Codex Sinaiticus, *which represents the bulk of the second-oldest manuscript of the Bible in the world, written in what's known as 'koine Greek'; along with the legendary Lindisfarne gospels; two Gutenberg Bibles; the personal copy of Tyndale's New Testament that belonged to Anne Boleyn; and two copies of the Magna Carta of* 1215 *which, following the fire two days ago at the Bodleian Library in Oxford, means that foundational document is now perhaps lost forever.*

Curators and staff have been arriving here during the night, many of them in tears at what they say is a truly irrecoverable loss. The BBC spoke to one librarian weeping over what she said was the destruction of one of Leonardo da Vinci's notebooks. Another said he was grieving over what had been the sole surviving manuscript copy of the poem Beowulf. *'It feels like the end of the world,' he said between tears, referring to the series of similar fires that have struck across the globe in just a matter of days. 'Soon there will be nothing left.'*

Our home affairs editor is there. In the last few minutes, reports are emerging of a similar blaze at the British Library's storage facility in Boston Spa in West Yorkshire. That building, largely out of sight of the public on a trading estate near Wetherby, houses many of the library's less frequently used documents, including much of its comprehensive collection of newspapers. A spokesman says he fears that the fire there has 'destroyed our record of the last two centuries'.

We had hoped to be joined now by one of the country's most eminent historians, but I'm afraid we've just learned that he's been taken ill in the last hour . . .

Chapter Forty

US Secret Service field office, Washington DC, 9.38am

'Let me say from the start: this will be pro bono. I won't take a cent of your money.'

'That's really not necessary, I can—'

'I insist. And that's final. Consider it a favour to Stuart. That said, if you decide at a later date to sue the Secret Service for wrongful arrest, unwarranted detention and gender bias, seeking damages of one hundred and fifty million dollars, then I will of course be only too happy to assist in your defence on a strict no-win, no-fee basis, taking either twenty per cent of damages or thirty million dollars, whichever is the greater.'

'I haven't really—'

'I'm kidding.'

'Oh. Right.'

'So you got some clothes, yes? I don't recommend you try out what they have here. Orange might not be your colour. I'm kidding! And did you eat yet? They give you something to eat?'

'I didn't really feel—'

'Course not. You've been up all night. Who wants to eat? Besides, you're in shock. Who wouldn't be?'

Maggie had met Andrew Goldstein just once, at the funeral of Stuart: his older brother, her mentor. He wasn't as physically large as Stuart – his stomach was the size of a seat cushion rather than an entire unit of upholstery – and his field was law rather than politics. But there was enough of Stuart in the accent, in the posture, in the dizzying pendulum swings from Catskills stand-up to earnestness and back again, that she automatically extended some of the ease she always felt with Stuart to his brother.

If you're ever in trouble, call Andrew. He's a sonofabitch, of course, but let him be your sonofabitch.

Maggie had spoken to him a few months ago, when she had to testify at those hearings on the Hill. But Andrew had handed her over to a colleague. His expertise, he said, remained 'down in the gutter, with all the low-lifes'. He was not a constitutional, human rights or even corporate lawyer. His field was crime. Usually based in Manhattan, he had taken the dawn shuttle to meet her here on L Street, where she had been in a 'holding room' – or cell – since just before five am.

'So obviously this is bullshit,' he said. 'And I say that because I know what my brother, *olev l'shalom*, said about you. Which is that there was no one, besides our grandmother, he trusted more. And maybe not even her. Said you were on the side of the angels. I'm on the side of the Mets, but all the same.'

Maggie offered an exhausted smile, her first for so long that she felt the muscles strain as she did it. What made it harder was the sheer frustration at being locked up like this today of all days. It was Friday, thc day of the verdict in the Keane trial. The Bookburner's deadline would pass today. And here she was, off the field and utterly useless.

'That said,' he went on, 'it's not what I thought it was.'

'What do you mean?'

'Swatting. When you called me – waking up Mrs Goldstein from her much-needed beauty sleep, I might add – I thought, OK, we know about this. It's a thing assholes do. They call 911, they say, "The woman in apartment seven is holding a hostage at gunpoint. Please, help me, help me, come quick!" And so the police send a SWAT team. Assault rifles, flak jackets, infra-red sights, the whole kaboodle. They have to. They can't take the risk that you're not some psycho who's about to blow your boyfriend's head off. No offence.'

Maggie gestured. *None taken.*

'But the asshole who made the call is doing that purely to fuck up your life. It happens. Neighbours fall out. They send in a SWAT team.'

'But this isn't that?'

'No. It's not. This time, the call came from the White House.'

'Why?'

'Because of this.' Andrew pulled out his laptop, tapped a few buttons, breathing heavily just the way Stuart used to, and finally pressed play on an audio file.

There was a beep, signalling the start of a voicemail message. Then Maggie heard her own voice.

This is Maggie Costello, former special assistant to the president in the office of the White House Counsel. I know a lot more about this president than any of you realize. Enough to bring him down. And if information won't do it, I'll just have to find another way. Remember, I'm a US citizen: the Second Amendment applies to me too!

Maggie fell back in her seat. Her body seemed to belong to someone else. And now her voice, saying those things.

'Play that again.'

Andrew pressed play once more and watched Maggie's face as she listened. The words hadn't changed, nor had their order. It was still Maggie's voice, clearly, unmistakably issuing a barely coded death threat to the President of the United States. The reference to the right to bear arms could mean nothing else.

'When was that message left?'

'Secret Service are saying they picked it up at,' Andrew checked his notepad, 'two forty-one am.'

'Where was it left?'

'On the direct line of the White House Chief of Staff. A number known to very few people, outside current and former employees. Where were you at that time?'

'I was in my apartment. In bed.'

'Any alibi who can confirm that?'

Maggie made a face, just to register the implicit intrusion into her private life, an area Stuart strayed into only very gingerly.

'I was in bed alone, Andrew.'

'Shame. So theoretically you could have made that call?'

'*Theoretically* I could have climbed the Eiffel Tower. But I didn't. I was fast asleep. Andrew, I was completely shattered.'

Andrew sat back in his chair, then pushed it further back until he risked tipping over – a signature Stuart move.

'I hear you, Maggie,' he said at last. 'Trouble is, I also *hear* you.' He nodded towards the laptop. 'We agree that's your voice, right?'

Maggie agreed it was.

Andrew suddenly leaned forward, his chair snapping back into an upright position. 'Hold on. There was a case, fifteen years ago. Chicago, I think. Sleepwalker. Murder, acquitted on grounds of diminished responsibility.'

He wasn't looking at Maggie, just thinking aloud, his eyes darting left and right. 'This would be different, sure, but the same principle. We'd just need to show—' He interrupted himself to make eye contact with his client. 'Do you have a history of talking in your sleep? Forget that. Do you have someone who might be willing to *testify* that you tend to talk in your sleep? Former lovers, ex-husbands, family members.'

Maggie thought of Liz, picturing her in a witness box as she detailed the sleeping arrangements of the bedroom they shared in Quarry Street. She then imagined Uri, telling the court of his nights with Maggie Costello. And then the clerk introducing a surprise witness: Richard . . .

'No one's ever told me I talk in my sleep.'

'All right. Maybe they've not *told* you. Doesn't mean you didn't do it.'

'You think that's our best line of defence?'

He was clicking the locks on his briefcase, readying himself for departure. 'Right now, I think it's the only line of defence. If you think of a better one, call me.'

Maggie said goodbye and returned to her cell. Her body was still crying out for sleep, the accumulated exhaustion of the last several days not relieved by the hour or two she had got before the SWAT team had battered down her door. She contemplated the thin, narrow, hard mattress and laid herself down.

That recording Andrew had played to her was conclusive, not only of her guilt but of her deterioration. That she could make such a call was itself shocking: to realize that she had that much anger roiling away within her, anger that she was clearly repressing during her conscious hours. But to discover that she could do such a thing – threatening violence against the president, for heaven's sake – and then *forget* she had even done it, that shook her to her core.

Was she losing her mind? Was that what this work was doing to her, was that what it had already done? She had always told herself that she thrived on pressure, that the urgency, the adrenalin, the constant high stakes – things that might drain someone else – instead fed and sustained her. *People who are not us don't understand that stress is not the same as pressure*, Stuart used to say. *Stress only comes when you have more, or less, pressure than you can handle. Don't forget the 'less', Maggie. Just as dangerous. Talented people who are underused get stressed out.* He then proceeded to tell her of the political consultant who had literally driven into a ditch during a North Carolina senate race, such was his despair at his boss, a candidate who wouldn't let the campaign manager manage the goddamn campaign.

But maybe Stuart was wrong. Perhaps the pressure had finally metastasized into stress. There'd been so much of it, after all.

Not just these last few days, but everything she had done these last few years. Was her unconscious seething with so much fury and, let's face it, unhappiness, that it had now taken to issuing death threats to former colleagues in her sleep? She closed her eyes and wondered what was coming next. Not just legal proceedings but, doubtless, psychological assessments culminating in a conversation with Andrew Goldstein which she could hear even now.

Maggie, I want you to listen to me. I think you need to plead guilty. On grounds of diminished responsibility. It means you won't go to jail. You'll be in a hospital. It'll be safe and then we can review . . .

She played back the tape in her head.

This is Maggie Costello, former special assistant to the president in the office of the White House Counsel. I know a lot more about this president than any of you realize. Enough to bring him down. And if information won't do it, I'll just have to find another way. Remember, I'm a US citizen: the Second Amendment applies to me too!

Jesus Christ, who talked like that? Did she? And yet it was unmistakable. Unlike the body in the porn video, this voice was hers. That was her accent – part Dublin, part too many years in Washington, DC. There was no one else who talked that way. No one could even impersonate it. Occasionally someone would try, but most American attempts at an Irish accent degenerated into Boston via the Kennedys.

Maggie felt a pulse somewhere in the back of her head, a low-voltage twinge that she understood only a second or two later as the stirring of a thought. It was a memory, prompted by that fleeting thought of the Kennedys.

Maggie had not yet demanded the right to a phone call with a family member. She demanded it now.

'Liz? It's Maggie. Long story, but I need your help.'

She proceeded to tell her sister as concisely and as calmly as she could that she was being held in a cell by the Secret Service. 'Jesus fuck,' was Liz's considered response.

'Listen, I need you to look something up for me. Are you in front of a computer?' Maggie gave sweet and blessed thanks that, where Liz was concerned, the answer to that question was almost always yes. And it was now.

'OK,' she said, giving her the string of four or five words she wanted Liz to search. Her sister listed the results and Maggie told her which item she should read out loud. It was an article from *The Times* of London, relatively recent.

Liz read out the first line. 'A Scottish technology company has used computers to recreate the speech President John F. Kennedy was set to deliver in Dallas the day he was assassinated.'

'That's it,' Maggie said. 'Keep going.'

'Sound engineers formed the 2,590 words of the address that Kennedy wrote but never gave by trawling through 831 of his speeches and radio addresses. From those, they extracted 116,777 sound units, each of which was then split in half and analyzed for pitch and energy. The half units, known as phones, were each about 0.04 seconds long and had to be tested next to each other to ensure that they did not clash. It was those phones the engineers used to form the words in Kennedy's text.'

Liz was doing her best, but her voice was trembling. Maggie had been careful to avoid the words 'jail' or 'prison' but 'cell' had just slipped out. She knew her sister well enough to know that, no matter what words were now coming out of her mouth, all Liz was thinking of was that cell.

As her sister read on, two lines of the *Times* story leapt out. The first was a quote from the founder of the tech company that had made the breakthrough, hailing its potential as a gift to those losing the use of their voice to illness. 'There are only forty to forty-five "phones" in English, so once you've got that set you can generate any word in the English language.' The second stated flatly that 'the technology needs only three to four hours of voice recordings to run clearly'.

They wouldn't even have needed that long, Maggie thought: it was a short voicemail message, no more than fifty or sixty words long. And recordings of Maggie's voice were out there. Given what had gone down in the White House, and how much material had been released during the congressional hearings that followed, it wouldn't be a surprise if just a few clicks took you to recordings of the phone calls she'd made when she worked there. Probably there were whole phrases that could be cut and pasted in their entirety, with no editing required. Now that she thought about it, she might even have once uttered the words, 'Remember, I'm a US citizen: the Second Amendment applies to me too!' Given the nature of office banter, she couldn't rule it out.

She almost admired the ingenuity of it. Probably if you listened a hundred times, through headphones, you'd notice tiny, microscopically uneven cadences here and there. But to the regular ear, you'd never know it wasn't real. It had convinced the

Secret Service and Goldstein. It had convinced Maggie herself. And why wouldn't it? It was her voice, after all.

So who had done it? Her first thought was the White House itself. Hadn't her evening with McNamara left her wondering about the sheer scale of the Alexandria project, a task beyond the reach of most, but comfortably within the scope of the US government? Cobbling together a fake voice message would have been easy for anyone within the government machine: they would have had access to the archived White House recordings and a hotline to the Secret Service, to say nothing of the Chief of Staff's voicemail. For them, it would have been a neat, in-house operation.

But the timing was crucial.

'Maggie, are you still there?'

'Sorry, yes. I was just thinking. Listen, Liz, that thing I asked you to do last night? Don't say what it was, but did you do it?'

'Yes, straight after we hung up. Why, has that got something to do—'

'Thanks, Liz. Thank you so much.'

That had to be it. Within hours of asking Liz to poke around in the Keane alumni chatroom, she had been swatted. In a way, her plan had succeeded. She had lured her quarry out into the open.

Maggie cleared her throat. 'Today's Friday, isn't it?'

'Of course it is. Fuck me, are you losing track of time in there or something?'

'No, no. I know it's Friday. I just mean, you're seeing your therapist today.'

'Are you about to take the piss out of me again?'

'No. I'm not. Listen, Liz. I've been thinking about what you said the other day, about being on the brink of a breakthrough. You know, about your childhood.'

'Yeah.'

'I think I know what it is.'

'You know? How could you know?'

'Because I was there, you daft cow. It's about . . . Ma.'

'I had a feeling it was something to do with—'

'Let me just say it. I'd rather you hear it from me than from Charles bloody Aznavour.'

'Yves.'

'Whatever. The thing is, Liz. Our ma was—'

The word stuck in Maggie's throat. She hadn't expected it to, but it wouldn't come out. Not without effort. When she finally pushed it out, it made a crack in her voice. 'Ma was an alcoholic.'

'What?'

'She had terrible trouble with drink, Liz. Especially after Dad, you know, when it was just the three of us. We'd get home from school, and she'd be slumped on the doorstep.'

'I don't believe you.'

'I wish it wasn't true, but it is. She'd get into fights in the shops, she'd fall over. She couldn't cope. That's why we were sent off to the convent.'

'But . . . you always told me she was ill. That she was having a bad day.'

'I know.'

'Or that she'd taken cough medicine that didn't agree with her.'

'I know.'

'You lied,' Liz said slowly, as if the meaning was only appearing before her now. 'You've lied to me all these years.' Her voice was trembling.

'I'm so sorry, Liz.'

'Why didn't you say anything? Why did you never tell me the truth?'

'I think I was trying to protect you. That's what I was *always* trying to do, Liz. Always trying to shield you from the situation. From her. You were only eight. You were barely older than Ryan.'

'But *you* were so young, Mags. You were eleven, for Christ's sake. Does this mean . . . that time, when your eye was bleeding. And I could hear her shouting in the kitchen. Had she . . .'

'Liz, it's such a long time ago.'

'Had she hit you?'

'There's no point. Not after all these—'

'And you took me to Nan's. You bundled me out of the house, even when you were bleeding. You were just a child.' Maggie could hear her sister's tears and snot through the phone.

'I had to keep you safe, Liz.'

'And you've been carrying this alone, all this time?'

'It wasn't like that.'

'Why wasn't it like that?'

'Because I hardly remembered it myself.'

'I don't believe that.'

'It's true. I think I buried it, Liz.'

'But that's so bad. It's so unhealthy.'

'I'm not so sure. I mean, look at you. Why did you need to

know any of this stuff? You were fine until you started seeing Yves Whatshisname. You were so much better off not knowing, so much better off not remembering.'

'But that never works, Mags.'

'It's worked for you! Look at you. You're a brilliant teacher, you're a fantastic mother – such a good mother, Liz.' Her voice faltered again. 'I wanted at least one of us to turn out OK.'

At that, Liz's tears turned into hard, convulsive sobs. 'But all these fires and everything. You always said history matters. The past matters. And yet . . .'

She couldn't finish the sentence. All she could manage was: 'I wish I was there with you. I hate living so far apart.'

'Me too, Liz. Me too.'

They spoke for a few minutes longer, agreeing to see each other just as soon as they could. When they were done, Maggie blew her nose loudly and wiped her eyes. And then she asked the officer on duty for permission to make one more call.

'I want my lawyer,' she said.

Chapter Forty-One

US Secret Service field office, Washington DC, 2.55pm

The television, Maggie concluded, was less a concession than a pacification measure. Having a TV set on, albeit muted and tuned to Fox News, was a way to stop the inmates getting restless.

Right now, Maggie was staring at it, transfixed. Maybe it was because this was a building she had actually visited, in a city she had been to several times. Whatever the explanation, the sight of the British Library in London reduced to a charred ruin reached her in a way the other fires had not. She felt her eyes pricking at the sight of it.

Perhaps it was the exhaustion. Or, more likely, the frustration – of being here, locked up, when this threat, this faceless menace, was still active and raging. The TV news had shown the image that now filled the British Library website: a single bottle, alone and fragile, hanging on that wall.

She tried to picture the person or people behind this rampage: killing historians, survivors and eyewitnesses, destroying archives, both physical and digital, all over the world. But in her mind, the threat had only one form. All she could see was fire: stealthy, silent but utterly lethal. She imagined herself in a cabin surrounded by a blazing forest, knowing that the flames were getting nearer, the heat rising and there was nothing she could do about it. She was trapped.

A detective came to interview her, but she just repeated her insistence that she had been asleep at 2.41am and that she had not left that voicemail message. All she would say is, 'I don't know how it was done, but I did not leave that message.'

She had decided to wait for the return of Andrew Goldstein before unspooling her theory. Better he hear it first. When he came, in the mid-afternoon, he listened patiently as she explained. For a moment she saw a look cross his face that she didn't like, the look the sane have when humouring the unhinged. She saw herself as she must have looked: the crazy Irish chick, unslept and unkempt, raving on about digital software and surveillance and JFK, for Christ's sake.

But that expression of indulgence passed as soon as it had come, like a cloud moving across the sun. A second later, Andrew was back, listening intently, scribbling notes.

'That's good,' he said. 'The only problem will be time.'

'Time?'

'This is not a quick argument to make. We'll need to find a technical expert, someone who—'

'But it's not that complicated, Andrew. Someone made a collage out of bits of my voice. Just like they stuck my face on a porn film. They're creating fake evidence. That's what this is about. It's the flipside of burning all these libraries. They're showing what they can do, what they *plan* to do. They'll get rid of all the real evidence, and then they'll replace it with whatever garbage they like. And technology lets them do it.'

There was that look again. Only fleeting, but sufficiently unambiguous, it made Maggie pine for Andrew's dead brother. Stuart would understand. Stuart would believe her. Stuart would see the danger.

Though even as she had thought that, she remembered the countless times her old mentor had made her prove whatever claim she had put before him. *Hunch is not enough, kiddo. I could care less about your instincts. If I want 'intuition', I'll take a yoga class.* Evidence and proof: he accepted nothing less.

So she did not protest when Andrew said he would have to make some calls and consult with colleagues. His main focus now, he said, was on bail: he needed to prove that Maggie posed no danger and would not try to abscond. 'We may need to surrender your passport.'

'That's OK,' she said, offering a thin smile. 'I've got another one.'

They said goodbye and she had more time to stare at the silent TV as it carried those pictures from London – a burned husk of a building; a black, acrid sky; grieving library staff; sober politicians; a visiting royal on the scene – on a loop. She read the subtitled words as they crawled, in broken English, across the screen. In among the punditry and speculation, one line recurred:

Of the dozen libraries in the Alexandria Group, only one remains left untouched.

An hour or so later – though it could have been much more – Maggie had a visitor. When she was led into the visiting room, she wondered if she'd ever been more delighted to see him than she was now.

'Oh, Uri.'

'What? Don't pretend you're surprised to see me. Where else would I be?'

She felt that same pricking sensation in her eyes. She dabbed at them and said, 'Sorry. I'm just so . . .' She wanted to say 'tired', and also 'grateful', and maybe a hundred other things, but nothing would come. Her voice crumbled into a croak.

'I know,' Uri said. 'I know.'

He moved to hug her, until the guard in the corner bellowed a reminder that 'Physical contact is prohibited'. Uri shrugged and sat down, on the opposite side of a table, as if he were another interrogator. But still she could catch the scent of him and feel the effect it had on her insides.

'I brought something for you.' He reached into his shoulder bag and pulled out a photograph. It was the Stanford class portrait that Maggie had found on her doorstep last night.

'Yeah, I saw that. I should have said. Thanks so—'

'No. I've got more information now. I've filled in more of the blanks.'

He pointed at each face in turn, offering names now for all of them. For each one, he offered a line of potted biography, one that served as a concise, common sense exoneration.

'This guy died in 2004. Just behind him, this one, was a star of the class, apparently: he now has early onset dementia . . . That guy is the administrator of the San Francisco Opera.'

Maggie pointed at a tall, smiling man with big eighties hair. 'What about him?'

'That's Clive Soderberg. Interesting. He became a regular, mainstream historian. Presented a podcast: "Your History".'

'Presented? Past tense?'

'Yeah. He was found dead in a boating accident last week.'

'An "accident"?'

'Exactly.'

Uri kept going, his finger hovering over each of the bright young faces. 'Him you know,' he said, as he reached Crawford McNamara. 'And him.' He pointed at Keane.

'What about them?' Maggie indicated the small peppering of women.

'Oh yes, I got more on them. These two I had already,' he said, explaining that the long-haired beauty on the left was an overseas student, now known as Anna-Sofia de Lance-Holmes, having married a London property magnate and become one of the pre-eminent society hostesses of that city. 'The only public involvement I can see is that she supports children's theatre companies. Drama groups, amateur dance.'

'Nothing in our area?'

'Not that I can see.'

'And this one?' She was pointing at the woman in the Coke-bottle glasses.

'She practises medical law in Toronto. Defends victims of hospital accidents.'

'Hmmm.' Maggie had picked up Uri's pen and was chewing the top of it. She could have killed for a cigarette.

'That one,' Uri said, picking out a striking woman not far from Keane. 'I did wonder about her. There was some talk of an affair with Keane, way back. But I couldn't nail it down.'

'Really?' Maggie's mind was turning over.

'Don't get too excited. It's not her.'

'Why not?'

'She died three years ago.'

Maggie's finger had stopped at the cool customer, her eyes and much of her face concealed by large, eighties sunglasses. 'And her?'

'That's Tammy French.'

'OK?'

'I know she was in the class, because she's mentioned in the records. She took the course. But she barely registers in the alumni blog. I think she was pretty peripheral.'

'Or they were all so sexist, they didn't notice the women unless they looked like models.'

'Definitely a possibility. But it's hard to know, because there's just nothing else on her.'

'How do you mean, nothing else?'

'Online. I've searched. I mean, there's people with that *name*, but they're not her. Wrong age, wrong place.'

'What about all those college alumni things?'

'Nope.'

'Seriously?'

'No.'

'Isn't that a bit weird?'

'I don't know. I didn't—'

'You're saying, the college newsletter or whatever mentions everyone else, but—'

'They don't *mention* exactly. Sometimes it's literally just their name and the dates they were at—'

'But she doesn't even get that?'

'No.'

Maggie stared hard now at the blurred face in the photo, trying to see behind those oversized dark glasses. 'I really do have to get out of here, Uri. We need to know everything we can about Ms Tammy French. And we need to do it soon.'

Chapter Forty-Two

Melita Island, Montana, 3.29pm

All previous boundaries of rank and status had now eroded entirely, so that Jason didn't hesitate to sit in Jim's chair and type into his keyboard as if it were his own. The demands on them had been so complete for so long, none of them had any energy left for social niceties, including deference to Jim as manager or the attendant sanctity of his workspace. Jason was looking for something and if that meant commandeering his boss's machine, so be it.

Irritated not to find the relevant file straight away, he began minimizing a few of the two dozen windows open on the screen. Eventually that exposed a graphic in the top left that Jason instantly recognized. It was an animation, the same wobbling GIF displayed on the websites of each of the libraries that had been destroyed. Now it showed a single green bottle resting on the wall.

'Just a little reminder.'

Jason jumped, his nerves shot by exhaustion. He hadn't heard anyone come near. Putting a coffee cup down on the desk by way of retaking his territory, Jim adopted a faux-narrator voice and, nodding towards the graphic, said, 'And then there was one.'

Jason got out of the chair, but kept jabbing at the keyboard: a signal that he was engaged in nothing that had to be concealed from his boss. 'I was looking for the Washington list,' he said.

'Sure,' Jim said, gently pulling the keyboard back to himself as his right hand shifted the mouse. 'Here you go.' The screen filled with a document in the same format as the other eleven they had used for similar reasons. Jason skimmed the items, listed for this last target: the Library of Congress.

He was unsurprised by the first objects: the US Constitution, along with James Madison's personal copy of the Bill of Rights which he had drafted and proposed, Thomas Jefferson's text of the Declaration of Independence, written and amended in his own inked hand, and the Gettysburg Address delivered by Abraham Lincoln. There was the original map used by explorers Lewis and Clark as they ventured into the American west, as well as a complete collection of *The North Star*, the mid-nineteenth-century newspaper published by abolitionist Frederick Douglass. Its slogan: 'Right is of no Sex – Truth is of no Color – God is the Father of us all, and we are all Brethren.' There was a snippet of primitive film, capturing an employee of Thomas Edison as he sneezed, evidence of the great innovator's first experiments with moving pictures, as well as the first ever film deposited for copyright.

Despite the fatigue gnawing at his insides, Jason found himself enchanted by the treasures listed and itemized. The laboratory notebook of Alexander Graham Bell. One of the earliest known baseball cards. Gershwin's full orchestral score for *Porgy and Bess*. And, Jason's favourite, the personal effects extracted from the pockets of Lincoln hours after his assassination. Among them: two pairs of spectacles, a lens polisher, a penknife, a watch fob, a linen handkerchief, and a brown leather wallet containing a five-dollar bank note – one issued by Lincoln's mortal enemies in the Confederacy – and eight newspaper clippings, including several warmly in praise of the president about to meet his fate.

What riches, Jason thought. Without asking permission, he struck the relevant keys on Jim's machine to send the document over to himself. Soon he would draw up the familiar battleplan, working out an order of priorities and a drill so that they would miss nothing. No point going to all these lengths and missing the crown jewels.

Back at his desk, he thought again of the graphic on Jim's computer. How over the last few days, as one after another of the Alexandria libraries were reduced to hot ash, the image would have changed: twelve, then eleven, then ten and on and on. And now there was just a single one left in the entire world.

What strange work this was, aimed at such completeness. From this cabin on Melita Island he was close to a process that demanded wholesale destruction, across the planet and back through the centuries. He imagined himself inches away from a blaze that was somehow capable of tearing through space and time. He could feel the heat of it on his face.

But there was that green bottle on Jim's screen, teetering on the wall. There was only one left.

Time to get to work.

Chapter Forty-Three

Secret Service field office, Washington DC, 5.33pm

Maggie could not have said how long she'd been asleep. The only clue was the way her clothes clung to her skin, her arms and neck coated in that film that tended to be the product only of deep unconsciousness. She didn't remember lying down on this narrow prison bed at all; maybe she had just keeled over, the last several sleepless days finally demanding what was rightfully theirs.

The door to the holding cell was now open and in came a guard. Female, hair pulled back in a severe ponytail, her shirt a colour that was not quite khaki but rather a deathly beige. Unsmiling, she did not let her eyes meet Maggie's.

She was carrying a tray, but there was no food on it. Instead, were several small items that Maggie could not identify, including a couple of white plastic cable-ties. The guard crouched down and began fiddling with the various pieces. It reminded Maggie of a toy Liz had once taken off one of their male cousins at Christmas in Cork: a physics kit involving simple circuits, batteries and lights. (Liz had said the boy had 'given' it to her, which was not quite true. But it was Liz's interest in the toy at all, rather than the honesty of its acquisition, that had troubled their nan: she'd wondered if it meant Liz was, you know, not like other girls. *Because I would like to be a great-grandmother one of these days.*)

'Can I ask what this is?' Maggie said.

'By order of the court,' came the reply. Maggie waited to hear the rest before realizing that was, in fact, meant as a complete answer.

'What is by order of the court?'

'This.'

'I know. But what is "this"?'

The guard looked up, but not at Maggie. She was fiddling with an item on the tray, a shiny disc the size of a nickel, which Maggie guessed was a battery. Oh. Now she understood.

'I need you to expose your right ankle for me.'

That confirmed it.

At that moment, with a sound that combined the bustle of a man carrying a briefcase, a stack of papers and at least twenty pounds in excess weight, Andrew Goldstein erupted into the room. His third visit of the day.

'Hold on, hold on, what's happening here? Officer, what are you doing to my client?'

'By order of the court,' she said again, blankly.

'Not until I've had time to disclose and discuss the court's order with my client.'

The guard glanced upward, thought about ignoring the lawyer who was now sweating and exhaling loudly and then took a different course. 'You have three minutes. Then I'm going to finish what I started.'

Maggie sat back in her chair, rubbed her eyes and, for no more than two or three seconds, allowed herself to enjoy the sensation of being back home, in her own sovereign space.

The apartment was in a state, still strewn with the debris of the last several days. The front door had been replaced with a thin, chipboard alternative that was repulsive to look at – Andrew had arranged it – while the contents of several drawers were on the floor, exactly where the SWAT team had left them. But she had never loved this place more.

She looked over at the bathroom door, delighting in the fact that it was both an actual bathroom and hers. The privacy, the autonomy, the *liberty*: she had not been deprived of her freedom for long, but now that she had it back she clung to it tightly.

She looked back down at the desk. On it, framed by her hands, was the group photograph Uri had uncovered. She went through each face one more time. She started, yet again, with William Keane. He was her Greenwich – the centre of the known world – and she worked out from there.

All of them were accounted for: McNamara, Kelly, the rest. The only puzzle was Tammy French, the woman with the sunglasses.

She reached down to her ankle, touching the spot where the plastic bracelet rubbed against her skin.

My advice is, forget it's there. That had been Andrew's suggestion as he explained that the court had granted her bail on condition that Maggie be fitted with an electronic tag. He'd been apologetic. 'It's a horrible thing, treating a person like a livestock animal. What are you, a goat? I'll be filing a complaint with the—'

But Maggie had cut him off, explaining that she could not have been more grateful. 'Andrew. So long as I'm out of here.'

So he had stood back as the guard completed the fitting process, testing the electronic connection and the GPS and the tamper-proof casing. As the woman in her sour beige shirt worked, Andrew explained that the court had allowed tagging because it had been persuaded – by him, of course – that Maggie posed no threat to herself or to anyone else. He had further persuaded the court that no limits needed to be placed on Maggie's movements, no curfew imposed. 'But you will be tracked and monitored, by the Secret Service and whichever federal agency they choose to share that information with. So I don't need to spell out, do I, that you must therefore abide by the—'

'No, Andrew,' she had said. 'You don't need to spell it out.'

Maggie was still staring at the picture, wondering what she'd missed. Once again, she started with Keane himself. Andrea Ellis had insisted that the FBI had eliminated him as the hidden hand behind the fires and targeted killings. They had been crawling all over him for months, if not longer, monitoring all his contact with the outside world, both physical and digital. She had to take their word for it: the culprit was not Keane.

But who else? She had ruled most of them out: they were

either dead, dying or else so clearly without the means to stage an operation of this scale that they were eliminated just as surely.

What about Mac? It was true that he had rich and powerful friends. His linguistic fingerprints were on that manifesto. And yet Maggie had found his denial of involvement convincing, not least because she knew that, given all that had happened, he too would have been under the constant and intense scrutiny of the authorities. He couldn't have pulled this off without their knowledge.

And so she came back, for the hundredth time, to the woman in shades. She was as sure as she could be that, once she found out more about her, she too would be ruled out. She'd be living a life of suburban blamelessness outside Tucson or Philadelphia, and Maggie would have nothing.

She checked her phone again. She was waiting for an update from Uri, any info he'd gleaned at all on Tammy French. Her own searches had proved futile, trailing down the same dead ends he'd already exhausted.

Maggie looked hard. Thanks to those sunglasses, there was so little to go on. If eyes were the window to the soul, here the curtains were firmly drawn. It was infuriating: she was the only person in this picture to have kept her shades on. If only Maggie could just reach in and take them off . . .

There was nothing else you could see. Tammy was wearing a T-shirt: a tight, seventies number with some kind of image on it. Most of it was obscured: all Maggie could see were two white blobs, indistinct curved shapes, one a few inches above the other. With a squint, you might just about see the higher one as a triangle, the lower looked more like a banana. Maggie remembered some of the tie-dye numbers her mum kept at the back of her wardrobe, with the swirling patterns and prints of that era, every one of them random. This T-shirt was going to give nothing away; it was as opaque as Ms French's sunglasses.

And yet, it was all Maggie had. She couldn't look away. Those two little white blobs were somehow nagging at her. They weren't familiar exactly, and yet some corner of Maggie's brain was worrying away at them.

She went to the kitchen to pour herself a whisky. As she felt the warmth hit the back of her throat, a memory returned of a hokey old quiz show which Maggie and Liz would watch as kids when they were spectacularly bored, mainly to laugh at the super-nerdy contestants. It pitted two epically swotty families against each other, as they were asked questions about science, history or general knowledge. The two sisters would roll around at the lank-haired daughters, spotty sons and bespectacled mothers. And, almost hidden amongst the giggling and excluded from their mockery, was their own ability to answer a good portion of the questions.

Not that they'd ever have admitted it, but a favourite round involved a close-up photograph. The contestants had to guess what the strange zig zag lines or jagged shapes signified, resolution coming only when the camera zoomed out to show the tread of a shoe or a front-door key. Both Maggie and Liz got rather good at it.

Now Maggie went back to the living room and that photograph. She was looking again at the white blobs, meaningless on

Tammy French's T-shirt. If the camera were to pull out, and if the man standing in front of French were to get out of the way, what would it reveal?

Hold on.

Suddenly Maggie saw a hint of coherence in those shapes. Were they not random after all, not even abstract, but one end of a line drawing? Indeed, not just any line drawing, but a logo?

Maggie reached for her laptop and typed in the single word 'logos' and then opted to see only the images. Instantly the screen filled with the emblems of soft drinks, hamburgers and shoes that would be recognized the world over. She scrolled through them all, but not one of them mapped onto the image on that T-shirt.

Think, she told herself. *Think*.

This woman, Tammy French, was young. She was a student. It was the 1980s. She wouldn't have been wearing a corporate brand. T-shirts were for causes.

Now Maggie typed in the words 'charity logos' and before her was an array of designs, most of them involving hearts, outstretched palms or children. And then she saw it, as clear to her as that moment of revelation on the old TV quiz show. An image of a skipping young deer, in profile.

Maggie grabbed for a piece of paper and held it to the screen, covering most of the animal, so that only the rightmost portion was visible. What you saw were two white blobs, one a soft triangle, the other a banana shape. They were, in fact, part of the deer's face and one of its front legs. This was the logo of AFN, the American Fund for Nature.

It was disappointing, no doubt about it. The organization was huge; support for it was generic rather than revealing; and it bore no relation to the project of destroying the world's memory of its past. Whatever satisfaction there was in decoding the image – the same pleasure she and Liz had experienced as TV viewers – had given way to the frustration of colliding with another dead end.

Going through the motions, Maggie now did a quick search of AFN. The organization was younger than she would have guessed, founded in the 1970s, which meant it would have been just a few years old when Tammy was promoting it across her chest at Stanford. Back then, it seemed, it was a fairly radical outfit: more animal rights than animal welfare. But these days AFN was all fluffy bunnies and cute pandas, safely mainstream. A quick survey of the current board showed a line-up of the great and the good, a couple of Hollywood names and some corporate chieftains, among them the prolific giver, society hostess and free speech enthusiast Pamela Bentham, the same Pamela Bentham who had endowed the centre that hosted that debate Maggie had attended at Georgetown several lifetimes ago. Of French, there was no sign.

Maggie clicked through each of the listed donors in turn, not even in hope let alone expectation. AFN was surely the tamest kind of corporate giving, a bland, inoffensive way to tick the 'social responsibility' box in time for the annual company report. Board members attempted to project some profound, long-standing connection with animals – *Walter spends his weekends riding herd on his Montana ranch* – but none of it was very convincing. Interestingly, Bentham was the one whose connection seemed deepest. *Now serving as our Life President, Pamela has been with AFN from the very start, supporting our work since our founding.*

Maggie scratched again at her ankle. How long had she spent at this now? It was pointless. All she had established was that Tammy French wore an AFN T-shirt back in the 1980s, when it was a bit edgier. There was no sign she was still involved. Her name did not appear anywhere on AFN's website, just like it did not appear anywhere else.

Maggie wondered again about Bentham. If she was involved from the beginning, back when AFN was quite niche, was it possible she had known French? Maybe the group was small enough then.

Now she searched for Bentham, and Wikipedia confirmed that the two women were about the same age: both in their mid-fifties. But the entry was very sketchy on her education. There was no sign of a college degree that Maggie could see.

Maggie went to a *Vanity Fair* profile of Bentham that referred to a 'college romance' and another that talked about a junior year abroad in Europe. But neither said anything about where exactly she had studied.

The *Vanity Fair* piece was accompanied by the requisite lavish photoshoot, in which Bentham posed with her husband and, in one picture, her billionaire father in their enormous, antebellum home, a sometime Virginia plantation. Alongside it was a gallery of smaller shots, including a black-and-white image of a young Bentham bottle-feeding a lamb as part of her work with AFN.

Maggie scrolled lower and now there was another cluster of pictures. The central one was from two decades earlier, showing

Bentham in a shoulderless ballgown, dancing at a New York fundraiser with her husband, then a rising star on Wall Street. Next to it was what seemed to be a holiday snap, the couple sunning themselves on the deck of a yacht near Antibes, France, shielding themselves with sunglasses and matching his-and-hers baseball caps.

Which was when it hit her with perfect clarity. *Of course, of course, of course.* It all made sense. She remembered Mac's words: *Follow the money.*

Her hands were trembling as she reached for the phone. She dialled his number and, thank God, he answered after one ring.

'Uri, it's me. I need you to find something out, right now. I'll explain but—'

'Slow down, Maggie. What's going on?'

'There's no time to slow down, I just need you to—'

'What's happened?'

'I've worked it out.'

'Worked what out?'

'Tammy French. I know who she is.'

Chapter Forty-Four

Court 73, Richmond, Virginia, 2.40pm

'Mr Keane, your closing argument please.'

For a moment, the courtroom, packed and hushed, wondered if William Keane had not heard the judge. Those jammed into the public gallery craned to see the man in the white suit arranging his papers at his desk, his head bowed. Only after four long seconds had become five, did he finally look upward – the lead actor who knows never to rush the final speech.

'Your honour, I'm grateful. As I am to you, ladies and gentlemen of the jury. How we have tried your patience these last few weeks! Myself especially. For it was I who brought this case. You could have been at home, tending your hydrangeas' – a warm snigger at that – 'coaching Little League, but I dragged you here for all this time. Once again, I apologize to each and every one of you.

'Why did I do it? I'm not a lawyer, as you know. I'm just like you, an ordinary citizen who never set foot in one of those fancy,

East Coast law schools. So why did I sue Miss Susan Liston, seated over there, for what she wrote about me in that book of hers? As you all know so well by now, I bet you could recite it in your sleep' – at that Keane all but winked at one of the older women in the jury, who responded with a blush – 'Miss Liston called me a "slavery denier". I sued her in this court because I believed this made no sense. For how can you deny that which did not exist? And I hope I've set out the facts which convince you of that.

'But that does not answer my question to you. Why did I do it? Why did I tug us from our beds and our homes and make us sit in this courtroom all these long days? I didn't do it for my reputation or my "ego".' He dragged out the last word as if it were somehow exotic or at the very least modishly modern.

'No, sir. I was happy in my study, with my dry, old books. I had no need of this circus. No offence, your honour. I do not seek fame or glory. I certainly don't seek money, which is good because I've not made any for a long time, thanks to this case.' More warm laughter from a corner of the public gallery.

'I brought this case because I believed my state, Virginia, and my country, the United States, needed to be free of a burden we have carried for too long. Oh, not people like us' – he gestured at the older members of the jury – 'it's too late for us. We've carried this all our lives, haven't we? It's got in our bones. It's in our marrow.' *Marrah*. 'No, it's the children I'm thinking of. The young. The next generation.

'Let them grow up the way we could not: without this terrible weight of history on their backs, without this stain of "slavery" on their clothes, without this mark of Cain on their faces. They need to emerge from out of this shadow.

'And a shadow is what it is, ladies and gentlemen. A ghost, a spectre.'

A voice bellowed out from the gallery: 'You lie! You're a liar!'

The judge banged her gavel and demanded order. Keane smiled, utterly unfazed.

'I know that feelings run high on this topic, your honour. But the truth is the truth, the facts are the facts. And that is what I would ask you, my fellow Virginians of the jury, to focus on. Don't be swayed by what you thought you knew about "slavery" before you came into this courtroom. Think only of the evidence that was presented to you once you were here. How Professor Barker could not rebut my contention that *Twelve Years a Slave* is a powerful, moving work of *fiction*. And remember the visit here of that wonderful lady Mrs Henderson – *Mrs*, I emphasize. Boy, she set me straight on that one, didn't she?' He gave another semi-wink towards the jury. 'We couldn't forget her, no sir! But she became forgetful, didn't she. A little confused. Just like all those documents we looked at. All those contradictions and mistakes. Time and again, they revealed that what looked like a firm, clear record was instead unreliable.

'Now, one last thing before you are taken from here to a room that will be sealed and quiet and away from jammering hammerjacks like myself. You will deliberate against a backdrop of disquieting events that have—'

'Tread carefully, Mr Keane.'

'I will, your honour, I will. There is no need to share with you the details of what's been happening in this state, this nation and around the world. We'll say no more than that there have been acts of violence. How's that? Acts of violence. But I want you to cast all that far from your mind. Do not be distracted by it. We don't know who or what is behind these acts, but none of it has anything to do with the arguments I've been making here before you. Nothing whatsoever. You can be appalled or worried or frightened by those acts, but it still has no bearing on the question you have been asked to decide. Was it fair for Miss Liston to call me those names? Or am I right to say that the past is not what we took it to be? That we are not the villains some of those folks – in the Ivy League colleges and in Hollywood and at the *New York Times* – would have us believe we were and are?

'That's now for you to decide. It's in your hands. The Commonwealth of Virginia, the United States of America and the people of the world are watching.

'Your honour, I rest my case.'

A spontaneous burst of applause greeted Keane as he sat down, with several in the public gallery rising to their feet. In response, another group broke into a chant: *Keane lies, Keane lies, Keane lies.*

And in the midst of it, calmer than the rest, was a young woman – lean, strong, athletic – whose focus had not been on William Keane but his opponent, Susan Liston. She watched Liston from above, her gaze steady. She seemed to be assessing her. Only occasionally did the woman in the gallery make the smallest, habitual movement, almost a tic – a finger reaching upward and rubbing her left eyebrow.

Chapter Forty-Five

The Mayflower Hotel, Washington DC, 7.23pm

The Mayflower Hotel was beautifully lit at this time of night, the entrance all but glowing under the enormous, rippling flag of stars and stripes. Standing on the opposite side of the street, watching the cabs, limos and SUVs arrive, Maggie could see the allure. With its buxus trees posted like sentries on either side of the doors, themselves discreetly illuminated, the Mayflower could have been a chateau on the outskirts of Paris, the faded stone suggesting an old-world grandeur that Washington often aspired to but only rarely reached.

She would have to get this right, she thought, checking again the ridge around her ankle. Putting tights on over an electronic tag had proved quite a challenge: she had snagged two pairs before gingerly getting these on. Now she just hoped the tag wasn't too obvious. She would only have one shot; she could not blow it.

More guests arrived, in a constant flow: the men in tuxedos, the women in gowns that usually erred towards black or safe, deep shades of purple or green. Even from here, she could see that almost all of them were white and seriously monied.

Not for the first time, she gave thanks for Uri who had within half an hour worked out where Maggie needed to go. Whether that was through his own shoe leather, or contacts who did the digging for him, hardly mattered. He had found out.

Maggie took a deep breath and another glance at her outfit, a black cocktail dress that had seen regular service at occasions like this. It was the one she had worn at White House dinners or diplomatic engagements, back when she was invited to those. She had once favoured the black trouser-suit, but over the years that had become the signifier for 'staff'. Maybe it was because she was younger than most of the guests, but when, at a reception for the French foreign minister, a woman had marched over to Maggie, handed her a mink and said, 'Would you be a dear and take this to the cloakroom for me?' she had decided that the pant suit was over.

She lifted her head, pushed back her shoulders and crossed the road. Confidence. It was all about confidence. She would walk into this dinner, raising funds for the Washington National Opera, as if she too were an honoured guest.

Her stride was purposeful, but she was still stopped as soon as she was through the revolving doors.

'Can I see your invitation, ma'am?'

'Oh no.' Maggie smiled warmly. 'I'm not here for the event. I'm here to meet a guest at the hotel.'

'Reception is that way, ma'am.'

Duly ushered away from the line, Maggie then simply walked

through the lobby, with its shining marble floors, twinkling chandeliers and gilt decoration, until she had rejoined the snake of guests as they headed to the Grand Ballroom. If anyone asked to see her invitation, she would say it was in her coat, now checked in at the cloakroom. For the sake of completeness, she then approached one of the twenty-something women – they were always twenty-something women – who were standing around with clipboards. Dressed in black pant suits.

'I'm just checking – do you know if my husband arrived? Name of Smith?'

The woman smiled keenly and started flipping pages until she came to a cluster of Smiths, which Maggie promptly skimmed through. (Of all the skills that had proved precious in the White House, reading upside down was perhaps the most valuable.) Spotting one of them as yet unticked, Maggie added, 'Robert Smith?'

The young woman found 'Smith, Robert' a half second after Maggie had seen it and then chirped, 'Seems you're the first to arrive! Table twenty-three.'

Maggie thanked her and then pressed into the ballroom itself, a cavernous space with Versailles pretensions, from the painted domed ceiling to the elaborate balustrades on the mezzanine level above. The room was heaving, but Maggie's gaze was now a tractor beam, searching for the top table and the woman who would be playing host.

In retrospect it was so obvious. Tammy French had indeed been a student at Stanford, a contemporary of Crawford McNamara and an equally enthralled student of William Keane.

French had left little imprint on the others, seemingly passing through without trace, never to be mentioned again in their alumni newsletters or even in the college records. And that was because Tammy French did not exist.

Oh, as Maggie had explained to a baffled Uri over the phone, Tammy was flesh and blood, all right. But 'Tammy French' was a pseudonym, an alias adopted for the four years of student life, and very possibly at boarding school before that. It was a common enough ruse at the time, if by common you meant widespread among the multi-millionaire classes. When the sons and daughters of the very richest were getting kidnapped in alarming numbers, the smartest money sent its offspring out into the world, or at least to be expensively educated, incognito. Which was how 'Tammy French' was born, the invented creation of her always inventive father.

From what Maggie could see, Tammy had stuck to her role perfectly. None of her student contemporaries had twigged who their classmate was. This was the age before social media, so there was no online database of images her face could be checked against, no Instagram posts that might have alerted would-be ransom-seekers to her whereabouts. A more innocent age.

And yet, she had not been careless or fancy-free. Even on a day that was sufficiently cloudy that not one other person in William Keane's history class had felt the need to shield their eyes from the sun as they posed for a group photograph, Tammy had worn sunglasses – ones large enough to obscure her face from view.

Which meant that she could study unhindered, taking classes, listening to lectures, scribbling notes and having her mind expanded, by Keane especially. His radical ideas about history had influenced so many of them, shaping them for years to come. Kelly alone in his cabin; McNamara spinning his theories in his Washington townhouse. All of them were still Keane's disciples. But only she had dared take their teacher's gospel truly out into the world, to implement it in its most radical form. Of all people, it had been the one few of her fellow students had noticed, the one Maggie herself had passed over without even a moment's thought.

Perhaps, Maggie reflected now, only one person had ever noticed her: Keane himself. Maggie heard again a remark the historian had made to her that day in the Richmond law office. It had meant nothing to her at the time, and she'd ignored it. But now Keane's voice sounded loud in her head. *You remind me of one of my most interesting students. Though she wasn't quite as bright as you. But the* passion.

Maggie was now perhaps three yards away from the top table. She watched as this group, the elite within the elite, the billionaires among millionaires, greeted each other. There was a generational divide of sorts. The older group, seventy-five and over, consisted of overweight men squeezed into black tie, their bony wives armed with Eisenhower-era hair-dos falling on semi-skeletal clavicles. While the younger rich, fifty and above, were pictures of glowing health, the men tanned and lean, silver hair trimmed short, the women sinewy, all gym arms and thick, salonned hair.

And there, effortlessly moving between both groups, was the woman Maggie had come to see. Her dress was surprisingly old-fashioned, a taffeta number that Liz would have branded instantly as 'meringue'. Her hair was a shade of auburn that seemed indebted to chemistry rather than nature. She was not pretty: her face was too long, her jawline too harsh for that. But she had confidence and poise and, when she rocked her head back in apparent delight, as she was doing now, she had the same flirtatious charisma Maggie had seen in that photograph.

Hovering nearby, in regulation pant suit, was a woman Maggie identified as an assistant. Beaming brightly, Maggie approached, touching the woman's elbow as she made her request to be introduced.

'And who should I say would like to meet her?'

Without hesitating, Maggie said, 'Why don't you tell her Tammy French is here?'

Chapter Forty-Six

The Mayflower Hotel, Washington DC, 7.55pm

Maggie watched the woman's face as the assistant announced her surprise guest, Maggie carefully lip-reading as the name – *Tammy French* – was spoken and then the reaction: the mouth dropping, both ends tumbling downward first in shock and then in a curl of . . . what was it? Fury? Fear? Both, by the looks of it.

It took less than half a second, a beat, for the rictus smile to reassert itself. Once it had, the painted, mask-like nature of that face struck Maggie afresh. The scarlet lips, the pale powder: it was part eighteenth-century courtesan, part harlequin. Maggie felt a chill in her blood: for the first time, she realized this woman terrified her.

The assistant was approaching, her demeanour more serious now. 'Why don't you follow me to this side room? She'll join you there.'

Maggie followed the woman, walking in single file in a channel between the outermost tables and the wall. But her eyes were darting, involuntarily, from left to right. They'd almost reached the side room when, in her peripheral vision, she spotted a man on the other side of the ballroom, dressed in a plain suit, cheaper than the others here. He touched his ear, the way she had seen security personnel do a hundred times before. His pace quickened ever so slightly. Every instinct told her the same thing: this was a trap.

Maggie turned on her heel and plunged back into the centre of the room, threading her way through the glitter and sparkle of the tables and the guests. She made two immediate calculations. First, those security guards would hesitate before shooting into a room of eleven hundred people. Second, she would be hard to pick out in a thicket of women dressed exactly like her. As she advanced towards the back of the ballroom, and not for the first time, she gave thanks for the little black dress.

She pushed at the first door she found, which took her immediately into some kind of service area, where a cluster of busboys were polishing wine glasses and retrieving cutlery. Ahead were two doors, through one of which emerged a stream of waiters and waitresses, all clad in identical black costumes – its centrepiece the Nehru jacket, now the ubiquitous server uniform at high-end Washington events – each one carrying a tray piled with identically minimalist plates of food: little whirls of salmon and a decorous twist of dill. They came out in such a stampede that Maggie had to dart to one side, just to avoid being crushed under foot. She moved forward and pushed at the other door.

Immediately she was hit by the steam and metallic clang of mass food production. In front of her was a long, polished counter illuminated by a series of lights dangling from above. Running the full length of the counter were two open metal shelves, behind which stood a parade of chefs, each one filling the space in front of them with plates ready to be picked up. In single file, a line of servers moved forward to pick up their consignment for despatch outside. It was a military operation.

Maggie made an instant assessment. She wanted to get into that kitchen area, behind the counter, but how to get past the two barriers, first the human line of waiters and then the metal structure itself?

She moved forward, doing her best not to run but to walk with authority, as if she had every right to be in the banqueting kitchen of a major Washington hotel. She looked over her right shoulder. *Shit*. Just in through the same door she had taken was one of the guards, carrying a weapon and steadying himself to take aim.

Maggie was past the counter now, with a doorway to her left. She ducked through it, where she was hit by more steam. A conveyer belt was pushing a line of plastic trays filled with champagne flutes into a tall, rectangular machine that she soon identified as an industrial dishwasher. In front of her, a squad of Latino men in overalls were grabbing at hoses dangling from the ceiling as they washed a series of enormous pots and pans. She could see another door, but that led straight back out into the kitchen: she'd be an easy target for the guard.

She would have to head back out of this room the way she came in, this time turning left again and moving further away from the kitchen, darting between two tall, mobile racks – their slots filled with trays – on the move, before taking the first door she could see.

A blast of frigid air announced this as the cold store, where metal shelves were stacked with oversized containers of strawberries and raspberries and cartoonishly large pots of mayonnaise. Again, there was no external door.

'Get out of my way, sir.'

She couldn't see him, but the tone and volume of that voice told her that the security guard was moving out of the cooking area and coming this way. Maggie had no choice. In that instant, she backed out of the cold store and opened instead the next door she came to, walking straight inside.

Except this was not a room. The size, added to the sharp drop in temperature, confirmed that she had stepped into a freezer. There were shelves to the left and right of her and straight ahead, arranged in a U-shape that left a small clearing in which she could stand. It was perhaps six feet across, and four feet deep. She felt the door close behind her.

The obvious thing to do was to turn around and get out, to find somewhere else – anywhere else – to hide. But the guard would have made up the ground by now. If she went back outside, she would walk right into him. She could not let that happen. She had somewhere she needed to be.

She looked around, searching for anything that might serve as a hiding place. There was a corner of the bottom shelf to her left that was in shadow. The space on either side of it was filled, which not only added to the darkness but which, Maggie reasoned, would make it plausible for there to be something there. That something would be her.

She approached, preparing to squeeze herself into the gap. Quickly, she saw that it couldn't be done with her shoes on. She needed to make herself smaller, with fewer hard edges. She slipped the shoes off and held them instead, as she crouched down and clambered into the space. Next she curled her chin into her chest and faced the wall.

She held her breath. Still, she could pick up the scent of the food next to her: vast vats of chocolate ice cream. The lights went out.

Perhaps two seconds later, the door opened.

'Anyone in here?'

Maggie kept her eyes closed, but she sensed a flashlight scoping the room. She held tight, willing her body not to tremble in this cold.

She could hear that the guard was still inside, his footsteps echoing against the cold surface of the floor.

He took a step closer.

And then three or four steps in quick succession, followed by the sound of the door opening and closing again.

She breathed out. But she would not uncoil just yet. He might come back in. Her eyes still closed, she strained to hear the sound from outside.

The guard was talking into the cold store, just next door. 'The police are on their way, miss. So if I were you, I'd come out quietly and we'll work this out.'

Her teeth were itching to chatter. It took an act of will to bite down and force them to stay quiet. There was a banging sound from outside.

'Ladies and gentlemen, I know you have work to do, but we need your co-operation. There is a woman hiding in this vicinity who we believe poses a security threat to guests at this hotel.'

The cold was beginning to bite into her bones.

'If you see anything unusual, you need to report it to us right away. To us or the police, who are on their way. And if you find the woman we're looking for – white, red hair, around five foot eight inches – you need to detain her, by force if necessary. Is that clear?'

Maggie could hear the sullen silence of the kitchen staff.

'Is that clear?'

There was a murmur, and then the sound of work resuming.

Maggie considered uncoiling herself, and breaking out of this icebox that was now making her convulse with cold. Her feet, sheathed in nothing but the gossamer-thin fabric of her tights, were pressed into the back wall of the unit, which made things worse. But she could still hear footsteps and noise outside: it wasn't safe to get out.

Even as she could hear the guard, apparently patrolling the space between the cold store, the pot-wash area and here, her nervous system switched focus, away from fear of this man and his gun, towards the cold that was burning through the shoeless soles of her feet. The chill was instant and extreme, an unbearable frost that threatened to turn both feet numb any moment now. She had to get her shoes back on.

She moved to uncurl herself, but as she did, she could see that her hands were not so much trembling as quaking, as if entirely out of her control. The skin on her bare arms became rough with goosebumps. The urge of her teeth to chatter was too strong to resist; once she succumbed, she seemed to vibrate with cold.

Perhaps it was because of all those uncontrolled movements, but as she moved her right foot, her tights snagged on the shelf, ripping the fabric from the heel to the toe. Not that she saw it in the dark. Realization came when she came to put her shoes back on, planting the bare sole of her right foot on the cold hard ground.

Her grip palsied by cold, it took Maggie longer than she'd anticipated to put the left shoe back on. As she moved to do the same for her right foot, she felt a sensation that sent a shot of pure alarm through her cerebral cortex. The shoe was in her hand and she had bent herself into the right posture, but she could not lift her foot off the ground. It wasn't a muscle failure or a deficiency of strength. It was the cold: in just a few seconds the sole had become stuck to the frozen floor.

She gave it another push, sending all her strength into her foot. But it was sealed tight. Another effort, though this time a new fear inserted itself: what if she tore her foot from the ground, but left her skin behind in the process? It seemed so fully cemented by the sub-zero temperatures she had no confidence that, in a test of strength between herself and the frost, she would win.

Instinct made her crouch down and attempt to slip her fingers under the sole of her foot, to prise it away. As she bent, she heard her knees click.

The voice from outside again, now speaking into whatever

room was on the far side of this one. 'Miss? You cannot wait this one out. You need to come out.'

But she wasn't paying attention to the guard, but to another sound she heard just as he spoke. It was distant and she could not be certain it wasn't some neurological trick played on her by the ice that seemed to have inveigled its way into her entire sensory system. But she thought she had heard a beep. Just a single one, but definitely there.

She willed there to be a second one, which might act as confirmation. But on the basis of what she had, she reckoned the sound came from her left. More important, and on this she was certain, the noise was not from inside this freezer or even the vast kitchen area. It was from outside. From the street. If she guessed right, it was the sound of a reversing truck.

The trouble was, there was no way to explore, not without leaving this hiding place of hers. It was clear: she had to get out. If she did not, she might freeze to death, if the guard didn't find her first.

She was still crouching, almost squatting, with her fingers desperately trying to work her foot away from the glacial floor. She made her palm flat and attempted to slide it under the sole, like slipping a spatula under a steak glued to a frying pan. She shoved at it, wriggling her fingers to keep the blood flowing and to ward off the numbness.

More noise from outside. 'The police have arrived, Miss Costello. You're all out of time.'

At that instant, and in an intense act of will, Maggie simultaneously slid her hand underneath with great force and devoted all her mental strength to the task of peeling her foot off the ground, forcing her mind to pay no heed to her fears about leaving her skin behind.

It worked, the foot finally lifting free of the ground, sending a strange, sickening pain through her. In the same motion, she put on the shoe which she'd been holding in her free hand, stood up to full height and rushed for the door.

But where was the handle?

She couldn't see it, not where she'd expected it.

Oh, please God, no.

She had thought of this place as a room, but now she wondered if it was, in fact, exactly like a freezer you might have at home – one that only opens from the outside.

Her hands, her jaws, her knees were trembling, as she searched for the way out. She looked left and right, though her sight was struggling in this cold. It wasn't the curling wreaths of vapour in the air that were the trouble, but rather her eyes themselves. They seemed to be moving more slowly, straining to process visual information. She wondered if the cold had simply dried up the film of moisture that was meant to cover them. Or, worse, was the jelly of her eyeballs itself beginning to freeze?

At last she saw it, a green hemisphere of a button on the right-hand side. She pressed her palm on it and, with a sound that sent relief into every part of her, the door mechanism was released. She pushed it open and with a glance left and right, she turned left, towards the sound of that single, hopeful beep.

She slalomed her way through more vertical racks and stainless steel counters, until she saw that her instinct had been right.

There was a loading bay at the back of this area, one that opened to the outside world. But it was not open now. And yet if she was right about that reversing truck, perhaps it was about to open at any moment?

Her eyes went to the far wall where, demarcated by a pattern of diagonal red and white stripes, was a red pull-down lever. She guessed – she hoped – it was the mechanism for opening the steel-shuttered barrier that would give out onto the loading bay.

She could hear male voices, a group of them, arriving from the main kitchen. Could she get to that lever without being spotted? And if she did, wouldn't the noise immediately give her away? And, her biggest worry: would the door take so long to open that the guard, now backed by police, would have time to grab her before she'd had a chance to get out?

The voices were getting nearer. She'd have to risk it. She took a breath and, her limbs still stiff from the cold, ran to the lever. Feeling the metal in her hand, she pulled it down.

The noise was fierce, a howling klaxon accompanied by clanging bells, while three flashing red lights immediately began turning directly above the barrier.

Simultaneously, the steel shutters began to rise towards the ceiling. The opening was tiny at first, but immediately after pulling the lever, Maggie had laid herself flat on the ground, ready to roll out as soon as the gap became wide enough. She did that now, finding herself on the other side, covered in the dirt of a delivery dock. She got to her feet and in that moment realized that she was on a concrete platform, set at the height of a truck bed. She contemplated the steep drop to street level, but did not hesitate. The alarm had probably confused her pursuers – masking the sound of the gate opening – but it had given her a head start of no more than two or three seconds. She had to jump. Now.

The pain in her right foot was intense as she landed, but she could not listen to it. Instead, she ran and ran, turning right as soon as she could, desperate to get out of this deserted back alley and out onto the main drag of Connecticut Avenue, where there would be the safety of people. As she ran, she wondered if that really was a shot she heard whizz past her ear and wondered too about the strangely damp, almost fresh sensation she felt in her right foot.

But she tried to put both out of her mind as she finally took in the blessed sight of traffic and, better still, an approaching cab. She was focused only on where she had to go next – and how little time she had.

Chapter Forty-Seven

Capitol Hill, Washington DC, 8.40pm

Just that little touch to the ear had confirmed it. Until then, Maggie could not be certain that the former 'Tammy French' was guilty. But that reaction to hearing the name again, that call to her private security detail, confirmed it. It meant Maggie was right.

It also brought back a line from the Bookburner's manifesto that had, on first reading, seemed like little more than a platitude.

Sometimes events have a momentum of their own.

As Maggie slouched low in the back seat of a cab racing along Massachusetts Avenue, occasionally peeking over her shoulder to check if she was being followed, that was the line that she replayed in her head, over and over. It had new meaning now.

Maggie reached under her left sleeve, where her phone was strapped in place in a runner's armband. She pulled it out and looked up the corporation that had 'Tammy French' on the billionaires' table. Maggie had read this entry a dozen times, but now a thought was forming.

Austin Logica is a multi-billion-dollar company specializing in financial systems and algorithmic innovation. It was established initially as a data processing firm in the 1980s . . .

She read on until she came to the key paragraph.

Besides data analytics, AL's breakthrough product was software that drew on machine learning, thereby automating processes that previously required a human operator. Widely seen as the first large-scale application of artificial intelligence in the financial sphere, AL benefitted from . . .

Now Maggie looked out of the window and bit her lip. She looked back at the text of the page in front of her, which was describing the breakthrough Austin Logica had made which massively increased its scale and wealth, developing the key bit of software widely credited with the advance of 'the internet of things'.

Sometimes events have a momentum of their own.

Maggie's mind was racing, but her body also demanded attention.

The change in temperature as she re-entered the world outside the freezer store had been a relief, but now her skin seemed confused by it: little goosebumps reappeared at intervals on her arms, almost as if they were remembering the intense cold. She rubbed her arms, up and down, again and again.

But her focus was on her foot. Only once she was safely in the car, and had closed her eyes for two or three seconds as she forced herself to take several slow, deep breaths, did she attend to the sensations that were coming from her right shoe. Gingerly, she tried to remove it but stopped before it was fully off. The shoe was gurgling with blood; it contained enough to fill a coffee mug.

She could see what had happened and the sight made her gag.

It was exactly as she had feared. The patch of skin that covered the ball of her foot had been stuck so tightly to the floor of the freezer that, in the tug of war between her and the frost, the frost had won. It had kept hold of the skin, tearing it cleanly from the sole. It was doubtless still there, on the floor.

She suspected that the cold had killed off her nerve endings, or at least dulled them. That, coupled with the adrenalin that was thumping through her system, had anaesthetized her: intense pain was coming, she was sure of it. She asked the driver for his box of tissues, used almost all of them to mop up the blood and form an improvised bandage, replaced the shoe and tried to focus.

Sometimes events have a momentum of their own.

When Maggie first skimmed past that line, she'd read it as no more than an abstract rumination on the forward propulsion of history, the way human events can seem to be driven by a force greater than any individual or even collective act of decision, the way they can seem to be pushed by nature itself. But now it struck her as more important, more concrete, than that. These words were a warning.

The thoughts were tumbling over each other now. The source

of 'Tammy French's' fortune, a company at the cutting edge of artificial intelligence. The fact that the CCTV from the various fires around the world had shown no intruders or attackers, no arsonists carrying cans of petrol. The fact that there had been no arrests. *Sometimes events have a momentum of their own.*

Maggie willed the driver to go faster as they moved along Constitution Avenue, the glowing white dome of the US Capitol looming over them. In a few seconds she would be at the Library of Congress. She knew exactly where she needed to go – somewhere that, for once, involved no people.

Chapter Forty-Eight

Capitol Hill, Washington DC, 8.46pm

She thrust a bill in the driver's hand and, seconds later, she was facing the mammoth, neo-classical facade of the Jefferson building of the Library of Congress, built with enough grandeur to be worthy of a spot directly opposite the Capitol and next to the Supreme Court. Except now it was not the architecture alone that made it an intimidating sight.

This building and the other two that made up the library were wholly encircled by a combination of armed police, military-grade vehicles and traffic barriers. She counted at least ten fire trucks. Overhead was the constant throb of a police chopper. It was the full ring of steel, put in place hours after the fires in Oxford, Paris and Beijing. The couple of daytime entry points, with airport-style walk-through metal detectors, were now closed.

Maggie got as close as she could, walking the sealed perimeter, looking for any hint of a gap. She approached the larger, more modern Madison building – each step bringing a fresh surge of pain, a red flash which forced her to picture the exposed, raw flesh of her right foot – but something told her that the prime target would be this, the oldest, most historic part of the library.

Maggie strode up to the first officer she could find, standing sentry by one of the traffic barriers sealing off the path to the Jefferson building's main entrance. He had a semi-automatic weapon across his midriff, and was bulked up with a bulletproof vest attached variously to a radio, a phone, a body-camera, a spray canister and a truncheon.

'Maggie Costello, White House,' she said, flashing her now-expired pass.

Without replying, he muttered into his radio. Minutes later a man she presumed to be a more senior officer appeared.

'My name is Maggie Costello from the White House, and I need access to this building. Urgently.'

'You got written clearance to be here?'

'No. This is an emergency. As we all know, this building is under imminent threat from a terror attack and I need access to prevent it.' She was aware of how ludicrous that sounded, especially coming from a woman in evening wear.

'No one gets in or out of this building, ma'am. Those are our orders. No exceptions.'

'But it's not about who gets in or out. That's not where the threat is coming from.'

'Well, feel free to take it up with the Chief of Police or the Director of the FBI. But the way we're dealing with this situation is to let no one in. OK?'

Maggie walked away, her head pounding in frustration. Her foot was throbbing, almost in sync. She reached for her phone and dialled Andrea Ellis's number. Mercifully, she picked up.

'Maggie?'

'No time to explain, but I need you to authorize entry for me into the Library of Congress. I need to get in there before—'

'There's no way I can do that, Maggie.'

'What? Why?'

'I can't put an untrained, unarmed, unequipped person into harm's way.'

'Oh, for fuck's sake, I can look after myself, you know that.'

'This is a counter-terrorism situation, Maggie. Given the pattern so far, after hours is exactly when the danger is greatest. It's night-time: there's no way I'm putting you in there.'

'Andrea, please. I think I know how this is playing out. I need to—'

'The answer is no, Maggie. And that is my final word.'

Maggie drifted away from the cordon and found herself pacing aimlessly. Her foot was screamingly painful. It was telling her what she did not want to hear: that it was time to go home, that it was time to give up.

As she approached the kerb, thinking how far she'd have to walk to have any chance of hailing a cab, her phone vibrated. It was a text. Where the name should be, it simply said *No Caller ID*. She read the message twice.

Go to the rear service entrance. Around the corner from the steel shuttered gate, there is a narrow side alley. Currently unmanned.

There is an unmarked door with a keypad mechanism. Enter the number 657843.

It would be lunacy to follow this advice: it was so obviously a trap. Whoever had sent this message either had some way of seeing that she was here, trying to get in, or had guessed that that was what she would do. She would be walking right into their lap.

And yet, what if this was a miscalculation on their part? Maybe the sender of that text did want to lure her in, but once inside the library she could look after herself, couldn't she? At least she'd be in, with a shot at stopping the fire. Out here she was useless.

She walked around the perimeter until she found the steel-shuttered entrance to an underground car park in an area populated with oversized bins. This had to be the service area, protected as far as she could tell by at least four armed officers. She kept walking until, as promised, she reached a gap in the cordon. It opened to a narrow alleyway between two brick walls: you'd walk straight past it if you weren't looking for it.

Maggie darted inside and came to a locked brown metal door. Even the keypad was barely noticeable. She had to squint in the darkness to type in the six numbers.

It opened with a clunk and, at last, she was in. She was standing in a bare, concrete stairwell, possibly a fire escape. She walked upward, pushing her way through double-doors and then a series of narrow corridors, hoping for something recognizable.

After several wrong turns, she pushed into what she guessed was a suite of back offices. Suddenly there was a sound, a movement from the floor above her. There was no doubt about it: there were footsteps.

Hesitantly, she emerged, looking in the gloom for a staircase. She took it, moving as noiselessly as she could up each step.

She was in a lobby, which led through to a vast reading room. That was where the sound had come from.

She moved inside and then called out.

'This is the FBI. Who's there?'

Nothing.

'I'm armed,' she lied, hoping there was no tremor in her voice. 'Put your hands in the air and reveal yourself.'

Maggie held her breath. Was she about to put a human face at last to the plague of fire that had devoured one great library after another, and that sought to destroy this one?

As quietly as she could, she pulled out her phone and activated the flashlight. The beam lit up stack after stack of books, scoping the empty space until, at last, it picked out a distinct, undisguised face. Maggie recognized it straight away.

Chapter Forty-Nine

The Library of Congress, Washington DC, 9.18pm

His hands were up and, Maggie could see, they were trembling. Even the whiskers of his long, biblical beard seemed to be quaking. Irving Herman, Principal Deputy Librarian of the Library of Congress, looked terrified.

'Mr Herman?'

'I'm sorry,' he said, shielding his eyes from the light. It was only then he made out Maggie's face. His expression changed. Something like a smile appeared. 'I told you, didn't I, Miss Costello? I'd do anything for these books. I've given my lifetime to them. Why wouldn't I give my life?'

'How long have you been here?'

'In the library? Every night since this started.'

'Standing guard?'

He looked sheepish. 'Trying to, yes.'

'And no one's seen you? None of them?' Maggie gestured at the armed presence outside.

'They're relying on the CCTV to see what's happening inside,' he said, 'and I don't think it's working. But I can see outside. That's how I saw you, through the window.'

'So that text was from you.'

He nodded. 'What can I say? You seemed to care.'

Maggie smiled. 'I do care, Mr Herman. I don't think we have much time and I need your help. I need you to take me to the server room.'

Instantly Herman turned and led Maggie through the reading room, out and down two flights of stairs to a lower ground floor level. They went past the coat check area and a locker room, until finally they faced a series of brown doors that were marked *Staff*, *Private* and finally *Authorized Entry Only*. Herman, who had an ID card on a lanyard around his neck, now tugged at it so that it stretched on a long string, enabling him to unlock a reader whose small red light instantly turned green.

The temperature increase hit her straight away, even before the lights turned themselves on. Fans were grinding away noisily, but still the air was thick and stuffy. She was in a room full of machines, stacks of slim black boxes – each one the size of a component from an old-school hi-fi system – held in vertical racks. All of them were flickering away, the lights signalling a code that to her was utterly opaque.

She tried to divine the logic that might govern this room. Several of the stacks were indeed labelled, but not in language that made any sense to her. One was marked *PHP Server*, another *SQL Database*. She guessed that *LOC Intranet* referred to the internal website of the Library of Congress. Otherwise, she was clueless.

Herman was looking at her hopefully, as if she might be able to unlock this puzzle.

'Listen,' she said. 'I think the threat is coming from the outside. I don't exactly know how they're doing it, but someone is hacking into the system that controls everything in these buildings – the heating, the lights, the air-conditioning – and using it to start a fire.'

'They're turning the building against itself.'

'Exactly. The only way we can stop them is if we just break the connection. Somehow we need to prevent any instructions they're sending – to the fire controls or whatever – from getting through. Which means this room. So Mr Herman, I'm asking you: do you know how any of this works?'

She knew the answer even before asking the question. He gave a shrug that told her he was as baffled by all this as she was.

'All right. I need you to call whoever operates this room. Ideally, whoever set it up.'

'I have a number for the head of IT?'

'Call them,' she said. Herman hesitated, as if awaiting more detailed instructions. 'Now, Irving. Call them now!'

His phone had no signal, so he stepped outside, his foot keeping the door ajar. She watched his face as he waited. And waited. 'Not even voicemail,' he said.

Maggie now pulled out her phone and dialled Liz's number, which she'd taken care to memorize.

'Come on, come on,' she muttered, as she waited for a ringing sound. After what seemed an age, there was a first ring, and then a second. And then a third. No reply and, once again, no voicemail. That was odd. Liz almost always picked up. Her phone was with her at all times, and even if she screened other people, she always took a call from her sister.

Were these calls – from her, from Herman – even going through? Was whoever – or whichever programme – that was doing this somehow jamming any phone signal that came from deep inside this building?

Whatever the explanation, she was on her own.

She looked again at each stack of servers, seeking to decipher these meagre labels. What the hell was PHP? Could the H refer to the heating system? And what of SQL?

Herman was standing next to her. She turned to him. 'Have you ever heard people refer to the electronic system for the maintenance of this building?'

'You mean the temperature and so forth?'

'Exactly. What do they call it?'

'Obviously curators and conservators and suchlike refer to "climate control". And sometimes, I think I've heard them say "environmental control". Does that help?'

Maggie was off looking through the racks, their lights dancing merrily. No sign of CC or EC or anything like it.

Perhaps it was the heat or the frustration or the raw throb coming from her right foot, but at last the frustration got to her. 'Jesus Christ, where the hell is it?' she said, pounding the wall.

'I could take you to the boiler room perhaps?' Herman said.

She looked at him, sure he was wrong. That would be the room full of dumb machinery – all pipes and tanks – when what she needed was the brain in charge. But she had drawn a blank here. She gestured for him to lead the way.

More corridors, more stairs as Maggie frantically checked her watch. It was late in the evening, approaching the hour when so many of the other libraries had been struck. And there was only one left. The machines that Austin Logica had programmed – or who had, themselves, learned how to wreak this havoc across five continents once given their broad mission – were doubtless readying to strike at any moment. Perhaps they already had: the fuse wire, or its electronic equivalent, had been laid in the last few days or hours or minutes and the match was about to be lit any second now. *Sometimes events have a momentum of their own.*

They'd arrived at the boiler room. As they walked in, no motion-sensitive lights came on to illuminate the room. Once Herman had found a manual light switch, she could see why.

Inside was an old furnace, including a coal oven of the kind you might find in the engine of a steam train. There was a copper boiler attached to an enormous cylindrical tank and a thicket of pipes. All of it was defunct. It looked like an exhibit in a museum. Which in a way, in a protected, historic building like this one, it was. This was the Library of Congress: even a disused boiler room was deemed to be of significance, and therefore had to be preserved.

She looked at Herman, who rather than looking downcast seemed to have a new resolve. 'I don't know what I was thinking. Please, follow me.'

He led Maggie to the basement level, to what seemed to be less a room than an oversized store cupboard. There was something that looked like an elaborate fusebox, and the rest was a series of electronic panels, glowing with various shades of cool blue light.

Her eye ran over each one: fire alarm, burglar alarm, lighting. Eventually, in the right-hand corner, she saw it: a sophisticated panel, displaying multiple squares, each window suggesting a zone of the library and dotted with numbers, which Maggie guessed indicated times, target humidity and the like. Even at a glance, she could see that the temperature setting was not normal: it displayed not a number, but the word 'Maximum', alongside a red warning triangle containing an exclamation mark.

She pressed at the touchpad, but that brought up a boxed message which covered most of the display: *Manual override disabled. Contact your system administrator.*

The box faded and she tried it again. The same message appeared. Whoever it was who had hacked into the central nervous system of this building, one thing was clear: their control was now total.

Maggie had already decided on the action she would deploy in this situation. She grabbed at the cable that fed into the climate control panel and which had been neatly stapled to the wall. She tugged at it once, then tugged at it again. On the second attempt, the cable broke free of its neat plastic brackets and was easier to grip. But it was still feeding power to the panel.

She pressed the palm of her right hand onto the device, pinning it to the wall, and with her left hand she gave a third yank to the wire, pulling downward. To her intense satisfaction, she felt it wrench away, its copper endings now exposed. The screen fell dark.

She turned to look at Herman, catching his smile. The pair stood there, enjoying the moment of stunned relief. 'Does this mean the books will now be safe?' Herman said.

'It should do,' Maggie said. 'Now, whatever instructions the hackers are sending to the equipment in this building, none of it will get through.'

'What was that?' Herman said, cupping his ear.

Maggie was about to say it again, this time shouting to be heard, when she stopped herself. *The fan in this room was still going.*

Without saying anything, Maggie ran out of the basement riser, up the stairs to the ground floor and into the corridor, running until she saw a grille in the wall. She held her hand up, to feel the breeze coming from the vent, stretching on tiptoes to reach. There was no doubt: air was still coming through.

Which meant she hadn't turned off the system. She had only prevented new instructions from getting through. Whatever settings had already been programmed, they were still in place, the building's fans and heaters dutifully obeying their command.

And that would include the most recent commands, issued just a few minutes ago by those bent on destroying the last of the world's great libraries. Now they would be implemented and she was powerless to stop them.

She turned back to find Herman, who was looking at her, baffled.

'Irving, I need you to think. What is the driest room in this building? What has the oldest books?'

'What? I don't understand.'

'If you were going to burn this building down, where would you start?'

Herman dipped his head and scratched the space just above his ear. Maggie felt the impatience pulse through her. Her foot seemed to be flashing red with pain.

'Please, Irving. Where?'

'Rare books,' he said at last. 'The Rare Books and Special Collections Reading Room. Second floor.'

They took the stairs together, galloping until they reached two wooden double-doors. Maggie hesitated for a second. What if this room was already on fire? What if opening these doors released a fireball that not only killed both of them but devoured the rest of the library? Perhaps there had been a moment like this in Paris, in Tehran and in Moscow: a moment when someone, in their desperation to save a library, had destroyed it. She thought of that librarian in Tokyo, giving his life to rescue a collection he loved – and doing so in vain.

But there was no time to pause. She pushed the door open and felt a marked increase in temperature. She looked for any sign of fire, but there was none. The heat was less natural than that: it felt like someone had left all the radiators on full blast.

Herman looked towards her, as if waiting for a cue. She was walking along one wall, past the antique maps kept under glass and the notices announcing future exhibitions and advising that last requests for books was at five pm, looking upward, waiting to see an air vent. She found one and indicated for Herman to bring over a chair. While he held it steady, she climbed up, letting out a yelp as she put pressure on the exposed flesh of her right foot.

As soon as she reached the right height, she could feel it: the heat seeping through the metal slats. She touched the grille, the first step towards an attempt at removing it. But it was too hot to touch. She was in the right place; she knew it.

She looked back down, presuming she would find Herman still gripping the chair. In fact, he'd already disappeared behind one of the librarians' desks, emerging a few seconds later carrying a slim, metal ruler.

'I was looking for a screwdriver,' he said, 'but I'm afraid this is all I could find.'

Maggie thought of summoning one of the men outside: they were bound to have tools. But there was no time. She took the ruler and began prodding and probing at the grille, looking for a weak point where she might prise it loose. To her surprise, the horizontal strips of metal bent easily. Perhaps they were melting in the heat.

Soon she had created an opening wide enough for her to put her hand through. She tugged at her sleeve to shield the skin of her fingers, forming a makeshift glove as she pushed her hand in and worked away at the edges. She pushed at the frame of the grille, her fingers working their way around its border. It was working, the metal rectangle becoming looser each time. Finally, and using the cloth of her sleeve, she grabbed hold of the grille by clutching several of the bent metal strips and yanked it towards her. It came away in her hand.

She let it drop to the floor and now closed her eyes to brace herself for what she knew would be a near-impossible exertion. Other women her age were at the gym four or five times a week, if not daily. Their arms were taut and sinewy: a pull-up bar would hold no terrors for them. But Maggie was not one of those women.

To her sister's irritation, Maggie remained slim with minimal exercise and she could take a flight of stairs without gasping for breath. But what fitness she had was native, rather than worked. Yet now she would have to pull herself up and into this small opening, a manoeuvre more demanding even than lifting her own body weight, for it also required a gymnastic pivot into a narrow space (and gymnastics had never been her strong point).

She looked down at Irving Herman's face, which was simultaneously hopeful and desperate. She looked back up at the vent, girded herself, closed her eyes for a second.

With all her strength she got herself up to the right height, her hands gripping the lower edge of the opening. Now she would need to plunge her head and shoulders in, inserting herself as far as she could.

But she hadn't reckoned on the blast of heat. It came at her like a punch, a thick jet of hot air that almost choked her. It made her lose her grip and plunge back down onto the chair, landing on the raw wound that was her right foot.

Herman attempted to comfort her but succeeded only in annoying her. She brushed him away, reset herself and assessed the opening one more time. She took a breath and made the leap again.

This time she allowed no interval between reaching the requisite height and making the pivot. She tried to combine it into a single movement: up and then folding her back so that she made herself into an L-shape as she pushed her head into the space as far as it would go. Then another surge of strength as her hands pushed along the duct to drag her torso and waist in behind her. Instinctively she knew when she had passed the fulcrum point, with more of her body in the vent than outside it. She exhaled, a half second of relaxation, before snaking her way inside on her front, commando-style.

Ahead of her she could see what she took to be the heating unit, a big pulsing metal box generating the roasting air that was now at an unbearable temperature. She looked down at the floor, at the dust and grime, at the accumulated debris of human skin and hair, all of it tinder-dry, and now could guess how each of these great houses of learning had been torched. These vents contained the perfect kindling. All the unseen arsonists had to do was remotely turn the heating units to their maximum setting and wait for them to strain beyond their capacity. Eventually they would be the spark that would light that pyre.

Suddenly, as Maggie inched her way closer, there was a new noise. It took her a second to identify it and then another second to absorb its meaning. A fan had just switched on, moving the stagnant, super-heated air directly into her face. Of course. This was surely how they got the fire out from the duct and into the building, fuelling the blaze with nurturing oxygen. It would catch any moment now.

She had drawn level with the heating unit. Her skin seemed to be burning up, as if she were blasted by a scorching sun. But she had to get closer. In the quarter-light of this narrow tunnel, she knew she hadn't found what she was searching for.

And then, at last, she saw it, emerging from the base of the steel heating unit: a simple white cable. She tugged at it, but couldn't get purchase on it. It seemed to be moulded into the machine. She pulled again.

Suddenly she had an image of what would happen if she succeeded. A live, naked cable exposed to this searing heat: it would spark. It would be she who had started the fire that would destroy this building – and take her life.

No. She would have to turn these machines off. But how? Blindly, and through touch alone, she traced the cable until she hit the side wall. The cable disappeared into it. There was no socket and no plug that could be neatly pulled out. She felt faint. She heard herself gasping for oxygen.

And then her fingers found it. Midway up the wall was a thick, large but simple switch. Even in this gloom, she could see it was held in position by a thin filament of wire, to prevent an accidental decision to move it. With a penknife she could have cut through the wire easily, but of course she had no knife. She removed her watch and, with its metal strap side on, used it as a makeshift and painfully blunt saw. She was gasping in the heat.

Finally the wire gave way. The switch was exposed.

Maggie hesitated. What if it was not as it seemed? But she had no choice. There was no time. She closed her eyes and flicked the switch.

Saturday

Chapter Fifty

FBI field office, Washington DC, 2.37am

'You OK?'

'Sure.'

'Do you want to take a moment?'

'No. no. I'll be fine.'

'You don't have to do this, Maggie. Really, I can do it. And you can watch.'

She and the Deputy Director of the FBI, Andrea Ellis, were standing just outside an FBI interview suite, by the two-way mirror which, from this side, served as a wide picture window. It allowed them to look at the prime suspect in the Bookburner case, arrested less than an hour earlier in connection with a global conspiracy to destroy the world's great libraries, to murder leading historians, survivors and eyewitnesses and to attack the foundations of global knowledge and information. Someone whose vast wealth, connections and command of technology extended all the way across the planet, even into the heart of the world's most powerful government, allowing her company to hack into the White House itself. She was there right now, calmly staring into space: the woman once known as Tammy French.

'I want to,' Maggie said.

'The doctors will kill me if they find out. The report from that so-called examination you had says you've suffered serious burns, skin damage, possibly grave psychological trauma and that you should be hospitalized immediately.'

Maggie's foot was throbbing and she was feeling light-headed, two facts she had concealed from the FBI paramedics who, on Andrea's orders, had checked her out. 'Doctors. Always over-anxious. They remind me of the nuns.'

'Maggie. With all due respect: they had to pull you out of a ventilation duct that was about to blow. The fire department said it was a matter of seconds before it went up. If you ask me, it's a miracle.'

'I was pretty lucky.'

'I don't think luck had anything to do with it.'

'So. Shall we go in?'

'If you're ready.'

'I'm ready. Actually, one thing before we go in. No one's explained to me properly: how did you know to pick her up?'

Andrea smiled. 'You led us right to her, Maggie.' When she saw Maggie's look of puzzlement, she lifted her ankle and tapped it. 'That tag on your leg, remember. We saw you'd gone in and been chased straight out. Didn't take long to find out who you'd been asking to see.' She smiled again. 'Come. It's time.'

Andrea led the way, opening the door and taking her place directly opposite the suspect. Maggie was at Ellis's side, which suited her fine: it meant she could stare at this woman's face without having her stare straight back.

As Ellis introduced herself, explaining that Maggie Costello had been a senior investigator in the case, Maggie's gaze remained fixed. There were traces of the Tammy French Maggie had seen in that Stanford photo, the young woman in the sunglasses. But that wasn't who she was seeing now.

Instead, she cast her mind back to the first time she had seen this woman in person, just a few days ago. So different then: demure, shy even. And, unexpected in a billionaire, clearly lacking in confidence.

But the woman at this table was, no less unexpectedly, calm, even serene. Her hands were crossed on her lap; they were not trembling. There were none of the nerves Maggie had spotted in that lecture theatre.

'I know you've already had your rights formally read to you, so I won't do that again, and you have also waived the right to have counsel present, including an offer of legal support provided by your father. That remains your position?'

'Yes.'

'For the tape, can you confirm that your name is Pamela April Bentham?'

'Yes.'

'And you know why you are here?'

'I do indeed.'

'Good. I'm going to run through the essential facts as we understand them, and then we'll have some questions. Is that clear?'

'Crystal.'

'As you know, federal agents have raided the headquarters of the company you own, Austin Logica, in Austin, Texas. They have commandeered the building and a team of infosec specialists have spent the last few hours working methodically to both dismantle and analyze the apparatus inside. Initial findings suggest that the attacks on the so-called Alexandria Group of libraries, archives and databases around the world were directed electronically from your company headquarters and indeed under your personal instruction. That will be the heart of the government case against you.

'We believe that your machine learning program was deployed to target a weakness in these libraries' HVAC, or heating, ventilation and air-conditioning, systems, taking control of them remotely and that, once the programme was up and running, no human hand may even have been involved.'

Sometimes events have a momentum of their own.

'We further believe that you, through Austin Logica or through hired agents acting for you, organized the murder of several individual figures, in this country and around the world. There is also clear evidence linking you and/or Austin Logica to the penetration and sabotage of Google and its global search function, as well as to a series of fires at book distribution centres in the US and around the world. As such, it is likely that you will face a series of charges including arson, conspiracy to commit arson, murder, conspiracy to commit murder and terrorism. I repeat my advice to you earlier: the forensic evidence my colleagues are gathering against you in Austin and elsewhere is so overwhelming, your best course of action – perhaps your only course of action – is to co-operate with us and our investigation. Is that clear?'

'Yes.'

'Is there any comment you would wish to make about the facts presented so far?'

Bentham said nothing, but her silence was not a hostile one. She was at ease, like a woman patiently waiting for a train or sitting in her box seat at the opera, preparing for the overture to begin. She did not meet either Andrea's eye or Maggie's, but even that did not seem to betray discomfort, let alone guilt. Rather she seemed content merely to contemplate her own thoughts.

'Could I ask a question about timing?' Maggie said, doing her best to seem calm, doing her best to repress the thought of all those precious documents destroyed forever, the thought of Russell Aikman and Judith Beaton and, most painful to Maggie, Martin Kelly.

Bentham turned towards her, her face polite if incurious, as Maggie said, 'Why was it important that these libraries be destroyed by Friday? Why couldn't it take as long as it took? Why the hurry?'

Bentham said nothing, though there was a hint of a smile.

Maggie tried again. 'You see, I think it has something to do with William Keane.'

Maggie could feel Andrea next to her, gazing as intently at Bentham as she was. They could see the change in her, the way her eyes widened, the way she moved in her seat. Just at the mention of his name.

'You were one of his students at Stanford, I think.'

'No need to say "I think" when you know. No need for games.'

'You were a student under the name Tammy French.'

Bentham said nothing.

'Is that right?' said Andrea.

Bentham nodded.

'And Keane was quite something, wasn't he?'

Again, the half-smile but no words.

'I know he had an enormous influence on all those who studied under him. Crawford McNamara was something of a protégé, I think.' Maggie had chosen her words carefully.

'Did he tell you that? I'm sure Crawford would like to think so.'

'Is he wrong?'

'Professor Keane didn't have favourites. He cared about all of us.'

In that moment, Maggie glimpsed the young Tammy French, shunted around by her corporate tycoon father from one boarding school to another, finally arriving, barely out of her teens, at Stanford and finding herself in the classroom of William Keane: a dazzling, whip-smart older man with the time to pay attention, even to her.

The pain in her foot was insistent now, demanding that Maggie listen to it. She was beginning to see colours that weren't there. But she pressed on. 'And then suddenly Keane was back, all these years later, fighting this big legal case. And you wanted to help him, isn't that right?'

Bentham was silent again, holding Maggie's gaze with a smile that was almost a smirk.

Ellis chipped in. 'I will remind you again, Ms Bentham, that the only hope for you is to answer our questions. This lack of co-operation might seem like a clever strategy but I warn you, any judge will see it as evidence of guilt rather than innocence. Your case would be best—'

'Surely you understand why I have no interest in helping "my case"? Surely you realize why I have no need of a lawyer? Oh, come on, you're both intelligent women. Isn't it obvious?'

'Isn't what obvious?'

'That I've *won*.'

Both Maggie and Andrea had the same instinct. *Say nothing: let her talk*.

'I admit nothing, of course. But look what's happened. All these libraries, vanished. All those documents, disappeared. The historical record will never be the same again. And let's say your agents have destroyed that little algorithm you say was working in Austin. Do you really think that will be the end of it?

'You talk about machine learning, Miss Ellis, but what about something much more powerful? What about *human* learning? What if human beings have witnessed the extraordinary events of the last few days and learned something from them? What if they decide they don't need my computers or anyone else's to continue this vital work, and they decide to carry it on themselves? Copycat attacks, the newspapers call them. And then there's a copycat to copy the copycat. And on it goes, expanding exponentially.'

She crossed her hands across her lap once more and pursed her lips with satisfaction. In her head, Maggie could hear Mac's voice, when he'd mocked her naiveté in looking for a single villain: her opponent was a *movement*.

Maggie was feeling faint, but she was determined to push on.

'And yet, Keane himself never called for any such thing, did he?' A thesis was taking shape in Maggie's mind. 'I mean, all those lectures, all those writings. He never once called for the destruction of the historical record.'

The tranquil repose of before was broken, a look of thunder passing across Bentham's face. 'You've got a nerve lecturing *me* about the ideas of Professor Keane. I've read every word that man has written, every speech he's given, every lecture he's delivered.'

'But you were going far beyond his teachings. You were contradicting them.'

'In *The Second American Revolution*, Professor Keane set it all out.'

'He didn't call for book burnings though, did he? He's been down there in Richmond arguing that key historical texts are bogus or misleading, but he doesn't say you should *burn* them.' Maggie was leaning forward, deliberately pressing herself into Bentham's space. 'Or did you think you'd give him a short cut, just in case he failed to nail it in court? Keane wouldn't need to explain away all those inconvenient documents, because you'd have got rid of them all.'

'Read Professor Keane's book. Or read *The Next American Revolution*. The position is perfectly clear in both volumes. The clue is in the titles, Miss Costello. He was calling for a *revolution*.

And if you're serious about making a revolution, if you really do want to make the world anew, then you have to clear away what's gone before. To create a new world, first you must destroy the old.'

The point was so clear to her, so transparent in its truth, her eyes were shining with its brightness.

'People get dragged down by the past. I've seen it for myself. When I was growing up, I barely spent more than a year in the same town or the same school. Each September, I'd start over. New place, new name. No friends, no history. It didn't do me any harm.'

Maggie clocked that too, but she was determined to keep pressing. 'All right. That may be what you think. Burn it all down, *tabula rasa*. But Keane never spelled it out like that, did he? He didn't dare make it explicit.'

'Sometimes people need help. Even Jesus needed his disciples.'

'And I suppose now was the right time?'

'It was the *first* time. The first time such a project could even have been contemplated, thanks to the technology.'

Maggie did not want to react to that admission, nor allow any glance to pass between her and Andrea Ellis. Instead she kept going. 'But still, what you've done is not what Keane explicitly called for, is it? You've now associated his cause with violence and death and destruction. Wanton vandalism. You've probably ruined his chance of winning that case in Richmond.'

'Why don't we wait and see?' Bentham replied, the smile returned.

'But you've discredited him. You've taken a scholar and

reduced him to the level of a terrorist. That's how William Keane will be remembered, thanks to you. As nothing more than a book-burning thug. And it's your fault.'

'How dare you?' Pamela Bentham said, slamming her fist onto the table. 'He will be proud of what I've done. He may not be able to say it, but I know that's what he feels. When I see him on the television, I can see that's what he's thinking. I can see that's what he's telling me. "Well done, Pamela. Well done, my clever, clever girl." '

Chapter Fifty-One

Walter Reed National Military Medical Center, Bethesda, Maryland, 11.42am

The first sensation she remembered was a smell. Or rather a combination of two smells, the second of which was strong enough to wake her.

The first to reach her as she stirred from unconsciousness was the scent of roses, not a flower she'd ever choose for herself. But the fragrance, with its hint of a Dublin spring and her grandmother's house, was unmistakable. And in her state of suspension between sleep and wakefulness, between the living and the dead as it seemed to her, it was so comforting as to be enticing, luring her to open her eyes.

But what woke her was the muskier, more human aroma of Uri Guttman. She did not need to see him to know he was there, to feel his presence. Even before she had worked out that she was in a hospital bed, her arms punctured with drips and needles, she understood that Uri was near.

When she saw him, fussing with a window blind, in jeans and a dark T-shirt, she couldn't help but smile. It was involuntary. She felt it come upon her, twitching the edges of her lips and giving her no say in the matter.

He must have sensed it, because he wheeled around to face her.

'Hello, there, Miss Costello. It's good to have you back.'

'Hello,' she said, her voice thin and dry.

He moved swiftly to the bedside table, where he poured her a glass of water, which he held just by her lips. It was such a sensual gesture, so intimate, that, unbidden, she felt a stirring of desire that caught her by surprise.

'Where am I?' she said. He smiled and then they both laughed at the Hollywood absurdity of it.

'You're in Walter Reed.'

'Walter Reed? That's for veterans. I'm not a veteran, Uri.'

'So the doctors were right: nothing wrong with your brain.'

'Seriously. Walter Reed?'

'The Deputy Director of the FBI insisted. Along with your friend, the governor. She pulled some strings. She said, "She's served her country as much as any vet." You're getting great care here. Including on that foot.'

The memories came back to her, a trickle at first and then a torrent. The hotel, the freezer, the library, Herman's face. The interrogation of Pamela Bentham.

'Though, I have to say, the foot made them a little bit confused. The rest of the injuries are from heat; that one is from cold?'

'It's a long story.'

He sat on the bed next to her and took her hand, placing his over it. 'I know.'

'How come I'm here? What happened?'

'After you were interviewing Bentham, you mean? Apparently, you closed out the interrogation, she left the room and you collapsed in a pile on the floor.'

'In a heap.'

'You don't normally correct my English: that means you're definitely sick. They say it's nervous exhaustion. Which is a fancy way of saying you're shattered. The good news is, you got lots of flowers.'

He went over to pick up a bunch of lilies in the corner, reading from the card. ' "To Maggie. With eternal gratitude and friendship, Donna." These are from the Director of the FBI.' He pointed at some tulips. 'I think the fruit came from the head of the Library of Congress.'

'The Librarian.'

'What?'

'The *Librarian*. That's what the head's called.'

'I'm telling the neurologist: they can cancel the brain scan.'

Maggie laughed and the effort brought a stinging sensation to her face, the pain you get when you've been out in the sun too long.

'The doctors are furious, by the way. They say that . . . what's her name?'

'Andrea.'

'Andrea had no business keeping you working, doing that interview, in your state. Sure, you got through on adrenalin. But she shouldn't have let you. All those machines – the heating equipment in the library – apparently they were red-hot when they pulled you out.' He sat back on the bed, putting his hand on hers. 'You were very lucky.'

She liked the touch of his hand, his skin cooling. But a moment later, he sprang back up and was across the room, fussing over his bag.

'You know, Uri,' she said. 'I'm really glad about the library. I'm relieved.' She could hear the thinness of her voice. 'But I keep thinking about the other eleven. All those precious books. All those archives. All gone. And it's my fault. I could have saved so many more. I wasted so much time, went down so many dead ends. It's my fault.'

He spoke with his back to her, as he pulled out a laptop from his backpack and began looking for cables. 'That is so typical of you, Maggie, I can't even begin to tell you.' He turned around, the computer now open. 'Look,' he said. 'There are a couple of things I thought you'd want to see.'

As he propped the machine on her lap, he was close enough that she could smell his skin.

The browser was open to the CBS News website and he clicked on a video that had been posted an hour or so earlier.

More on that breaking story now, as we cross live to the Detroit suburb of Sherwood Forest where correspondent Philip Jeremy is reporting on an extraordinary reunion. Phil?

That's right, Bob. Emotional scenes here as Esther Gratzky, a survivor of the Holocaust who had been missing and presumed dead, was reunited with her family, safe and well. You might remember, Bob, that Mrs Gratzky – well-known in the Detroit area for her talks to schools and community groups, telling the harrowing story of her wartime experience in Poland – disappeared earlier in the week, just as many Holocaust survivors were found dead in mysterious circumstances here in the United States and around the world. When Mrs Gratzky went missing, her son and daughter feared she too had suffered a similar fate.

But today she emerged in good health following what police say was an abduction. Family members are disputing that choice of word this morning. Here's what Michael Gratzky, Esther's son, told local station WDIV. Let's listen in.

'We're just so glad to be back with my mom. It's such a relief, for all of us. Especially the grandchildren and great-grandchildren. We're just so happy.'

'And can you tell us, Michael, what happened? Was your mother kidnapped?'

'Well, it's pretty surreal. She was certainly taken from her home last week. And she was prevented from communicating with any of us. But she says she was incredibly well treated and that the people who took her, she says that basically they looked after her. They said they were hiding her in what was kind of a safe house, because they believed her life was in danger. And now that we know that other survivors were getting killed, I believe them. I wish it hadn't happened this way. I wish we could have known what was going on. But my mother thinks these people saved her life. And my mom has pretty good survival instincts, you know? She . . . she . . . I'm sorry. It's just that we . . . I'm sorry.'

'That's OK. You take a moment. Everyone at WDIV is just so happy she's safe. Can you tell us, the people who looked after your mother, do you know where they are now?'

'We don't know. They drove my mother back to her house. They dropped her off. And then they just clean disappeared.'

'Could she describe them?'

'She says they were young. And she just keeps saying they were so kind to her.'

'All right, Michael. Thank you and stay safe.'

So that's the interview our colleagues over at WDIV here in Detroit ran earlier. Mrs Gratzky now back with her family, in good health – her life apparently saved by some mysterious guardian angels. Bob?

Maggie looked at Uri, whose cheeks were wet. She took his hand.

'This story, you know?' he said, his fingers at his eyes. 'This damn story. I grew up with it, every day hearing about it. Mothers of friends, grandmothers of friends, aunts, uncles. In my country, you cannot escape it.' He found a tissue and blew his nose. 'And you tell yourself you're over it. There's nothing about the Shoah you don't already know. And then, you hear something like this.'

Maggie squeezed Uri's hand and felt three words make the journey towards her lips. But she didn't say them. Instead she kept his hand in hers until, eventually, she said, 'I don't understand. Who could have taken her?'

'Now look at this. I noticed this just before you woke up.' He took back the machine and searched for the archive of video testimony of Holocaust survivors, the website the two of them had seen all but melt before their eyes just a few days earlier. It appeared promptly and apparently in full working order. He typed in the name of Esther Gratzky and was greeted by a page complete with a video playback screen, ready to roll.

'It's working.'

'So are these.' He opened a new tab for the Yad Vashem archive of the Holocaust. And a new tab each for the libraries of Tehran, Paris and Moscow. Websites that had been destroyed were now back.

'How come?'

'I have no idea. But look what I saw a few minutes ago.' He went to yet another tab, open to a Reddit forum, dedicated to the nerdy business of the mechanics of the internet itself.

There were too many words on the screen for Maggie to take in. 'Tell me what it says.'

'The basic story is, all of these sites seem to have been cached or mirrored. Somebody was storing back-up versions, keeping them safe.'

'Who?'

'No one knows. The only clue is this.' He took his cursor to a paragraph, which he highlighted.

The main IP address seems to trace to Melita Island, Montana. Anyone know it?

Chapter Fifty-Two

Melita Island, Montana, 8.48am

Jason Ramey had read about champion cyclists and how they taught their bodies to delay exhaustion. They would collapse in a heap one day, they told themselves; but it couldn't happen just yet. They become masters of delayed gratification and, for the purposes of the task in hand, basic human rest was deemed to be gratification. Sleep would be indulged eventually. But that day had not yet come.

This, he realized, was how he had approached the strange, endless days in this cluster of Scout cabins on Melita Island. He had pushed himself to the limits of his endurance, and then far beyond those. He had seen his colleagues – his comrades, his brothers and sisters, for that's how he felt about them at this moment – do the same. His admiration for Jim, his boss, especially was bottomless.

But now, suddenly, the fatigue was flooding in, as if the levees had broken at last. The cue had been the moment Jim told them the threat was over, that their work was done. Although Jim had not put it so definitively. 'The threat has receded,' was his formulation. But they could read the news. They could see the live pictures of the raid on Austin Logica and the arrest of Pamela Bentham.

Above all, they could see what was happening on their own screens. They could see how, within minutes of the Feds announcing that they had dismantled the apparatus inside Austin Logica HQ, the denial-of-service and other attacks on the world's digital databases slowed down. To these volunteers' well-trained eye, the link was obvious and undeniable. As for the caution that made Jim describe the threat as 'receded', rather than 'defeated', that only made Jason respect him more.

Now Jim was focused on the de-rig. 'Folks, we need to be out of here in one hour. Two vessels will be at the jetty in exactly fifty-five minutes, and we will be loading every last piece of equipment into the self-assembly boxes you see arranged before you. If each of you takes care of your own terminal and screens, and then goes to the cabin to pack away your personal items, we can do this. Anyone who finishes early: join me in de-rigging cables and other comms. Clear?'

That left no time for speeches, a celebratory drink or any form of valediction to Melita Island, their home for this extraordinary, sleepless period. It was not until they were on the boat, crossing the water to Lindisfarne, where they would be picked up in four separate SUVs and driven to the airport, that Jim gave any kind of address.

'Folks, I know we're all too exhausted to listen to any kind of speeches. I know I am. But I wanted to say two things. The first is that what you have all done is nothing less than a great service to humankind. You have been involved in identifying and then protecting some of the most precious objects in human history. We called it "filing", which didn't sound very heroic, but what you did helped protect and guide to safety some of the individuals whose memories are a crucial part of the human story. And you have preserved a digital record that others wanted destroyed. You didn't do it for money. At least I hope you didn't.'

Jason and the others laughed at that.

'And you didn't do it for glory. Given the means that were necessary for this work, it will probably have to remain secret forever. But you signed a contract that promised you "the greatest possible reward" for your efforts. That reward is the knowledge that you did something important for the sake of your fellow human beings. That you did it for history. And for truth.'

There was loud applause for that. Jason high-fived the two people next to him. Maya rested her head on his shoulder, in silent affirmation.

'And here's the second thing. None of you ever knew the person behind this effort. That was how he wanted it. I confess I never met him myself, though I was in contact with him until very recently. I won't violate his wishes by revealing his name. But it was down to his determination, his insight and his sheer genius that we did what we did. He spotted the threat early. He anticipated each move the enemy would make. And he knew how to guard against it. He recruited me, and he trusted me to recruit you. He even suggested the place we've just left behind, a place he knew well. If you had a glass in your hand, I'd ask you to raise it and join me in drinking to a truly great man.'

The rest of them took their cue and mimed lifting their invisible glasses to make an invisible toast. 'To a truly great man!'

Chapter Fifty-Three

Walter Reed National Military Medical Center, Bethesda, Maryland, 1.18pm

Uri's phone rang. He talked into it and headed out of the room, leaving Maggie alone with the laptop. She was so exhausted, her eyelids seemed to be made of lead. And yet, she couldn't help herself.

She pulled the machine towards her, opened up a new tab and typed the words *Melita Island*.

> *Uninhabited, undeveloped and completely surrounded by water, Melita Island is just as it was in the late 1940s when the Scouts first began participating in summer camps there. Its wooded acres . . .*

Maggie stopped reading and closed her eyes. A thought flickered somewhere, several layers deep. She read on.

> *The sixty-four-acre island has two and a half miles of shoreline on*

Flathead Lake. Our Scout camp makes use of powerboats, sailboats, rowboats . . .

There it was again, like a comet against the sky. A thought, a memory, she couldn't place.

She opened her eyes again to look at the page on the Boy Scouts of America website. It showed two boys, from the back, sitting on a jetty and framed by a simple wooden canopy, looking out onto the water. It seemed like an idyllic summer evening, one of those childhood memories anybody would cherish . . .

Hold on. It came again, like a word on the tip of her tongue. She tried desperately to retrieve it, fighting not just the fatigue but the limits of her own memory. Come on, come on.

And then it reached her, touching her synapses and forming itself into a visual image. It was Edith Kelly, sitting in her lawn chair at the Shady Lanes retirement village. Recalling her son, Martin.

'*Terry, my husband Terence, was convinced Martin would be president one day. I never thought that for one single moment. Never. He was far too shy. And he was a thin-skinned child. Hated being teased. He went on Scout camp in the summer, but I'm not sure he ever fitted in.*'

Maggie turned towards her bedside table, wincing at the pain as she twisted. Her skin felt raw. But there was her phone.

She turned it on and was relieved to see it still had power. She went through her recent calls, until she saw a number that looked like Shady Lanes. She dialled and, summoning her strength, asked to be put through to Mrs Kelly. There was resistance – 'This phone has been going non-stop' – but Maggie said she was part of the investigation into the death of Mrs Kelly's son. She was calling from Washington, DC, and this was of great importance. It required all her strength not to sound like a woman sitting up in bed. She could hear the call being transferred.

'Mrs Kelly, it's Maggie. Maggie Costello. I'd understand if you never wanted to speak to me again.' She paused. The phone had not been hung up. 'I'm calling to say how sorry I am about what happened. How sorry I am about your son.' She paused again. 'But I'm also calling to say there's something important I need to ask you.'

A second, another second, another and then a reply. 'You don't need to say sorry. What happened is my fault, not yours. Martin made his choices, I made mine – and the Good Lord made his.' Her voice was steady, but the stoicism was not fooling anyone. Maggie could hear the grief.

'Mrs Kelly, I know that this is painful, but I need to ask you something about Martin.'

'He's at peace now, my love.'

'I know. But there's something I need to know about Martin's childhood. Something that might . . . help.'

'Help? How could it help?'

'When we met, you said . . .' Her voice was drying up, it was becoming a croak. 'You said that Martin went camping, with the Scouts.'

'What's that?'

'Scout camp. Martin went on Scout camp.'

'That's right. When he was eleven. Or maybe twelve. His father was the one who pushed him. "It'll make a man of you!" he said.'

'My question is, where was it? Where was the Scout camp Martin went to?'

'I don't follow. Why would this—'

'Please. Where was it? Do you remember?'

'I do remember. It was a lovely place. It looked fine. Martin sent me a postcard each week. Always the same. A picture of an osprey, flying—'

'Where was it, Mrs Kelly?'

'It was out west. Far away from New York. He had to fly across the country, even at that age. Montana, it was. Melita Island, Montana.'

Chapter Fifty-Four

Walter Reed National Military Medical Center, Bethesda, Maryland, 2.39pm

For no reason Maggie could discern, Uri was tidying up the hospital room. He was topping up the water in the vases, throwing out discarded envelopes and papers, removing the used water glasses.

'You're up to something.'

'I'm not. I'm making it nice.'

'But why?'

He turned around. 'You need a reason not to throw out a banana peel? You want to keep it?'

Maggie smiled, the domesticity of this moment warming her. She could hear Liz's voice in her head. 'This is your problem, Maggie. The only way you can behave like a halfway normal person is when you're nearly killed and forced to sit still in one place . . .'

Liz had been in touch, Maggie sparing her the details of the injuries, the collapse and the fact that she was in hospital. Her sister didn't need to know. Instead, Maggie said she was catching up on her sleep at home. Liz had replied by sending her a link to an article she'd just come across in a women's magazine. Her message said: *Just read this and tell me it's not you.*

The article was headlined *The Ten Defining Traits of Children of Alcoholics*. Maggie skimmed through it, refusing to look at more than the first few words of each paragraph.

One: Fear of Losing Control.
Two: Taking on a High Burden of Responsibility. Feeling a 'super-responsibility', as if they are duty-bound to take care of all those around them, even to take on the cares of the world.
Three: Inability to Relax and Have Fun.
Four: Harsh Self-Criticism and Constant Sense of Guilt.
Five: Difficulties with Intimacy.
Six: More Comfortable Living in Chaos or Drama than in Peace.

If she could have, her sister would have circled and underlined that last one. 'Adrenalin junkie with a Messiah complex': the verdict she'd passed on Maggie years ago.

Maggie put the phone away.

She closed her eyes and an image of Martin Kelly filled her head. She pictured him in his cabin, the loner alone yet again – hammering away at his keyboard, listening in to the online debate among William Keane's followers and disciples, as slowly he grasped what was underway. Steadily, he'd understood that a plan was forming, in the mind of one person at least. Who knew what it was – maybe an offhand remark in that closed forum, maybe a whistleblower from inside the company – that made Martin look at Austin Logica and Pamela Bentham, but something did.

Martin must have realized at that moment that the threat was genuine. Maggie wondered if he'd already been moving away from the ideas of his youth. Or was it the prospect of those ideas, which once shone so brightly in the academic seminar room, turning now into lethal and unpalatable reality that repelled him? She imagined the anguish of a man who'd been happy enough to discuss the notion of erasing history in theory, now appalled by the thought of it happening in practice.

And then, God alone knew how, from behind his keyboard, he must have recruited a group of people to help thwart Bentham's plan as best they could. Not by stopping her burning down libraries – they surely had no idea how she was doing that – but at least by salvaging what, and who, they could. And doing it in a secret place he knew well.

The irony of it, and its bitterness, did not escape her. All that computer activity, as Martin Kelly had attempted to save the world's memory, had made him look less like a saviour than the prime threat, at least in the eyes of the FBI. It had suited Bentham perfectly. She had crafted the manifesto so that it could plausibly have been Kelly's handiwork, creating a trail of crumbs that would lead to his cabin. He, by his own frantic efforts to track down the most precious documents and witnesses, had added to that trail. And it had been Maggie that had followed it, leading a team of federal agents to his door – and to his death.

Eyes still closed, she let out a deep sigh: guilt seemed to stalk her, from one chapter of her life to the next. Now it was attached to Martin Kelly. The world owed him a great debt. Somehow Maggie would have to make that known. She would start with his loving, patient, heartbroken mother: Edith Kelly deserved to know that her son had not died a failure, but a hero.

When she next opened her eyes, the TV, muted in the corner, had sparked into life, a 'breaking news' logo zipping across the screen. The picture showed William Keane on the steps of the federal courthouse in Richmond, a cluster of reporters and cameras surrounding him. Beyond them were two large crowds of supporters and opponents, apparently jostling. Maggie could hear the chant: *Don't know, don't care/Nothing happened, nothing's there.*

The camera only showed the pro-Keane group briefly, so it had gone almost as soon as it had appeared, but there, unmistakable among them, was the face of Crawford McNamara.

Maggie reached for the clicker and turned up the volume. Keane was just getting started.

'Ladies and gentlemen of the press, I thank you. Thank you. Hush now. All right. OK.

'With your permission, I'd like to make a short statement. I want to begin by thanking the good people of the press for your patient, not to say dogged interest in this case. I know there are those who like to deride you as the fake news media, and, Lordy, you often deserve it. But you've been here at this courthouse day after day, and I thank you for that courtesy.

'As you know, twelve good people of the Commonwealth of Virginia have just ended their deliberations and communicated that fact to the judge, who has taken the unusual and gracious step of allowing this outcome to be known right away, even outside regular court hours. I offer my sincere and true thanks to those citizens. They are the foundation of this great nation of ours.

'They listened as I tried to make a crucial argument for the life of this republic. I told them that we had been weighed down too long by a legacy that was undeserved, by a story that was written from fever dreams and hot imagination – rather than cold, hard facts – and which has cast a shadow over us for generations. I presented my case as well as my modest gifts would allow. And they did the honour of listening to me, a simple fellow Virginian by the name of William Keane, with solemn respect. I am grateful to them.

'I am especially grateful because they did not allow themselves to be swayed by the extraordinary and dramatic events that have swirled around them these last few days. Why, fire has rained down from the skies over this land and over distant lands that speak in other tongues. It has seemed like the very end of days as great storehouses of records and documents were put to the flame.

'Some unkind souls were uncharitable enough to suggest that your humble servant might have played some role in these apocalyptic events. You know of course that that is false. I am a historian, for gosh's sake! I may have argued with aspects of the historical record of this nation, that is plainly beyond dispute. But I am no arsonist. Heaven forfend.

'History matters. We need history. But we need to get it right. Which is why I am so grateful and so proud of those six fellow Virginians who sat inside that courthouse and raised their hands to say, "Aye, William Keane speaks the truth."

'Of course, six did not. But this result – a hung jury – is not the outcome any of the pundits or the experts or the establishment predicted. They thought I would be humiliated, laughed out of court and despatched faster than a rooster at a rodeo. No, sir. That's what the people of Virginia have said today: No, sir'ee. Not so fast. Not so fast.

'I thank you for that applause. Too kind. Thank you, friends. But this is a truly historic day, if you forgive a historian using that much-abused word. Today a jury was asked if so-called "slavery" really happened and they did not say yes. They said they were not sure. They had doubts. They wanted to see more and better evidence than the pile of myths and fables that has built up over two hundred years.

'That, my friends, is a victory. It means we go on to a retrial, a second chance for me to make my case and for the world to hear this argument anew. And, though I played no part in creating the new reality I am about to describe, the plain fact is that my opponents, Miss Susan Liston and her high-powered team of clever New York lawyers, will find the coming rematch harder than our first bout. For some of the papers and texts they relied on no longer exist. They are but as ash and smoke upon the winds.

'Ladies and gentlemen, my thanks once again. A milestone in our nation's journey has been reached. A great burden is about to be lifted. Together, we have made history!'

Chapter Fifty-Five

Walter Reed National Military Medical Center, Bethesda, Maryland, 3.23pm

Maggie must have dozed, because when she awoke Uri was hovering over her, his bag over his shoulder, readying to leave.

'It's been a long day,' he said. 'You should get some rest.' He bent down to kiss her softly, on the lips.

Once he'd gone, she curled herself into a position ready for sleep, trying not to think of the smug face of William Keane, McNamara at his side, and the apparently never-ending battle that stretched ahead. Whatever punishment came down on his devoted student, Pamela Bentham, Keane would be fine. Bentham had almost anticipated as much. In that windowless interview suite, Maggie had insisted Keane would be ruined. The older woman had simply smiled. 'Why don't we wait and see?'

Maggie was about to drift off when she noticed a small piece of paper, folded in half, on the nightstand.

It was from Uri.

Maggie,

We haven't had much time to talk about us. Now is not the time either, not while you're fighting to get better. So I want to say just one thing. I know you might think all we have is what we used to have. But I think that's a big thing. It means we have a foundation that we can build on.

Maggie, I think we have a future because *we have a past.*

U x

She read it again and reread that last line three times over. *I think we have a future* because *we have a past.*

And she felt herself fill up with hope that maybe this time it was the truth.

THE END

Acknowledgements

This is a book about truth, and while it is fiction much of it is rooted in fact.

When William Keane grills Professor Andrea Barker in court over *Twelve Years a Slave*, for example, he cites an essay she's written: 'The Redemption of Solomon Northup'. The text that Keane quotes is, in fact, 'The Passion of Solomon Northup' by Eric Herschthal, published in the *New York Times* on 6 November, 2013.

I owe a great debt to the work of David Rieff. The Bookburner's manifesto draws several of its most pertinent examples from Rieff's excellent 2016 polemic, *In Praise of Forgetting*. The arguments Uri makes about the virtues of amnesia are similarly in line with Rieff's thinking.

The harrowing experience on the train from Auschwitz to Nordhausen, attributed in the novel to Judith Beaton, is not made up, but was told to me by one who endured it: Joseph Kiersz. I reported his story and that of other Holocaust survivors in 'Safe House', published in the *Guardian* on 14 May, 2011.

The Times report, found by Liz, on the computer-generated recreation of an undelivered JFK speech was published in that newspaper on 15 March, 2018. Meanwhile, Jen Goodwin's act of penetration testing is based on the remarkable testimony of a real-life and ingenious pentester, who pseudonymously recounts her adventures under the Twitter name of Jek Hyde.

The book whose title Mac so admires – *Nothing is True and Everything is Possible* is very real. It is by Peter Pomerantsev and deserves its high reputation.

I am, of course, indebted to many others. Between them, Tom Cordiner, Steven Thurgood and my *Guardian* colleague Alex Hern were hugely generous with their expertise on all matters digital. David Menton and Lisa O'Carroll guided me on tricky questions of Irish idiom, while Richard Alman was a patient instructor on the technical aspects of fire and fire prevention. Jonathan Cummings remains an indefatigable ally, able to hunt down information that eludes lesser mortals. Steve Coombe is not just knowledgeable on questions of intelligence and security, when it comes to projects like this one, he has become something of a co-conspirator.

I'm hugely grateful to the team at Quercus whose enthusiasm for this novel has been such a source of encouragement. Jon Butler and Stefanie Bierwerth have been both supportive and insightful from the start, improving the story at every stage: I feel very lucky to be under their wing. Once again Rhian McKay proved herself to be a copy editor with a frighteningly sharp eye.

I'm glad to have another chance to thank my friend and agent,

Jonny Geller, and always with good reason. There is no greater ally a writer could have.

A last word goes to my family, whose patience is tested every time I start a new novel. My wife Sarah, and our sons Jacob and Sam, ensure that our home is never quiet, but always humming with talk and laughter. That's not a distraction, but the soundtrack of my life. I love all of them more deeply with each passing day – and that is the truth.